PRESS

WHITE HOUSE MEN BOOK 1

NORA PHOENIX

Press (White House Men Series 1) by Nora Phoenix

Copyright ©2020 Nora Phoenix

Cover design: Vicki Brostenianc www.vickibrostenianc.com

Model: Jon S.

Photographer: Eric McKinney

Editing and proofreading: Tanja Ongkiehong

All rights reserved. No part of this story may be used, reproduced, or transmitted in any form by any means without the written permission of the copyright holder, except in case of brief quotations and embodied within critical reviews and articles.

This is a work of fiction. Names, characters, places, and incidents either are the products of the author's imagination or are used fictitiously. Any resemblance to actual persons, living or dead, businesses, companies, events, or locales is entirely coincidental. The use of any real company and/or product names is for literary effect only. All other trademarks and copyrights are the property of their respective owners.

This book contains sexually explicit material which is suitable only for mature readers.

www.noraphoenix.com

To Allison Janney

Thank you for giving us CJ Cregg. Even after all these years, she remains one of the strongest, smartest, funniest female characters ever portrayed, and you brought us so much joy with that role.

PUBLISHER'S NOTE

This is a fictional book, set in the White House as it exists in reality, though obviously with a fictional president and staff. Any resemblance to real people, living or dead, is a pure coincidence.

I've tried to be as accurate as possible in portraying the inner workings of the White House as well as the several federal agencies, but for the sake of clarity and suspense, I've taken some liberties. I've included a list of all the terms used.

Please note this book has a trigger warning for a detailed description of a terrorist attack and violence, particularly the prologue.

LIST OF TERMS USED

ATF - Bureau for Alcohol Tobacco and Firearms
ASAC - Assistant Special Agent in Charge
CAT - Counter Assault Team, part of the Secret Service
Chief of Staff - the right hand of the President, basically the CEO of the West Wing. Other high government officials often have a chief of staff as well, including the vice president and the First Lady.
CIA - Central Intelligence Agency
DoD - Department of Defense
DoJ - Department of Justice
East Wing - a building adjacent to the White House where offices are located, including that of the First Lady and her staff
EEOB - Eisenhower Executive Office Building, where the offices of the vice president and his staff are located. The vice president himself also has an office in the West Wing.
FBI - Federal Bureau of Investigations
HUMINT - Human Intelligence (intelligence learned through direct human contact)
NCTC - National Counter Terrorism Center

NSA - National Security Agency
NYPD - New York Police Department
OEOB - Old Executive Office Building
PIAD - Protective Intelligence and Assessment Division, part of the Secret Service
SAC - Special Agent in Charge
Secret Service - the agency that protects the President of the United States, as well as the First Lady, the vice president and multiple other dignitaries
SIGINT - Signals Intelligence (intelligence learned through picking up digital signals, eg phone calls, emails, etc.)
West Wing - the building where the president and his staff work, which includes the Oval Office. Technically, this is not part of the White House, but is an adjacent building
White House - technically, the White House includes several public meeting rooms like the State Room and the East Room, as well as the personal living quarters of the president and his/her family

PROLOGUE

"This is Levar Cousins, reporting live from the New York Pride Parade. As you can see, the weather is beautiful on this June day, the sky blue and the temperature a crisp seventy-two degrees with a slight breeze. But the parade itself is burning hot with some of the best participants and the biggest floats yet to come. Here's a quick recap of last year's highlights."

Levar kept smiling until Claire, the assistant producer, told him through his earpiece they were off the air. He quickly dabbed his forehead with a cotton handkerchief, then took a sip of water.

God, he loved New York. The fast pace was in sharp contrast with the California laid-back atmosphere he'd grown up in, but he'd adapted quickly. This city truly never slept, and something was always happening. But nothing brought out the exuberant flamboyance of Greenwich Village like the Pride Parade.

The streets were packed, the crowds ten rows deep alongside the route of the parade. The rainbow was everywhere from flags to shirts, hats, body paint, and more, and

Levar basked in the celebration. One day a year, he'd let himself believe that equality was achievable, that someday soon, they'd manage to eradicate homophobia and transphobia.

"You're doing great," Robert, his cameraman, said over the sound of the tinny music in the background as he plucked a bit of confetti out of his hair.

"Thanks. At least it's not in the nineties, like last year."

They smiled at each other in mutual understanding. They'd both been there last year, though Levar had participated, not reported on it. After covering five parades as a cameraman, Robert was a veteran, and Levar was grateful to be working with him. Robert had given him some good pointers already, a welcome reprieve from the hostility he often got from others at the station.

Was it his ambition and the fact that he'd gotten a lucky break early on in his career and landed this gig? Or was it mixed in with low-key homophobia? He suspected that for all its corporate blah-blah about diversity and inclusivity, the station still had a long way to go before those lofty words would become day-to-day reality.

"Fifteen seconds to live," Claire warned him, and Levar wiped his mouth, then quickly checked his shirt, as had become his habit. He was wearing a light blue shirt that made his eyes look extra blue, and as a bonus, it also highlighted he was in good shape. Vain? Maybe, but he didn't care. He was on TV, so damn right he wanted to look good. Besides, every time he'd worn that shirt, he'd scored a hookup, so clearly, it worked. His best friend, Rhett, had called it his get-laid shirt, and he wasn't wrong. Claire counted off the last three seconds, and Levar's smile was camera-ready.

"I'm excited to see this year's outfits, floats, and signs,

and we have the perfect spot to view, right across from the Stonewall Inn, where the infamous Stonewall Riots broke out that birthed the pride movement."

He waited as Robert slowly panned to the right, showing the inn.

"Because for all the fun and extravaganza of the Pride Parade, let's not forget the battle for equality that started it... and that's still going on. At the core, Pride is as much a protest as it is a celebration."

There, he snuck that one right in. One point for the gay agenda. His boss might get on his case about it, but if they hadn't wanted a personal opinion mixed in, they shouldn't have sent in a gay reporter. And a gay cameraman, he thought as Robert panned back to him. Too bad Levar had a firm policy on doing coworkers, or he'd hit that hard. Or maybe let Robert hit him hard. The man looked like he knew what he was doing, and it had been a while since Levar had experienced a good dicking. The kind that left him slightly sore the day after.

"This year, the organization has chosen to spread out the most extravagant participants throughout the parade, and we've seen some amazing floats already. If you're just tuning in now, we're about to see familiar groups that participate every year, including the NYPD, the NYFD, the employees from the city, and many more. It's—"

BOOM!

The deafening blast stunned him, but then a force coming from behind him knocked him off his feet. He went flying forward, slamming into Robert and crashing down with him. His body smashed into the pavement, and for a second or two, he couldn't breathe, his lungs refusing to fill. *Breathe.* His ears were ringing so loud he couldn't hear anything else.

Breathe, dammit. Breathe!

Finally, he sucked air in with a gasp, his lungs aching as they expanded. He blinked a few times, but his vision remained hazy. Smoke. Something was burning. The sharp smell stung his nose, making his eyes water.

What the fuck had happened? The music had stopped, and instead, keening and crying drifted in the air, muffled through the ringing in his ears that hadn't subsided yet. People were shouting, screaming, sobbing. He grunted in pain as he moved.

Robert. Was he okay?

"Levar...Levar!" Claire yelled in his earpiece. Had her voice always been that shrill? God, his head hurt.

He groaned in response. "I'm here."

"What's happening? We can hear you and see you, but we took you off the air. Are you okay? And Robert?"

Levar pushed himself up onto his knees. White-hot pain lit up his right wrist, and he cried out. "Fucking hell!"

"Are you hurt?" Claire shouted

Why was she shouting? He shook his head, but it didn't clear his vision, which remained blurry.

Someone moaned. Close by. Robert. Levar crawled toward him on his knees, holding his wrist against his chest. Was it broken? "Robert! Are you okay?"

Finally, his eyes lost the blurriness. The explosion had thrown the cameraman against the iron fence they'd been filming in front of, the one around Christopher Park. He was lying like a raggedy doll amid blackened debris from god knew what, his left arm bent at a weird angle, clearly broken. He must've tried to brace himself. His eyes were open, and when Levar reached him, he grunted. "I'm alive. Everything hurts, but I'm alive. What the fuck happened?"

They looked at each other, and their eyes widened at the

same time. "A bomb," Levar said way too loud, his ears still ringing. "That was a bomb."

A bombing. And he was here, with a camera. A switch flipped in his brain. "Claire, we're okay. You said you still have our feed? Video and audio?

"Yes. We've been rolling B-tape the whole time. Are you good to go?"

Levar didn't hesitate. "Yes. Robert's arm is broken, though, so I don't know if—"

"I can do it," Robert cut him off. "Gimme a few moments."

Levar pushed himself up, his legs shaky but holding. With his good arm, he pulled Robert up. Thank fuck it was him and not two-hundred-eighty-pound built-like-a-truck Martin, who he usually worked with. Robert winced, but he quickly lifted the camera, wiped off the lens, and hoisted it onto his shoulder.

"Video check?"

"Levels are good," Claire said.

"Audio?"

Levar picked up the mic he'd dropped. "Testing one, two, three."

"Audio isn't perfect, but good enough. You boys ready?"

"You're bleeding." Robert gestured at Levar's neck.

Levar touched it and came away with bloody fingers. "How bad is it?"

Robert stepped closer and studied it for a moment. "It's a gash. Looks like you'll need stitches, but you're not bleeding out anytime soon."

"Stitches can wait," Levar decided. "Do we know anything yet, Claire?"

"No, but we're on it. Police scanners are going nuts, but nothing concrete yet. I'll keep you posted."

Rhett. He'd been on assignment, taking pictures. Was he okay? *Please, let him be okay.* He'd have to text him right after.

He breathed out slowly. "Okay. I'm ready."

He checked himself out of habit, his breath hitching when he took in his shirt, now spattered with blood, probably from that gash, and with dirt. It would have to do. He was *alive*, dammit. Nothing else mattered right now.

"Live in five, four, three…"

"This is Levar Cousins, reporting live from the New York Pride Parade, where an unknown explosion just rocked through the crowd here across the Stonewall Inn. We don't know what happened, but we'll show you what we're seeing."

BOOM!

Another blast hit from farther away, but Levar almost lost his footing. He frantically grabbed a traffic sign to hold on to. The camera shook as Robert struggled to stay up as well. "That was another explosion!" Levar shouted over the wails that rose around him.

He had to ignore them. If he didn't, if he let the sheer agony in those screams get to him, he wouldn't be able to do his job. And the world needed to see what was happening here.

"This one seems to have come from our right, farther down the parade route. We don't have any confirmation yet of what's going on, but people are panicking and trying to get out of here."

He turned around, and as the smoke cleared, he got his first look at the site of the initial explosion. His breath caught in his lungs, and he stood frozen, unbelieving as he took in the carnage.

And then the third bomb went off.

∽

HENLEY PLATT SHOOK HIS HEAD, but the ringing in his ears wouldn't subside. That would be sure to give him a migraine for days, he thought, then wanted to slap himself for the stupidity of that line of thinking. People had *died*, and he was worried about a migraine?

Get it together. Take a deep breath.

Around him, panic had erupted, and even with the loud beeping tone still wrecking his ears, the screams came through loud and clear. God, the *screams*. People were dying, suffering, in pain. Yelling, wailing, shouting. A stampede. People pushing each other, falling, picking each other up, then pushing some more. Burning confetti was raining down on him, and he brushed it off with slow, painful moves.

He had to get out of the way, or he'd get run over. He crawled to the side, careful not to cut himself on the broken glass all around him. As far as he could see, the blast had knocked out all the store windows. Some frames too, doors half-hinged, and windows sills half-caved in.

He found shelter in a doorway. God, his body hurt. And his ears. Okay, self-check. He took another deep breath, then ran his hands over his body. His palms were bleeding, as were his knees. The second blast had propelled him forward onto his hands and knees. He'd scraped off the skin, but the wounds were superficial. Bloody and dirty, but not serious. His wrists hurt, but he could still move them. Not broken, then. He hadn't hit his head, so that was good.

His bag seemed okay, but then again, he'd paid almost as much for it as for the camera inside because it was guaranteed to withstand anything, according to the manufacturer. Well, if it had survived this, he'd write them a damn thank-you note and suggest they'd promote the bag as bombproof. He opened it. His camera looked undisturbed. Thank fuck for that.

He closed the bag again, then pushed himself up, letting out a curse at the pain that shot through his hands and wrists, but he made it up. He swayed, so he grabbed the doorpost and held on until the dizziness had passed. His ears finally stopped ringing, and the other noises came in much louder now. More screams. Moans. Crying. People shouting at each other, yelling, asking questions no one knew the answers to.

Something buzzed in his pocket. His phone. He pulled it out, cursing again at his stupid wrist, then accepted the call. His editor. "Henley, are you okay?"

He'd never heard the veteran editor like this, almost panicked. "I'm alive, Julie. Minor scrapes and bruises. What do we know?"

"It's okay to take a moment and—"

"I'm good. I promise. Tell me what you know."

"Three blasts. The first one right in front of the Stonewall Inn, the second two minutes later about 900 yards up the route, and the third one a minute after that 900 yards in the other direction. Where are you?"

"Crossing of 7th, 4th, and Christopher, close to Christopher Station. How many dead?"

"They don't know, but Channel 11 has a news reporter on the scene who's been reporting live since right before the second blast, and the carnage is such that they've switched to a thirty-seconds-delayed broadcast to blur out the worst. It's... It's bad."

His mom. She knew he was going to the parade. She'd be scared to death if she saw the breaking news and the reports. And she'd watch because she always has the TV on.

"Julie, can you ask someone to call my mom and tell her I'm okay? Number is in my personnel file."

"On it."

She called out to someone and repeated the request. Good. That was taken care of. He hated worrying his mom. She'd suffered enough for a lifetime.

He took a deep breath and forced all thoughts of his mom down. He had a job to do. "I was a hundred feet or so from the second bomb. It knocked me off my feet, but I got lucky because an NYPD armored vehicle shielded me, taking the direct force of the blast."

The truck, once so imposing, was now a blackened, dented wreck, looking gloomy and apocalyptic.

"Thank god. Henley, can you report? Are you able to do your work? I know you're off today, but—"

"Yeah. I hurt my wrists, though, so I'm not sure I can write anything."

"Don't worry about that. Is your phone battery charged?"

He let out a short laugh. "Always, boss. You trained me well. Backup charger in my bag."

"You have a camera on you?"

"Yeah. Brought my Nikon to take pics of the parade. I don't have my big zoom with me because it was too damn heavy to lug around all day, but I should be good."

"All right. Get your camera ready and shoot as much as you can. Put on your headset, stuff your phone into your pocket, and talk. We'll record the call, and André will work with you on this. Your name will be first in the byline."

"I don't even care, Julie."

"You will a few days from now. Do your job, Henley. We'll listen."

He took a deep breath. Okay. He could do this. He'd never been fond of live reporting and hadn't done it in ages, but he had experience. All he needed to do was shift his head into the right gear, turn his emotions off, and become a reporter, an observer. He opened his bag again and lifted the camera out, then took off the lens cap and put it in his left front pocket. Thank fuck he'd decided to bring his camera when he'd made plans to attend the parade.

His wrists protested against the weight of the camera and the moving around, but he pushed down the pain. They weren't broken, so it wasn't an emergency. Whatever was wrong with them would have to wait. Work came first now. He closed the camera bag again, locked his phone, and stuffed that into his right front pocket. Showtime.

"I'm walking toward the site of the third blast. People are still running away." He checked his watch. "It's been six minutes now since the third explosion, so I think we're all hoping this was it. The armored vehicle in front of me took the full hit of the blast, shielding me and the NYPD officers inside it. The streets are littered with glass from broken windows and all kinds of debris."

He swallowed. "I...I see the first wounded. It's chaos here, but amid all that, people are helping each other. A few feet from me lies a man, a participant in the parade, judging by his outfit. His right lower leg has been ripped off. Someone's using his belt to make a tourniquet."

"911 is getting flooded with calls," Julie said. "They're trying to get to everyone, but with so many people there and three different bomb sites, it's gonna take emergency services a while to get through."

Sirens wailed in the distance, the piercing sound only adding to the surreal atmosphere. What had been a joyous celebration only minutes before was now a...a gruesome, harrowing wreckage. The city that had once been home to him now felt like a war zone. The usual sounds of traffic were missing, the honking horns, cab drivers yelling, and the *beep-beep* of delivery trucks backing up.

Even the smell was off. *Wrong.* New York always smelled of exhaust fumes, a strangely comforting scent that Henley associated with being home, but now his nose was filled with smoke, whips of sharp, toxic odors...and the nauseating stench of burnt flesh.

He took a steadying breath. "I see a few first responders. They must've been stationed here as one of the first aid posts for the Parade."

He kept walking, describing what he saw and taking a ton of pictures. When he got closer to the blast site, his stomach roiled. "I can't even guess how many have been killed, but...bodies are lying in the streets, some of them missing limbs."

A lean man sat on the sidewalk, dressed in a pair of jeans shorts and an "I'm his" T-shirt that had once been white but was now covered with bloodstains. In his arms lay a big man, lifeless, his broad, naked, furry chest showing large wounds and copious amounts of blood. Henley was no doctor, but no way was that man still alive.

"Matthew, Matthew..." the lean guy wailed as he held his boyfriend or husband close.

Henley swallowed as he watched them through his lens, taking multiple pictures. He felt like a vulture preying on death, but he had to. It was his job to present the news, no matter how horrible it was. Across the street, another photographer, holding a camera with a much bigger zoom lens, shot pictures of the two men as well. They lowered their cameras at the same time. Henley didn't recognize him, but that didn't mean anything. He raised his hand in acknowledgment, and the other guy did the same.

"Many people have large chest wounds." He picked back

up his report. "Either from the direct blast or flying objects as a result of the explosion. Head wounds, lots of injuries to limbs, legs especially. People are taking off shirts and ripping them into pieces to use as temporary bandages."

He lifted his camera again, clicking away. Praise Jesus for digital cameras. "The glass has been knocked out of the windows in the whole area. Thank god I'm wearing sturdy boots, or the glass would cut straight through my soles. I'm now close to the blast site, about thirty feet away."

"Can you tell where and how the bomb was positioned?"

"No. The FBI and the ATF will have to send forensic experts to determine that. There's nothing left here. Everything is leveled. The...the pavement is stained with blood, as are the buildings. People have been smashed into the walls."

"Henley..." Julie's voice was filled with horror. Thankfully, she left it at that because he wasn't sure he could've held it together had she shown more sympathy. He had a job to do, and that required disabling his emotions. He'd grieve later, whenever that was.

"I see the first cops. They're cordoning off the blast site, which seems smart if they want to preserve evidence. Hold on. Let me take some more pics."

He kept walking, painting the horror he was witnessing, and often stopping to record the scene with his camera. "People are helping each other. Right now, I'm watching a guy coordinating a group of people who want to help, telling them what to do." He raised his camera, zooming in a little to get a better view. The guy looked familiar. He took a picture, then zoomed in a little more. "It's Senator Shafer, the Democratic senator for Massachusetts. He was walking in the parade today."

"Can you get his reaction?" Julie asked.

Henley hesitated as he lowered his camera. "He's saving

lives, Julie. I'm not comfortable diverting his attention. People are literally dying in the streets."

"I trust your judgment, Henley. Your call. We can always contact him later for a statement."

Henley kept watching the senator as he pointed at people and gave them a job to do. It was an amazing sight to see and a classic example of natural leadership.

"This guy is destined for more," he said to himself.

"What did you say?" Julie asked.

"Nothing. Just a... Nothing."

He went back to work, reporting on the horror that would become known as the New York Pride Bombing.

1

Five Years Later

Levar glanced around the conference room in the Eisenhower Executive Office Building, where he usually held press briefings, mentally counting and checking off names. It looked like all the big players were there. Good. That would make his boss happy, and far more importantly, it would please Vice President Shafer. And that, as far as Levar was concerned, was the ultimate goal. He served at the pleasure of the vice president after all, not at the whims of his direct boss, who wasn't known for setting a high standard. Any kind of standard, really.

"Don't touch your scar," Nicole, his assistant and right hand, whispered.

Levar turned sideways. "What?"

She leaned in even closer. "Your scar. You tend to touch it whenever we talk about it."

She appeared uncomfortable, and Levar frowned. What was she referring to? "I don't—"

"Whenever we talk about the commemoration, you rub your scar."

Levar froze. Did he? His hand flew up to his neck before he even realized it. The rough ridge of the scar was a comfort beneath his fingers, a tangible reminder he had survived. One hundred and fifty-three people had been killed, but he had made it out unscathed save one permanent scar.

"If this stirs up bad memories, maybe you should—"

"I'm fine," Levar said. "And I'll make sure to stay away from the scar."

Her eyes were compassionate. "Levar, it's okay if this is hard for you. It was a traumatic experience."

He briefly patted her shoulder to soften the impact of his words. "I'm fine. I promise. It's not hard for me at all. Just another day at the office."

She studied him for a few seconds more, then smiled at his lame attempt at a joke. Working for the vice president meant typical days didn't exist, and they both knew it.

"Okay, everyone, let's get started," Levar said, raising his voice.

The reporters all took out recording devices and various media to take notes. This wasn't a formal briefing, not like Katie Winters, the president's press secretary, did. Levar couldn't complain. At thirty-two, he was assistant press secretary to the vice president, and one of his senior advisors. Still, he had his eyes on the ball, and one day, it would be him in the White House, doing press conferences in the James S. Brady Press Briefing Room. With millions of people watching.

"The vice president will be flying to Norfolk today for

the christening of the aircraft carrier USS Jefferson Shafer, named after his grandfather, Jefferson Shafer, gunnery sergeant and former long-time senator for the state of Massachusetts. The vice president is honored to christen the ship. Nicole will hand out copies of his speech after this meeting."

"Will the vice president's father attend?" Danny, the senior White House correspondent for the New York Times, asked.

"Yes, he will, as will several other members of the vice president's family, including Mrs. Shafer and their son, Kennedy."

Levar went over the details of today's trip, elated he didn't have to come. Usually, he didn't mind, but he was slammed with work. And exhausted, but that was nothing new. He hadn't had eight hours of sleep since the day he'd started working for the vice president. Hell, he counted himself lucky if he got in six.

"Next on the agenda is the five-year commemoration of the New York Pride Bombing next month. The vice president will attend a ceremony in Christopher Park, across from the rebuilt Stonewall Inn, where he'll reveal the memorial designed by architect and survivor Elizabeth O'Donnell. She lost her right leg when the third bomb went off. Her wife, Erin, who attended with her that day, suffered multiple injuries to her chest and arms."

He caught a gesture from Nicole from the corner of his eyes and dropped his fingers, which had been rubbing his scar. Dammit. She'd been right. Why did he keep doing that?

"Why is Vice President Shafer attending the ceremony and not the president?"

That was Henley Platt, the White House correspondent

for the Washington Times. Levar frowned. It seemed like an obvious question, especially coming from someone like Henley. The guy was sharp as a tack, and Levar had learned the hard way to word things carefully around him and to always be on guard. The man had an unbelievable talent to make people say far more than they had intended to. He was fair, but he buried you alive if you fucked him over. Levar could live with that.

"Mayor Ben Goldstein of New York City personally invited the vice president for this ceremony, knowing how dear this event would be to his heart. As a survivor himself, the vice president has been dedicated to advocating for the rights of all survivors and to ensure they're looked after, financially as well as legally and emotionally."

Levar rattled off the answer without hesitation, having iterated similar statements too many times to count. That answered Henley's question, but to his surprise, the reporter raised his hand again. "A follow-up, if I may."

Levar nodded. What follow-up question could Henley possibly have about this?

"So there's never been any mention of the president attending rather than the vice president?"

Levar's heart rate sped up. He *knew* that look on Henley's face. The reporter's eyes had grown sharper, and he had that feigned innocence about him as if he were asking about the weather. All Levar's alarm bells were going off. Henley smelled blood...but about what? What did he know?

"Not as far as I'm aware of," he gave his standard diplomatic answer. It allowed him to present new information later on without coming across as a liar.

"Could you check on that for me?" Henley's voice was sugary sweet, which only made those alarm bells blare even louder.

"Sure. I'll get back to you on that. Now, the tentative schedule for the ceremony is as follows."

Levar walked them through the schedule, then spent another ten minutes answering questions. "That's all for now. Those of you who'll be joining the vice president to Norfolk, please make sure to be at the press bus by noon sharp. As you all know, the vice president likes things to run on time."

They all laughed, as it was well known that Vice President Shafer's four years in the Army had left him with a deep appreciation for planning, schedules, and punctuality. Henley packed up his notes and stuffed them into his binder while the room cleared out. He was all for going digital, but if he had to scribble stuff down fast, paper always won.

"I gotta run," Nicole said and hurried out. She'd be accompanying the press on today's trip, and Levar let out a breath of relief. A whole afternoon to get shit done. He'd finally be able to catch up. Somewhat, at least.

"Levar."

Levar looked up. "Henley. Anything I can help you with?"

Henley perched on the edge of the conference table, his long legs stretched in front of him. His brown eyes were laser-focused on Levar, and Levar resisted the urge to look away. "I have a source who claims that the president wanted to attend the commemorative ceremony and was upset the vice president accepted without checking with him first."

Dammit all to hell. Where the fuck had that come from? "This is news to me," Levar said, holding Henley's gaze.

"Mmm."

Levar almost rolled his eyes. Did Henley really think that tactic would work on him? As if he'd fall for an interview technique he'd learned in journalism 101. He waited as Henley studied him.

"Was that all, or did you want to spend the rest of today staring at me in a futile attempt to get me to say more?" Levar snapped when he got tired of the game.

"I'm waiting for you to give me a real answer."

"I told you. This is—"

"That's not an answer. I'm not interested in whether or not you knew about this."

"If I'm not aware, that's usually a pretty good indication your source is unreliable."

"Are you denying it, then?"

Levar's jaw ticked. As much as he wanted to, he couldn't. He might be a senior advisor to the VP, but that didn't mean they never kept him out of the loop, if only so he could claim plausible deniability. "I'll look into it."

"Please do."

"I'm sure it's idle gossip," Levar added. "You know the president asked Senator Shafer to be his vice president because of his strong record on advocating for diversity. He knows of the vice president's firm ties to the..."

Henley was staring at something, and Levar followed his eyes. His scar. He was touching it again. He dropped his hand, and Henley's face mellowed. "The New York Pride Bombing," he said softly.

Levar swallowed. Did Henley feel the same way whenever those words were uttered, that slight jolt to his nervous system? "Yeah."

He couldn't ask him. He and Henley were... Enemies wasn't the right word because the vice president believed in keeping good relationships with the press. That didn't mean they were on the same side, though. So what did that make them? Rivals? Competitors?

"If you ever want to talk..." Henley said, and his words hung heavy in the air.

Levar shoved his hands into the pockets of his tight-fitting dress pants. "Off the record?" he said, then regretted it immediately. "Sorry, that was—"

"Mean?" Henley suggested, but he didn't sound angry.

"I was thinking along the lines of low, but mean works."

The corners of Henley's mouth pulled up. "So that would make you a mean..."

Levar held up a finger. "If the next word out of your mouth is *girl*, you and I are gonna have a problem."

Then he grinned, and Henley's face split open in a broad smile as well. He'd never go there, and they both knew it. Levar had been profiled by the liberal media as one of Vice President Shafer's *gay squad*. Anyone who had missed his inadvertent outing during his emotional reporting during the bombing—not that he'd been in the closet, but the network hadn't wanted him to flaunt it—had learned he was gay as a rainbow flag-carrying unicorn.

Of course, the conservative media had vilified him and the other queer members of the vice president's staff, but the result was that the whole country knew Levar was gay. Henley had experienced his own five minutes of unintended fame when media had picked up on him being the first openly pansexual White House correspondent for a major news outlet. He had a boyfriend and was reportedly happy, so Levar never had to fear homophobic digs from him.

Henley's face sobered. "I mean it, though. Talking helps."

Levar shrugged. "I know. My roommate and I talk. Rhett Foles? He's a news photographer."

"I know who he is. The guy won a World Press Photo award for the pics he took there. They were incredible."

Levar's heart grew warm. "They were, and so is he."

Henley lifted an eyebrow. Was he seriously asking if Levar was dating Rhett?

"We're just friends," he said, then wanted to slap his head. He'd fallen for Henley's damn trick after all. Fuck him and his puppy eyes. Ugh.

"I wasn't asking."

Levar rolled his eyes. "Of course you were, just not with words."

Henley had the nerve to wink, and how did Levar stay mad at a guy who winked? So Levar just rolled his eyes again, with a little more dramatic flair this time, and Henley chuckled. Damn, the guy was cute when he grinned like that. Totally off-limits, but hella hot with his tanned face, his dark eyebrows, those piercing brown eyes, and a beard that looked so soft it made Levar want to run his hands through it. Theoretically.

Levar grabbed his binder. What the hell was he doing, checking Henley Platt out? "I assume we're done for now?"

Henley's face grew serious. "My sources say President Markinson is jealous of the vice president, of his popularity. You guys better watch your back."

2

By the time Henley made it home, he was wiped. "Hey, babe," he called out as he kicked the front door shut with his foot. He dumped his messenger bag onto the floor, wincing when it dropped harder than he'd intended. Thank fuck his laptop was in a case that could survive a tornado. It had once, in fact, when he'd gotten caught in one during a trip to Oklahoma. Or had that been his previous one?

"I brought home Chinese. Wasn't sure if you'd had dinner yet, and you didn't answer my texts."

He walked into the kitchen and set the plastic bag with the food on the counter. Damn, he was hungry. No wonder. It was way past eight already. "Babe?"

He took two plates out, the forks and knives. Hey, where had the Nespresso machine gone? Its place on the counter was empty.

"Logan, what happened to the Nespresso?" Henley frowned, then turned around as footsteps came up behind him. Whatever he'd wanted to say died on his lips when he spotted the weekend bag Logan was carrying.

Uh-oh. Again? Why did this keep happening to him?

He held back the deep sigh, forcing himself to keep his voice level. "I take it you didn't pack for a weekend in Virginia or something equally innocuous?"

God, he was tired. Bone-tired. The kind where he felt every single one of his thirty-nine years.

Logan raised his chin. Henley recognized the signals. He was gearing up for a fight. Granted, the makeup sex was usually spectacular and almost enough to make Henley forget about the drama, but not quite. "I'm going to stay with Bradford for a while," Logan said, his tone as icy as Elsa's.

"I assume this is where I ask why? Or beg you to stay?"

Logan huffed. "This is where you do anything, really, anything at all to prove to me you're still in this relationship. I'm not asking for you to propose or make a big theatrical gesture, but would it be too much to ask to see you still care? I'm walking away, Hen. This is not the time for sarcasm."

Shame filled Henley's insides. He hated it when Logan was right. Logan in one of his drama moods he could dismiss without difficulty, but a reasonable Logan was much harder to ignore.

"Sorry, babe." The endearment rolled off his lips too easily. A habit, that was what it had become, much like Logan's standard "Hen," which, for the record, Henley hated with a passion. "What happened? Did I do something wrong?"

Logan crossed his arms. "You'd have to actually *be* here in order to do something wrong."

Henley massaged his temples, his stomach rumbling. Eating his Chinese while arguing probably wouldn't do him any favors, right? He was so damn hungry. "You know what I do is not a nine-to-five job." He barely held back the "babe."

"You said you didn't have regular hours, that you sometimes had to work evenings and weekends too."

"Yeah, and was I lying?"

"Hen, you haven't been home in the last six weekends. Not for more than a few hours, half of which you spent on your phone."

"It's been a busy few weeks. You know the White House has been focused on the Supreme Court nomination and the Whittle scandal. I'm the White House correspondent. I need to be on top of things."

He almost smiled at that double entendre, but one look at the thunder in Logan's eyes had him reconsidering. No sarcasm, no dirty jokes. Noted.

"The White House will always be focused on something, and unless you make different choices, you'll always be chasing the scoop."

What was he supposed to say to that? He couldn't deny it. Not that he even wanted to. "This is my career, Logan, not some hobby. What do you want me to do? Tell my boss to send someone else when something is going down?"

"Yes! Isn't that why you have a team? You're always saying how good Adriana is. Why don't you send her sometimes?"

"She's a fucking baby! She's twenty-five, barely out of college, and you want me to send her to a White House briefing on her own?"

"Send Luther with her, then. Didn't you tell me how proud you are of him?"

On some level, Henley was impressed that Logan even knew those names, knew who they were. He'd have a hard time himself coming up with the names of any of Logan's coworkers other than the congressman he worked for. He supposed that was telling, and yet he didn't even feel bad about it. Had he grown numb, or was he simply too tired and too hungry to care?

"Luther is amazing. He's also ambitious as fuck and would step over my dead body with a smile to take my spot. This world is ruthless, babe."

Dammit. He had to stop calling him that.

"So when will it be enough? When will you be willing to take a step back and focus on your personal life...on your boyfriend?"

"Do I still have one?"

"That's up to you. I love you, but I can't go on like this. So you have to make a choice."

Was that dread he was feeling in his stomach? It didn't feel like it, though. The thought of Logan leaving didn't fill him with anything even close to dread, sadness, or despair. It felt more like...annoyance? Frustration definitely because he'd been here before. Repeatedly.

"Are you asking me to choose between you and my career?" he asked, his voice carefully neutral.

Logan's chin rose higher. "Yes. I've played second fiddle long enough. I don't think it's unreasonable, do you?"

Henley pushed out a tired exhale. They were just postponing the inevitable now. If this was the end, could they at least get on with it so he could eat his damn orange chicken, take a long hot shower, and crash? If he'd learned one thing from his previous relationships, it was that trying to patch up what was irreparably broken only made things worse.

"I'm almost forty, Logan. I've been White House correspondent for not even two years. That's not something I'm willing to give up. I've worked too hard for this. So I'm sorry, but the position of first fiddle has been taken."

Logan's eyes filled with tears. "At least I know where I stand now. I guess you never really loved me."

"Or we have a different definition of love," Henley suggested. "Because to me, love also means cheering each other on, being supportive of each other's career."

"That's not love, Henley. That's being good friends. Roommates. Which makes sense, in hindsight, because that's what we really are. I feel like I barely know you. You never talk to me."

"I talk to you all the time. How else would you even know the names of my coworkers?"

Logan let out a sigh. "That's sharing information, Hen. I'm talking about sharing your heart, getting to know the real you. You always keep me at arm's length. You're what my therapist calls emotionally unavailable."

Emotionally unavailable? Talk about an empty buzz word. How was that even a thing? Whatever. Henley didn't even know how to answer that one, so he said nothing, and the spark of hope on Logan's face dissipated.

Logan took a step back, then picked up his bag. "I'll be by later this week to get the rest of my stuff."

Henley eyed the empty spot on the counter. "I suppose I have to go shopping for a new coffeemaker, huh?"

Logan's laugh was humorless. "Why bother? You're never home to drink it anyway."

He had a point there. Not that Henley was feeling magnanimous enough to admit it. "I'm sorry things didn't work out between us."

"I swear to god, I promised myself to keep the drama to a minimum, but if you're about to suggest we should stay friends, I'm gonna lose it."

"I wasn't. I don't have time for friendships anyway."

"Which is why you've become such a grumpy, lonely asshole. Good luck with that."

Henley watched as Logan walked out, hauling two suitcases and his weekend bag. He pulled the door closed without another word, and Henley sighed. That could've gone better.

It wasn't until later, after wolfing down reheated Chinese food and taking the hottest shower in world history, that he felt human enough for a little introspective moment. That feeling in his belly he thought had been dread? Not dread. Not even close. It was relief.

He speed-dialed his mom.

"Hey, honey," her warm voice said.

"Hi, Mom. How have you been?"

"Good. I almost beat your brother at chess today. Someday soon, I will, and it will be glorious."

Henley laughed. "I have faith in you, Mom."

"Everything okay, honey? You sound tired."

"I am." He rubbed his temples. "Logan broke up with me."

"Oh, honey... How are you feeling about it?"

"I don't know. Isn't that awful? Pretty sure I'm supposed to be heartbroken, but I am not."

Silence filled his ear.

"You know I don't believe in telling people what they're supposed to feel anyway," his mom finally said. "But in this case, I can think of a few reasons why you'd feel this way."

"Really?"

"Honey, Logan was nice, and I really liked him, but he wasn't right for you. He loved you, clear as day, but you... liked him."

"I loved him, Mom," Henley protested. "I wouldn't have asked him to move in with me if I didn't."

"You asked him to move in with you because it was more convenient. With your work hours, it meant at least seeing him in the mornings and when you got off work."

Henley's heart clenched painfully. "That makes me sound very calculated."

"Not calculated, because that would imply intent. I don't think you were consciously aware. You liked him, honey, enough to take the next step. But if the thought of losing him doesn't break your heart, I think it's safe to say you didn't love him."

Henley let out a long sigh. "Like you losing Dad."

"It killed me. You know it did. You saw it."

Henley winced as he remembered the day his father had walked out on his family. One day, they'd been happy, and the next, he'd decided he was tired of the suburban life and had left his wife and three kids behind. Henley had been fifteen, his siblings even younger. His mom had been absolutely devastated.

"What's wrong with me that I didn't love him?"

"You can't tell yourself to love someone, you know that. Love doesn't work that way. Besides, neither of you was at fault. You can't help who you are, but neither can Logan. He needed something you weren't able to give."

"My time, or so he told me," Henley said, not able to keep the sarcasm out of his voice.

"Was that why he broke up with you?"

"Mmm. That, and apparently, I'm emotionally unavailable."

His mom was silent a long time. "He's not wrong."

Henley almost choked on his breath. "What? How can you say that?"

"Because it's true. Be honest, honey. The trust in your relationship was one-sided. You were there for Logan, but you never leaned on him. You don't lean, Henley. You don't. In all your relationships, you never have. You don't trust people to be strong enough to hold you."

Henley swallowed, his throat suddenly tight. "Mom…"

"Hush, it's okay," she said, her voice warm now. "We'll talk about this some other time. I'm sorry, honey. I know this is hard for you."

His mother's words kept playing through his head when Henley went to bed right after the phone call. Was she right? He was too tired. Whatever the cause of their breakup had been, Henley hoped Logan would find someone else, someone better. He was a good guy who deserved to be someone's priority. Just not Henley's.

3

Levar took a deep breath, then knocked on Ethan's door. He loved his job, his coworkers, dealing with the press. He loved working for the vice president and playing a part in helping him get his message out. His boss? Not so much.

"Yeah," Ethan called out, sounding annoyed as always, and Levar took that as permission to come in.

"Ethan, can I bother you for a few minutes?" he asked. Why did he always feel like a kid reporting to the principal whenever he was in Ethan's office?

"Is it urgent? I'm busy," Ethan said without looking up from his screen.

What on earth could the man possibly be busy with? If a world championship for delegating existed, Ethan would win it hands down.

"During the briefing yesterday, Henley Platt had a question I couldn't answer, so I wanted to run it by you. I promised him an answer today."

Ethan merely grunted. That wasn't a flat out no, and

Levar plowed on. "It's about the commemorative ceremony for the Pride Bombing."

Finally, he had Ethan's attention. The vice president's press secretary looked up, his eyes sharp now. "What about it?"

"Platt has a source who claims the president wanted to attend the ceremony himself and that he's upset the vice president accepted the invitation without talking to him about it."

"Bullshit," Ethan spat out. "Absolute nonsense. Why would the president want to go himself? This is clearly Shafer's turf. He's the big hero of the Pride Bombing, so the president would want to milk that for all its worth. Besides, the president's calendar is pretty full at the moment, and it's not like this would be that big a priority. It's sad and all, and I'm sure the memorial will be beautiful, but he has bigger events to attend."

By the time Ethan was done, his cheeks had grown red, and he wiped away some spit that had flown out with the last few words. Wow. He sure had given a long-ass answer to what was supposed to be an innocent question, hadn't he?

"That would be a no, then," Levar said.

Something flashed in Ethan's eyes, but just as quickly, it was gone again. "Tell Platt this has no factual basis whatsoever. And if you can find a way to tell the press to stop trying to stir up trouble between the president and the vice president, that'd be good. They're always trying to create problems where there are none."

Stop stirring up trouble? What was the man talking about? This was the first time Levar had ever had a direct question from the press about this. Should he say something? One look at Ethan's less-than-friendly expression made him nix that idea. "I'll talk to Platt."

"And you'll tell him his source is feeding him lies."

Okay, Ethan was acting straight-up weird now. Why was he so fixated on this? If it was BS, as Ethan claimed, then why the lengthy defense and the micromanagement of what to tell Henley?

"I'll make sure he understands." Levar intentionally left it vague what exactly he'd make Henley understand. He was nowhere near ready to have that conversation yet. No, Levar needed a second opinion. From someone he could trust.

He cornered him outside, near the Starbucks where they both always went for their midday caffeine fix. The coffee in the Eisenhower Executive Office Building, the EEOB, where the offices for the vice president's staff were located, was, slightly put, not the best, and they were both coffee addicts.

"Hey, Calix," he greeted the deputy chief of staff to the vice president.

"Hey, yourself. Did Kelly talk to you about the Good Neighbor project the vice president and Mrs. Shafer want to announce?"

"Yeah. I'm coordinating with Mrs. Shafer's communications staff."

"Good. I like the idea. Could get us some positive PR. Not that we desperately need it. The VP has been on a roll lately."

That was as perfect as an opening as it was ever going to get. A quick check confirmed no one was paying attention to them as they walked back to the EEOB. "Calix, can I run something by you? Something confidential?"

Calix slowed down and nodded.

"Is there tension between the president and the VP? Tension I should know about?"

Calix gave him a sideways glance. "Not that I'm aware of. Let me put it this way. Nothing out of the ordinary. There's always gonna be tension between the man who holds all the power and the man whose role depends on the goodwill of the former."

Levar let that sink in. If even Calix knew nothing about it—and he rarely missed anything—maybe Ethan had been right, and nothing was going on. But Henley's sources were usually excellent, so how had this rumor gotten started? And why had Ethan been so weird about it, so aggressive?

Calix stopped him with a hand on his arm. "Why are you asking? Is something wrong?"

Levar's hesitation was brief. He could trust Calix. "Henley Platt asked about it. He has a source who told him the president had wanted to go to the commemorative ceremony for the Pride Bombing."

Calix's face tightened, and a wave of guilt barreled through Levar. He shouldn't have dropped that so carelessly. If the triggers were bad for him, he could only imagine what they had to be for Calix, who'd lost his husband that day and had been injured himself.

"I'm sorry. I—"

"It's okay. It's always jarring, but I'm sure it's the same for you. But back to the topic, which is concerning. Platt has reliable sources, and he isn't often wrong."

His tone made clear he didn't want to discuss it further, so Levar let it go. "Ethan was weird about it. Wanted me to squash it hard. He said the press should stop stirring up trouble between the president and the vice president."

Calix raised an eyebrow. "I wasn't aware that's what they were doing."

"Me neither."

Calix took a sip of his coffee, his forehead wrinkled with what Levar always called his thinking lines. "I don't like this.

Why would the president want to go himself? The ceremony has always been the VP's territory."

"Maybe that's why? It's gotten him a ton of positive press."

"You think the president wants to tap into that for himself?"

"Sounds plausible."

"And Ethan told you to kill it?"

"Kill it hard."

Calix took another sip of his coffee. "Let me run this by Kelly and see what she thinks."

"What do I tell Henley in the meantime?"

"Deny it, but leave some wiggle room in case the source was partially right. But if you feel like you can trust him or have an opening for a different approach, go for it. I trust you."

They started walking again. "Thanks for the heads-up," Calix said. "Keep me posted, would you?"

They chatted until they reached the building, then went their separate ways. Levar returned to his office and closed the door behind him. How would he handle this toward Henley? If only he could wait until Calix had talked to Kelly Brockson, the vice president's chief of staff. Even though Ethan was his direct boss, they all reported to Kelly. She was a no-nonsense, get-shit-done, type A personality, and Levar loved and feared her in equal measure. Did she know about it? There was no love lost between her and Ethan, to the point where Levar sometimes wondered why Ethan still had a job.

He texted Henley. *Stop by my office when you have a chance.*

Only a few minutes later, Nicole knocked on his door. "Henley Platt is here to see you."

"Yeah, send him in. Thanks."

Henley sank into the comfortable love seat without being asked. Levar checked to make sure the door was closed, then sat down across from him. Henley didn't say a word as Levar studied him. "You're really good at making people talk," he finally said.

Henley grinned. "You called me into your office to tell me that?"

"I didn't call you into my office. What am I, the principal? I invited you to pop in."

"Either way, here I am, so what's up?"

He looked washed out, his face colorless and his eyes, which were usually razor-sharp, duller. Was he okay? They didn't have the relationship in which he could ask that. A press secretary couldn't be friends with a reporter. It would be a recipe for disaster. But he did know he could trust him, at least professionally. Henley wouldn't screw him over.

"Can we talk, off the record?"

Henley nodded. "Sure. This about the ceremony?"

"Ethan told me to deny it. Hard."

Ah, there it was, that look in Henley's eyes, like a shark who smelled blood in the water. "But you're not, or you wouldn't be sitting here, talking to me off the record."

"I talked to some people. None of them know anything about it."

"And yet you're still not denying it. Why?"

"Because your sources are usually reliable, and you wouldn't have brought this to me if it bore no credibility."

"My source is very reliable," Henley confirmed. "And it's so out of left field that it's plausible, to say the least."

"Is it?" Levar asked.

"Out of left field?"

"Mmm. This was the first you heard of a conflict between the president and the VP?

"What are you gonna give me in return? Sources close to the vice president?"

Levar scoffed. "You're joking, right? That'll lead straight to me. Make it senior White House official."

"They'll think it came from the president's staff."

"And your point is?"

Henley chuckled. "Fair enough. No, it wasn't the first time. Over the last few weeks, I've picked up rumors, but nothing specific, and no one wanted to talk."

The leak was coming from President Markinson's staff, then. If Calix didn't know about it, it couldn't be one of their people. Unless it was Ethan. But would he go that far to undermine the vice president? If so, that was a risky move that could cost him his job. No, Levar doubted Ethan would be that stupid.

"I'm not officially denying it, but it's the first we've heard of it. If it's true, it's surprising, since the president is well aware of Vice President Shafer's ties to this event and the community it represents. As the first openly bisexual vice president and not only a survivor but a hero on that horrific day, the vice president belongs at that commemoration. It would be unwise for the president to step into a role he hasn't earned."

Henley's hand flew over the paper as he wrote down Levar's words. When he was done, he looked up. "Thanks."

"Thank you. We're on top of this now."

Henley rose, his eyes sparkling. Gay humor, always a double entendre in every innocent word. "Good, because I intend to dig to the *bottom* of this."

Levar rolled his eyes as he let out Henley, whose laugh boomed until he was halfway down the hall. Fucker.

4

The plus side of not having a boyfriend anymore was that Henley no longer wrestled with guilt for working late. But as Henley poured himself a glass of wine—red because what else would pair with the Panera soup bread combo?—and settled on the couch to watch CNN, he also became aware of the downside. He didn't have anyone to talk to when he came home, and how awful was he if that was what he missed most?

He took a spoonful of the creamy tomato soup—always his favorite, though Panera's squash soup in the fall was amazing as well. Had his mom been right with that whole spiel about him not trusting people? Not leaning on them? The idea didn't sit well with him, but no matter how hard he tried, he couldn't deny she had a point. Maybe not as extreme as she'd put it, but he did have trust issues.

He didn't need to be a psychologist to figure out why. His dad walking out like that had forever changed him. Not only had he become an adult at fifteen, taking care of his younger siblings while his mom worked full time to support their family, but he'd also lost his faith in people. Not in his mom. Never in his mom. She'd been like a rock, an anchor. She'd grieved beyond words for the life she had lost, for the dream that had been shattered, but she'd straightened her back and had done what was needed to survive. Henley would never buy into the ridiculous idea of women as the weaker sex, not after what he'd seen his mom do.

So yeah, he did have some trouble trusting people. Logan had made the right call. He really did deserve much better. And Henley would have to settle for hookups again. Sigh. He was getting too old for that shit...and definitely too tired.

The idea of going back on Grindr or some other stupid app, with all the privacy issues he foresaw, considering his job—he was exhausted at even the thought. Plus, it would cost time and energy, and he'd have to groom and prep and do the whole who's-topping-and-who's-bottoming dance, and he just couldn't. Too much work. He should become celibate instead. And god, *that* was a depressing thought.

He'd just finished dinner when his phone rang. An unknown number—not unusual when many sources protected their identity as best they could. "Henley Platt."

"It's me."

He recognized the voice instantly. "Larry, how are you?"

That wasn't the man's real name, of course, but Henley would happily call him Deep Throat for all he cared, as long as the man kept talking to him. He'd provided Henley with solid tips so far. It had to be someone pretty close to Markinson, considering the access he had, but Henley didn't pry. An anonymous source who talked was worth way more than a known source who clammed up because he'd lost anonymity.

"I didn't see anything about the Pride Bombing ceremony in your paper this morning."

Henley pressed Record on his recording app. Recording with one party's consent was legal in DC, and it provided him with some necessary proof in case he ever needed it. "I'm still doing follow-up research on that. So far, no one has been able to confirm it."

"The vice president's people denied it?"

"Yes."

Larry laughed. "God, they're idiots. Completely out of the loop."

"Are they?"

"You have no idea."

Men liked to brag, and Henley gladly used that to his advantage. "I guess you're fooling them all, then."

"We sure are. Then again, they're pathetic, the whole lot, so there's that. They're all just a bunch of…"

Henley stayed silent. That sentence could've ended in many ways, but somehow, he suspected the intended ending had some kind of homophobic slur.

"You're gay too, aren't you?" Larry asked, confirming Henley's suspicions.

"Not gay. Pansexual."

"Same difference."

Actually, it wasn't, but this wasn't the time for *How to be an Ally 101*—not that he thought Larry would've been interested. "Why?"

Larry hesitated. "No reason," he finally said. "Just curious."

"What else can you tell me, Larry?" Henley wanted this conversation to be over with. "I'm gonna need more details to get this fact-checked."

Larry huffed in annoyance. "What else do you need to know?"

"You said the president wanted to go to the ceremony himself. How clear was this? Are we talking about a casual remark, something uttered to a small circle of confidants, what?"

"One of his people put out feelers with the organizers, but they were told that Mayor Goldstein wanted the vice president there and that he'd already informally asked him. The president was irritated that this had been decided behind his back and through back channels."

Henley didn't believe that even for a second. These things were always done through back channels to minimize potential loss of face. But he would let Larry in the illusion he believed him, since antagonizing him had zero benefits.

"Why would the president even want to attend in the first place? No offense, but this isn't really his scene, his crowd."

The most LGBTQIA+-supportive thing Markinson had done so far was make Shafer his VP, and he'd only done so for the political benefit of cozying up to the hero of the moment. His previous VP had resigned due to health reasons only nine months before reelections, and Markinson had wanted to cash in on Shafer's rapidly rising popularity. Plus, Shafer came from the most prestigious political dynasty in the country. He was the new Camelot. Had that enthusiasm waned, even though they'd won the reelection?

"The president feels the vice president is too much in the spotlight, that he's claiming the glory and honor for that day, thus downplaying and minimizing the live-saving efforts from the first responders."

Jealousy. Markinson was jealous of Shafer's hero status. Would Henley ever stop being amazed at how small and petty the most powerful could be? Obviously, not something he'd utter out loud. "Mmm."

"Look, no one denies that what he did was heroic, but that doesn't mean he should keep milking it, you know? He needs to share the limelight with others."

Like the president? The man who hadn't even been there that day and who'd needed a crash course in correct terminology before his press conference? *Right.* Also something that would never be more than a thought in Henley's head or maybe a watered-down op-ed. "Mmm."

"Right?" Larry took Henley's affirmative sounds as agreement. "The president has been fully committed to bringing the terrorists behind the Pride Bombing to justice."

Henley swallowed, unable to make a sound now. No matter how often he wrote those two words, read them, or heard them, they always made him shiver.

"And he should get the credit for that, which, let's face it, is a far bigger accomplishment than what Shafer did."

"Mmm."

Henley had discovered years ago it was possible to say that while grinding his teeth with annoyance. Some days, he hated his job, especially when he had to listen to self-inflated people spouting absolute nonsense and had to pretend to agree. Or at least listen. Which he did, but god, it cost him at times.

"It's thanks to the president that the bombers were caught. I mean, they're dead, but that wasn't his fault. No one knows how they were able to commit suicide."

"Not all of them were caught," Henley pointed out. "Hamza Bashir is still at large."

The three students from Kashmir who had placed the

actual bombs had been caught thanks to intense cooperation between various agencies within the intelligence community. As far as Henley was concerned, Markinson hadn't played a role in that. That had been extensive intelligence work for which the president shouldn't get the credit.

"Bashir's gone underground in Yemen, but the CIA has intel on his whereabouts."

Oh. My. God. Had Larry just...?

"But that's off the record, of course," Larry added hastily, a note of panic in his voice.

Yeah, no shit. The man had revealed classified information. Top secret, most likely. To a reporter, for fuck's sake.

That the CIA was still trying to get a firm location on Hamza Bashir, the leader of Al Salaahin and the alleged mastermind behind the bombing, the Al-Quaeda splinter group that had claimed responsibility for the bombing, wasn't news. Of course they were, and they had been since they knew who had been behind it. Larry had merely confirmed they might be a step closer to being able to send in a Special Forces team. Now Henley had to decide if that tidbit was worth more than keeping Larry as a source.

If he published it, he'd lose him for sure. Hell, Larry would get fired. But way more importantly, by revealing this information, Henley would compromise the efforts of the intelligence community to apprehend Bashir. If he slipped through their fingers because of Henley's warning and planned another attack, Henley would never forgive himself. As much as he chased a scoop, the safety of others came first. And so did justice for the victims of the Pride Bombing.

"No worries, Larry. We'll keep that last bit between us," he said, ramping up the brotherhood-vibe in his voice.

"You're a class act, Platt. That's why I want you to have

the information. The public deserves to know, and if we can both benefit a little at the same time, then no harm done, right?"

Kill. Him. Now.

"Couldn't agree more, Larry. Was that all for now?"

"That should help you get this out there, no? I'll find you when I have more."

Larry hung up without another word, and Henley stopped the recording and saved it to the cloud. What a moron. Then again, idiots like Larry seemed to be his bread and butter, so could he really complain? At least he had more info on Markinson and the deal with the commemorative ceremony. What a twat. Henley hadn't been a fan of him before the bombing, but his respect for the president had sunk gradually lower over the years. Being jealous of Shafer for saving lives? How small and petty.

But the new information meant another chat with Levar, and Henley was looking forward to that. He could deal with Ethan Haffley—Levar's boss—of course, but all reporters despised the man. He was a weasel, that one, and Henley had wondered on more than one occasion why Kelly Brockson hadn't gotten rid of him yet. Henley wasn't sure if Ethan knew what loyalty meant, but if he had any, it sure as hell wasn't to the vice president.

No, Henley would deal with Levar...and enjoy the view while he was at it because damn, the guy was *hot*. Levar had a pair of amazing blue eyes, so light they were the first thing Henley always noticed about him. He was much leaner than Henley, who, at thirty-nine, had acquired a bit of a dad bod, but he still radiated strength. And sexiness. Sexy strength, was that a thing? If not, it totally should be because it fit Levar to a T.

Nothing was ever gonna come from it—hello, conflict of

interest—but that didn't mean he couldn't look. And now that he was single again, he could even look a little longer and harder.

Harder. Henley took a big gulp of wine and laughed at his own joke. Some things never got old.

5

"I'll get back to you on this," Levar promised Henley, eager to get him out the door so he could talk to Calix. This latest info from Henley, only two days after his first question about the Pride Bombing commemoration? Not good. Trouble with a capital T.

"Make sure you do."

Levar suppressed an annoyed sigh. "Come on, Henley, you know I will."

Henley winked at him. "I know, but I like riling you up."

Oh, for fuck's sake. Was he serious? "If what you're saying is true, I don't consider that something to joke about."

Henley, who had his hand on the doorknob, turned around again. "He's on his way out, Levar. The president is in the last two years of his presidency, and like many before him, he's getting worried about his legacy. He wants to bask in the spotlight. That's all. He's the past. Shafer all but has the party's nomination sewn up for the elections."

"Even if the president actively works against him? If he handpicks another candidate and endorses him?"

Henley frowned. "Do you really think it'll come to that? Traditionally, presidents have always stayed neutral until after the primaries and a candidate had been elected."

"Officially, yes, but we both know what has happened behind the scenes. The president wields tremendous power, even if he does it unofficially."

Levar caught himself. He was revealing way too much, but Henley waved dismissively. "Not everything we discuss is on the record. You know that. This is just two guys talking politics. You have a sharp political mind."

Levar gently shook his head. "Just two guys talking politics? Come on now. Neither of us is that naïve."

Henley's face fell, and he sighed. "True. I wish it could be, though. Don't you miss it? Being able to talk politics without having to weigh your words, without being on your guard the whole time? Just for fun?"

What kind of question was that? "Isn't that what friends are for? Or, just a suggestion, partners?"

Sadness filled Henley's expression. "I don't know if I have many of those left."

"Partners? Usually, one will do, but if you're poly, power to you."

"It turns out I couldn't even hold on to one partner…"

That explained Henley's somewhat dreary demeanor the day before. Levar's heart flooded with sympathy. "He broke up with you?"

Henley shrugged halfheartedly. "Can't blame him."

"What we do isn't easy. Long days, weird hours, always on call. Not many partners would understand that. He works for Congressman Gibson, right?" Henley seemed surprised Levar knew this. "I keep files on all of you guys. You never know when it may come in handy."

"Ah. Right. Yeah, he's a junior staffer for Gibson. He likes it, but he's not the hungry, super ambitious type…"

"Like us." Levar shared a look with Henley that felt like they connected, like they somehow belonged to the same club.

"And you?" Henley asked.

"Me what?"

"Partner? Boyfriend? Husband?"

Levar shook his head, grinning. "As if you wouldn't know if that were the case. Nope, single and very happy rooming with my best friend, Rhett."

"At least you have someone to talk to, right?"

Dude, that's just sad, Levar wanted to blurt out, but he held back.

"I know. I'm pathetic," Henley said with a sigh.

Levar held his thumb and index finger up. "Just a little." He widened the distance. "Also a little dramatic."

Henley's eyes sparkled again, which made Levar strangely happy. "Now scram because I have work to do."

As soon as Henley had left, Levar stepped out of his office. He'd better talk to Calix right away.

"Was that Platt leaving your office just now?"

Levar's heart skipped a beat, and he turned around to Ethan, who had sneaked up behind him. "Yes."

Never answer more than the question. It had been hammered into him in his public relations training.

"Did you talk to him about the ceremony?"

"Yes."

"And you're sure he got the message?"

Levar thought of Henley's sharp gaze, the way he'd read between the lines. "One hundred percent."

Ethan awkwardly patted his shoulder. "Good. Glad to see you're a team player."

With a toothy smile that was probably meant as an encouragement, Ethan walked into his own office and shut the door firmly behind him. What was he doing there all day anyway? He delegated most of the meetings and briefings to others, with the bulk falling on Levar's shoulders. Levar shrugged it off. That was a problem for another day. One crisis at a time.

He hurried over to Calix's office.

"Sheila, is Calix free?" he asked Calix's assistant.

"They're wrapping up the security briefing."

"Can I wait?"

Sheila tapped a few keys on her computer. "Yeah. His next is at eleven, so you have ten minutes max."

Levar waited impatiently and, as soon as the briefers had left, rushed into Calix's office. He closed the door behind him. Calix looked up from his phone, where he'd been speed typing a message. "Uh-oh."

"Yeah. Uh-oh indeed."

He filled Calix in on the new information he'd gotten from Henley.

"Dammit. Is he gonna run it?" Calix asked.

"Yeah. And we can't ask him not to. This is more than salacious gossip. He's got a solid source. Did you talk to Kelly?"

Calix nodded. "It was news to her, and I've got her permission to take this to the VP." He sighed. "There goes my schedule." They walked out together. "Sheila, can you reschedule my eleven o'clock? And tell Max we're on our way to see the vice president ."

Sheila nodded, already reaching for the phone.

"Did you talk to Ethan again?" Calix asked as they walked.

"No. I went straight to you."

Calix's voice dropped to a whisper. "Keep it that way."

"You don't trust Ethan?"

"Do *you*?" Calix fired back.

"No. He's one of Markinson's men, always has been."

"Exactly. His loyalty is with the president, not with the VP."

They'd reached the vice president's office, and Max, his assistant, gestured they could walk in. Calix closed the door behind them.

"What's up?" Vice President Shafer asked, pushing his chair back and joining them in the comfortable seating area.

"Sir, have you heard anything about the president wanting to attend the commemorative ceremony for the Pride Bombing himself?" Calix asked.

Shafer's eyes grew sharp. "No. Should I?"

"Henley Platt has a source." Calix gestured at Levar.

He shared what he'd learned, Shafer listening intently. Levar respected him for his ability to listen and process information fast, then analyze it.

"So the tl;dr is that it's most likely true, since Platt's sources are always reliable," Shafer said.

Levar's eyebrows rose. "Tl;dr?"

"Too long; didn't read, the executive summary, as managers would call it."

Levar's cheeks heated. He and his big mouth. "I know, sir. I was merely expressing my... Never mind."

Shafer chuckled. "I try to keep up with the times, Levar. I'm not *that* old."

Where was a nice, big hole in the ground when you needed one?

"Stop teasing the poor kid, sir, so he can get his foot out of his mouth. We need to contain this," Calix said.

"Do we?" Levar said, desperate to get back on topic. "I'm

not sure this story would be to our disadvantage. If we spin it right, the president will come off as petty."

Shafer sat quietly for a while. "I hear what you're saying, and it could work for now, but we may need a broader strategy."

"Sir?" Calix apparently was as confused as Levar was.

Shafer folded his hands. "The president has been keeping me more and more out of the loop, and by now, I'm convinced it's intentional."

"Is it his staff or himself? You know they can get territorial, but that doesn't mean he authorized it," Calix said.

Shafer looked from Calix to Levar, then back. "We're entering a new phase now, one where I need to establish a voice independent of the president. If I want to have any shot at becoming the nominee, I need to lay the groundwork now."

Levar nodded. Where was Shafer going with this?

"I've always been loyal to the president, and I will remain so, but at the same time, I need to look out for my own future. And I need a staff who is fully committed to that. To me."

Ah. Levar understood now. "You have my loyalty and commitment, sir. I'm not going anywhere, and I'm on your side."

Shafer nodded, sending him a powerful smile. "Glad to hear it. I like you, Levar, and you're exceptionally talented at what you do. I'm happy to have you on my team."

Levar grew warm inside. "Thank you, Mr. Vice President. It's an honor and a privilege."

"Good. Now, I don't think a little distance from the president is a bad idea, but I don't want to get saddled with all the shitty tasks he doesn't want or that are potentially explosive."

"Yes. We need to stay away from Social Security reform for now," Calix said. "That's one topic the president would like to dump into your lap, and nothing good can come from that."

"Unless we can control the narrative," Levar said. "If we position the VP as the man with the vision and the guts to tackle this crucial problem, we could use it to our advantage."

Calix jotted something down. "I like that idea. Let's schedule a brainstorm and come up with some topics we think the president may want to send our way that we could spin in a positive way. For now, how do we handle this article Platt will be writing? Can we deny it?"

"Yes." Levar leaned forward. "If we're agreed we didn't know about it."

"I knew he wanted to push me back in the ribbon-cutting, ship-christening, groundbreaking kind of ceremonial activities, but this was a new one for me. To be honest, I feel a tad hurt by it. Surely, he must understand how much this ceremony means to me." Shafer sounded genuinely upset but also baffled.

"Henley thinks it's jealousy," Levar said.

"*Henley*?" Calix's tone held an edge.

"You know I'm on a first-name basis with all White House correspondents."

God, why had he gone on the defense instantly? He had nothing to hide, but now Calix would think he did.

"I was more curious as to why he'd share his theories with you. Was he asking for your opinion? For a quote?"

"No, he... I exchange information with certain trustworthy members of the press sometimes, when it's to our mutual benefit. Henley and I were trading information. If not for that, we wouldn't have known about this."

Calix studied him a bit longer, then nodded. "Fair enough. Do you think denial will work?"

Levar considered it. Henley had his source. All denial would do was make them look like idiots that they'd been kept in the dark. "Let's call it a miscommunication between the president's staff and yours, sir," he said to Shafer. "We'll add that you're looking forward to the ceremony and that the president is more than welcome to join you."

Calix grinned with approval. "Smart. That way, we confirm we're going and that the vice president is primary here. He'll never go if he's only attending and not taking your place, sir."

Shafer looked at his watch. "I like it. But let's schedule that brainstorm soon."

"I'm on it, sir," Calix said.

Shafer rose to his feet, and Calix and Levar followed his lead. "And, gentlemen, this does not leave this room."

6

Miscommunication, his ass. Henley couldn't blame Levar for that diplomatic answer, but that didn't mean he had to stop digging. Something more was at play here than miscommunication between the president's and the vice president's staff, and he would find it. He always did. Hungry Henley, his first editor had jokingly called him, a compliment for his drive and passion for delivering the best story possible. He'd lived up to that nickname over the years—and to his more recent moniker, Henley Hound—and he had no intention of letting up anytime soon.

All thoughts of Logan, the breakup, and the concept of emotional unavailability were forgotten. What the fuck did he care anyway? He had his career, and he'd invest his time and energy into that. Way more rewarding than someone who could walk out on him on a whim at any moment. Not that Logan's decision had been a whim—he wasn't the type for that—but the principle stood. Work was far more reliable than people ever would be, as Henley's long list of ex-partners could attest to.

He hadn't heard from Larry since their last conversation two days ago, but since he still hadn't run the story, he had no doubt Larry would contact him again. Larry had an agenda, and Henley wasn't entirely sure what it entailed, but Larry wouldn't stop until this story was out there.

That didn't mean Henley had to write it the way Larry wanted, though. In fact, he wouldn't, if only because a story based on one source wasn't news. It was gossip, speculation. No, he needed a second source to confirm it, someone with intimate knowledge, eager to share their thoughts with him.

He'd spent the morning reaching out to his contacts in the White House, but none of them were willing to talk. The White House press briefing was uneventful. Katie Winters, President Markinson's press secretary, wasn't Henley's favorite person, as she was notoriously blunt, but she did run a tight ship and kept briefings fast and efficient.

But Henley didn't even try to get her to comment on his source. She'd feed him BS anyway. No, he needed an advisor a little lower in the hierarchy. Someone who would feel important when approached, who'd reward Henley by saying too much. He'd struck dirt with Markinson's key advisors, though, so who was left? Who would have inside information on the Pride Bombing ceremony story?

He froze. He was thinking too small. If he was right, if Larry's hints at a more prominent issue were correct, this wasn't about the ceremony at all. Hadn't Levar said it himself? What if the president handpicked another candidate? He needed to look at the bigger picture, and with that, he knew who to approach.

The man was a creature of habit, and as he'd expected, Henley caught him at McDonald's, walking in for his daily small vanilla milkshake. "Bryce," Henley greeted him, getting up from his spot right next to the door so he'd see him enter.

Bryce's eyes widened in surprise. "Henley. It's good to see you." He took Henley's extended hand and shook it. "Or am I going to regret I said that?"

Henley grinned. "That depends on if you're willing to talk to me or not."

Bryce sighed as he let go. "What would we be talking about?"

Henley leaned in. "The elections."

Bryce frowned. "I'm not involved in the midterms."

"The presidential elections."

"I should've met you at an expensive restaurant rather than let you pay for my milkshake."

"Give me fifteen minutes of your time, and I'll throw in a ten-piece nugget meal."

"I really need to raise my standards. I'm way too cheap a date," Bryce grumbled, but his eyes sparkled.

Henley ordered, then found a spot for them to talk, all the way in the back.

"What do you need to know?" Bryce said, then popped a nugget drenched in barbecue sauce into his mouth.

"Who will the president be supporting in the next elections?"

Bryce stopped chewing. "What the hell kinda question is that? You know he'll support whoever gets the party's nomination."

"Officially. But who is he supporting unofficially? Who's getting his behind-the-scenes support?"

"I don't know what you're talking about." Bryce lowered his eyes, gazing at his milkshake as if it was about to birth babies.

Henley spoke softly. "You're the party's single best

polling expert. You know the polling data of everyone who would have a chance at running in two years. I'm asking you if the president asked you to run numbers on anyone else but the VP."

"Jesus, Henley, do you know what you're asking?"

"I've only just started. Tell me I'm completely off the mark here, and we'll chat about your beloved Red Sox for the next ten minutes...and you know how much that pains me as a Yankees fan."

Bryce slowly shook his head, sighing deeply. "We're gonna be here a while, aren't we?"

"I'll order you more nuggets."

Bryce rolled his eyes and shoved another nugget into his mouth. Henley waited patiently. "The request came from Victor Kendall, not from the president," Bryce said.

Bingo. Henley kept his face blank. "I doubt the president's chief of staff would do that without the president's approval."

Bryce gave a one-shoulder shrug. "Maybe, but it's still an important distinction to make."

"And what was the request, exactly?"

Bryce took his time sipping on his shake. "To create a shortlist of the five most likely candidates to beat Shafer in the primaries."

Henley softly whistled between his teeth. He'd called it. "So the president is selecting another heir apparent. What does he have against Shafer?"

"Off the record?"

"Background only. I'll get it confirmed through other sources, but I need to know what to look for."

"The president had expected Shafer to help him win the elections two years ago."

Henley frowned. "They did win."

"Yeah, but they lost the House and the Senate."

"We're talking two seats in the House and one in the Senate. That's all the Democrats lost, which was way less than expected. They ran with an openly bisexual senator with strong ties to the LGBTQIA+ community. What were they expecting?"

"Oh, trust me, I warned them. Shafer's initial numbers were good, but they were soft."

"Of course they were soft. People like to think of themselves as progressive, so they say they'll vote for a bisexual vice president. Doesn't mean they're actually gonna do it on election day."

Bryce threw his hands up. "You're preaching to the choir, man. I told them, but the president wanted Shafer."

"He wanted his hero status and popularity, you mean."

"Same difference. But it turned out to be a mistake—at least in his eyes. Shafer did better than I had projected, but the president still blames him for the loss of seats."

"Or maybe he's just jealous because no matter what he does, Shafer's favorites are much higher than his."

Bryce sighed. "The president's approval rate is fifty-two percent right now. Shafer's at sixty-nine. Even Republicans like him. He's got the military experience, the political connections. He knows how the game is played…"

"Plus, it's easy to ignore him being bisexual when he's married to a woman and has a son. And never so much as a rumor of him stepping out on his wife."

"There's that too."

"So Markinson has decided to support someone else than Shafer?"

"I don't think we're at that stage yet. I've only started running some numbers for him."

"Just out of curiosity and strictly between us, how are Shafer's numbers looking? Should he decide to run?"

Bryce met his gaze straight on. "Good. Really, really good. He's built up a lot of goodwill and political capital in the three years he's been vice president. He's proven himself. And he'll always be the Pride Bombing hero, the man who saved lives." Bryce emptied his shake, slurping out the last bit. "Weren't you there when it happened?"

"I was."

"Did you see him?"

"Briefly. I even took some pictures of him, but I didn't talk to him. He was too busy saving lives."

Bryce shook his head, clicking his tongue. "I still can't comprehend it, you know? How people can hate so deeply they're willing to take innocent lives."

"Be glad you can't get it. It shows you'll never sink to that level despite the crap we deal with every day."

"True that. So you got enough?"

Henley went through what he had learned in his head. He definitely had enough now to dig further and get people to go on the record. "One more thing. The vice president's staff seems to be unaware of any tension. How is that possible?"

Bryce wiped his hands off on a napkin, then dabbed at his mouth. "No way Shafer hasn't picked up on this tension. From what I hear, the president has been on an active campaign to shut him out. So if his staff claims they're unaware, either they're lying, or Shafer is a class act and protecting the president. My money's on the latter."

Bryce got up and threw his trash into the trashcan, then came back. "You owe me at least ten milkshakes."

Henley chuckled. "Thanks, Bryce. You've been more than helpful."

He got himself a coffee and sipped it as he slowly walked to his office at the Washington Times building. Had Levar lied to him? It didn't sit right with him. Levar could be evasive when he had to be, and he could spin with the best of them, but to Henley's knowledge, he'd never outright lied to the press. Or at least if he had, he'd never been caught. But deceiving didn't fit his character, his approach.

And what was more, why would he lie about this? If there was tension and he'd been aware, wouldn't he have taken the opportunity for a subtle dig at the president? No, Levar hadn't lied to him, which meant either the vice president hadn't known—which seemed highly unlikely—or he'd chosen to keep this from his staff. Why would he do that? What reason could the vice president have to keep this under wraps? Was he hoping to mend the apparent rift between the president and himself?

Henley all but rubbed his hands as he threw his empty coffee cup into the trash and stepped into his building. It seemed he needed to have another conversation with Levar. He couldn't wait.

He caught him later that day after contacting Levar's assistant to see if he had a minute. He did. As Henley walked into his office, Levar rolled his eyes at him. "We really should stop meeting like this. One more visit from you and people will start to talk."

Henley grinned at Levar's dry wit. "Since it seems to be the only way we can meet, you don't leave me with much choice."

Wait, that had come out way flirtier than he'd intended, and the slight widening of Levar's eyes proved it. Crap. Would he take it the wrong way? Had he just risked the great working relationship he had with Levar?

"Yes, unfortunately my dance card is completely full...

for members of the press."

Thank fuck he'd taken it well. Henley inwardly sighed with relief. "That's a shame because I think we'd have made a dashing pair on the dance floor. Just so you know, I do a mean rumba."

They were both laughing now. "Personally, I'm more of the dirty dancing variety," Levar said, then looked shocked as if he couldn't believe he'd said that. Well, neither could Henley, so that made two of them. Somehow, they'd slid into flirting territory, and now that they had, Henley found himself reluctant to leave.

"Trust me, nobody would put you in a corner," he said, his voice just a little breathless because holy shit, this was *Levar* he was flirting with. Supersexy, superhot Levar, who was also super off-limits for too many reasons to count. So why did he want to keep flirting with him just a bit longer?

"What are we doing?" Levar asked hoarsely. "We can't do this."

Henley shrugged, holding his eyes. "Of course we can. It's just...talking."

"You were flirting," Levar pointed out.

"So were you."

"And you think that's okay?"

"If this stays between us? Sure it's okay. It's harmless, Levar."

Levar swallowed, his gaze lingering as he took in Henley. "Yeah, somehow I doubt that. You don't come equipped with a 'harmless' setting."

Henley chuckled. "Is that a compliment?"

"If that's how you wanna take it. I'm just saying I'm not falling for your harmless routine. You make great white sharks look like potential pets."

Henley put a hand on his heart, staggering back. "You

wound me, sir. I'll have you know I'm generally speaking a nice guy."

"Says the guy whose nickname is Henley Hound because once you smell blood, you don't give up."

Henley waved his hand. "Those rumors are greatly exaggerated." When Levar put his hands on his hips, Henley held up both hands. "Okay, okay. I'll admit there might be a kernel of truth to that."

"A kernel of... Remember who you're talking to here. I *know* you. I know exactly what you're capable of."

Henley lowered his hands. "You know the reporter Henley. Not the man."

Why was he even making that distinction? Of course Levar only knew him like that. They weren't friends, and they sure as hell would never be more than friends. Anything between them was impossible, and why that thought made him sad, he didn't know.

"Unfortunately, that's all I will ever know," Levar said, and Henley latched on to that one word.

"Unfortunately?"

Levar avoided his gaze, and damn, he looked cute when he was flustered. "It's an expression. Nothing more."

"Oh."

"Why? Were you expecting a marriage proposal and everlasting love?"

Levar had gotten his footing back, and Henley grinned. "I usually start with a date, but everlasting love sounds good."

Levar rolled his eyes at him. "Let me know if you figure out where and how to find that because clearly, I'm clueless."

"And you're asking the man whose boyfriend dumped him for being a shitty boyfriend?"

"True. Let's stay married to our jobs, then. Much safer and less risk of getting hurt."

"Amen to that."

"Speaking of our jobs, I assume you didn't come here just for flirting and cute banter."

Henley's face fell. "No, though that was an unexpected bonus. I need your official comment on some things."

Levar sighed. "Yeah, I figured. Hit me with it."

7

"We need to talk," Levar told Calix, closing the door of Calix's office behind him.

"Experience has taught me nothing good ever comes from that opening line."

"You're gonna see that affirmed once again." Levar pulled up a chair. "I had another conversation with Henley this morning. He's got a source, and you're not going to like it."

"Does the VP need to be here for this?"

"Yeah, he does."

"Okay, give me a few minutes. Don't go anywhere. I'll see if I can get Kelly to sit in as well."

Levar nodded, grabbing his phone as soon as Calix had hurried out. Fifty-two new emails in the last hour. God, would it ever end? He quickly read through them, deleted a few newsletters, and typed out rapid responses to some others. He really was married to his job, wasn't he? He and Henley had that in common at least.

But what the ever-loving fuck had he been thinking, flirting with him? Henley had flirted right back, though.

Come to think of it, hadn't he initiated it? Yeah, he had. Not that the "he hit me first" approach still worked at their age, if it had ever been effective. So once again, what the hell had he been thinking?

He hadn't been, which was the problem. He'd gotten caught up in the fun of it, in the game, the challenge of outwitting him. Henley was smart and quick-witted, and sparring with him had been the most stimulating conversation Levar had had in ages. And if that wasn't the saddest proof ever of his utter lack of a social life... *Sigh.*

Voices sounded in the hallway, coming closer, and Levar put his phone away. Vice President Shafer walked in first, with Calix on his heels. Levar expected Kelly to follow, but Calix closed the door after himself.

Shafer sunk into a chair, looking tired. "Calix said you had new information."

"Yes, sir." Levar gave a quick summary of what Henley had shared with him about Markinson asking for polling numbers from possible contenders for the Democratic nomination. "He's running this, and he's asking for an official statement."

Shafer let out a deep sigh. "I guess the cat's out of the bag."

"Did you know all this?" Calix asked Shafer.

"Some of it. I knew he wasn't happy with the election results and that over the months, he's put the blame more and more on me. But I wasn't aware he's basically recruiting potential presidential candidates behind my back. It's..."

"It's tasteless, is what it is. Backstabby." Calix dragged a hand through his hair, looking annoyed as fuck.

"He's jealous, sir," Levar offered. "Your approval ratings are much higher than his. You're one of the most popular vice presidents in history, if not the most popular one of all."

"I can't help but feel like it's not entirely deserved," Shafer said. "If I hadn't been at that Pride Parade…"

"People love their heroes," Levar said. "There's nothing wrong with that."

"No, but I understand it must be frustrating for the president that he isn't getting that same approval and validation for the work he's doing."

Then he should do a better job, Levar wanted to say, but of course, he didn't.

"No offense, Levar, but why are you running point on this? Where's Ethan in this?" Shafer asked.

Levar glanced at Calix, who nodded he should tell the truth. "I asked Henley why he hadn't approached Ethan, and he laughed at me. The consensus among the press is that Ethan gives them the runaround, denies everything, or only speaks up when it's something critical of the president."

Shafer's face tightened. "Can you confirm this?" he asked Calix.

"Unfortunately, yes. I've had my doubts about his loyalty for a while."

"He worked for the president in his first campaign," the vice president said. "In fact, he was one of his primary spokespersons then. My guess is he's still sour the president chose Katie Winters over him."

Levar scoffed. "Not just Katie, but Paulo as well as her deputy. Ethan got stuck with the far less glamorous job of working for the VP." His cheeks heated as his gaffe registered with him. "I didn't mean to imply working for you is somehow less glamorous or less of an honor," he stammered, but Shafer held up his hand.

"I don't take offense easily, and let's face it. If you think you're gonna be the president's press secretary, ending up working for me is a disappointment."

God, he wanted to die of embarrassment. What a stupid thing to say, even though Shafer seemed to take it in stride.

"That may be so, but it's been six years since Markinson became president. That's a long time to hold a grudge and stay in a job you hate," Calix said. "So why is he still here?"

The room grew quiet. None of them had an answer.

Calix sighed. "Let's keep him out of the loop on this. Levar, you take point on this issue. Report anything you hear back to us."

"Will do. But what do I tell Henley?"

Calix looked at Shafer, who rubbed his temples. "There's a reason I'd kept this to myself for now. If we're not careful, this will become a scandal—the next whatever-gate. It would drown out our entire message."

"I understand, sir, but if we don't tackle this, you'll be seen as weak, which will hurt your chances in the elections in two years," Calix pointed out.

"Henley's not gonna give up. He smells blood in the water, and he's got sources to back it up," Levar said.

"Do we have any idea who his sources are?" Calix asked Levar.

"Not until I've read the actual article, but he's got to have some senior advisor to the president. He has inside information."

"Which means that either the president has ordered the leak or he's silently condoning it because we all know his advisors don't go against him, or they'll get fired."

Shafer brought up a valid issue.

"Why would the president want this leaked?" Levar wondered. "What's in it for him? Usually, the White House tries to keep a lid on stuff like this, so why not this time?"

Shafer slowly shook his head. "I wish I had the answer

to that. I guess all we can do is keep a close eye on this and monitor it carefully. Levar, you got a good handle on this reporter?"

A good handle on Henley? He wished. "I have a great relationship with him, sir. Working relationship, I mean. I'll make sure to stay in close contact with him. Professionally close."

God, he needed to stop talking right fucking *now*. He was babbling, and moreover, he was making a complete fool of himself. Again.

Calix looked at him funny, then said, "Okay. I think our answer to Henley should be that the vice president has always strived to have a good working relationship with the president and that as far as he's concerned, that's still the case. The vice president respects the president and looks forward to serving the country together for the next two years. And don't go into specifics."

Levar nodded, quickly jotting down some notes in the notes app on his phone. "Gotcha. I'll contact Henley and let him know."

As soon as he was back in his office, he called Henley, who picked up after the first ring. "Hey, it's me."

Henley chuckled. "Hi me, it's hey."

Levar groaned. "*Dad jokes*? We're at that level now?"

"Well-timed dad jokes are in a league of their own, I'll have you know."

"We'll chalk it up to the age difference," Levar said, and that got an immediate protest out of Henley.

"I'm not that old!"

"I'm thirty-two. Pretty sure that was a while ago for you..."

"Ouch, that hurts. I'm almost forty, which is the new thirty and all that."

Levar laughed. "When you do what we do, I'm pretty sure forty is the new fifty."

"True," Henley said with a sigh. "But it's worth it, right?"

"I guess so. Haven't really thought about it."

"You will. Trust me. Anyway, I assume this is not a social call, as welcome as that would be?"

Was he flirting again? Levar had better not get sucked into that again. No matter how much he wanted to. "I have an official statement for you about the alleged tension with the president."

"Okay. Shoot."

Levar rattled off the statement Calix had given him, and when he was done, Henley clicked his tongue. "Smart statement."

"Yeah?"

"It makes you look dignified and makes the president look like he's slinging mud."

"Obviously, I'm not going to comment on that."

"I wasn't expecting you to. This will run as soon as I have everything confirmed, just FYI."

"Thanks for the heads-up. Let me know if you have any more questions."

Henley was quiet for a few beats. "I will. I'm sure we'll talk again soon."

Henley ended the call, but his parting words kept playing through Levar's mind the rest of the day and even during his commute home, a half-hour MARC ride north to the somewhat boring but efficient suburb of Rockville, Maryland. Henley's words had sounded like a promise, like something he was looking forward to. And if Levar was honest, so was he.

When he got home—an apartment he shared with his best friend—Rhett was cooking. Delicious aromas wafted in from the kitchen, overpowering the usual smell of vanilla that had become their normal, and Levar's stomach growled.

"How was your day?" Rhett asked as Levar kicked off his shoes and loosened his tie.

"Long. That smells good, babe. What are you making?"

Rhett was stirring in a large pot. "Beef barley soup. Not exactly spring fare, but I was in the mood for something hearty."

Levar hugged him from behind and pressed their cheeks together. "Smells delicious. Thanks for cooking."

"If we had to rely on your kitchen skills, we'd be dead by now."

Levar slapped his ass. "Smartass. Nice ass too, by the way. Have you been working out again?"

He unbuttoned his shirt, then unbuckled his belt. The most glorious moment of the day was when he could swap his suit for a pair of sweatpants and a hoodie. And exchange his boring if decent-looking Calvin Klein boxer briefs for his silk panties, which made him feel sexy, even if no one saw them. Panties and sweatpants might be a strange combination, but it worked for him.

Rhett shrugged. "It's quiet at the moment, and the gym here is empty during the day."

"No new leads yet?" Levar called out from his bedroom, where he quickly got changed. He picked black silk panties today, the lace against his cock making him half-hard instantly. It would wane off soon enough, but that first touch with silk never failed to arouse him.

"A few, but nothing tangible. I sent out my portfolio to everyone by now, but no one's biting..."

"Yet," Levar said, stepping back into the kitchen. He eyed the soup. It should be almost ready by now, so he put out bowls and small plates, then grabbed crackers and cheese. "Beer?"

"Sure."

Levar popped open his beer and took a few gulps. God, that tasted good.

"I'm always amazed by how much faith you have in me," Rhett said. Levar gave him the bowls, and he ladled the soup into them. "It's been five years since I won the World Press Photo. No one remembers me anymore."

For a while, they were quiet as they sat across from each other at the kitchen table, eating dinner. "You took a long time off after that," Levar said softly. "And it was completely necessary, but it prevented you from capitalizing on your relative fame."

Rhett sighed, his shoulders dropping. "I didn't even attend the ceremony for the victims."

"Stop blaming yourself for that. You needed time to heal. We all did. You're so talented, babe. Something will open up for you. I know it."

Rhett nodded, even though he didn't look like he believed Levar. "Let's talk about something else. Something fun."

"A reporter flirted with me," Levar blurted out. Oh, shit. Why the hell had he said that?

Rhett's eyes widened. "Tell me more."

"He's this guy who works for the Washington Times, Henley Platt. He's following a story that involves the VP, so we've talked multiple times. But he was flirting with me today."

"Henley Platt was flirting with you..."

"You know him?"

Rhett rolled his eyes. "He won a Pulitzer Prize. Of course

I know him. Also, he's hot. Like, not exactly a bear but ruggedly handsome. And gay, right?"

"Pan, but yeah. He's...attractive."

Rhett shook his head. "Hell no. He's way beyond attractive. He's hella hot."

Damn right he was, but Levar wasn't gonna admit that. He should never have even mentioned the harmless flirting. Not that he couldn't trust Rhett. They'd known each other since high school, both coming from a suburb of sunny Sacramento, California. They'd been the two gay kids in their freshman year and had instantly bonded.

After one kiss when they'd been sixteen, they'd decided they'd stay friends, and they'd been super close since. No, Levar trusted Rhett blindly. Didn't mean it was smart to mention Henley. Rhett might be a total dork at times, but he was way more perceptive than most people gave him credit for.

"Then *you* tap that." It came out snappier than he had intended.

Rhett tilted his head as he studied him, and Levar practically squirmed under his scrutinizing look. "You *like* him," Rhett finally said.

"Don't be ridiculous. He's a reporter. Things could never work between us."

"Hence your absurd and frankly poor attempt at deflecting by suggesting I go after him. I've never *tapped* anything in my life, and I have no desire to start now. Trust me, your crush is safe from my feeble efforts to turn in my V-card."

Few people could make him feel as small as Rhett could. "Sorry," Levar mumbled, feeling properly chastised. "I didn't mean to imply that... You know... Whatever. Forget it."

Rhett reached for his hand and squeezed it. "No, babe.

You need to forget it. Nothing good can ever come from flirting with the enemy. You know that."

Levar sighed and emptied his beer. "He made me feel alive. Funny and witty and *alive*."

"Yeah," Rhett said, and that one word held a world of emotion. "But you still need to forget about him."

8

Henley was furiously typing, the words pouring from his brain like a wide-open faucet. He loved moments like this, when he experienced true flow. His phone rang, and he scowled. Every. Single. Time.

"Dammit," he swore loudly, then picked up with a sigh. "Hello?"

"Mr. Platt?" A woman's voice.

"Yeah. Who am I speaking with?"

"Mr. Platt, I'm Dana Taylor from CTV Media."

CTV Media? They produced documentaries or segments for news outlets. What did they want with him? "Okay." His curiosity was piqued now.

"We're shooting a long segment about the New York Pride Bombing for NBC News, which they're planning to broadcast during the week of the Pride Bombing commemorative ceremony. We were hoping to interview you."

"Interview me? It's usually the other way around."

She laughed. "Yes, this must be unfamiliar territory for you. But we're bringing a group of survivors together, all with different experiences of that day, and interviewing them as a group."

Henley let that sink in. A group interview. That meant sharing his memories with a group of complete strangers. Yeah, that didn't sound appealing at all. "I'm not sure if I'd be the right person for this." "Before you make up your mind, let me tell you one more thing. All proceeds of this production will go to the Rainbow Coalition in honor of the victims. We didn't feel like it would be appropriate to make money off this horrific tragedy."

Dammit. She knew how to get to him, didn't she? "Am I the first one you're approaching?"

"No, but you are on our first-choice list. Three people have committed so far, including the deputy press secretary to the vice president, Levar Cousins."

Henley sat up straight. "Levar has agreed to be interviewed?"

"Yes. Do you know him personally? Oh wait, you're a reporter. You must know him professionally."

"Both." Why on earth had he shared that? "We actually ran into each other on that day for the first time." He swallowed back the dryness in his throat.

"Oh, well, even better. Does that mean you agree?"

"When would this take place?"

"Saturday a week from now. We'd pay for your plane ticket to New York, of course."

"Train ticket," he said automatically. "Not a fan of flying."

"Train ticket, in that case, as well as two nights in a hotel in Manhattan. Maybe you'll have the opportunity to do some sightseeing."

Henley swallowed again. "Dana, I hope you'll think twice before using that line with any of the others. After what happened, New York City is the last place many of us survivors want to be. Just wanted to point that out."

She remained quiet for a few beats. "I sincerely apologize, Mr. Platt. You're absolutely right, and I'll make sure I'll be more sensitive in the future."

She wasn't flippant about it, her tone conveying she was truly sorry. "Thank you," Henley said. "I'm from Connecticut, and I used to visit the city all the time, but ever since that day, it holds very different memories for me."

"I understand, and I apologize for my insensitivity. I hope you won't hold this against us in your decision to come."

Henley could think of a long list of reasons to say no, not the least of which was that he was crazy busy. But what else was new? He hadn't taken a weekend off in a long time, as Logan had brought up recently, so he was long overdue one. Of course, Levar coming didn't factor into his decision at all. *Right.*

"I'll be there," he heard himself say.

Dana let out a happy sound, then went over some details with him. As soon as she'd hung up, Henley pulled up his texts.

Looks like we'll hang out in NYC next weekend, he texted to Levar.

The answer came in under a minute. *I wondered if they were gonna ask you. You flying?*

No. Train. Don't like planes.

Same. Can't get any work done on a plane unless you fly first class. CTV doesn't cover that.

Word. What train are you on?

Haven't booked yet. What are the options?

If we take the 7 pm, we'll be at Penn Station just before 10.

We?

You're gonna let me sit by myself for three hours? He was pushing it again, and Henley held his breath. How would Levar react?

Sitting with you means not getting any work done.

I'm sure the VP will survive if you take a weekend off.

Wow, you just went from three hours to a weekend. That escalated quickly.

So? Are you saying you can't take a weekend off?

Dude, when was the last time you took a weekend off?

What is this, you show me yours, and I'll show you mine?"

More a case of pot and kettle, but if you wanna whip it out and compare, bring it...

Henley grinned. Sparring with Levar was fun. The guy had a sharp mind and gave as good as he got. *I thought gays had decided a long time ago that size doesn't matter...*

This time, it took longer before Levar replied. Henley watched those three little dots appear, then disappear. Had he gone too far? He was about to apologize when Levar's answer popped up.

IMHO people who say that are usually exclusive tops who overestimate the size of their dicks and don't know how to use them.

Henley laughed out loud. *Are you size shaming?*

Not at all. Just saying that no matter the size of the equipment, the owner needs to read the manual.

Not that you'd know anything about that.

Obviously. Always asking for a friend.

Henley thought about his next one. He didn't want to push too hard, but somehow, the idea of spending three hours on a train next to Levar was...appealing.

So, the 7 pm, then?

Sure.

That one was in the bag. Dare he hope that Levar was

looking forward to it as much as he was? No way was he asking that. They weren't in high school anymore, though the giddy butterflies in his stomach certainly reminded him of the crush he'd had on the captain of the lacrosse team back then. God, he was playing with fire. They both were, but Levar didn't seem to be able to stop any more than he was.

Any suggestions for a hotel? I haven't been back since I left the city two weeks after...

He read Levar's text twice, a mix of compassion and nerves settling in his belly. The confession part he felt in his soul because even though he had been back twice, it was still hard for him. But the first part, the asking for a hotel recommendation, was that a passive-aggressive way to find out where Henley was staying?

I know a few places, but I haven't booked yet. He sent it, then hesitated. Should he? Why the hell not. They'd crossed that line ten texts ago anyway. *Want me to book a room for you as well while I'm at it?*

The dots teased him for almost a minute. *Sure. Thx. Queen, please. And not to be picky, but nowhere near Greenwich Village.*

No worries. Same here. I got you.

Thx for understanding. It's not always easy to explain to others.

I know. You can't really blame them. They can't understand unless they were there.

Right. I feel awful sometimes for coming across as difficult, but there's things I can't do.

Same here. If you ever want to talk, I'm here.

That's an offer you may come to regret, considering we'll be on the same train for three hours.

Henley smiled. Six years ago, he would've replied with

"I'll survive," but he'd never use that expression callously again. *Strangely, that doesn't deter me at all.*

Good. See you next Friday. If we don't run into each other before then.

I hope so. Henley stared at the words for a while. What the hell was he doing? He deleted them again, but the excitement inside him wasn't so easily doused. In fact, he hadn't felt this energized since he'd stumbled across the Supreme Court Justice scandal a few months ago. What did that mean?

It meant that he needed a life. He needed to get laid, possibly. And maybe he should hunt for some kind of scandal, a new *gate*, so he could focus his energy on that. Nothing like a thorough investigation to get his blood pumping. That should get his thoughts off Levar.

9

Henley's front-page, above-the-fold article on the tension between the president and the vice president caused a shit storm of catastrophic proportions. He'd found multiple sources willing to go on record—anonymous of course—but the picture that emerged was not a flattering one for the president. He'd come back to Levar for more comments on stuff he'd discovered, and Levar had shared it all with Calix and the vice president, both of whom were upset about what Henley had found out.

None of them blamed Henley. He was doing his job, and they all recognized that. But the fact was that this was bad publicity, even if it had become crystal clear the fault didn't lie with them but with the president and his staff. As a result, tensions between the president's staff and theirs rose high, and Levar even endured a chewing-out by his boss that he should've prevented Henley from running with the article.

"If you had denied it when he first asked, this would've

never happened," Ethan raged to Levar the day Henley's article released.

"It's hard to deny something when it's the truth." Levar was pissed off as fuck. Had Ethan learned nothing in the six years he'd been the vice president's press secretary? Probably not, since the man had always had highly capable deputies. Levar had been hired when Shafer had become VP, but his two predecessors had been more than qualified. Ethan had always been good at letting others do the work.

Ethan threw his hands in the air. "That's such a twentieth-century approach to what we do. The truth is what we make it out to be. All you had to do was deny, and Platt wouldn't have had a leg to stand on."

Levar mentally counted to ten. "He had sources from *inside* the White House. That left little to deny, and if we had, we would've looked like idiots."

"Rather that than embarrassing the president like that," Ethan snapped, and any doubt Levar had possessed about where his loyalty lay went out the window. He wanted to remind him they worked for the vice president, not for Markinson, but he let it go. It would be useless anyway.

"This won't look good when I inform Vice President Shafer," Ethan said, and Levar double-checked to make sure he wasn't joking. This time, he couldn't keep his mouth shut.

"Considering my statements to Platt came directly from the vice president, I'll take my chances. Was there anything else? I have a train to catch."

Ethan's eyes spewed fire, but he waved Levar out the door without saying another word. Levar had steam coming out of his ears as he walked out. That incompetent, disloyal asshole. He was so riled up about Ethan's attitude that his heart was racing, his body flooded with adrenaline. He'd have to find a way to channel Elsa more. Let it go and all that crap. That queen had known how to handle shit.

Good thing he'd brought his weekend bag to work so he didn't have to go home first. He locked the door of his office and took his suit off, then hung it neatly on the coat rack he had in the corner so it wouldn't wrinkle. He pulled his jeans out of his weekend bag, and as he did, out fell one of his favorite panties—a soft pink thong with lace trimmings on the legs and embroidered roses on the silky fabric.

He hesitated for a moment as he looked at his boxer briefs, which were far more practical. Also far more boring. Fuck it, he wanted to feel *good* right now. It had been one hell of a week, and the shitty convo he'd just had with Ethan was the proverbial insult to injury. He dragged down his underwear, then stuffed it into the side pocket of his bag. He could barely hold back a little moan as he pulled on the panties, the soft silk caressing his skin. His cock got hard instantly.

It never failed to arouse him, the sight of himself in those frilly panties. They were so pretty, and they stretched around his hard cock almost obscenely, hiding nothing. Yup, this had been the right choice. He wanted to feel beautiful. No one would see, but it didn't matter. *He* would know, and for now, that was enough.

He never let others see anyway, except for Rhett. Not that he'd had much time lately for hookups, but even when he had, he'd worn normal underwear. Or what others would consider normal underwear. A guy had ridiculed him once, and that had been enough to make him decide to keep this part of his life to himself.

He pulled a T-shirt over his head, then put on a pair of jeans and sneakers rather than the dress shoes he always wore to work. There, so much better. He did a last check of his office to see he hadn't forgotten anything, switched off the light, and headed out. He'd told Ethan he wouldn't be available this weekend. To make sure the message had come across, he'd also told Liz, Ethan's assistant, and he'd informed Calix. It would have to do.

He was stupidly excited. He and Henley had shared looks all week. Looks and witty banter, quick remarks while handling the business side of things. The tension between them was a constant, always palpable, and it was equal parts exhilarating and terrifying. When was the last time Levar had felt a connection like that? An attraction?

Maybe he needed to score a hookup. Do the proverbial dusting-off of the Grindr app on his phone and find someone to release his pent-up sexual energy on. But even that thought made him tired. As easy as they sounded, hookups were hard work. Finding a safe place to fuck, discussing logistics, having a backup plan in case the guy turned out to be a total twat—which had happened to him before, and he'd had to fake an emergency to get the hell out of there. Somehow, the mental energy it required was too much for him.

He checked his watch. He was on time to catch his train, but he didn't feel like taking the Metro, so he hailed a cab and let it drop him off at Union Station. The grandeur of that building never ceased to impress him. Aside from Grand Central in New York, it had to be one of the most iconic train stations in the country, if not in the world. The outside was already imposing with its arches and the symmetrical, classical design, but the great hall always made him stop in his tracks for a moment. The light spilling in through the arched windows, the ceilings that stretched endlessly high above him, the contrast of the old design with the hustle and bustle of the modern-day commuters, it took his breath away.

He got a prepackaged sandwich from Pret A Manger, along with a little bag of chips and a bottle of water, then studied the information sign and headed to the right track. A line had already formed, with Henley standing almost at the end. Judging by how quickly Henley noticed him and waved him over, Levar figured he'd been on the active lookout.

He smiled as he walked toward him, then dropped his bag onto the floor. "Hi."

Clearly the most brilliant opening line ever.

"Hi," Henley said.

At least that made two of them engaging in this awkward conversation. "God, this feels like the start of a really bad first date." He snickered, and Henley laughed.

"Glad to hear I'm not the only one who finds this a tad complicated to navigate."

Levar stepped a little closer to him and lowered his voice. "Maybe we should have some ground rules. Just so we both know where we stand. I don't know about you, but that would make things easier for me."

Henley cocked his head as he studied him. "I assume you're talking about the not reporting on anything you tell me?"

Levar jammed his hands into the pockets of his jeans. "Look, I don't want to offend you, but the fact is that you're a reporter. If I have to weigh every word the whole weekend, it's not going to be fun. So if you could just give me your word that anything we say, starting now until this trip ends, is completely and utterly off the record, including on deep background and all that shit, that would help me relax."

"I think I can agree to that," Henley said. "But I'm hoping it goes the other way as well."

Levar frowned. "What could you possibly tell me that I could reveal to others?"

"Let's say I tell you about a story I'm working on. I need to trust you not to feed that information to other reporters or to start working actively to shut that story down."

The man had a good point. "Fair enough. Starting now?"

Henley smiled at him. "Starting now."

They both stared at each other, saying nothing, and then they both laughed. "So far, it's not really helping," Levar said, still laughing.

"We'll get there. Just give it some time."

The train pulled into the station, and they had to wait until all the passengers had disembarked before they were allowed to get on. The line was long, but they got lucky and found a good spot to sit next to each other and dumped their bags under the seats. Levar ended up with the window seat, which he didn't mind at all.

"So you're not a fan of flying either?" Henley asked him.

Levar shrugged. "I'm not saying I hate it, but considering how much time it costs, it's not the most efficient way to travel for such short distances. Especially in New York, where the airports are not easy to reach from Manhattan and vice versa. Plus, like I texted you, you can't get any work done on a plane anymore."

Henley rolled his eyes. "I know, right? Once upon a time, you could use the tray table to put your laptop on, but the space between the chairs has gotten so small that if the person in front of you leans back even an inch, you have no room left."

"That's why I prefer the train. At least I can work a little."

Levar opened his sandwich and placed it on the little

tray table with his chips and his water. "Didn't you bring anything to eat?" he asked Henley with his mouth full.

"No. I wasn't sure if I'd have the time. I was running a bit late."

Levar hesitated for a moment, then pushed the carton with the remaining sandwich to Henley. "I have an egg salad sandwich on whole-wheat bread for you. And we can share the chips if you want. And the water."

Henley chuckled. "The water convinced me. So generous of you."

His eyes sparkled as he grabbed the sandwich and took a big bite.

"Did you read the questions they're going to ask us?" Levar asked.

Henley nodded. "They're pretty much what I was expecting."

Levar finished his sandwich, then wiped his hands off on the napkin. "I'm hoping they won't manipulate us into getting too emotional. A few questions gave me concern because they could easily turn into making us cry, if that makes sense."

"Yeah, I see what you mean. I don't think it should be a problem for you or me, considering we're both smart enough to recognize those kinds of questions and either deflect or refuse to answer, but I'm not sure about the others who will be there."

"Did you know any of the other people on the list?"

"I recognized some names, and I met the councilman they'll be interviewing in person years ago, but he's not like a friend. More like someone I know professionally."

"Like me," Levar said. Why had he said that?

Henley calmly finished his sandwich, then took a few sips of the water. "I'm not sure if I should stress that you were wrong and that what we share is more than a professional relationship or pretend I don't know what the hell you're talking about. It's a fine line to walk."

Levar let out a sigh. "You know what I like about you?"

Henley grinned. "My sparkling personality? My witty banter? My hot, irresistible body?"

Levar smiled. "Obviously, all of those too, but you don't play games. I don't know why I made that remark, but you could've easily ignored it or, like you said, could have pretended you didn't know what I was talking about. But you didn't. I like that. I like that you acknowledge we're both finding this hard to navigate."

"Yes. And what makes it hard is that I don't even know what 'this' is. Are we becoming friends? Could we be friends, given our professions? Are we engaging in a little harmless flirting? Or...?"

Levar's stomach did a funny jump. "Or what?"

"Oh, come on, Levar. You just complimented me on not playing games. Then don't you dare to pretend either."

"You know what I don't like about you? How often you are right," Levar said with a sigh. "But yes, I did know what you meant with your statement. The answer is that I don't know either. I have no definition for this. What I do know is that us being friends is already a questionable endeavor, so that pretty much rules out anything more than that, I would say."

Henley bumped his shoulder gently. "You forgot to add *unfortunately* to that statement."

That made Levar smile all over again. "The *unfortunately* was implied."

"That leaves us with the option of a very careful friendship," Henley said. "And considering we're both workaholics who barely have time to call our mothers, let alone to invest in a relationship, maybe that's not such a bad option. It's not like either of us would have the energy for more. Plus, I'm fresh out of a relationship, and I've been told anything I get into now would only be a rebound thing."

"True," Levar admitted. Why then did his heart ache a little at that conclusion?

"Yeah, you agree with the rebound theory?"

"I don't know. Never been in a relationship long enough to test it."

Henley looked surprised. "You're thirty-two, and you've never had a serious relationship?"

"Nope. Never missed it, to be honest. After college, a lot of guys my age were party animals, you know? I liked hooking up as much as the next guy, but I didn't want to have to hang out in bars and clubs every weekend. I hooked up, but I never dated seriously."

"Right there with you. I was focused on my career."

"Exactly. I was interning with a local TV station, doing every job they asked me to. Nothing was too menial for me, and I learned tons. Then when I was shadowing one of their reporters, she took a fall and broke her ankle, and I took over her segment on the spot. The station loved it, and when they had an opening, they hired me. After that, I had even less time for a boyfriend."

"You worked so hard to get where you are today. I admire that."

Levar smiled. "Right back atcha. Though you did try the boyfriend thing."

Henley chuckled. "*Try*, huh? That was a nice, subtle dig, man. Well done."

Levar grinned. "I was proud of that one myself."

"I don't know how I feel about a relationship, about the

relationships I had. None of them lasted longer than two years, so I'm sure that speaks volumes."

"Ouch."

Sadness flashed over Henley's face. "Yeah. Someday, I'll have the time and energy to face why that is, but not anytime soon."

Levar's heart ached for him. Henley might not be heartbroken over the breakup, but the whole thing clearly hadn't left him unaffected either. "Back to hookups, then?" he said, opting for a lighter tone.

Henley rolled his eyes, the sadness leaving his expression. "If I can muster the time and energy."

"Even more reason why I do hope we can share a fun weekend. As careful friends."

Henley's eyes sparkled, alerting Levar that something witty was coming. "Well, you've always said your goal was to maintain friendly relationships with the press."

"True. So let's be friends, at least for this weekend."

"Friends." Henley reached out with his left hand. Levar didn't even think about it. He put his right hand into Henley's, and Henley laced their fingers together. The simple contact sent a rush of arousal through Levar, which in itself was a sad testament to how badly he needed to get laid. He'd expected Henley to let go, but about ten seconds in, he still had a tight grip on Levar's hand.

"Do you usually hold hands with your friends?" Levar asked.

Henley looked down at their joined hands as if he hadn't even realized he hadn't released Levar's. "Not usually, no, but I think I should if it feels this good."

This whole careful-friends thing was going to be a disaster, wasn't it?

10

They had decided to arrive separately at the theater where the documentary would be filmed. Henley had wanted to protest at first when Levar had suggested that, but then he'd realized Levar had a good point. People might not be able to place them right away, but Levar still got recognition from his live reporting of the parade.

Every time the Pride Bombing was mentioned on TV, they used his feed because he'd been the only one who had reported shortly after the first blast and who had actually caught the second and third blast on camera, if from a distance. And with his job, arriving at the same time as a well-known reporter was not smart. Henley understood. Didn't mean he had to like it.

The hotel had sported the same continental breakfast every decent hotel in New York City had: cereal, bagels, a few stale muffins, and as a bonus, scrambled eggs, bacon, and sausages. Henley had done what he usually did and had brought his own oatmeal, so he could resist the temptation to eat too much crap.

He showed his ID at the door of the theater. A security guard let him in and told him to report in the Sinatra Room, wherever that was. Someone had been helpful enough to hang signs, however, so he easily found his way. When he walked into the room—the many portraits of the famous singer immediately showing he'd found the right room—Levar was already there, chatting with a woman. He made eye contact, and they shared a quick nod of recognition.

Along one of the walls was a table with coffee on it, and Henley helped himself to some. He had no doubt it would be crappy, but even that was better than no coffee at all. He was surprisingly groggy, considering he'd slept for nine hours. He couldn't even remember the last time that had happened. But he and Levar had gone to their rooms instantly after arrival, and Henley had been so tired he'd fallen asleep while watching the evening news. His mom had always said that sleeping longer than her customary six hours made her more tired than just sticking to that routine, so maybe she'd been onto something.

"Good morning, everyone," a friendly-looking black guy in a bright pink shirt and a pair of tight jeans called out. "According to our records, we're complete, so we'd like to get started. No worries, we're not jumping right in, but we would like everyone to take a seat so we can test the sound and the lighting."

Henley ended up across from Levar in the circle of chairs they had set up. Eleven chairs: ten survivors and one for Natalie, the woman who would be interviewing them. He hoped she'd done her homework. This production company had a good reputation, but that didn't mean they'd be able to get this sensitive subject right. Then again, both he and Levar were there to intervene, should they feel something was wrong.

They were asked to introduce themselves while the sound engineers tested the sound levels. The ten survivors came from all walks of life. A drag queen from the Bronx. A retired NYPD detective from New Jersey. A housewife and mother of four children from Maryland, who had celebrated her tenth anniversary with her wife. They were mixed races and genders, with one woman who Henley thought was transgender. Not that it mattered to him.

"We want to keep this as natural as possible, which means we'll be working with several cameras at the same time, and we'll roll continuously. That way, we can easily edit it into one fluid documentary, catching both the person talking and the reactions from the rest of you. If at any time you need a break, just say so. Continuous rolling doesn't mean we can't stop in between. Try to let each other finish as much as possible, but feel free to react to each other's stories. We want this to be a conversation, not a formal interview."

Henley liked the sound of that. The mood in the room was good, positive. He hoped it would stay that way. The first questions were easy. What were you doing there on that day? Were you walking in the parade? Watching it? Working?

"I guess none of us have to ask you what you did or why you were there," Natalie said to Levar, who smiled sheepishly. "Your report from the scene has been broadcasted all over the world."

Levar nodded. "It's still surreal to see myself pop up like that. You have to remember that I was an unknown reporter at the time, working for a local affiliate. The Pride Parade wasn't considered big news. It was soft news, a human-interest filler, something easy and happy to add to the evening news. I'd expected it to be reduced to nothing more than a flash if something bigger had happened. As it turned out, this became the news."

"Did you ever hesitate before you initiated the broadcast?" Natalie asked.

"Not really. We started immediately after the first explosion. All we did was make sure we had survived, that we weren't bleeding out, and that our equipment was working. I went into a strange mode. Even now, looking back, it feels like a dream. It was me, reporting, but at the same time, it wasn't."

"How were you able to turn off your emotions?" Henley asked him, and Natalie nodded in agreement with his question. "Because that's what I struggled with when I walked around. I saw so much suffering that it was hard to do my job."

Levar looked straight at him as he answered. "The advantage, if you can call it that, of TV reporting is that you look at the camera, not at your surroundings. As long as I kept my eyes trained on the lens, I could keep it together. But when Robert, my cameraman, started shooting what we saw, I had trouble speaking at times. The good news was that I wasn't in view then, so I simply stopped talking and let the viewers interpret the images themselves until I had control over my emotions again."

Gus, the retired NYPD detective, hummed in agreement. "I was close to the third bomb when it went off, so I'd already heard the first two explosions and was on high alert. I'd been a cop for over twenty years when it happened, and I'd served multiple tours in the Army, so I thought I'd seen a lot. But was I wrong. This was by far the worst thing I'd ever seen. In combat...that feels professional, like war in a setting where you'd expect it. This came out of nowhere. I felt myself switch to a different mode. I was working, and that's what it felt like as I was helping people trying to get away, was assisting the wounded. You wear the uniform, and it helps you to turn off your emotions. Of course, that also has its downsides."

"Such as?" Natalie asked.

Gus let out a deep sigh. "Such as not talking about it afterward either. As law enforcement officials, as men, we still wrestle with a macho culture that tells us that talking about your feelings is for girls, that it's weak, and that you just have to suck it up. It doesn't work that way. If you don't talk about a traumatic event like that, it will stay with you. It will haunt you. I didn't talk until three years later, and that was because my wife forced me to seek help. I'd started drinking, hitting the painkillers hard, anything to numb those pesky feelings I couldn't talk about. It was hell, absolute hell. It almost cost me my marriage, and it affected my job, the relationships with friends, even with my kids."

Henley nodded slowly. Wasn't it interesting how different he had experienced that? Maybe because reporting meant processing in a way. He'd written countless articles about it in the weeks after, and it had forced him to deal with his own emotions about the subject. He had hated it at the time, but maybe he should've been glad.

The interview continued, and Henley appreciated the atmosphere in the room. People were warm, respectful, and when someone got emotional, they found support. Hopefully, this would translate on-screen as well.

"When I realized that the only reason they planted these bombs was out of hatred, that still shocked me," Jorge, a flamboyant and wonderfully vibrant man from Puerto Rico, said. Henley loved watching him, his face showing every emotion. "I thought that after 9/11, we'd seen what people are capable of in the name of hate, but then this happened, and it's just unimaginable. I can't comprehend how you can hate so much that you're willing to kill others for it. Random people, people you don't know. Complete strangers."

A rush of murmurs of agreement went through the room, Henley's included. He'd felt the exact same way. To see what hate had cost had made him cry. How could people do that to each other?

"To me, it also shows how far we still have to go in true equality," the housewife said. "They chose the Pride Parade because, in their eyes, it represented the liberal morals of the US. And let's face it, they're not alone in that opinion. Every day, members of the queer community still face harassment, discrimination, abuse, all because we don't fit a certain mold. This was merely an extreme expression of that same judgment, that same hate we still see in our own country."

That was a strong political statement, but Henley couldn't agree with her more. Not that he would make a similar statement in public. And neither would Levar. Both of them had a job in which they couldn't afford to get this radical and, as a result, alienate people.

"One subject we haven't talked about yet is the terrorists," Natalie said. "The three men who planted the bombs were arrested three months after the bombing, and then they all committed suicide within days of their arrest. How did that feel?"

"I was shocked. Absolutely shocked," the transgender woman said. "I'd hoped that their arrest would give us some answers, but it didn't. I was fiercely disappointed they were able to take the easy way out rather than stand trial for what they'd done."

Earlier, she had shared she'd just finished her transition and was celebrating her new identity at the parade, confirming Henley's intuition about her. She'd been at the parade with her wife, who had been amazingly supportive of her transition and who had stayed with her. Sadly, her wife had lost her life in the attack when a piece of concrete had hit her in the head and had pierced her brain.

"I think most of us share that feeling," Natalie said, her tone warm.

"What still bothers me is how little we know about that terrorist group," the drag queen—who was nonbinary and had asked to be called Jordan—said. "They came out of nowhere, and no one has heard from them since. And of course with those three students committing suicide, we're none the wiser on a lot of the details. That still doesn't sit well with me."

Henley frowned, but before he could say anything, Levar beat him to it. "What do you mean by that, exactly? I'm not sure I'm following."

"I'm sure you have information you're privy to that the rest of us don't, and I understand the reasons for that. But for us ordinary folks, there were no warning signs. After 9/11, all these reports came out about how the CIA and the FBI had missed signals. How they'd failed to communicate with each other, which had led to Al-Qaeda being able to plan the attacks. But we knew, at least in hindsight, they'd been active already. And after 9/11, they were still active. It wasn't their first terrorist attack, and it wouldn't be their last. For this radical terrorist group, the Pride Bombing was their one and only attack. That's the part that still baffles me."

Levar and Henley looked at each other, and Henley saw his own curiosity about what Jordan had said reflected on Levar's face. They brought up an interesting point. Henley had reported extensively about the three bombers, all students from Kashmir, the disputed region in India. All three from poor families, radicalized by Al Saalihin, a terrorist group with ties to Al-Qaeda, to fight for an independent Kashmir. At the time, it had felt like the new 9/11, and it had dominated the news for months, but Jordan was right. Al Saalihin had gone completely quiet since.

"That's an excellent point," Natalie said. "I am looking at our two political men to see if they can shed some light on this. Levar?"

Levar gave her a faint smile. "As Jordan already indicated, my job prevents me from speaking out on this topic publicly. I wish I could say more, but I can't."

"I understand." She turned to Henley. "What about our political reporter? You wrote tons of articles on the bombing and the trials. Has this topic ever come up?"

"I haven't reported on this recently, but I agree that Al Saalihin seems to have disappeared is curious. It's definitely something I'll be looking into."

"They've never caught Hamza Bashir, the alleged mastermind behind the attack either, just the bombers," Jordan said.

"True, but don't forget that it took many years before Osama bin Laden was found as well. It's a big world, and hiding is relatively easy," Henley pointed out.

"If you do find out anything, keep me posted. I have my thoughts on this as well." Gus looked at Henley intently when he said this, almost as if he was saying more. Interesting. Henley would have to make sure to get his contact information. A former NYPD detective was always a good source to have on file.

By the end of the afternoon, when they were done, it almost felt like the ten of them had become friends. Wasn't it special that even though they were from different cities, different genders and sexual orientations, various walks of life and educational levels, they had this one big thing in common that brought them together? They had survived something horrible, and that would always be a part of who they were. Henley exchanged hugs with those who offered, including the burly detective.

Gus glanced around them as if to check no one was listening in, then put a hand on Henley's shoulder and brought his mouth close to Henley's ear. "I didn't want to say this on camera, but this whole case stinks. I worked for the Joint Terrorism Task Force until I retired last year, and there were too many how and why questions about the bombing we never got an answer to, especially about Hamza Bashir. If you ever want to dig deeper, come find me."

Henley nodded. "I will, Gus. Thank you."

11

Levar was exhausted as they made their way out of the theater. A whole day of sitting and talking had been more tiring than a regular workday for him. Not that he was naïve enough to believe that was all it had been: sitting and talking. He'd done some heavy emotional work, and if he had to take a guess, he hadn't been the only one.

"Can we at least walk back to our hotel together?" Henley asked softly as he stepped up next to him.

Levar did a quick look around him, but everyone was spreading in different directions. "Sure. You don't want to take a cab?"

Henley shook his head. "I need to walk for a bit, clear my head."

"I feel you."

For the first few minutes, they said nothing as they strolled shoulder to shoulder, almost touching, but not quite. While they'd been inside, a thunderstorm had drenched the city, and the smell of the ozone in the rain mixed with car fumes. The pavement was damp, puddles quickly evaporating in the clammy heat. Hordes of tourists packed the streets, carrying wet rain ponchos and umbrellas. They'd stayed away for a few weeks after the Pride Bombing, but then they'd come back as if nothing had ever happened. Strange how that worked.

For Levar, New York had never been the same again. He and Rhett had moved to DC two weeks after the attack, Levar impulsively taking the job offered to him after a station in DC had seen his live broadcast. He'd done it as much for Rhett—who'd turned into a shadow of himself after the bombing—as for himself. A fresh start, an environment that wouldn't remind them of what they had survived, had been what they'd needed. Three years later, he'd started working for the vice president, and he'd never looked back. New York was his past, and being here made him on edge.

Little by little, Levar's head stopped spinning, his thoughts slowing down, and the pressure headache receding. "That was intense," he said.

"It never ceases to amaze me how tired you get from emotional effort. Sometimes even more than from physical exertion. I don't get this exhausted from a thirty-minute spinning class, you know?"

Levar took a quick look sideways. "You take spinning classes?"

Henley's mouth pulled up in a grin. "The truthful answer is that I should have a hell of a lot more spinning classes than I manage, but about once a month, you'll find me soaked in sweat in the spinning studio."

"Attractive picture you're painting there."

"It's really good for a tight ass," Henley said, and Levar chuckled.

"If that was some backhanded way to get me to check out

your ass, there's no need. I've already seen it, checked it, and approved it."

And they fell right back into this flirty banter that had quickly become their habit. What was it about Henley that made Levar forgo all his usual carefulness, his reserve at mixing work and pleasure? Henley got under his skin, somehow, and it amused and terrified Levar in equal measure.

Henley stopped walking, but Levar didn't notice right away. When he did, he halted too, and Henley caught up with him. When Levar looked at him questioningly, Henley shrugged. "I had to return the favor, didn't I?"

Levar's cheeks heated up. The idea of Henley checking him out, specifically his ass was...appealing. If he studied him closely enough, would Henley be able to see that Levar wasn't wearing regular underwear? He shouldn't, and yet the idea got Levar excited to the point where his cock stirred. Not good.

"And what's the verdict?" he asked, keeping his tone light.

"You don't need any spinning classes," Henley said with confidence, and Levar laughed all over again.

"Do you want to grab a bite somewhere?" Henley asked.

Levar hesitated. He'd love to, but what if people recognized them? After all, this was New York, where the chance of running into paparazzi was not out of the question. "How about we order takeout and eat in our room together?"

Henley frowned. "Are you really that scared to be seen with me? We shot a documentary together. It's not like we don't have a valid reason to be in the same place at the same time. Plus, it's just dinner."

Levar sighed. "It's not just dinner, Henley, and you know it. Anyone watching us or overhearing our conversation would immediately pick up on the flirting. That's all fine and dandy when it's just the two of us, but I can't have anyone reporting that the deputy press secretary to the vice president is cozying up to one of the best-known political reporters. It would cost me my job."

Henley's frown disappeared, and he looked guilty. "You're right. Sometimes it's easy to forget that I'm not the one who could lose his job. No one would care about a reporter cozying up to someone from the White House. Worst-case scenario, they'd paint me as an opportunist who would wine and dine someone to get better information. But yeah, it could cost you a lot more."

"Takeout, then?" Levar asked.

"Takeout it is. Are you a pizza person, a Mexican fan, Chinese, Thai? What are you in the mood for?"

Levar licked his lips. "Honestly, Chinese sounds really good."

"I think I spotted a Chinese restaurant close to the hotel, right? Like, across the street from where the cab dropped us off when we arrived?"

It turned out his memory had served him right, and half an hour later, they walked into the hotel, carrying several cartons of Chinese takeout, two bottles of water, and two cans of beer.

"Your room or mine?" Henley asked.

Levar thought of the messy way he'd left his room and the chance that some silky underwear might be lying around. "Your room," he decided.

Henley wiggled his eyebrows. "Hiding something from me, are you?"

Levar nodded, keeping his face serious. "Yes. I've got a whole room full of secrets."

"Are they good secrets? Like, the naughty kind?"

Levar couldn't keep his laughter in. "A whole room full of naughty secrets? What, like I'm shooting a porn movie there?"

They were still laughing as they walked into Henley's room, which was only marginally neater than Levar had left his and just as small. A queen-size bed, a stamp-sized bathroom with a toilet and shower, a TV mounted to the wall, and the world's tiniest desk holding a Keurig with paper cups, pods, and sugar and creamer, and that was it. It smelled the same too, like old carpet and bleached towels, though the food soon overpowered the less appetizing odors.

It also had a flimsy, foldable table with two foldable chairs, and they settled down knee to knee with the food. Attached to the wall was a plexiglass holder with colorful fliers for New York attractions that threatened to spill out. Levar had zero desire to see them anymore.

For a while, they were quiet as they ate, but then Henley said, "Today went better than I'd expected. Natalie was clearly well prepared, and the questions were respectful toward us."

Levar nodded. "I was concerned it would get too sensationalized, but she never crossed that line. And the few times where people truly got emotional, she gave them space."

"She didn't bring it up, but did you know our paths crossed that day?" Henley asked.

Levar looked up from his plate with a sharp move. "What? Are you serious?"

"Yeah. You were reporting, and I walked by. I was on the phone with my editor, doing a live report of what I was seeing. She was recording it so they had my raw, first impressions. We ran into each other and made eye contact."

Levar slowly shook his head. "I don't remember that. Are you sure it was me?"

"Look at the footage sometime. If you can stomach watching it. You'll see me pop up in the background."

"That is so strange that I don't remember." Then he caught himself. "Actually, it's not. I've never told anyone this outside of some good friends and my therapist, but for a long time, I couldn't remember anything about the first hours after it had happened. It was a big black hole in my memory. What was surreal was that I'd look at the footage of myself describing what I was seeing, and I couldn't remember being there, couldn't remember saying those things. It was like watching someone else."

Henley's eyes were soft and kind. "That doesn't surprise me. I had trouble placing things in the right order at first as well. In hindsight, I was grateful my editor recorded that whole call so I could listen back and piece together what had happened. It's how the brain protects us from trauma, and if you think about it, it's pretty cool."

Levar finished his plate with sesame chicken, then checked the cartons to see what was left. "Mind if I take some more General Tso's chicken?"

"All yours. I'll finish the sesame chicken, and then I'm good."

"What did you think about what Jordan said about Al Saalihin never having claimed another attack?" Levar asked.

Henley swallowed the last bite, then pushed his plate back. "Intriguing. When we were done, Gus told me he still had plenty of questions about the how and why. It turns out he used to work for the Joint Terrorism Task Force here in the city."

Levar shoved his plate aside as well and took a sip of his beer. "I don't know about you, but for some reason, I've never been that focused on the background of the bombing. Experiencing it was traumatic enough. Reporting on it made me the network's darling, since the ratings went through the roof, but I always focused on the human stories. The hard news, the political implications, I tried not to think too much about those. I don't know why."

Henley looked pensive. "I did write about it. I remember thinking at the time that it was nothing new, you know? We've known Al-Qaeda for years, and they've been active for years, so to me, this was just another example. After all, the way it was presented to us was that this was an offshoot from Al-Qaeda, closely connected. That was the official viewpoint of the intelligence community, and I never questioned it."

"Do you now?"

"I don't know. Enough to take a second look, I guess, though I don't have anything concrete that makes me wonder. From the beginning, some aspects were distinctly different than previous Al-Qaeda attacks, but terrorist experts always explained them away."

"Such as?"

"Such as that Al-Qaeda usually does suicide attacks, not remotely detonated bombings. The FBI stated that they could be changing their tactics after the relative success of the Boston Marathon Bombing."

"Right. And didn't they say Al Saalihin was too new to pull off an attack this big?"

Henley nodded. "That suggested experienced members, which doesn't gel with how new this cell is. Plus they can't seem to find any known established connections, like financial ties or training camps. They're a ghost cell, which is worrisome in itself. And what bothered me about what Jordan said was their point about there not being any warnings of this attack. That's quite unusual. Every large bombing, every successful terrorist attack has always had warning signals, even if just in hindsight. With this one, the intelligence community has stated it came out of nowhere. None of their usual channels of monitoring terrorist activity had shown any chatter, any leads. That's the only part I don't like about this."

"Maybe they had warnings, but they're not willing to share this because it would compromise the investigation."

"That could very well be the case, considering they're still on the hunt for Hamza Bashir, but it did tickle my curiosity again."

"I wish I could tell you that you were on the right track or give you a hint on where to dig, but I genuinely don't know anything more than you," Levar said. "Despite what Jordan said about me having access to classified information, I haven't come across anything so far. Granted, I'm not need-to-know on a lot of this—or at least, I wasn't—but I haven't even heard hints."

"Somehow, I suspected that already, though your answer to Jordan was very politically correct. Then again, you have some experience in answering difficult questions." Henley winked at him.

Levar pushed his chair back and got up, patting his stomach. "Damn, I'm full. Let's clear this up before your whole room smells of Chinese food all night."

Henley shrugged. "I've had worse smells in a hotel room, trust me."

They worked together in throwing the containers into the trash and clearing the table. Levar tied the trash bag so it wouldn't continue to reek, and then they looked at each other. He didn't want to go. Not yet. It was too early to go to sleep, and he had zero desire to go out. He was too tired, and besides, New York had lost its charm for him five years ago. But staying here with Henley seemed dangerous. How would he even suggest it?

"Wanna watch some TV together?" Henley asked, his tone a little too neutral to hide that he was feeling as insecure about this as Levar.

Levar smiled. "Sure."

"Can I use your bathroom first?"

"Of course," Henley said as he installed himself on the queen bed, then switched on the TV.

Levar did his business but left his shirt untucked to alleviate some of the pressure of his waistband. Damn, he'd really eaten a lot. He awkwardly climbed onto the bed and settled next to Henley, making sure not to touch him.

"What are you in the mood for?" Henley asked.

"Do you mind if we watch the news first? I just want to make sure the White House hasn't burned down while we were gone."

They watched in companionable silence as the news reported that President Markinson had made some remarks about the economy being in a good state and showed pictures of flooding in the South due to heavy rainfall.

"The White House hasn't burned down. Imagine that." Henley smirked.

Levar yawned, then stretched his arms high above his head to relieve the tension. "Always good to realize that life goes on, even when we're not there."

When Henley didn't answer, he turned his head toward him. Henley was staring at him, but not at his face. He was looking at his...

Oh God. How high up had his T-shirt ridden when he'd stretched just now? He was wearing jeans that were pretty low cut, which meant that the gorgeous white lace panties he had on peeked out from under his waistband. "What?" he snapped.

Henley finally lifted his eyes, but rather than the disgust Levar had expected to see, they showed something else entirely. *Hunger.* Raw, unbridled hunger.

12

Can we hang out today?

Henley had looked at his text for minutes before he hit the Send button. How would Levar respond? Chances were he'd reject him. And Henley would understand. He would've understood before yesterday, but even more after last night, after he'd spotted Levar's choice of underwear.

Levar had scrambled up from the bed and all but fled out of the room. Had he been embarrassed? His cheeks had been bright red, and he'd looked flustered as fuck—a first, since he usually had a tight grip on his emotions. He clearly hadn't meant for Henley to see his underwear, those gorgeous, sexy-as-fuck panties. Even a glimpse had been enough to get Henley so fucking aroused, and as soon as Levar had left the room, he'd jerked himself off hard to the memory. The orgasm had been the best he'd experienced in months.

And then he'd fallen asleep and had slept for close to nine hours. Apparently, he'd been a tad tired. Still, the day was young. He'd fallen asleep early, and it was only eight in the morning.

His phone dinged, and he mentally fortified himself before reading the reply.

To do what?

That wasn't an outright no.

I don't care. Just hang out. We can stay in the room if you want.

Not sure that's a smart idea...

Yeah, good point. Now that Henley knew what Levar had been hiding under his clothes, that vision wouldn't leave him alone. Being in a private room with him for hours might be asking too much of his restraint and self-discipline. No, he had to find something else to do. Something Levar would be comfortable with, and that would give them an opportunity to chat...and flirt. Someplace where no one would be able to overhear them.

How about we go for a walk through Central Park? We can grab breakfast along the way.

Won't anyone recognize us?

Hmm, Henley doubted anyone would look at them twice, but he had to find a way to reassure Levar.

I'll find us some disguises

Disguises? You setting up a covert operation?

Just some stuff that will make it harder for people to recognize you

And he knew just the thing. The MLB fan store across the street from the hotel would come in handy.

OK.

Henley air-pumped his fist. Yes! *I'll pick you up in 20 minutes or so.*

He hurried across the street and got what he needed, sporting a big grin that didn't leave his face until he knocked on Levar's door. Levar opened almost immediately, and after one look at Henley, he started laughing. "That's your idea of a disguise?"

"The Yankees are playing the Red Sox today. I can damn well guarantee you half of New York will be wearing white and blue today, including caps. And since it's bright and sunny, the sunglasses won't stand out either."

Levar slowly shook his head. "You're killing me here, man. The Yankees? You want me to wear a fucking Yankees shirt? Three generations of Cousins are now rolling around in their graves, let me tell you. We're Dodgers fans. If my dad saw me, he'd slap me silly."

Henley grinned. "He'd better not find out, then."

Levar rolled his eyes, but he accepted the shirt, cap, and sunglasses Henley was holding out. He stepped into his room, and Henley hesitated, then walked in after him and closed the door. Levar gave him a look but pulled his shirt over his head, revealing his toned body. He wasn't ripped or even muscled but lean, with just the right definition and endless planes of smooth skin, unlike Henley's own hairy chest and belly. He had his back waxed monthly to make sure it stayed hairless because nope, he drew the line there. But Levar looked like he was naturally smooth. If not for the fact that his ears were just a little floppy, he'd almost be pretty. The overall combination was still more than a little attractive.

"Great job not undressing me with your eyes," Levar said.

Henley pointed at the shirt he'd taken off. "Pretty sure you did that, not me."

"You know that's not what I meant."

"I have no idea what you're talking about." Henley winked.

Levar straightened his shirt, then put on the cap. "Right."

Henley held up his hands. "If you want to talk about—"

"Shut up, asshole."

"I'll take that as a no, then."

"Damn right. Now, let's go."

The temperature was perfect, sixty-five degrees with bright blue skies. The thunderstorm from the day before had cleared the air, the muggy weather giving way for a much more pleasant warmth. New York City in the summer was hell, both because of the heat and the hordes of tourists, but spring was perfect. Besides, tourists wouldn't be up this early, so they and the joggers would have Central Park to themselves.

They walked north on Seventh Avenue, the stores preparing to open as the coffee shops and breakfast delis were bustling already. Starbucks was packed, but the baristas worked through the line fast, and a few minutes later, Levar and Henley walked out with coffee and croissants. Henley had treated himself to a slice of banana bread, which was nothing but fat and sugar and yet tasted so damn good.

They said little as they sipped their coffees and made their way toward the entrance of Central Park at 59th Street. As Henley had expected, the park was still quiet. Runners with zoned-out eyes passed them to their left, while sleepy-looking people walking their dogs barely spared them a glance. The sounds of traffic and the wail of an ambulance faded into the background as they ventured deeper into the park, and Henley breathed in the air, which was so much fresher here. It smelled greener, like trees and fresh-cut grass, especially on a day like this.

He'd almost forgotten how much he'd loved New York. Growing up in Connecticut, he'd visited countless times, and when he'd moved here after getting a job at a New York-based paper, he'd quickly settled in. He'd loved the fast pace of the city, the queer-friendly subculture, the gay bars where he could score a date. Or a partner.

New York had been home to him, a place where he'd felt welcome and accepted. Safe. The bombing had taken that away from him. Sometimes he wondered if people realized the true damage of that day was so much more encompassing than the people who had died and gotten wounded or those who had lost loved ones.

Levar shot him a sideways glance, and Henley pushed down the sad thoughts. He wanted to focus on the now, on being in the moment. "Where did you live when you lived here?" he asked.

"Brooklyn. Rhett and I shared a crappy one-bedroom apartment that had roaches."

"You make it sound so appealing."

Levar shuddered. "God, it was ten kinds of awful, but we couldn't afford anything else. He was a freelance news photographer, doing weddings and bar mitzvahs to stay afloat, and I was an intern at first and then a lowly reporter, paying off a ton of college debt. I still am."

"Tell me about it. I paid the last bit off two years ago, I think."

"Where did you go to college?"

"UConn. It made the most sense for me as an in-state student. I did my master's there as well, since they gave me a good scholarship. You went to UCLA, right?"

Levar nodded. "Me and Rhett both."

"What's the story with you two? Never been more than friends?"

"We shared one kiss, but it felt like kissing my brother, so we decided we wouldn't ever speak of that again. He's special to me. Like a best friend mixed in with a younger brother. I've always been protective of him, but even more after…after that day. He's my soulmate, just not in the romantic sense."

"More like Dawson and Joey."

Levar raised an eyebrow. "Not sure if I should be worried or impressed with that reference."

Henley laughed. "I had an ex-boyfriend who was addicted to that show. I've watched more episodes than I'd ever feel comfortable to admit."

"How many exes do you have exactly?"

Henley frowned as he did a quick count. Logan, obviously, and before him, Pierre, the French intern at the paper. Then came Aggie and Christa, both of whom hadn't even lasted a year. And Spencer had been before that, a nonbinary artist who still held the record with two years and three months. They'd broken up with Henley for not wanting to commit, which, come to think of it, was eerily close to Logan's emotionally unavailable accusation. Plus Timothy, his first serious boyfriend.

"Six?"

"Was that a question or a statement?"

Henley checked his count. "Pretty sure it's six." He looked sheepish. "That's quite a bit, isn't it?"

"Between the two of us, we're right on the average, I think, so whatever. I don't shame people for relationships. Or sex. You do you and all that as long as you're not hurting anyone else."

Henley let that simmer for a bit as they continued their walk. "I'm pretty sure I hurt them," he finally said.

"On purpose? Like, did you cheat?"

"Hell, no. I'm loyal to a fault, probably why they all broke up with me and not the other way around."

Levar stopped, holding Henley back with a hand on his shoulder. "You're telling me that all your six exes broke up with you?"

Why was he even telling him this? He was never this open to people, but for some reason, Levar was so easy to talk to. "Yeah. A therapist would have a field day with that, I imagine."

"Huh. Interesting." Levar let go of Henley's shoulder and resumed walking. Henley hurried a few steps to catch up with him. "Did they all give the same reason?"

What had been the reason they'd broken up with him? Logan's was easy to remember, and Spencer's had come to mind earlier, but what about the others? Hell if he could remember, and that made him mentally pause for a moment. Why couldn't he recall? Had it made that little of an impression?

Levar bumped his shoulder, his blue eyes kind. "Let's talk about something else. I didn't mean to make you feel bad."

Henley gladly jumped on that escape. "Yes, let's talk about you. What do you do for fun?"

"Fun? What's that?"

The joke was lame, but Henley laughed anyway, relief flooding him. "I know, right?"

"In the sparse free time I have, I just hang out with Rhett, watch a movie or a documentary."

"Not a fan of the club scene?"

"Been there, done that. After New York..." His sigh was sad.

"The bombing changed everything," Henley said. How he longed to take his hand, but he wouldn't risk it.

"We lost a lot more than friends that day."

Henley was strangely comforted that Levar's experience

paralleled his. Hadn't he thought the same thing only minutes ago? So few people understood, but Levar did.

They chatted as they walked past the Lake, then even farther north. "You're not getting tired yet?" Henley checked.

"Not at all." Levar gestured at his feet. "I brought my running shoes in case I'd have the chance to get a run in."

"You're a runner?"

Levar grinned. "Not as much as I'd like to be, but yeah, I run whenever I can squeeze one in."

Henley opened his mouth, the joke almost making itself, but Levar jabbed a finger at him. "Don't say it."

Henley laughed. "You're making it too easy, man."

They exited at the Met. "Want to grab something to eat?" Henley asked.

"That bakery is amazing." Levar pointed at an Italian bakery. "Rhett and I used to go there all the time. We spent way more than we could afford, but no regrets."

The doorbell chimed as they walked into a narrow space, the shiny tile floor as old as the man behind the counter, wearing an old-fashioned baker's uniform. "Bon giorno," he greeted them, sending them a toothy smile.

Henley's mouth watered as he took in the display cases, stuffed to the brim with the most-delicious-looking treats. And god, the smell. Lemon, bread, vanilla, and roasted nuts, all wrapped into one tantalizing aroma that made his stomach growl.

He'd already had banana bread, so he really shouldn't, but Henley got a portion of zeppoli, Italian fried dough treats that were simply heavenly, especially with raspberry sauce. Levar laughed at him, shaking his head as he opted for an espresso and two sandwich cookies dipped in chocolate. It probably explained why Levar was still slim while Henley had the padding around his waist. Whatever.

They found a spot at the window where they could people watch.

"God, this is amazing," Henley said with his mouth full after the first bite. "I love pastries and cakes. And cookies."

"So basically you love butter, flour, and sugar, is what you're saying."

"Don't ruin it for me, man."

Levar held up his hands. "I wouldn't dare."

"I know I shouldn't." Henley patted his stomach, looking guilty.

Levar's eyes roamed over Henley's body. "Not sure what you're referring to, but you look *fine* to me."

"Yeah?" Henley was stupidly pleased with that remark.

"I can appreciate a little extra softness. Hypothetically speaking."

And...they were right back at it, their eyes locking until Levar deliberately looked away, checking his watch. "I need to get back to the hotel and grab my stuff. I'm on the three o'clock back to DC. You?"

Henley swallowed back his disappointment. Levar was right. They needed to drop it. "My mom is meeting me at four to hang out and have dinner, and then I'll take the early morning train back. I couldn't come down here and not see her."

"You close with your mom?"

Henley nodded. "She's amazing. Didn't bat an eye when I came out, first as bi, then as pan. Took it all in stride. Are your parents okay with you being gay?"

"God, yes. I came out at thirteen, and my dad said he'd known since I was ten or so. My mom just cried and hugged me. California has its benefits, I'm telling you. Well, generally speaking, the East Coast isn't bad either."

"Nope, we could've done a lot worse."

They needed to leave, but Henley didn't want to. He wanted to walk more or go to the Met together or just sit here and chat. None of those things was an option, but the awareness that they were about to step back into real life ached inside him.

Levar's expression reflected some of his own sadness. "This was... I had a good time."

"So did I."

Levar sighed, averting his gaze. "Guess we'll be back to our professional relationship tomorrow."

Henley took his hand for just a moment. "Thank you for this. For yesterday and today."

Levar met his eyes again. "Right back atcha."

Then he abruptly got up and walked out. Henley watched him until he couldn't see him anymore. Why the hell did it have to be Levar he was feeling a connection with? God, he sucked at relationships. He really, really did.

13

Taking a few days off always sounded amazing, but Levar never failed to regret it afterward when he saw how much work he had to catch up on. Technically, he was off on the weekends, but the reality was that he usually worked at least half a day every Saturday and Sunday. But with spending the weekend in New York—as wonderful as it had been—he'd actually managed to not only take off but not even think of work. Hell, even after he'd come back, he hadn't so much looked at his email until Monday morning.

Of course, reality had crashed hard into him then. Hundreds of unread emails in his inbox, a whole stack of papers on his desk that Ethan had dropped there as usual, and a call sheet a mile long from reporters who needed information and had been brushed off by Ethan. Happy times.

He spent the first hour furiously reading through his email, ruthlessly deleting anything that didn't require his attention. He delegated as much as he could to Nicole, forwarded some stuff to Katie Winters, and made a list of the things he really had to do himself. No chance in hell he'd get that all done within the next twenty-four hours, but at least he had a full overview again.

In an informal briefing, he answered most questions reporters threw at him, apologizing a few times that he wasn't completely caught up yet. They took it in stride, probably because it was unusual for him not to be on top of things, and they gave him a lot of latitude in this case. Once that was done, he rushed back to his office to plow his way through his to-do list.

He'd been working in blessed silence for about an hour when Calix poked his head around the corner. "Walk with me," he said, and Levar was once again amazed at the man's ability to make something sound like a request when it really was an order.

He didn't say a word as he got up and followed Calix out the door, then down the hallway to Calix's office, where the deputy chief of staff closed the door firmly behind them. "Grab a seat," he said. "I didn't want to go through Nicole, as this is not something I want to be leaked to Ethan."

That sounded mysterious, and Levar's heart rate sped up as he took a seat.

"We've had some long and hard conversations over the weekend." Calix sat down behind his desk. "And by we, I mean the vice president, Kelly, and me."

"About the tension between the vice president and the president?"

Calix nodded. "That was what started our conversation, but we got into things a little deeper. First off, I'm going to ask you not to repeat this conversation to anyone else, including Ethan. You've promised the vice president your loyalty, and I hope that is something we can continue to count on."

Levar swallowed. Holy crap, Calix made it sound as if they were about to ask him to plot a foreign war. "Of course, Calix. You know I support the vice president, and it's an honor to work here."

Calix's face relaxed a little. "Good. Forgive me the dramatics, but it's been a rough weekend."

"I'm sorry I wasn't there," Levar said, feeling guilty, though maybe that was also because of who he'd spent part of the weekend with. God, if Calix only knew... But he could never know. Their time in New York had to stay between him and Henley.

Calix waved his words away. "That's ridiculous. You wouldn't have been able to do a lot for us anyway. And more importantly, we wholeheartedly condone your participation in this documentary, so we were glad you were able to travel to New York. I hope the interviews went well?"

Levar's cheeks heated. Why couldn't he stop thinking about Henley? As soon as Calix had said the word documentary, Henley's smiling face had popped into Levar's head. The way he'd looked at him as they had meandered through Central Park, as if Levar was the only other person on the planet. Those warm brown eyes from under his Yankee cap, his booming laugh, and how his mouth could pull up in an irresistible grin. And the hunger in his eyes when he'd gotten a peak of Levar's panties. God, why was he thinking about *panties* when he was talking to Calix?

"Yes," he said, his voice croaking a little. "The interview went very well. The woman interviewing us was respectful, had clearly prepared herself well, and the group she had assembled had great chemistry."

"Good, good," Calix said. "She approached me as well, but..." He stopped talking, and a look of sadness passed over his face. "I couldn't do it. It's still too raw for me."

The man had lost his husband that day. *Raw* was probably an understatement. "I completely understand. It wasn't easy for any of us to talk about it, but it did help. But I know you're not the only one who declined to be interviewed. They asked Rhett as well, my roommate. He's the one who—"

He abruptly cut himself off. God, he was such an idiot. Why hadn't he thought of this before he opened his mouth?

Calix's face grew even sadder. "He's the one who took the picture of me and Matthew, I know."

"I'm sorry," Levar said quickly. "I shouldn't have brought it up. I didn't think about it when I said it."

Calix sighed. "It's okay. You didn't do it on purpose, and you shouldn't have to weigh your words that carefully. It's just that... It hurts. It hurts less than it did five years ago, but it's still painful. I'm glad Rhett took that picture. In fact, I'll be forever grateful that everybody had seen it. First, I was upset because it felt too private, but then I realized I wanted the whole world to know what the consequences of hate are. Hate took my Matthew from me, and people need to see that. It's easy to think of attacks like this in terms of numbers, of casualties, of wounded. But they affect people, real humans, like me. Like you."

Levar had to swallow again to get rid of the tightness in his throat. "And like Rhett. He struggled for a long time, and I feel like he's only now clawing his way out."

Calix cocked his head as he studied Levar. "In what way?"

"They asked him for the documentary as well. Actually, they approached him before they asked me, but he couldn't do it and recommended they call me. He refuses to talk about it. Not sure if you're aware, but for the first year or so after the bombing, he didn't leave his house aside from our move. We lived in New York at the time, shared an apartment in Brooklyn, but we moved to DC two weeks after. We couldn't stay, so I jumped on a job offer. Once we were here, I'd hoped things would get better for him, but he developed agoraphobia. That has improved over the last year, but it's still hard for him. Plus, he has trouble finding work. He can't do hard news anymore—too many triggers."

He wasn't sure why he was sharing so much about Rhett to Calix. Technically, the man hadn't asked for it, and it was debatable if the information was even useful to him. But Calix didn't seem to mind, judging by the way his expression had changed from sadness to sympathy.

"I'm so sorry for him. You know, everyone deals with events like that in a different way. I know for many of us, working for Senator Shafer, now Vice President Schafer, helped us to channel our emotions into something productive. I hope Rhett can find his way out of the depth he's in."

A warm feeling spread through Levar's heart. This was one of the reasons why he loved his job. He was working with some amazing people. "I hope so too. But anyway, yeah, I'm glad I did the interview. I'm not sure I'll be able to watch the segment, but I have no doubt it'll be good."

"Glad to hear it. To circle back about what we were talking about, the vice president, Kelly, and I are all on the same page that Ethan isn't functioning the way a press secretary to the vice president should. And I know we'll both agree that's an understatement. You've been loyal to him in the sense that we've never heard you complain about him, which speaks volumes about your character, but we've seen it with our own eyes, and we're getting signals from all directions. He needs to be replaced."

They were *firing* Ethan? Was he a horrible person to be

happy about that? Strike that. Happy wasn't even the right word. He was ecstatic, barely able to hide it.

Calix smiled. "You're allowed to be relieved."

Oops, maybe Levar hadn't hidden his joy as well as he thought.

"I can't deny I'm glad about this outcome."

"This means two things. First of all, we need to find a way to either fire Ethan or move him to another position in a way that doesn't draw too much attention. I'm sure Ethan doesn't want the drama of us announcing we're firing him for doing a crappy job, so sometime this week, Kelly will sit down with him and negotiate a good way to terminate his employment for us. We may have to put him to work elsewhere or help him find a position in corporate life, but that's Kelly's concern."

"That's smart. The last thing we want is for this to become a headline. Although I doubt reporters would want to make it one, considering most of them will be all too happy to see Ethan go."

"Yeah, you're probably right about that. The second issue, of course, is that he'll need to be replaced."

Right. Who would become his new boss? Would it be anyone he knew? Levar went through a quick list in his head, but no one popped into his mind. They wouldn't want someone from the president's staff, not under these circumstances, what with the tension already running high.

"Do you have someone in mind? I'm assuming you don't want anyone with strong ties to the president."

"No, definitely not. We're looking to find someone who can grow in his role here so that when the vice president hopefully wins the election, he could move with us to the big stage."

God, what an opportunity. Even with what Levar knew

about the president actively trying to undermine Schafer's bid for the presidency, Levar still believed the man could win. He was a strong politician with an incredible network, enough money to attract big donors, and with a wealth of experience from being vice president, even if Markinson often tried to keep him on the sidelines. So whoever they would appoint as press secretary now would have a big shot of becoming the White House press secretary if Shafer won the elections.

"You don't get it, do you?" Calix asked, smiling broadly now.

Levar frowned. What had he missed? He tried to think of anyone Calix could've been hinting to, and it took him way too long before it registered. "Me?" It came out a squeal.

Calix nodded, grinning.

"You're asking *me*?"

"Yes, Levar. We all agree you would be the right choice for this job."

Levar's mouth moved like that of a fish gasping for air as he desperately tried to find words. "Are you sure? I don't have that much experience. I mean, I've only worked here for two years, and before that, I was a news reporter. Are you sure I am not too lightweight for this?"

Now Calix laughed out loud. "God, Levar, don't ever do a job interview, would you please? You suck at it." Then his face grew serious. "Yes, we think you'd be perfect. As the vice president put it, you have the three things he's looking for in a member of his core team. You're smart, you're loyal, and you fully support his agenda. Anything else, you can learn. Besides, let's face it. You've been practically acting as the vice president's press secretary anyway. Don't think we don't know how much you've been doing that should've been on Ethan's plate."

Levar blinked a few times, then dragged a hand through his hair. "I'm sorry. I know I'm not selling myself really well right now, but I'm just...flabbergasted. Absolutely floored."

Calix leaned forward. "But will you do it?"

Levar didn't even need to think about it. This was everything he'd dreamed of. Only he was offered the position much earlier than he'd ever expected. "Yes. Hell, yes."

At least that had come out strong and confident. Hopefully, that would erase his blustering idiot performance of the minutes before.

"Good. The vice president will be overjoyed to hear that. We were really hoping you'd take the job. Is there anyone you need to confer with before you can give us your final answer?"

Levar shook his head. "No. I'm single, so I don't have anyone else to consider, except Rhett maybe, but he's already my roommate, so..."

"Even better. I'll let the vice president know. We're trusting you won't mention this until we set Ethan's departure in motion."

Levar nodded.

"We also talked about Henley's article and the tension between the president and the vice president that has now become front-page news."

"If we don't feed it, they'll move on to something else."

Calix let out a deep sigh. "The problem is that the tension isn't lessening. Over the weekend, the vice president had a...let's stay polite and call it a difference of opinion with the president. There were witnesses, so don't be surprised if someone asks you about it."

Oh god. This couldn't be good. "About what?"

"They had a difference of opinion on the Secret Service protection. The bottom line is that the vice president feels the Secret Service is stretched too thin and that they haven't addressed weaknesses that have been pointed out before."

"Didn't the president request broader protection than his predecessors?"

Calix nodded. "Yes, and that's part of the problem. Usually, only the president's direct family gets protection, meaning his wife and his children. Since the president has four grown children, that's already a lot. But President Markinson also requested protection for his two brothers and their families, which has put a lot of strain on the Secret Service."

"Have they gotten extra budget because of the increased required capacity?".

"No, on the contrary, and this is what the vice president pointed out. Look, you know he has his own Secret Service detail, and they're doing a damn good job. But he started to notice the hours they were making and the sacrifices they're being asked to make to do the job. Some men haven't had a day off in a month, and that's unacceptable."

"Why did the president ask for protection for his family?" Levar wanted to know. "I assume he had a reason for it, considering how much it costs."

Calix leaned forward, and his voice dropped to a lower level. "That's exactly what the vice president asked, and the president blew him off. The increased protection for his family started a few months after the bombing. That's five years ago, which is a long time to have extra protection without any specific reason. If there had been an increased threat at the time, which is not outside the realm of possibilities, it would make sense that threat had been neutralized by now and that the protection could've been reduced. But it hasn't. And the president refuses to say why. And obviously, the director of the Secret Service can't divulge this information to the vice president. And there's also the issue of several weaknesses that have been identified within the Secret Service but that haven't been addressed."

It sounded familiar. Where had he heard about this before? "Like what?"

"Like the president appointing people without the proper qualifications in key positions purely as a political favor. It puts the Secret Service at risk and thus the safety of those they protect."

Levar leaned back in his chair, scratching his chin. That was a tough spot to be in for him if the reporters got wind of this. He couldn't comment on Secret Service procedures. That was a hard rule, set in place to protect both the people who were under the protection of the Secret Service and the Secret Service agents themselves.

"What do you want me to say if this comes up in a briefing or if a reporter approaches me? Because I don't comment on Secret Service procedures, and we both know the Secret Service doesn't give briefings themselves, which will leave the reporters with nothing."

Calix nodded, his expression grim. "For now, unfortunately, that's exactly the strategy we have to employ. Don't deny but steadfastly repeat that you cannot comment on Secret Service procedures on account of protecting the safety of everyone involved."

"That's not going to hold them off for long," Levar warned.

"No, but hopefully long enough until we can get some answers ourselves. So those are your marching orders for now. If it does pop up on your radar, please let me know. This is something we really need to stay on top of."

Calix rose to his feet, then extended his hand to Levar. He quickly got up as well and took it. "Levar, we're glad you're on board, and we have every confidence in your ability to do this job."

"Thank you. I promise I won't let you down."

He almost floated through the hallways as he walked back to his office. *Press secretary.* He had just been promoted to press secretary to the vice president. Holy crap, what an amazing day this was. God, he needed to tell someone.

He came to a sudden stop when the first person who popped into his head wasn't Rhett. Or his parents. Or his brother. No, the first who came to mind was the one person who had just become even more off-limits than he already was. So far for a careful friendship...

14

Henley sat in the front of the room, in the middle of the first row. He'd always been more of a middle-row person, but lately, he'd switched to sitting more up front. He wasn't even trying to convince himself that change had any other reason than being able to make eye contact with Levar.

The day before, he'd noticed a difference in Levar. He'd been more energetic, a little hyped. Henley had expected a big announcement, something that would explain why Levar was so pumped, but nothing had happened. Maybe it was something else? Something personal? Or was he still energized from their weekend together, like Henley himself?

He leaned back in his chair, stretching his legs in front of him. He was early, another sign that should give him pause. He kept telling himself that it was all fine as long as he wasn't acting on it. And he hadn't. He'd behaved Sunday, when they had spent such a fantastic time together, just talking and hanging out. He hadn't kissed him, not even held his hand, so why had it felt so special? Nothing about this made sense.

But he hadn't acted on his urges and feelings. He hadn't touched him all weekend, not after they'd held hands on the train. Not when Levar had looked all kinds of cute that Sunday in his Yankees outfit. Not when his blue eyes had sparkled every time he'd fired back some witty comeback at Henley. And not even when he'd caught a glimpse of those lace panties, the ones he'd wanted to strip from Levar's body with his teeth before...

Okay, definitely not the most opportune moment to think of this. Hiding an erection in the front row of the press briefing was damn hard—har, har—especially considering he was wearing nice slacks and a button-down tucked-in shirt. He'd better think of something else.

The image kept playing through his mind, though. God, that small bit of silk and lace had been the sexiest thing ever. So unexpected and yet it completely fit Levar, the man who was so comfortable with his own sexuality. Henley had jerked off to it then, and if he kept reliving that memory, he might have to do it again soon.

When Levar walked into the room, Henley couldn't help but let his eyes trail over Levar's ass in those nice dress pants. Was he wearing panties again? What color would they be? Black would look amazing on him as well. The idea he was hiding something so sexy and frilly underneath that boring business attire was...

No, he really needed to stop thinking about this. He was a few seconds away from embarrassing himself in public, the likes of which he hadn't experienced since he'd been a teenager who had gotten an unfortunate hard-on in the swimming pool. He forced himself to look away.

Video, vides, videt. Videmus, videtis, vident.
Videbam, videbas, videbat. Videbamus, videbatis, videbant.
Running through conjugation of Latin verbs always

worked. If Father Gregory had known how his perfect student Henley was using Latin he'd drilled into him, the poor man would instantly die of a heart attack. Then again, maybe he had already been reunited with the saints, or whatever it had been he'd been looking forward to. Jesus, Mary, and Joseph, plus a few apostles, probably. If Henley thought hard, he could even recite them. See, that Catholic education had totally paid off. And that was the end of his unfortunate boner. Problem solved. If only he could move the problem of Levar and himself that easily...

"Good morning, everyone," Levar said as he took his position at the podium, spreading out two papers in front of him. "I have a special announcement to start with, then a couple of practical things, and after that, I will open the floor for questions."

Henley sat up straighter. A special announcement to start with? Okay, he was officially curious. Was this what had made Levar so hyper the day before?

"The office of the vice president is sad to announce that effective immediately, Ethan Haffley, press secretary to the vice president, has accepted a job as director of communications for the Henry Kissinger Institute for Foreign Policy. The vice president thanks Ethan for his years of dedicated service, and he respects Ethan's wish to lessen his workload in light of personal circumstances."

Ethan had *quit*? No fucking way. They'd fired him; Henley would put money on it. Ethan would never have decided to leave himself. They'd shipped him off to the institute and good riddance. But the bigger and way more important question was, who would become his successor?

As soon as he asked himself that, Henley knew the answer. *Oh my God.* Of course they'd asked him. He deserved it. Hell, he *had* practically been doing Ethan's job at least for the last year. His suspicion was confirmed when Levar dragged a hand through his hair, then cleared his throat. He was never nervous, but of course, this was a different kind of announcement. This was about himself.

"The vice president has asked me to take Ethan's position, and I have gladly accepted. Effective immediately, I will be acting as press secretary to the vice president, and all press relationships will run through my office. My relationships with all of you have been amicable, and I hope to continue these in the years to come. I look forward to working together on informing the public about the policy and projects that are so close to the vice president's heart. It's an honor to serve him as he continues to carry out his commitment to better the lives of the American people."

Henley was the first to applaud, but the whole room joined in, in seconds. A quick look around him showed that everyone shared his genuine enthusiasm for Levar's appointment. It was good news for all of them. Sure, they'd pretty much contacted him for everything anyway, but every now and then, Ethan had become territorial and had gotten on their case about bypassing him. At least now, Ethan was out of the picture officially.

As the applause died down, Levar said, "Thank you all for that response. I'm grateful to have such great working relationships with all of you."

He'd stressed the word "working," and Henley hadn't imagined his quick look in his direction either. Was that a hint? If so, he couldn't blame him. With this, he'd stepped into an even bigger spotlight. Anything between them had been impossible anyway, but now even more. And with Vice President Shafer soon gearing up to start his election campaign for president, Levar's job would become even more public. Half the country already recognized him from the Pride Bombing, but if Shafer won the elections and Levar became the White House press secretary, everyone and their mother would know who he was. There would be no more anonymity for them. For him, not for them. There was no *them*. As happy as he was for Levar, that thought soured Henley's mood.

"Two weeks from now, the vice president will travel to New York City to attend the five-year commemoration of the Pride Bombing. His wife, Sarah, and his son, Kennedy, will join him on this memorable day. Several congressmen and senators have announced their attendance, including delegations from New York, New Jersey, Pennsylvania—who all lost citizens in the attacks—and Massachusetts, the vice president's home state. Later today, Nicole will email you the preliminary program for the commemorative ceremony. The vice president is one of the main speakers."

Levar ran through a few more questions, and then he opened the floor for questions. They were softballs for the most part, though some reporters tried to get more information on the personal circumstances surrounding Ethan's departure. As expected, Levar kept repeating that for privacy reasons, he couldn't comment on those. Smart move. Personal circumstances hinted at a disease or something similar sensitive, which would help reporters back off.

"Will you attend the commemorative ceremony?" one of the TV reporters asked.

Levar nodded. "The vice president has asked me to travel with him. He'll be available for a brief Q&A after the ceremony."

"How does it feel for you to return to New York City, considering your own experiences on that day?" another reporter asked.

Levar hesitated. "As you can understand, I'm grateful to

be able to attend this ceremony. Grateful that I'm alive, that I survived that day, but also grateful that I can serve my country. Vice President Shafer has always been vocal in his support for LGBTQIA+ equality, and he has worked hard over the last two years to defend and expand the rights of the LGBTQIA+ community. I'm proud and honored to be a part of that."

He had deflected that one nicely. Henley debated with himself if he should confront him with the fact that he hadn't answered the question, then decided against it. Levar wasn't news. At best, it was the human-interest story, something for a junior reporter to work on. Not something Henley would spend time on.

Levar answered the last questions, then wrapped up the meeting. "Levar, could I ask you a question in private?" Henley called out.

Levar's eyes drilled into his, and then he nodded. "Make it quick. I have a to-do list the size of a CVS receipt."

Henley smiled as he followed him into his office, where it was Levar who closed the door behind them. He stuck his hands into his pocket, shuffling his feet as he asked, "What's up?"

Henley leaned against a wall, crossing his arms. "Congrats on the promotion. Well deserved, if you ask me."

Levar loosened a little. "Thank you," he said, and his smile was real. "It's a true honor, and I'm still on cloud nine."

He hadn't stated his remarks were off the record, and Henley liked that. Maybe they'd come to a point where they both understood that what happened in conversations like this was automatically private. "I'm excited for you. You've basically been doing Ethan's job for a while now, so I'm glad to see you get the official recognition and the accompanying responsibilities and salary."

Levar laughed. "I'm still a federal employee, so the bump in salary is just enough to buy me a couple of extra cups of coffee a month, but that's fine. I love working for the vice president."

"Hopefully for the soon-to-be president," Henley said.

Levar's eyes sharpened. "It's too early to make statements about that other than that Vice President Shafer intends to run, as far as he has communicated now. But we both know he hasn't made a formal announcement yet."

Henley shrugged. "It's way too early for that. But he will. And unless he runs the most stupid campaign in history or makes some big gaffe, he will win, which will make you press secretary to the president."

Henley didn't miss the excitement that flashed in Levar's eyes, the color it brought in his cheeks. "As I said, it's too early to talk about that. Besides, we don't know who else will run, and the vice president may be a strong candidate, but he's still bisexual. We both know that's a strike against him."

Henley sighed. "Yes, there's that. But let's face it. If ever a member of the queer community was likely to be the first president of the United States, it would be a bisexual senator with his pedigree who has been married to his wife for twenty years or so. The man is about as close to sainthood as they come."

"Maybe, but plenty of conservatives within the Democratic Party are upset with him for coming out. They felt it was unnecessary to declare himself as bisexual, considering he was in a committed relationship with a woman."

Henley rolled his eyes. "Let's not forget that for a lot of so-called allies, being gay is actually easier to understand than being bi or pan. The bi erasure is real."

"I know," Levar said. "Obviously, not from personal experience because I'm as gay as a freaking unicorn, but I have plenty of friends who have had nasty experiences after coming out as bi or pan. Even within the queer community, the B in the acronym isn't always accepted."

They stared at each other for a while. "Was there a reason you wanted to talk to me?" Levar asked.

"Yes." He had a reason to talk to Levar, right? Something he wanted to ask him. Did he? God, he couldn't even remember. He'd wanted to congratulate him in person, but admitting that had been the only reason would be embarrassing. "Right. I wanted to check in with you about the commemorative ceremony."

Levar raised an eyebrow. "Yeah? What about it?"

"Well, I'm going."

"I was assuming you would be, considering you're the White House correspondent for the Washington Times, as well as a survivor yourself. I would've been highly surprised had your editor not sent you."

"Right, right."

Levar frowned. "Was that all you wanted to tell me? That you were attending as well?"

God, he was such an idiot. What had he been thinking? "Because we're both going, I thought that maybe we could..."

He stopped talking, too flustered to continue. He was being ridiculous. What had he wanted to propose? That they traveled together? Of course they wouldn't. Levar would accompany the vice president, or he'd be on the press plane. And even if both of them would travel individually, they couldn't be seen together, not on the plane or the train or in New York.

"I'm not sure what you're trying to say," Levar said softly.

Henley shook his head. "Forget it. I was about to say something stupid, as you've probably figured out by now.

Pretend this didn't happen. That's probably better for both of us."

He finally looked up and met Levar's eyes, which seemed to mirror the sadness he felt himself. "Henley, I can't. I know we've —"

Henley held up his hand. "I know. Trust me, Levar, I know. I've told myself a thousand times, so don't even bother to explain. We both know this can never work. It's just..."

Levar smiled, a smile full of regrets. "It's hard when you want it so much."

The air between them zinged with electricity. "You want it too, right?" Henley said, his voice almost dropping to a whisper.

Levar hesitated for a second, then nodded. "Yes. Under other circumstances, if you and I hadn't had the jobs we have, I would've..."

"You would've taken me up on my not-so-subtle invitation."

"Yes. Or you would've taken me up on mine."

Henley swallowed. "I'll try to forget."

"Forget what?"

"Forget that I know what you hide beneath your clothes."

15

The commemorative ceremony was beautiful and brutal at the same time. They'd kicked things off with a private ceremony for survivors and their families in Christopher Park, where the vice president revealed the new memorial designed by one of the survivors. After that, they traveled to the auditorium of NYU, where more people had gathered.

The whole event had lasted two hours, and Levar felt completely wrung out afterward. The organizers had done a great job bringing together survivors, family members, first responders, and others who had been involved in the tragedy of that day, one way or another.

The vice president had talked about his own experiences but had focused mostly on the lives that had been cut short. He'd highlighted a few people who had lost their lives, showing their pictures on the big screens, sharing details about their lives that painted a picture of real people rather than names and ages on a list.

Various survivors had spoken, like an EMT who'd had

flashbacks to his time in Iraq for many months after the bombing. The 911 operator who was to this day still haunted by the calls of dying people she'd been unable to help. A woman who'd held her dying son, telling him over and over again she loved him. Family members who had been left behind.

Levar's throat had become so tight from fighting against his emotions, against his tears, that by the time it was finally done, he could barely swallow. He wasn't the only one. The vice president himself had gotten emotional during his speech, and throughout the service, sobs and quiet cries rose in the auditorium.

"That was beautiful, and I hope I never have to attend another one of these ever again." Calix shuddered as they walked out of the auditorium.

"My feelings exactly," Levar said. "I've discovered once again that you can wholeheartedly agree that something is crucially important and yet hate every moment of it."

Calix laid a quick hand on his shoulder. "You know where to find me if you ever need to talk."

Levar nodded. "I can say the same to you."

They shared a look that had become common in the last five years. It was the survivors' look, the meaningful wordless communication between people who knew how the other felt. The *only* people who knew how it felt because they'd been through the exact same thing. Different backgrounds, different stories, different experiences on that day, and yet they all understood. They were part of a unique club, a club that no one wanted to belong to.

"I'm gonna go ahead. I promised the press a few minutes with the vice president for a Q&A," Levar told Calix, who nodded.

"I'm sure they'll be nice after an experience like this."

Levar hurried out. He found the vice president with his wife and son waiting for him in the room the NYU had provided them as a personal space. "Are you ready for the Q&A, sir?" Levar asked.

"Yes." The vice president turned to his wife. "How do I look?"

Sarah Shafer brushed a lock of hair off his forehead, then straightened his tie. She pressed a brief kiss on his lips. "Handsome as ever."

Levar smiled at the obvious affection between those two. He hadn't had much personal contact with Mrs. Shafer yet, but according to the gossip among the staff, she was wonderful. Smart, easy to work with, and willing to listen to advice. The latter had endeared her to the staff, who was used to first and second ladies who didn't want to follow anyone's advice except their own.

Levar took the vice president to a room they'd organized as a briefing room. When they walked in, lights flashed, and several cameras were set up on the podium.

"Ladies and gentlemen, the vice president of the United States," Levar announced him, then moved aside.

Vice President Shafer stepped onto the podium and looked around the room. "First of all, I want to thank you all for coming to this ceremony. Five years ago, we witnessed a tragedy. We witnessed a horrible attack on our democracy, on our values, on our freedoms. Like 9/11, this event has become a watershed moment in our history, and we must never forget. I'm grateful to each and every one of you reporting on this, and I ask that you put the survivors and those who have lost their lives front and center. I'm now available to answer some of your questions."

Shafer always did well with press questions, which made Levar's job easy. He still monitored the questions so he could step in if necessary, though he didn't expect he'd have to. Like Calix had said, an event like this was not the moment to play hardball, and the press knew that too.

Henley sat in the front row, which had become his standard spot in the last few weeks. He was scribbling notes on the yellow notepad he always carried with him. He had a little dictation device on him at all times as well, but in many ways, he was old-fashioned in that he preferred pen and paper. Funny how Levar knew things like that about him.

They hadn't spoken since that last encounter in his office, and Levar wasn't sure if he was relieved or sad about it. Maybe both? At least they'd both shown where they stood, and that, strangely enough, had been a comfort. Knowing that he wasn't the only one who had wanted to explore the chemistry between them *meant* something.

And of course, Henley's reference to his panties had been...arousing. He'd never met a man who had reacted to his choice of underwear the way Henley had. God, the way he'd *looked* at him in New York, like he'd wanted to eat Levar alive. Why, oh why did it have to be the one man he couldn't have?

Well, technically, that wasn't true. He could think of plenty of other men who were equally unavailable, but those were all hypotheticals. Henley was real. Henley was sitting right there, in the front row, his head bowed as he wrote, those brown eyes that could be so sharp or resembling a cute puppy hidden for now, and every cell in Levar's body wanted to reach out to him. Bad idea. Bad, bad idea.

The vice president handled the questions with ease, and ten minutes later, Levar called it quits. "We thank you all for being here. Safe travels. The bus to LaGuardia will leave in twenty minutes, so don't be late, or you'll miss the plane."

Reporters packed up their stuff, and one of them called out, "Levar, will you be available on the plane for more questions?"

Levar shook his head. "I'll be traveling back to DC by other means. This is a full lid for today. I will see you guys tomorrow."

The room emptied within minutes. The vice president had already left with his family, accompanied by the Secret Service. Levar grabbed his things, then checked to make sure he had everything. God, he was tired. He felt as exhausted as if he'd worked ten days in a row. His head was just...full. Tense. Twisting and flipping with so many emotions he couldn't express, couldn't let out that he had a headache brewing.

When he looked up, Henley was standing there, the only one left in the room. Their eyes met, and Henley appeared as wiped and washed out as Levar felt. "Don't miss the bus," Levar said.

"I'm not taking the press bus and plane back. I'm staying the night here and catch the early train back tomorrow morning."

Levar swallowed. "Me too."

Henley took a step forward. "You have? Did you...?"

"No, I didn't know you wouldn't be on the plane. I just told you not to miss the bus, remember? I didn't check the list of reporters who would be flying. That's Nicole's job."

"So why did you decide to spend the night here and take the train?"

Levar let out a tired laugh, then pointed at his face. "Look at me. After the week I've had, after these hours of emotional hell, the last thing I wanted was to be stuck in a bus and on a plane with forty reporters."

"Yeah," Henley said, his voice hoarse. "Same. I had a feeling I'd be emotionally wrung out after the ceremony. I didn't want to have to talk about it with my colleagues, all of whom would've asked me about my experiences and emotions during the service, considering they all know I was there that day."

Levar sighed. "Yeah, that's the other reason. I've had a lot of questions from you guys this week about me, about my feelings, and I don't want to be the news. I serve the vice president, and it should be about him, not me."

They stared at each other for a bit. Henley cleared his throat. "Which hotel are you staying at?"

"The same one you booked for us last time. It seemed easiest, since I knew where it was."

"So am I."

Well, fuck. This just complicated things, didn't it? How was he supposed to handle this? He'd tried to stay away from Henley, and considering how successful he'd been, he suspected Henley had attempted the same thing. But the two of them, staying in the same hotel? Away from everyone else? They were asking for trouble.

"I can't travel back to the hotel with you," Levar said. "No matter how much I would want to."

"I understand, and I wouldn't ask you to."

God, they had to stop staring at each other like this, these long, meaningful looks that were so heavy, so emotionally charged. It almost felt like they were stuck in a teenage drama series, like an endless rerun of Dawson's Creek Henley had referred to last time.

"How about dinner together? In my room?" Henley asked, so soft that Levar had to lean in to hear him.

He closed his eyes. He shouldn't. He really, really shouldn't. "Okay." He opened his eyes again.

"Okay." A smile broke free on Henley's face. "I look forward to it."

God help them both. "So do I."

16

What were they doing? Henley kept asking himself that as he sat in the cab back to the hotel. Every time he sought Levar out again despite his best intentions not to. He was drawn to him like a moth to a flame, like Icarus to the sun. That last analogy was apt because one of them—if not both of them—would end up crashing if they continued this crazy dance, and yet neither of them seemed to be able to stop.

The radio was playing softly in the background—an eighties station, by the sounds of it—and the cab driver hummed along. His cab was worn, the leather seat cracked but clean, but it still looked neat, even this time of day. Henley appreciated the unmistakable smell of Febreze.

"You tourist?" the cab driver asked in heavily accented English. He was from Somalia if Henley had to take a guess.

"No, for business. And I used to live here. I loved it here, but now..."

The cabbie made eye contact in the rearview mirror. "Why you move? Is best city in the world."

It had been, once upon a time. Hell, six years ago,

Henley would've bet he'd never leave. Why would he? Lots of work, gay-friendly, every convenience known to man. What was not to like?

"The Pride Bombing," he said simply.

The cabbie's eyes lost their smile. "I came after. But that was bad. Very bad." He hesitated. "Is not okay to kill people because you don't agree with them. I'm Muslim, but it's okay to believe in other god, in other rules. We still neighbors. We can still be friends. Not everyone has to think the same."

Henley smiled. "Exactly. If everyone felt that way, the world would be a much better place."

After that, the cabbie left him to his thoughts, but Henley appreciated the short conversation, and he tipped liberally when he'd reached the hotel. "I hope you love New York again," the cabbie said when Henley got out.

"I hope so too."

He'd given Levar his room number, and they'd agreed to meet an hour later for dinner. Chinese again. They'd both smiled when Henley had proposed that. He loved knowing what he had to order for Levar, loved that he knew him well enough for that. Such a little thing, and yet it made him warm and giddy inside. So stupid. So unbelievably stupid.

He'd already called the Chinese restaurant before he grabbed a cab, so he popped across the street to pick up the food. As soon as he walked into his room, he took off his suit and got changed into a pair of comfy sleeping pants and a shirt. That, too, felt good, the knowledge that he could be himself with Levar. He wouldn't mind Henley being in what were basically his pajamas.

When the knock on the door sounded, Henley had just set up dinner on the little table. He smiled when he took in Levar, who was wearing a ratty 49'ers T-shirt and jogging pants. See? They were of the same mind. Relaxation, that was all they wanted.

Though he couldn't help but wonder what Levar was sporting under those jogging pants. Had he opted for more sensible underwear after getting caught the last time? Or was he wearing something lacy and frilly again? Something that would have Henley stroke his cock at the memory, his mind conjuring up a picture of Levar's hard shaft, barely held back by soft silk, stained with his precum. His balls, hanging heavy in the lacy trimming, threatening to spill.

"Let's eat," Levar said. "I'm starving."

Henley swallowed. He was starving too, but not just for food.

They barely spoke the first few minutes, both attacking the food. "God, why does Chinese always hit that comfort button?" Henley leaned back, rubbing his belly after he'd finished his plate.

Levar pushed his plate back as well, then wiped his mouth with a napkin. "I think it's because I can tell myself it's not as unhealthy as fast food, so it doesn't feel as bad and still satisfies that craving."

"Mmm, that sounds about right." Henley checked his watch. "Wanna catch the news?"

"Yeah, that'd be good. I'm curious to see what the networks are broadcasting about the memorial."

As if by unspoken agreement, they settled on the bed, pillows propped in their backs, their legs stretched out, and their shoulders almost touching. The faint whiff of the deodorant he must've refreshed before coming to his room tickled Henley's nose. The urge to put his head on Levar's shoulder was overwhelming, but he couldn't. Icarus and all that.

CNN had broadcasted the memorial live and was now

showing a shorter report with the highlights. Henley's throat closed all over again as he watched the vice president's speech for the second time that day, only this time on TV rather than live.

"He's so good at this," he said to Levar, whose eyes were glued to the screen.

"Yeah, he is. I may be biased, but he sounds more presidential than Markinson does."

Henley hummed in agreement. "Markinson can come off as distant, patronizing. Shafer makes you feel like he's at your level. He excels at connecting with people."

Levar let out a deep sigh. "I love working for him."

"How's the new job going?"

"I don't have to tell you that pretty much the only thing that changed is that I no longer have Ethan to deal with and have another title. In terms of what's on my to-do list, I don't see much difference."

"You're doing great."

Levar's face broke open in a wide smile. "You think?"

"Yeah. You have a sense of humor, but you also know when to put your foot down. It's a rare mix."

"Thank you. Coming from you, that's a huge compliment."

Henley raised an eyebrow as in the background, CNN continued their coverage. He'd lowered the volume so they could talk easier. "Coming from me? Like I'm the most critical person ever?"

"Are you telling me that impression is false?"

Henley thought about it, then grinned back. "Nah, you're right. But you're really doing a great job. The way you handled the Markinson-Shafer feud, for example, was perfect."

Levar looked at him for a few beats, his upper body

turned toward him. "I ought to thank you for bringing that up with me. It helped bring things in the open that the vice president hadn't wanted to share out of loyalty to the president."

Henley clicked his tongue. "He should be careful with that loyalty. It's definitely one-sided."

"Yeah, so I'm discovering. Apparently, they had another clash..."

He suddenly stopped talking, and Henley had no trouble understanding why. "You're talking to your friend, Henley, not reporter Henley Platt from the Washington Times," he said softly.

"Can you separate those two so easily?"

"No, not easily and I rarely do, but with you, I want to. If I don't, if all I am is reporter Henley, you and I can't hang out, and that's unacceptable to me. So we'll make this work."

"If you screw me over on this..." Levar's voice was raw.

"I won't. I promise, Lev." The little nickname fell off his lips as if he'd never called him anything else, and when he grasped Levar's hand, the other man didn't pull his away. Their fingers laced together as they sat in silence.

"Shafer and Markinson had an argument about the Secret Service protection. Apparently, the Secret Service is getting stretched thin because Markinson has requested protection for his extended family. Shafer questioned him about that, as well as about some other issues that aren't being addressed, and the president got snappy with him."

Henley realized the magnitude of what Levar was entrusting him with, and he squeezed his hand he was still holding. Thankfully, he could level the playing field instantly. "Remember those three articles I wrote about the Secret Service, about a year ago?"

Levar's eyes lit up. Henley's articles. That was why Calix's remarks about issues within the Secret Service had sounded so familiar. "Not in detail, but didn't you point out several weaknesses?"

"Yes. And I didn't even use all the information I had. It was bad. Really bad. You should look them up for some background info in case this new argument leaks and it's brought up again."

"I will, but give me the Cliffs Notes version?"

"It started with an acquaintance of mine, mentioning that her partner, a Secret Service agent, hadn't had a day off in three weeks. I thought that was curious, so I put some feelers out. The first thing I discovered was, like you said, Markinson requesting extended protection for his family, which was uncommon. What was interesting was that he didn't do it when he became president. He made the request a few months after the Pride Bombing. At first, it made sense to me, you know? Who wouldn't have gotten scared after that in his position? You can bet your ass that the Secret Service tightened the security around George W. and Cheney as well after 9/11. But it wasn't immediately after the Pride Bombing, and it lasted way beyond what could be considered reasonable. As a result, the Secret Service was overwhelmed."

Levar frowned. "He cut their budget when he got reelected. Why would he do that if he knew they were understaffed?"

"People were starting to ask questions, and he wanted them off his tail," Henley said. "And you know the Secret Service. They'll make it work, even at the cost of the personal lives of all their agents."

"Yeah, that pissed me off when I heard that. That some agents haven't had a day off in weeks is unacceptable, and that's what the VP communicated to the president, but he wasn't open to the feedback, to put it mildly."

"It gets worse. According to a reliable source, they're unable to protect the president the way they want to because they lack the manpower and the budget. When he's attending a public event, like at the Kennedy Center or a campaign rally, they're supposed to screen everyone in attendance. Every single person has to go through a metal detector. But that takes forever, so every time the president showed up somewhere, the event was delayed because of the time needed for that security screening. Markinson caught flak from the public about that, so he told the Secret Service to stop checking everyone and only do random checks."

Levar's mouth dropped open. "That's…that's incredibly stupid. And risky. You didn't put that in the articles, did you?"

"No. I wanted to, I really did, but it would've endangered the president and his Secret Service agents. But I did report on something else that was even more dangerous. Markinson had appointed two of his political donors to key positions within the Secret Service, and neither of them had the qualifications for it. Worse, they don't have a law enforcement background or any experience with top secret data, and both have been sloppy with their cybersecurity."

"I remember that. Something about them using open networks?"

"Ronald Truman, the NSSE director within the Secret Service, was caught using the hotel's Wi-Fi on a trip he took rather than setting up a secure VPN connection. My source said he wasn't compromised, but it's clear proof that Markinson installed unqualified people in key positions.

Truman is sixty-two. He's old school, barely literate with a cell phone."

"God, yes, I remember reading those details. That scared the crap out of me. Though I'm not entirely sure what NSSE is again. He coordinates the security for large events, right?"

"NSSE stands for National Special Security Event and refers to large events that Homeland Security deems high risk, like an inauguration or a big sports event, like the Super Bowl. The Secret Service is the lead federal agency for coordinating, planning, and security, and Ronald Truman is in charge. Now, as I pointed out in my articles, he has terrific people working under him, so I'm not worried about the security itself. But he has access to some top secret information...and uses public Wi-Fi. Anyway, I pointed out a number of critical deficiencies in my articles, which caused a shitstorm."

"Those briefings weren't fun for Katie Winters. I remember watching them and thinking how lucky I was I didn't have her job."

"Markinson was furious. He wanted Lisandra James to find out who my source was. She assured him she would, then let it die a slow death."

Levar whistled between his teeth. "That's a risky strategy for the director of the Secret Service."

Henley grinned. "She's got balls the size of Texas. Look, Markinson hates her and wants her gone, but she's relatively new to the job but highly qualified. He's already getting criticized for not having enough women in a leadership position, let alone a black woman...and she's both. Plus, firing her would've been all but an admission the articles were true, so he had to suck it up. She's just lying low now, waiting for him to go so she can hopefully build a better relationship with the next occupant of the White House.

The problem is that Markinson is not giving her the resources she needs to fix the issues. No extra budget and he refuses to fire his appointees. And trust me, I had a hell of a lot more information that I chose not to publish."

"They must've leaned on you to reveal your sources," Levar said.

Henley shrugged. "They tried, both with me and through my editor and even his boss, but they've got my back. This is at the very core of my profession—don't reveal your sources. Once we do that, no one will ever trust us again."

They were still holding hands, both of them relaxed in that touch. Henley stroked the back of Levar's hand with his thumb. He felt comfortable, simply by holding him. Wasn't that strange?

"Why are you telling me all this?" Levar asked.

"Because I like Shafer, and I'd like to see him become the next president. He needs to know what he's getting into with Markinson. But more importantly, I trust you. You'll do what's right with this info without revealing me as your source. It's public info, all documented in my articles and the blog storm that erupted after those. It's not hard to find once you know where to look, and now you do."

"Thank you." Levar swallowed, and Henley squeezed his hand.

They sat like that for a while, silent, their hands doing the communication for them. On TV, CNN was showing footage of the bombing once again. Levar tensed when his face appeared.

"Does it ever get easier for you to see yourself?" Henley asked.

"No. I thought it would, but it doesn't. It feels jarring, unreal, like I'm watching another me."

"It *was* another you. Just like there's a me before and after that day. We're not the same, and we never will be."

Then Levar did what Henley had wanted to do that whole time. He bridged the inch that separated their shoulders and put his head on Henley's shoulder, sighing softly. Henley lifted their hands and pressed a kiss on Levar's hand. Such an old-fashioned gesture, but one that came from his soul. Levar leaning on him hit him on a level he found hard to put into words. Like their souls connected.

"Sometimes, I'm so tired of it all. Tired of grieving, of waiting for it to pass. Tired of explaining what it was like, how it felt, how it has impacted me. Just...tired," Levar said, his voice breaking near the end.

Henley let go of his hand and wrapped his arm around Levar as he sank a little lower in the pillows. With a soft nudge, Levar gave in and rolled onto his side, settling his head on Henley's chest. He slung his arm around Henley's stomach, giving him goose bumps all over.

"I know," Henley said. "And you can't really talk about it because the people who weren't there don't want to hear this, or they don't understand, and the people who were there are already dealing with their own grief and emotions."

Levar crawled even closer against him, and his shirt was riding up, revealing the lacy band of a red thong. What a contrast it formed with his old shirt and those super casual jogging pants, and yet it fit him to a T. So sexy. So perfect. Henley couldn't even see the shape of his ass in those loose pants, but he could picture it with ease.

"Exactly," Levar whispered. "And I'm tired of it all."

Down boy, Henley told his cock, which was showing a lot of interest in exploring the rest of that strip of red lace. But it wasn't happening. Even if they hadn't been doomed to crash and burn, Henley would never have started something when Levar was so vulnerable.

He turned off the TV, then threw the remote onto his nightstand. "So talk to me. I know, and I understand...and I'm here."

"Thank you." It came out as more as a breath than a whisper, and the next thing Henley knew, Levar had closed his eyes and was asleep.

Henley watched him for a long time, his soul more at peace than it had been in years, even when his body protested the lack of action with a man in his arms. It took some maneuvering to turn off the lights without letting go of Levar, but Henley managed, and once he settled down again, Levar crawled right back into his arms, never waking up.

17

Mmm, he was so nice and warm, so comfy and safe. Levar's transition from sleep to waking up was slow, and he refused to open his eyes. He hadn't slept that well in ages, and he knew that as soon as he allowed himself to wake up fully, he'd shift right back into work mode. Into stress mode. Into worrying-about-everything mode.

Nope, he wanted to slumber a little longer because this feeling was amazing, and he needed to hold on to it. He tended to get cold in bed, and he was so toasty now, his whole skin radiating heat. His hand traveled to his cock, which was probably the most awake part of him right now, straining his panties. He slipped his hand below the lace, stroking himself gently.

Mmm, yes, a slow orgasm, that would make this morning even better. One where he teased himself for a long time before finally allowing himself to come. And then he'd wipe himself off with his panties, which others might consider a waste but always exhilarated him. Even more because he faithfully waxed his pubic hair and balls, reveling in the feel of the silk against his bare skin. Something about the combination of his spent dick, of his cum on the frilly fabric was so sensual and erotic.

"If you continue doing that, I can't guarantee I'll be able to keep my hands off of you."

Levar's eyes flew open as his body froze. Holy shit. Where the fuck was he? That heat was a male body he was plastered against, his almost bare ass cheeks pressed against warm skin. Henley. Oh shit, he was in bed with Henley. Had they...?

No, impossible. He hadn't even had a drink the night before, just water. But he'd been so tired, and being held by Henley had felt so fucking good and safe, and he'd...he'd fallen asleep. In his arms. And now that he thought about it, he vaguely remembered getting incredibly hot during the night and taking off his sweaty jogging pants and his shirt. That had left him with nothing but his underwear...his very lacy, sexy thong.

He yanked his hand from his dick, his cheeks flushing with embarrassment. Oh god. He was in bed with Henley, and he was wearing nothing but a pair of red lace panties. A *thong*. How the hell could he have been this stupid? He should never have put them on yesterday. He'd been wearing his boring Calvin Kleins all day, but when he'd gotten back to the hotel, he'd switched them out, knowing he'd be hanging out with Henley. He'd wanted to feel sexy.

"Are you gonna say something at some point?" Henley sounded amused. "Pretending it didn't happen isn't gonna make it so, in case you wondered."

"That sucks because I was really hoping that would work," Levar said, his voice croaky from sleep.

Henley chuckled. "Sorry to burst your bubble there."

"Do I need to apologize for anything?"

"Not unless you feel the need to apologize for offering me the most tantalizing view ever with you in that red lace. Or for making me wake up with the mother of all hard-ons and practicing my self-control."

Despite the situation, Levar smiled at the classic Henley response. Always a witty repartee. He took a deep breath, then turned around and faced him. Henley was sitting up against the headboard, his phone in his hand, his chest bare, revealing a broad, soft frame thinly coated with dark hair all the way to the waistband of his boxer briefs. Levar's ass had been pressed against his legs, and the only consolation was that Henley had also undressed to his underwear, if a much more sensible pair. And damn, the man had a pair of thighs that made Levar swallow, so big and strong. Mmm, yes, he appreciated a little meat on his men.

Out of everything he could've said, his brain latched on to one thing Henley had mentioned. "You like my panties?"

Henley shot him a questioning look. "You sound surprised. Wouldn't every man in my situation appreciate them?"

Levar propped himself up on his elbow. "Some men feel they're too feminine."

"Really? Let me have a better look."

Before Levar realized what he was doing, Henley had whipped the covers off him, exposing him and his still-hard dick in all its glory. Henley took him in, then licked his lips with a smack. "Nope, nothing feminine about that, and that's coming from a man who can appreciate feminine curves as much as a male hard body and anything in between. You're all male, baby, and those panties are delicious on you. Absolutely edible."

He dropped the covers back onto Levar, who lay stunned for a moment. What the hell had just happened? But then he cracked a smile, which morphed into a full laugh. "You're nuts."

Henley winked at him. "True, but that doesn't mean I'm wrong."

Levar grew serious. "I rarely let other men see me like this. Only Rhett knows, but he doesn't mind. Or I should say, he's fully supportive."

Henley put his phone on the nightstand, then sank lower and turned onto his side as well, mirroring Levar's pose. "I'm sorry you have such lousy taste in men."

"What?" Levar frowned.

"Clearly you must have because no good man who's attracted to other men would ever object to you in those sexy bits of lace. I've been thinking about them ever since our last trip to New York, when I saw them peep from underneath your pants."

Levar raised an eyebrow. "You've been thinking about my underwear?"

"I know, right? I totally transitioned into the creep zone there, but sheesh, man, can you blame me when you tease me like that?"

Levar's mouth curled up into a smile again, something that seemed to happen a lot when he was around Henley. "Thank you."

"For being a creep?"

"For being sweet and affirming me the way I am." Levar sounded probably much more serious than he'd meant, but the warmth spreading inside Henley was real, and it soothed some of the stings the careless remarks of others had caused.

"You know how you could thank me?" Henley wiggled his eyebrows.

"I have a sneaky suspicion which direction this will take, but bring it."

Henley pointed at his mouth. "One kiss. That's it. One kiss."

"You know this has catastrophe written all over it."

"Come on, Lev. We're two grown men. Surely we can control ourselves... One kiss can't hurt."

Levar grinned. "I bet many a baby was conceived that way."

"Well, that's one worry we don't have."

"True, but there are enough potential issues left to make this a really bad idea."

"The most fun things usually are a bad idea."

Levar's body zinged with the electric charge between them, with the adrenaline flooding his system at the idea of kissing Henley. Taking that step was most certainly a spectacularly bad idea and yet harder to resist by the second. "One kiss," he warned Henley.

"Just one," Henley promised.

Levar resisted for a few more seconds, then surrendered to the inevitable. He leaned in, and Henley did the same. They hovered with their mouths a breath apart, as if they wanted to make it last as long as possible. He shouldn't do this. He really, really shouldn't do this. Then Henley closed the distance, and Levar's mind went blank.

Henley's lips were warm, careful. A fluttering touch as light as a whisper, a promise of more. Levar inched closer, and the pressure increased. The kiss became moist, hotter, and a little moan floated from the back of his throat. His tongue peeped out, at first just to lick his lips, but as soon as he tasted Henley, he wanted more.

He wasn't sure who made the first move, and it didn't matter. Their tongues met as their mouths opened, and that innocent kiss became an explosion, hot, wet heat twirling, sliding, chasing each other from one mouth to the other. He scooted closer, and Henley yanked him on top of him, holding him with want and possessiveness.

Alarm bells were blaring in the back of Levar's head, but he was past caring. Then Henley's hands cupped his bare ass cheeks, and he moaned, instinctively gyrating his hips into him, seeking the friction. Henley was as hard as he was, their dicks only separated by a thin layer of cotton and a bit of lace.

He wanted to feel more of Henley, and when he couldn't, he rolled them over so Henley was on top of him. His hands immediately found their target, grabbing Henley's ass, first through the cotton, then slipping underneath to feel his bare skin. Now Henley moaned, and the sound fired Levar on even more.

He lifted his hips, circling them upward, and Henley ground into him. The lace rubbed his cockhead with enough friction that he was teetering on the edge. Those alarm bells became dimmer and dimmer as he spread his legs, inviting Henley to press his cock against his crotch even harder.

They were both panting, their lips never letting go, even as his body tensed up, his balls painfully heavy, and his cock so, so hard. Henley slipped his hand between them and clasped Levar's dick through the lace, and that touch was so sensuous and hot that Levar lost it. He pushed against Henley's hand, which squeezed with just the right amount of pressure, then rubbed again, his hips shamelessly propping him forward. His cock pulsed, his muscles going stiff and his vision white as his orgasm barreled through him, and he emptied himself against the lacy fabric...and Henley's hand.

"God, Lev..." Henley grunted. "So fucking hot."

And then Henley tensed himself, and the wet spot between them grew even wetter as Henley released as well, letting out a guttural moan, low and deep in his chest as his body convulsed. Their kiss became softer, losing that frantic edge. Levar kept his eyes closed as they descended from their high with sweet kisses, soothing and savoring until they finally let go.

Henley pushed himself up on his elbows, and Levar opened his eyes. Henley's lips were swollen, his hair was a hot mess, and his beard looked a little disheveled from where Levar had rubbed his own stubble against him. His eyes were still dark with emotions as he licked his lips. "I lied," he whispered.

"About what?"

"I didn't want just one kiss."

Levar leaned his forehead against Henley's. "What the fuck are we gonna do now?"

18

The Baltimore Convention Center was decently filled with flag-waving Democrats, who cheered and chanted his name as President Markinson took the stage. The president waved back enthusiastically, a broad smile plastered on his face that didn't quite reach his eyes.

The man should bask in the glow of the crowd's support. His ratings were abysmal the last few weeks, and the coverage of the Pride Bombing commemoration had boosted Vice President Shafer's numbers through the roof. That morning, another newspaper had reported on the feud between Markinson and his VP, and it was becoming clear who was at fault here. They had multiple sources confirming the bad blood on the president's side, with no quotes other than support from Shafer's side. Shafer inspired loyalty, and that was hard to come by these days.

Henley sighed as President Markinson shook hands with Senator Laura Kessler, the senior senator from Markinson's home state of Maryland. She was up for reelection and feeling the heat from her Republican challenger, so she'd called in a favor from the president to stump for her at a large rally in Baltimore.

They were old friends, so this was not a favor Markinson could've refused, even if he'd wanted to, which Henley didn't think was the case. This was about as friendly a crowd as he could get. Besides, he was two blocks away from Orioles Park, where his beloved Orioles had played earlier, crushing the Miami Marlins. If nothing else, that should've been cause for celebration for the president.

Markinson started his speech, and Henley tuned out. He'd already sent in his first article so he'd only have to add anything interesting that happened during the speech, and he doubted that would be the case. Markinson wasn't a bad public speaker, but after six years on the job, things were bound to get a tad repetitive.

Usually, Henley wouldn't even have attended a rally like this, but it was a slow news day otherwise, so his editor had sent him, just in case. That was news for you in a nutshell. One never knew when news would happen. If nothing else, the Pride Bombing had proven that. And of course, that brought him right back to Levar.

How could he be in a convention center packed with people and yet miss the one person who wasn't there? Henley checked his phone, even though it would've vibrated with an incoming message. Nope, nothing. Still nothing. Not that he'd expected differently.

He hadn't heard from Levar since their morning in New York a week before. After that amazing encounter, they'd left on good terms with the solid promise to keep their distance, and both of them had stuck to that so far. But damn, staying away from him proved to be much harder than he'd anticipated. He'd still attended the press briefings Levar held, but he'd deliberately sat in the back, although his body had ached to be closer to him. What the hell was that weird attraction?

He'd been off for the Fourth of July two days before, and all day, he'd debated texting Levar and asking him to meet. When had he become that person? He was thirty-nine years old, for fuck's sake. Way past the age for infatuations, and yet that was exactly what it felt like.

Should he send him a message? Just a quick "how are you?" Or maybe an "I can't stop thinking about you"? No, that would be too personal again. He had to keep his distance. "Just checking in," then? Or "wanted to make sure you're okay"?

He was still debating what to send him, his phone in his hand, when he caught movement from the corner of his eye. A man was sprinting toward the stage, and Henley's heart stopped. After that, everything happened in slow motion.

His brain disconnected from his body, turning him into an observer, watching everything from a safe distance.

The Secret Service agents on the stage dove on the president, pulling him to the ground. They were shouting, yelling orders.

Multiple shots fired simultaneously.

The man threw something.

More shots.

The man's body jerked, and he cried out something in a foreign language.

His body blew up in a thundering blast, disintegrating into pink mist as Henley sat frozen.

A second explosion rocked through the convention center, making the floor vibrate, and then it became quiet.

The silence lasted a second, maybe two. Then pandemonium broke out.

Henley sat motionlessly in his seat as screams erupted

and people started running, climbing over chairs, over each other to get out. He couldn't move. He was in New York again, on that pavement, his ears ringing as his body hurt. His knees, his hands.

No, he wasn't in New York. Where was he? Baltimore, Maryland. Convention center. A rally with the president.

A bomb. A bomb had gone off. Oh my god. The president. How many were dead? His heart was pounding, and he drew in desperate breaths.

Calm the fuck down. You're okay. You're not hurt. Breathe, goddammit. Breathe. You survived once. You can do this again.

He kept repeating it until his mind reconnected with his body, and his chest finally relaxed until he could control his breathing. Holy shit, he was *alive*. He'd survived a second bombing. How the hell was this even possible? What had happened? Was the president okay?

His head spun when he got up. All the chairs around him were empty, the entire press corps having escaped to somewhere safe. Or they'd moved in closer to whatever had happened to report. On what was left of the stage, the mist slowly subsided, revealing a stack of bodies, some unmoving. Other agents came running, weapons drawn, and shouting instructions. He must've been farther away this time because his ears didn't ring as much as five years ago. Or maybe it had been a different kind of bomb. Less powerful.

He was still holding his phone, and he looked at it in bewilderment for a few seconds. Then his mind switched into gear. He had to call his editor. But instead, his fingers pressed the Messages icon, and he fired off a quick text to Levar.

Two bombs at rally. President hurt, possibly dead. I'm okay.

Then he speed-dialed Toby, who picked up after three rings.

"Henley, what's—"

"Suicide bomber at the rally. Bomber is dead, multiple wounded. The president was hit, as were several Secret Service agents."

"Oh god..." Toby said. "Oh my god. Are you okay?"

He had to give Toby credit for thinking of Henley first under these circumstances. "Yeah, fine. I was too far away."

"Is the president alive?"

"I don't know. It's pure chaos on the stage right now with Secret Service agents everywhere."

"You're saying two bombs?"

"Yeah. One was on the bomber himself, most likely a vest, and the other was something he threw at the president. It was too loud and explosive for a grenade."

"Are the cameras still rolling?"

He hadn't even checked. His body still shaking slightly, he walked to the front. The press had been sitting to the right side of the president, and he slowly made his way around to the stage to get a better view. His eyes glanced over the bodies of the dead and the wounded on the ground. He didn't look too hard. Couldn't.

"The cameras got knocked back in the blast. Hold on," he told Toby. "Donna!" he called out to the CNN reporter who was standing there, looking dazzled. They'd hooked up a few times, years ago, and they'd managed to stay friendly after. "You okay?"

She slowly turned toward him, then blinked a few times. "Yeah. Just shaken."

Henley came closer. She looked fine, just disheveled. "Is your cameraman good?"

She nodded. "He's running an equipment check right

now, and we should be broadcasting in a minute or so. We have the blast on tape. We weren't rolling live, but we have it, so they're checking it now to see if it's suitable to be broadcasted."

The longer she talked, the more she sounded like herself. "Good," Henley said. "Did you bring other clothes with you?"

She looked down at herself, her eyes widening in horror as if just realizing her pale blue shirt was covered in dirt and blood. "No. I'm…no."

"You wearing anything underneath that?"

She would. Every female reporter did in case they got wet. No woman wanted her coverage to turn into a Miss Wet T-shirt contest.

"Yes. But it's just a white camisole."

Henley was already unbuttoning his shirt. "Take my shirt. Roll up the sleeves and leave the first two buttons open. You'll be fine."

"Henley…" Her voice was thick with emotion, but she pulled her blouse out of her pants, then whipped it over her head.

Henley took a wet wipe from his bag. He always had them on him. Always. They were good for cleaning your hands, your shirt, equipment, anything. You could even wipe your butt with them if you had to. They had saved his ass on more than one occasion—literally. He stood in front of her, then carefully cleaned her face, removing all dirt and gore as he spoke.

"This one matters. People will be watching this footage for decades to come, so take a deep breath, gather your thoughts, and go get 'em. Do your job."

She steeled herself, her eyes growing focused. She took the shirt from him, then buttoned up, and he helped her pull it straight, then quickly fixed her hair. "Thank you," she said softly, then leaned in and kissed him on his cheek.

He stepped back and raised his phone to his ear again. "Sorry, I was—"

"You were being you. I'm proud of you, Henley. Ridiculously proud," his old curmudgeon of an editor said, and a warm glow spread through Henley's body despite everything. "Now, can you do your job?"

He swallowed. "I can't look at the victims, at the carnage. It's too much after…"

"I understand. Turn your phone camera on and record it. That gives you emotional distance, and we'll look at it and have someone fill in the description. I'm sending someone over to take over from you, okay?"

He applied the advice he'd given Donna and took a deep breath, mentally focusing. "Okay."

19

"All right, folks, we'll take one last question," Levar said to the reporters as he checked his watch. Two more minutes and they had to be out of there.

He was happy with how the event had gone, considering it had been thrown together at the last minute. The vice president had been scheduled to speak at the Naval Academy in Annapolis for a graduation ceremony and the commissioning of this year's class. Unfortunately, the Academy had reported an outbreak of salmonella that morning, and they'd had to cancel. Instead, he'd done a virtual speech from the Roosevelt Room, followed by a meeting with an organization of spouses of sailors to continue the theme. He'd done great, as always adapting quickly to the changing circumstances, and the press was throwing him softballs in the Q&A.

"Vice President Shafer, do you feel that your background—"

The door behind them burst open, and Secret Service agents stormed in, immediately forming a protective wall around the vice president. "You need to come with us, sir," one of them said, his voice holding an edge Levar had never heard before.

Within seconds, they'd whisked him out of the room. Levar stared after them, completely bewildered. What the hell had just happened? His phone buzzed in his pocket, and he was so stunned that he took it out. A text from Henley. The blood drained from his face as he read it.

Two bombs at rally. President hurt, possibly dead. I'm okay.

Oh god. Oh god, oh god, oh god.

Should he say something? He had to. He couldn't be in a room with reporters and not say anything, not about something this big. He cleared his throat, finding it constricted and tight. "Guys, something seems to have happened at the rally for Senator Kessler, which the president attended in Baltimore."

The room grew quiet instantly. "What happened?" Sam from NBC asked.

"I don't know. A friend who was there texted me, but I don't have any details. I don't want to speculate."

"Give us something," Sam pressed. "What are we talking about here? A shooting? A fight?"

"Bombs. We talking bombs. But don't you dare quote me as your source. I'm sure more details will become available soon. I have to go."

Ignoring the reporters shouting questions at him, Levar hurried out the door and closed it firmly behind him. What did he do now? Calix. He had to talk to Calix. He started walking, then broke into a dead run. He barged into Calix's office without even acknowledging his assistant, who called after him.

"Levar, what the—" Calix started, but Levar cut him off.

"Something happened to the president. Bombs went off at the rally. He may be hurt…or worse."

Calix gasped, and the sound mingled with a sharp intake of breath from a woman Levar hadn't seen, Senator Riggs of New York, who'd apparently been in a meeting with Calix. "Do we have details?" Calix asked.

"No. A friend who was there texted me. The Secret Service just whisked the vice president away."

Levar was barely done talking when Calix's phone rang. "Kelly, you're on speaker," Calix said to his boss. "I have Levar here and Senator Riggs."

"The president was hurt in a bombing and is being rushed to Johns Hopkins in Baltimore." Kelly sounded like she was running. "Calix, I need you to liaise with Victor Kendall to decide which office is doing what. Someone needs to call the White House Counsel's office and tell them to send people over. The twenty-fifth amendment will have to be invoked. Call Chief Justice Hawk. Tell her she needs to come to the White House in case we need her. Send uniformed agents to get her."

Calix snapped his fingers at Levar, and he instantly grabbed a pen and notebook from Calix's desk and jotted down Kelly's instructions. The White House Counsel made sense. If the president was in surgery, the vice president would have to assume power temporarily. But why would they need the chief judge of the Supreme Court?

It sank in. In case the president was...dead. Judge Hawk would have to administer the oath of office to Vice President Shafer.

"Levar, for some reason we can't reach Katie Winters or her deputy, so you're acting as press secretary for the president now. Get your ass over to the White House and get ready to start briefing the press. Victor and I spoke, and we agreed that no one else is briefing the press but you. All departments will be given a gag order until further notice. I know we're throwing you in at the deep end now, but we have every confidence in you."

He was *what*? Acting as press secretary for the president? Holy shit. "Thanks, Kelly. I got this," he said with ten times the confidence he was feeling inside.

"I'll get you all the information as soon as possible. You'll be assigned a point person from the Secret Service who will brief you on what you need to know and what you're allowed to share. The president's personal physician was with him, so he'll talk to the treating trauma surgeons at Johns Hopkins. The vice president is being brought to a safe location, and the White House is under full lockdown until further notice. I gotta go. Keep your phone on you at all times. Use cell phones for alerts only and restrict all communications to secure phone lines."

She'd hung up before he could say anything, and the three of them stared at each other, horror painted all over their faces. "Oh my god," Senator Riggs said, her face ashen. "What can I do?"

"Call the Senate majority leader, the Senate minority leader, both leaders from the House, and the Speaker of the House. We'll set you up with a secure line in the Cabinet Room. Tell them to sit by their phone and answer when we call," Calix said. "And don't answer any questions. We don't have answers yet."

Levar's phone dinged again. Henley.

CNN is live reporting now. It's bad. They have it on tape.

"It's on CNN," Levar said.

He quickly texted Henley back. *Thx. Thank fuck you're okay. TTYL.*

Calix turned on the TV in his office, then changed the channel to CNN. Levar's stomach swirled violently at the images shown. Then Donna McKee stood up, and Levar could barely hold back a gasp. He knew the pale blue shirt she was wearing. The low shoulder seams made it clear it was a men's shirt in the first place, but he'd teased Henley with that shirt because it had little pink flamingos on the inside of the collar. She'd borrowed it from Henley, and somehow, that made Levar feel close to him, even at a distance. He was alive, and judging by how clean his shirt was, he truly was okay.

"Let's do this," Calix said, and Levar nodded.

The next half hour passed in a whirlwind of hurried calls, meetings, scribbling notes on a notepad, and putting Nicole to work to verify details as much as possible. Levar called a press briefing for ten PM, then worked to gather as many facts as he could.

Kelly had been right that Victor Kendall was on board with Levar taking over. Victor had appointed himself the single point of contact on behalf of the White House, with Calix as his right hand. Levar wasn't sure why Kelly wasn't there, but he didn't ask. All information streams ran through Victor, which made it easy to get accurate information. Victor had looked distraught when he'd given Levar a briefing at fast-forward speed before hurrying off again.

Levar received a call from Seth Rodecker, his newly appointed Secret Service liaison, who turned out to excel at spitting out the prudent information at record speed. Levar wrote everything down as fast as he could, praying with all his might he'd be able to read his own handwriting because he didn't have the time to type out his notes.

Seven minutes before ten, his phone rang. Victor. Levar picked up.

"The president was pronounced dead at nine forty-nine this evening." Victor choked up. "He sustained multiple penetrating injuries from the blast. He was in critical condition when he was wheeled into the OR, and he never made it off the table."

Levar gasped, his throat closing up. "Oh my god," he croaked. "The president..."

"Yeah," Victor said. "I know. I just had to call the first lady. She was still on her way back from an event in Virginia. Just...just try, Levar. Try to do your job."

"Yes, sir. Anything else I need to know?"

Victor rattled off some more details. Levar wrote it all down automatically, his brain barely able to keep up. "We need you to announce this. The vice president will be sworn in as soon as possible. Chief Justice Hawk is in the White House. Pick a few trusted reporters to be present. And you wouldn't know a photographer who could take official pictures, do you? We need this recorded for posterity, and we can't rely on the media."

"I do. Rhett Foles. He won the World Press Photo for his series on the Pride Bombing."

"Can you vouch for him?"

"He's my best friend and my roommate, sir."

"Call him and tell him to get over here as soon as he can. Send me a text with his full name, address, and Social Security number so the Secret Service can get him a visitor's pass. We're on lockdown, so someone from your office will have to escort him in."

"Yes, sir."

"Godspeed, Levar. You have a tough job right now."

He hung up before Levar could answer. He didn't give himself time to think because that would trigger all sorts of emotions, and he didn't have time for those. He called Rhett, who picked up almost immediately.

"Are you okay?" were his first words.

"Yeah. You saw the news? Where are you?" A TV played in the background.

"I'm in the Subway on the corner of 20th and East Street. I was on my way home from that corporate shoot I told you about, and I stopped to get a sandwich when I saw the news."

He was close, and he had his equipment on him. Thank fuck. "You cannot react in any way in public, you hear me? This cannot leak before I go on live TV a few minutes from now."

"What do you need?" Rhett was all business.

"I need you to text me your social. After that, you need to grab your gear and report to the West Wing entrance of the White House. Someone will come get you. Be prepared for extreme security. They'll want to search your bags."

"What...what am I shooting?"

"The next President of the United States taking the oath of office. Don't fuck this up."

"Oh god... I'm... You can count on me, Levar."

"I know. Get here fast."

He hung up, then sent off another text to Henley. *Where are you?*

The reply came immediately. *On my way back. ETA thirty minutes.*

Get back to the WH. Text me when you're here.

His hands shook as he put his phone in his pocket. He balled his fists, then relaxed them again and breathed in deeply. This was the single most important press conference he'd ever do in his life. He straightened his tie and opened the door to the James S. Brady Press Briefing Room. He'd always hoped to make it to this podium one day, but not like this.

He'd expected pandemonium, but he was greeted with a

hushed silence as if the group of reporters in front of him knew. The room was packed to the max, people standing all along the walls as well, all of them looking at him expectantly, though somewhat surprised. They must've expected Katie Winters.

He stepped up to the lectern, spread his notes out in front of him, and sucked in a deep breath. "My name is Levar Cousins, and as of now, I'm the acting White House press secretary. It is my sad duty to announce that at nine forty-nine this evening, President Markinson was pronounced dead at Johns Hopkins Hospital in Baltimore, Maryland, following a suicide bomber attack at a rally he attended there this evening."

A wave of gasps traveled through the room, and he waited a beat to give everyone the chance to process.

"We are heartbroken by this unimaginable loss, and our thoughts and prayers are with the first lady and their four children, their partners, and the president's grandchildren and other family and friends. His passing has rocked us to our core, yet we remain determined to preserve the spirit of democracy and freedom President Markinson embodied in his years of service to the American people."

He paused another beat, his heart rate slowing down.

"The cause of death was determined as several penetrating wounds sustained in the blast. Dr. Reginald Yarwood, chief of trauma at Johns Hopkins, will be available later this evening for questions, as will Colonel Dr. Hammer, the president's personal physician. Vice President Shafer was immediately placed in protective custody by the Secret Service and remains at an undisclosed location until the authorities are confident the threat has been contained. Preparations are underway for his swearing-in ceremony, which will happen as soon as possible. Chief Justice

Meredith Hawk is en route to the White House. Select members of the press will be invited to attend this ceremony."

There would be bitching about that one, but he didn't care. He was playing favorites here, and he wouldn't apologize for it. He needed reporters in there he could trust, people he knew would behave professionally.

"Aside from the president, we have seven confirmed deaths. We will release their names as soon as we have ensured their families have been notified. Ten people are in critical condition, but we are not releasing their names either as their families are still being contacted. As of now, we have fifty-six injured, varying from superficial to severe. The FBI has cordoned off the bomb site and already started their investigation, assisted by the Secret Service and all other government agencies. The United States government is determined to find the terrorists responsible and bring them to justice."

He looked up from his notes, meeting the eyes of the reporters in front of him. "I will now take your questions."

20

Henley's first stop had been Target. For some reason, his brain had focused on the stupid detail that he couldn't show up at the White House in just a white T-shirt. He suspected why Levar had told him to get back there. If the president was dead, Vice President Shafer would be sworn in. Henley wouldn't attend such a historic moment in his Hanes T-shirt with the faded yellow collar.

This time of day, upscale stores were closed, so he got off the 95 at an exit that promised him a Target, then rushed inside. He bought himself a dress shirt, asked the cashier to remove all the security tags, and got changed in the restroom. Yes, the shirt had creases from how it had been folded, but this was as good as it was going to get.

God, he was so grateful he'd decided to drive to Baltimore rather than take the press bus. He rarely drove himself as it meant wasting time in traffic, but he hadn't felt like being stuck on the bus with that many people. As a result, he was now on his way back while most of the other reporters would be scrambling to get to DC. Or maybe they weren't even trying, reasoning it made more sense to stay at the place of the bombing.

The bombing. How on earth was it possible he'd been present for a second bombing? That he'd witnessed two of these horrific events? He wasn't sure if he should call it good luck or bad luck, considering he'd survived both. God, he furiously hoped he'd never have to witness anything similar ever again.

He sent his mom a quick text, using voice to text, so she wouldn't worry when they saw the news. *I'm okay. Turn on the news. Love you.*

Her reply was fast. *Oh my God. Thank God you're okay. Love you too, honey.*

Leave it to his mom to use proper punctuation, even in a text. He didn't get his flair for words from a stranger. She'd been a paralegal, and after his father had walked out on them, she'd worked her way up until one of the most prestigious law firms in Hartford hired her. She kicked ass, even now that she was recently retired, and Henley couldn't be prouder of her.

He drove as fast as he dared, not wanting to get pulled over for speeding. For once, luck was on his side, as the beltway was blissfully clear of the traffic that usually congested it. He made his way to downtown DC much faster than he'd expected and parked in the parking garage of his paper. Luckily, that was only a few blocks away from the White House, and he ran the last bit of the journey, flashing his press credentials and ID-ing himself to get through. He'd expected the White House to be on full lockdown.

The Secret Service agent who guarded the entrance searched Henley's bag and patted him down, and he waited patiently. As soon as he set foot into the West Wing, he stepped into utter chaos. Crying people. White House aides running around frantically. Secret Service agents with pale, withdrawn faces. His stomach sank. Had the unthinkable become a reality?

A quick look at his phone showed him the breaking news. President Markinson had been announced dead. Oh god. They'd killed the president. How had they even gotten in with the bomb?

His stomach soured. He'd known the Secret Service had significant weaknesses. Hell, he and Levar had talked about it only a week before. But how had the bombers found out about these weak links? How had they been able to exploit them and get a suicide bomber in?

When he read the next line in the article on his phone, his eyes widened. The news had been announced by acting White House press secretary Levar Cousins. Acting press secretary for the president? How had that happened? But what an amazing opportunity for him.

The rush of joy Henley felt only added to the confusing mix of emotions inside him. Yes, he was devastated at the loss of President Markinson, though not so much because he personally liked the man as because of what he represented. For the first time in sixty years, a president had been assassinated. Not since that horrible day in Dallas, Texas, had this happened. This was a devastating blow to the country, to their sense of safety.

He took a deep breath. His mind wanted to jump on that, theorize and speculate about who was behind this attack. The parallels with the Pride Bombing were so easy to make, but they'd have to wait. It couldn't be, could it? He couldn't even let the thought in. Not if he wanted to be able to work.

Right now, he needed to focus on what was about to happen. He sent a two-word message to Levar. *I'm here.*

The reply was instant. *Report to the president's secretary at the Oval Office.*

The Oval Office? He'd been there twice. Once when he'd been officially named White House correspondent for the Washington Times on which occasion the president welcomed him. And once when he'd done an exclusive in-depth interview with Markinson, two years ago.

He rushed over to the West Wing, glad he knew his way because it was like navigating through a beehive. Fascinating how people could be in shock, emotional, distressed, and yet crazy busy at the same time. He saw red-rimmed eyes, colorless faces, heard quiet sniffles and broken voices. He felt their despair and grief, but he also noticed determination, people straightening their shoulders and digging in. The country would survive this. Of course it would. They were stronger than one man, even if that man was the president, but damn, it hurt.

When he set foot into the secretary's office, a room right next to the Oval Office, several other reporters were there—two TV crews, two major political bloggers, and Danny, the White House correspondent for the New York Times—talking to each other in hushed tones.

"Oh my god, Henley, are you okay?" Robyn, the CNN reporter, asked him. "Donna told me what happened, that you were there."

"I'm okay," Henley said. What else could he say? Hell, even if he had to, he couldn't possibly put into words what was going through his mind right now. "Is Donna okay? Did her report go well?"

"She did brilliantly, thanks to you. You're a class act, Henley."

"She had a job to do, and I just wanted her to be able to do it well." He smiled wryly. "I have some experience with reporting after an event like that. Though not on TV, thank god."

"Thank you all for coming," Levar said as he stepped into the room, and Henley's heart skipped a few beats at that all-too-familiar voice. He slowly turned around, his eyes meeting Levar's. He, too, looked paler than usual, and his mouth was set in a grim line, but the fire in his eyes was unmistakable. Adrenaline was fueling him, but he was on edge, and a strange rush of pride filled Henley.

"You're about to witness a historical moment, sad as it is," Levar said. "Because we have very limited room in the Oval Office, you're the only news crews and reporters allowed in. I expect you to behave professionally and report in a dignified manner that does justice to the gravity of the situation and the extraordinary circumstances under which this swearing-in ceremony takes place. I'm sure you'll understand we can't allow time for questions afterward, and I strongly suggest you don't even try. I won't look kindly on those who break these rules, and you may find yourself ignored for weeks to come. Now is not the time to piss me off."

That right there? That was the reason why reporters loved Levar. He was a straight shooter. He knew when to joke, when to take a firm stand, but he also knew when to be brutally direct, like now. Henley didn't doubt that his colleagues would stick to Levar's clear instructions. Probably just as much because they respected him as out of understanding for this situation and what was needed right now. Levar was right. They had a responsibility toward the American people to do justice to this moment and project confidence in their new president.

Levar ushered them into the Oval Office, where Supreme Court Chief Justice Meredith Hawk was waiting already. The tiny woman—she was only five foot one if Henley remembered correctly—stood quietly in her robes, holding a Bible, exuding strength despite her stature. She'd been on the bench for fifteen years now, five of which as chief justice. Henley prayed she'd last another fifteen years because she was fierce, smart, and amazing. But this situation was a first for her as well, and one she'd probably never hoped to have to experience.

Levar positioned them against the back wall, both camera crews placed on sides where they'd have the best view possible, with the newspaper reporters more in the back. Henley wasn't upset about that. It made complete sense.

"It'll be just a few more minutes," Levar said. His phone beeped, and he took a quick look at the screen, then swiped and typed out a short message. Henley couldn't even imagine his responsibilities right now. Where even was Katie Winters? Or Paulo, her deputy, for that matter? Had they been present at the rally? He couldn't recall seeing them, but that didn't mean anything. To be fair, he hadn't paid that much attention. Not until that bomb had gone off.

"Rhett Foles is here. Can you please escort him to the Oval Office?" Levar said in his phone.

Rhett Foles. What was he doing here? Wait, no, of course. They would need their own photographer. Levar had invited news crews who would record the event for posterity, but they'd also need their own photographer. Levar must've called his friend, and Henley couldn't blame him.

The pictures Rhett had taken that day of the Pride Bombing would forever be etched into Henley's brain. He was, without doubt, one of the most talented news photographers Henley had ever seen. How he'd managed to do it,

Henley still wasn't sure, but his photos from that day had been intimate, showing human suffering in a way that made you *feel* it. A few months after the bombing, a book had been published, featuring Rhett's photos, and Henley had bought it. It hurt to leaf through it, but god, those pictures were amazing.

A door opened, and Mrs. Shafer was brought in, her son, Kennedy, on her heels. He looked shaken, his hands trembling slightly as he took position next to his mother. How old was the guy now, twenty? What a way to grow up. Mrs. Shafer was dressed in a navy ensemble that seemed fitting for the occasion. Classy but simple and elegant. The color was perfect for the sad reason behind this swearing-in.

They stood in silence, the only sounds coming from the TV crew setting up and testing sound and picture until they were satisfied. Henley's eye caught the famous Resolute desk, still sporting a picture of Mrs. Markinson and another one of the whole presidential family. This room had been the backdrop of many significant events, but it had never been the site of a swearing-in. Not the kind of history to aspire to, but still.

The door opened again, and Rhett Foles was ushered into the room. He might be slightly underdressed in just a button-down shirt and a pair of Dockers, but considering how fast he'd shown up, he had to have been somewhere in DC when Levar had called him. Besides, the man would be behind the camera and not in the pictures anyway. He and Levar exchanged a few whispered words. Then Rhett lifted his camera out of his bag and changed lenses. He took a few test pictures, adjusted some settings, and then waited, just like everyone else.

Only a few moments after, a Secret Service agent opened

the door again, and Vice President Shafer stepped into the room. Much to Henley's surprise, he had a woman on his arm, and Henley had to swallow. Mrs. Markinson. The president's widow. Dressed in a simple black dress, wearing her signature pearls around her neck and in her ears, she was as elegant as ever. The only difference with her usual appearance was her red eyes and the blotches on her cheeks that even the most expensive makeup in the world couldn't hide. Or maybe she hadn't even tried. After all, no one would expect her to look perfect and unaffected by her husband's violent death.

Victor Kendall closed the door behind them. "Thank you all for coming. We will now commence the swearing-in ceremony for Vice President Shafer."

Chief Justice Meredith Hawk took a step forward, then handed the Bible to Mrs. Shafer, who dwarfed her. "Please hold this," she said, her voice surprisingly steady.

Mrs. Shafer took the Bible and, as if she'd done it a thousand times, held it out with both hands.

"Please place your right hand on the Bible and raise your left hand," Chief Justice Hawk said to Vice President Shafer, who calmly obeyed her instructions. "Repeat after me. I, Delano Abraham Shafer, do solemnly swear that I will faithfully execute the Office of President of the United States and will to the best of my ability preserve, protect, and defend the Constitution of the United States."

Vice President Shafer's voice was crystal clear as he repeated the words. "So help me God," he added.

Chief Justice Hawk nodded, then extended her right hand. "Congratulations, Mr. President."

"Thank you, Madam Chief Justice."

Henley had to admire his poise and steadiness under these crazy circumstances. Then again, the man was a decorated war hero, so maybe this wasn't the most pressure he'd ever been under.

The newly minted president first turned toward Mrs. Markinson. "Annabeth, I am so sorry for your loss. Thank you for being here. I can't even imagine how difficult this must be for you."

A single tear meandered down her cheek as she took President Shafer's hand, then accepted the kiss he pressed on her cheek. "Thank you, Dell. I am grateful for the knowledge that the country is in such good hands with you. I'm confident that you will continue Bill's legacy and be a worthy successor. I just wish it could've been under better circumstances, but I hope you know how proud he was to have you as his vice president."

Wow, Henley hadn't expected that statement from the first lady. Or former first lady, he should say, since Mrs. Shafer had taken that role as of two minutes ago. Maybe Mrs. Markinson hadn't been aware of her husband's issues with the vice president? It had been reported on widely, though. Didn't she read the news?

She'd never been a very hands-on first lady, at least, not in a political sense. She'd focused on childhood literacy as well as literacy in general, setting up programs all across the country to help children and adults read better and give them access to appropriate reading materials. One of her most successful initiatives had been a program that now ran in prisons throughout the nation and provided prisoners with books and suitable magazines. But she hadn't been the type of wife to get directly involved with her husband's work, so maybe she hadn't been aware of his deteriorating relationship with Vice President Shafer.

President Shafer. Hell, that would take some getting used to.

"Thank you, Annabeth. Your kind words mean the world to me, especially now. Please know that we're committed to helping you in any way we can. Whatever you need, we are here."

Mrs. Markinson smiled at him. "Thank you. I appreciate that. If you'll excuse me, I'd like to retire to the residence now and spend time with my children and grandchildren."

Everyone was quiet as she left the Oval Office, escorted by Secret Service agents.

After she'd exited, Victor Kendall turned toward all the journalists. "Thank you all. We request that you consider Levar the sole spokesperson for the White House. Please don't approach anyone else. It will take us a few days to adjust to the new situation, so we kindly ask that you don't take inappropriate advantage of this transition period."

"If we may ask, what happened to Katie Winters?" Danny, the New York Times reporter, asked.

Victor's mouth set in a grim line. "We'll have more information for you about that in the morning, but both Ms. Winters and her deputy are no longer working for the White House, as of now."

Henley had been watching Levar while Victor talked, and at that last line, Levar's eyes widened. Then he caught himself. So that had been news to him as well. Did that mean they were making him the official White House press secretary? Holy shit, that would be one hell of a promotion, going from assistant press secretary to the vice president to the main job in just a few weeks.

Henley followed the others out of the Oval Office. He wasn't even sure if he'd deliberately been the last one or if he'd unconsciously hoped Levar would say something, but when Levar grabbed his arm and pulled him aside in the hallway as the others walked back to the press room, his heart filled with relief.

"You okay?" Levar asked, and this time, Henley wasn't inclined to give the polite, expected answer.

"I don't know, but probably not."

Levar's eyes softened as he put a hand on Henley's shoulder. "I can't believe you were witness to another bombing."

"I know, right? Probably not a good time for me to buy lottery tickets. The odds clearly aren't in my favor."

"I'm so glad you weren't hurt." Levar's voice had dropped to a whisper.

"Thank you. It took a while for my body and brain to reconnect with each other after it happened, but I got there."

"That was a classy thing you did, giving Donna your shirt."

Henley raised his eyebrows. "You recognized it?"

Levar's soft chuckle sent sparks through Henley's body. "The shirt with the pink flamingos on the collar? Yes, I recognized it. I can't imagine many more men having the balls to wear that."

"I'll have you know pink flamingos are incredibly manly and sexy."

"On you, they most certainly are," Levar said, and there they were again, staring at each other with the air practically crackling between them.

"Are you the White House press secretary now?" Henley asked.

"No one has said it officially, but I think I am. Crazy, right?"

A warm rush raced through Henley at the realization that Levar had entrusted him with that personal remark without hesitation. Maybe they were getting better at separating their jobs and personal lives. "It would be one hell of a promotion for you, and I couldn't be happier."

"It doesn't feel like I've earned it. Does that make sense?"

Henley nodded. "I get where you're coming from, but they wouldn't have entrusted you with this responsibility if they didn't think you could do it. You're a natural at this."

Levar's smile was sweet. "Thank you. Sometimes it feels like you have more confidence in me than I do myself."

"Isn't that often the case, that others can see what we've become blind to? At least you'll step into a good structure. Katie ran a tight ship."

"I don't even know what happened to her. Victor hasn't said anything other than that they couldn't reach her or her deputy when this happened. I haven't heard anything about it since."

His eyes widened, his cheeks growing red, and Henley had no trouble understanding what had just happened. Levar had been talking to a friend, not to a reporter, and even though this was a story, Henley would have to let it go. "No worries, Lev. I won't say a word."

Levar closed his eyes, gently shaking his head. "I can't believe I just said that to you. I must be more tired and in shock than I realized. I'm sorry for putting you in the position where I told you something that you might want to act on."

"It's fine. Don't worry about it. You needed a friend, and I'm here. And I agree it's weird. I can't remember whether or not she was at the rally. I don't recall seeing her, but that doesn't mean anything."

"She wasn't. Or at least, she wasn't supposed to be. This was a nonevent. Actually, I was surprised you were attending."

Henley rolled his eyes. "You and me both, but my editor

insisted I go, just in case Markinson said something shocking or revealing. Pretty sure he wasn't expecting him to get killed right before my very eyes."

They stood staring at each other in silence. "I have to go," Levar said. "I don't even know what I'm supposed to be doing right now, but I'm pretty sure I should be doing *something*. So I'll...see you later?"

Henley didn't want to let him go, but of course, that was impossible. So he smiled at him. "Count on it."

21

"You can do this, honey."

His mom's voice was warm and affirming, and Levar felt it flow through him. As a social worker, she'd always excelled at giving him confidence, but he'd never needed it more than now. He'd FaceTimed his parents around two in the morning East Coast time, knowing that with the three-hour time difference with California, they'd still be up. They would be anyway, after this news. He'd needed to hear their voices, to know that they had faith in him.

"We're so proud of you, kid."

His father's face was serious, the man still in shock over what had happened to the president, but his words rang with pride.

"Thank you, Dad. It's an incredible opportunity, but I don't feel ready yet. I became the vice president's press secretary not even three weeks ago."

"They believe you can do this. Otherwise, they wouldn't have asked you. And your press conference went great," his mom said. "The way you announced the president's death...

And then all those reporters asking questions they had to know you couldn't answer."

Levar smiled at the indignity in his mom's voice. Always standing up for her kids with an intolerance for injustice that made her so good and passionate about her work and that had always defined her.

"They know, but it's their job to make me reveal more than I want to. It's my job to prevent that from happening."

"I couldn't do it," his mom said.

His father chuckled. "Darling, the minute someone started tearing up, you'd tell them everything they wanted to know. You're a sucker for a sad face...and I love you for it."

His parents shared a look of love, and Levar's stomach went weak, as it always did when he witnessed the strong relationship his parents had. "I gotta go," he said when they focused back on him. "It's gonna be a madhouse here the next few days, so I'm not sure when I can call again."

His father waved his hand dismissively. "We understand. Do your job, kid. We'll be watching every press conference."

"Thank you, Dad. It means the world to me to know I have your support."

"Always," his father promised.

"We love you so much, and we couldn't be prouder. Hang in there and take good care of yourself, honey, okay?" his mom added.

"I'll try."

His parents' encouragement gave him the will to soldier on, but fourteen hours later, he was beyond exhausted. Adrenaline could only keep one awake and fueled for so long, and he'd reached the limits of what his body and brain could handle.

He hadn't slept that night. Probably no one had. Throughout the night, more details had come in about the bombing, and Levar had done several press briefings. He'd talked to the chief surgeon of Johns Hopkins, making sure he was aware of what he could tell the press. He'd had at least ten phone calls from Seth Rodecker, his Secret Service liaison, who kept him continuously in the loop about any developments.

By dinnertime, Levar's brain shut down. Not that he blamed himself. It had been one hell of an experience, and that was an understatement. He was so tired he fell asleep on the MARC, grateful when he woke up on time to get out at Rockville station. He dragged himself to the commuter's parking lot, yawning repeatedly on the five-minute drive to home.

He'd spoken to Rhett, who had stayed through the night until about three in the morning, then had gone home to grab some sleep. He'd been back at it around ten or so. Levar wasn't even sure what Rhett's assignment was, but he trusted that someone—Victor, probably? Or Kelly? Calix?—had told him what was expected of him. Despite the horrific circumstances, Levar was grateful he'd managed to get Rhett involved. Hopefully, this could lead to more assignments for him.

Climbing up the stairs to his second-floor apartment took effort, his muscles protesting. *Wait.* Who was that? A man was sitting in front of his front door, his back against the wall, his legs pulled up. His face was hidden as he leaned his head on his arms, but Levar recognized him anyway. Henley.

"Hey," he said, and Henley jerked up. Had he woken him?

Henley blinked a few times, then rubbed his eyes. "Shit, I must've fallen asleep."

Levar extended his hand and pulled him to his feet.

"What are you doing here?" He frowned. "How do you even know where I live?"

"I'm a reporter, Lev. Finding out an address is really not that hard."

Right. Levar opened his front door. "That still doesn't answer the first question."

He stepped inside, then hesitated. Inviting in Henley was akin to inviting in trouble. But did he have any choice at this point? He could hardly have a conversation with him in the hallway. First of all, that would mean they had absolutely no privacy, and second...

Was there even a second? God, he was too tired for this. He wordlessly held open the door, then shut it behind Henley. He dumped his bag onto the floor, taking a moment to breathe in the familiar smell of vanilla. Home.

"I don't know why I'm here," Henley said softly, and Levar didn't doubt the truth of that statement.

"You look just about as exhausted as I feel. Maybe you didn't want to be alone?"

Henley let out a long sigh. "Do you want to be alone?"

Levar didn't have to think about that one. "No. But I'm too tired to talk. I need sleep."

"Do you want me to go?"

They kept circling the same issue, didn't they? No, he didn't want him to go. Yes, he should go. Stupidity didn't even begin to cover this, and yet Levar said, "No. Stay."

They barely spoke another word as Henley followed Levar into the apartment, where he hung his jacket, kicked off his shoes, and then set course straight for his bedroom. The two of them undressing shouldn't feel as familiar as it did. Silently, Levar handed Henley an unopened toothbrush.

They crawled into bed together, still not speaking, but

when Henley held open his arms and Levar sought his embrace, words weren't necessary. How could something so monumentally stupid feel so good? He put his head on that soft shoulder, nuzzled Henley's chest hair, and fell asleep.

He woke up shortly after midnight, according to his projection clock, groggy and confused. His head was throbbing, reminding him of the early days of his college years, back when he'd thought it was a good idea to go on a drinking binge and then get up early for classes the next day. Only he hadn't been drinking, had he?

Shit. The president. The bombing. Henley.

He was asleep beside him, holding on to Levar as if he had no intention of letting him go. His breaths were so deep and quiet that Levar had to strain his ears to hear them. He could feel the rise and fall of Henley's chest, but the man made barely a sound as he slept.

Should he check his phone? Make sure nobody needed him? He'd turned it off, but he'd programmed it such that the White House operator would always be able to break through his do-not-disturb setting, and so would Calix. No, if they'd needed him, they would've called. He required more sleep if he wanted to not only look presentable for the briefings tomorrow but sound intelligible as well. Decision made, he closed his eyes, snuggled back with Henley, and allowed sleep to drag him under again.

When he woke up for the second time, it was hours later, and Henley's changed breathing told him he was awake as well. Levar yawned, then turned onto his other side. It was pitch black in his bedroom, exactly the way he preferred it, so he could barely make out Henley's shape. "Did you sleep well?" he asked.

"I did. Thank you for letting me crash here. I...I didn't

want to go home. I couldn't bear the thought of being alone."

Levar's hand cupped Henley's cheek as if it had a mind of its own. "Are you okay?"

"I don't know. I will be, but right now, I'm...unbalanced."

Levar caressed his cheek. "It's gotta bring back a lot of bad memories for you."

Henley put his own hand over Levar's, then leaned his head into the combined touch of their hands. "It does. Not so much specific memories as it reminds me of how I felt after the Pride Bombing. So confused. Lucky to be alive yet guilty at the same time. Furious. Scared."

Levar left his hand where it was, resting against Henley's cheek. "It's perfectly normal to feel that way."

Silence hung between them, but it was a comfortable silence. "I wanted to be with you because I knew you would understand," Henley said finally.

"I do understand. I wasn't there, but I've seen the footage, and that was enough to give me the chills."

"Yeah. I'm not watching TV right now. Watching it live was bad enough. No need to repeat that."

"So, now what?" Levar asked. "Do you want to talk? Do you need a listening ear?"

"Honestly? I don't know. I don't know what I want. I don't know what I feel. I don't know anything anymore."

The hurt and utter despair in Henley's voice hit Levar deep. The man was in pain, but it wasn't the kind of pain that was easy to fix. It would need time. Therapy, maybe. Someone to help him process and label his feelings. Levar couldn't be that person for Henley for a million different reasons. But he could do something else for him, something they both wanted. "How about what you need right now? What do you need, baby?"

The word slipped from Levar's lips as if he'd said it a thousand times, completely natural. Or maybe inevitable. They'd been working toward this moment, hadn't they? Like two comets, destined to crash and burn.

"You," Henley said, his voice rough. "God, I need you."

Levar could make a list a mile long why this was a spectacularly bad idea, but right now, none of them mattered. The only thing that was important to him in this moment was making Henley feel better. He couldn't be his therapist, and even being his friend would be hard, considering his new job. But maybe, just maybe, he could be what Henley needed right now.

"You have me, baby," he said softly, and then he leaned in and pressed his lips against Henley's.

22

Their first kiss back in the hotel in New York had been sweet, the simmering tension between them resulting in a passionate kiss. This, this was different. The first contact, a mere brush of Levar's lips against his, stole his breath. Henley parted on instinct, letting him in, and then that slick tongue slipped into his mouth. Heat pooled in his belly, his cock, at the sensation of that warm tongue against his own.

The kiss grew hungry within seconds, almost desperate as they both fed on it, their tongues sliding and seeking, sloppy, wet sounds filling the room.

"Lev..." Henley rasped.

"I'm here, baby. Let go."

He did. Levar took over, and Henley let him, content to follow rather than lead, to let Levar set the pace. The kiss grew even hotter, Levar devouring his mouth, and nothing had ever felt this good. He was *alive*.

Levar rolled on top of him, and Henley moaned at the contact. He rubbed up against the hardness of Levar's body, the friction of his cock against Levar's sending sparks through his entire body. He wanted him inside him. He felt hungry. Empty. He'd never wanted anything more, but he wouldn't say the words. He couldn't. Levar was already giving him so much more than he should. It had to be enough. Whatever Levar would give him would have to be enough.

Levar snaked his hands between their bodies and cupped Henley's balls in a tight grip. His pulse jumped, and his hips bucked, seeking more. "Ungh..." he moaned.

Levar leaned up, watching him with eyes that were now dark blue and blazing. "Mmm, I know. You feel so good, baby."

He held Henley pinned with that burning gaze that said everything that couldn't be expressed in words. And Henley's eyes must be flashing that same wordless message. Hunger. Want. Desperation fueled by the knowledge that whatever they'd share now would be a onetime thing. The tension crackled, sparkled, his nerves all firing off eager requests for more, more, more. His heart raced, and his hands grew clammy, like he was about to jump out of an airplane.

Levar bent in and nuzzled Henley's neck, his stubble sanding his skin. Would it leave burn marks? Henley shivered. He wanted it to. God, he was fucking crazy. What was happening? Why did every touch, every kiss, every look only made him want Levar more?

Levar plunged his tongue back into Henley's mouth, greedy and eager, as if he couldn't get enough of him. Well, Henley had nowhere near enough of him, so that made two of them. Henley clung to him as Levar kissed him deeply again, his hands on Levar's shoulders, then his back. His skin was blazing hot, and Henley's body hummed with pleasure.

The always simmering attraction between them had once again combusted, enflaming them. The fire burned searing hot inside him, this inferno of want and need. Nothing felt real anymore after what had happened, but this did. He and Levar, that was real. He sensed it, sensed *him*, body, mind, and soul.

Levar's hand slipped into his underwear, and he circled Henley's cock, his hand soft, but his grip tight. A growly moan flew from Henley's lips as he shuddered. He wrapped his arms around Levar's neck as he arched his back and ground into his hand. "Touch me," he begged, his voice raw. "Please touch me."

Levar's hand tightened around his cock, and Henley closed his eyes, his lips parting as he blew out a shivering breath. His mind went hazy with pleasure, all thoughts gone but the sensation of that warm hand on his cock, of their bodies pressed against each other, of Levar's thumb gently rubbing his slit, spreading his precum.

Another needy moan escaped him, but Levar kissed him again, drinking in the sound before it even fully formed. His hand went to work, stroking, touching, teasing his cock. Henley kept his eyes closed and leaned into it, surrendering to the flood of emotions and sensations and feelings inside him. They all merged, one whirlwind of thoughts, and he couldn't process any of it. All he could do was *feel*.

Levar didn't stop, didn't even slow down, his hand picking up speed as he worked Henley toward his release. It was too fast and yet exactly right because he wouldn't have been able to stand it much longer, this pressure inside him building and building. His body needed to release, but so did his mind, like a pressure cooker that was at its peak.

"Look at me," Levar whispered. "I want to see your eyes when you come."

Henley's eyes flew open, unable to resist that quiet request, and then he exploded. His eyes froze as his body jerked, his muscles all tense. His cock spurted out his cum, and Levar kept gently pumping him until every last drop had been spilled.

The air left Henley, his body sagging, boneless. And then tears filled his eyes, and he cried. First gentle sniffs, but when Levar made a sound of distress and pulled his cum-stained hand out of Henley's underwear and held him tighter, his sobs turned violent. Levar rolled onto his back, taking Henley with him so he was lying on his chest, his face buried against his neck. His body shook as he cried hot tears, his lungs gasping for air, his throat so tight it caused even more tears.

He squeezed his eyes shut, sending a river of tears down his cheeks, then dripping onto Levar's skin. "I'm sorry," he half wailed, but Levar shushed him.

"Let it out."

"I don't even know why I'm crying!"

"Does it matter?"

He was tired. He'd just slept for hours, and yet he was exhausted. "I never cry."

"Well, maybe it's time you change that."

"I don't want to cry."

"Yeah, I'm gonna take a wild guess and say that's probably why you're crying now. Shit's gotta get out. You can't keep this in."

"I hate this. I hate crying."

"Stop fighting it. Let it out."

Henley lost the will to fight, and he surrendered to the flood that crashed into him, wave after wave after wave of sadness, of anger, of feelings god only knew Henley had no hope of ever untangling. He was a fucking mess, an embarrassing, blubbering mess, and on any other day, he would've been mortified, but not today.

Levar made it so easy, simply holding him and not saying a damn thing. As if he knew Henley could shatter at the wrong word. Henley clung to him, his knuckles turning white at the ferocity of his grip, but Levar never complained. He rubbed Henley's back, caressing his skin, scratching his neck like one would a cat to make it purr, making soft humming sounds in his chest until Henley finally calmed down.

He took a shuddering breath, then another one. Once he was certain his voice would hold, he said, "That was..." He didn't have words because he had no idea what had happened. "I promise I don't usually cry after an orgasm."

"Don't," Levar said, his tone sharp. "We don't need to talk about this, but don't make light of it."

Henley felt small. "I'm sorry."

Levar kissed the top of his head. "Don't apologize either."

"Will pretending this never happened work for you?"

"Since we've done a stellar job of that so far, why the hell not?"

Henley breathed out a sigh of relief. The first daylight flirted through the curtains, the promise of a new day. "I need to go."

"And I need to take a shower and get my ass back to work."

Henley inched off Levar's chest, then leaned in for one last kiss. "Thank you. I'll see you...later."

Levar's smile was sad. "Yeah."

Henley got dressed within a minute, and Levar stepped into the shower before Henley had even left the room. It made leaving easier, and maybe that was why he'd done it.

When Henley slipped out of Levar's room, he came face-to-face with Rhett in the hallway. Oops.

Henley opened his mouth, then thought better of it. The this-is-not-what-you-think routine was ridiculous here and also highly inaccurate, since it was exactly what it looked like.

Rhett gave him a stern look. "You two are playing with fire."

Henley sighed. "I know."

"Please be careful. Don't let this cost him his job."

What could he say? Nothing both of them didn't know already. "Take care of yourself," he said instead, then walked out. Not until he stood outside did he realize that Levar had never come, focusing purely on Henley.

23

The Oval Office looked so much bigger in pictures and on camera than it was in reality. Sure, compared to the tiny offices in the rest of the West Wing, the room was still pretty spacious, but it wasn't exactly big. That being said, Levar couldn't help but feel impressed all over again by the grandeur of the room he was in.

When President Markinson had taken office, the first lady had spearheaded a small-scale redecoration project, and Levar had to admit she'd improved the look of the room. The mustard-yellow curtains and upholstery had been replaced by burgundy-red curtains and ivory couches and chairs. In combination with the blue carpet—sporting the presidential seal, of course—the effect was a subtle red, blue, and almost white that was pleasing to the eye.

President Shafer was on the phone, finishing up a call with the British prime minister, looking very presidential behind the Resolute desk. He hadn't even been in office for forty-eight hours, and already, the White House staff had moved his personal effects from his vice presidential office to the Oval Office. Several pictures decorated the antique console table behind him: his wife, his son, the president with his parents and grandparents.

They'd ask him about his preference for paintings and other decorations as well, Levar remembered. President Markinson hadn't been a fan of presidential portraits in his office, instead opting for a landscape by Thomas Moran, an Edward Hopper painting of red barns, a gorgeous impressionist painting depicting American flags—Levar couldn't recall the name of the painter—and a painting that had to be a Thomas Kincaid.

He'd done a bit of reading on the White House and its history when he'd started working for Vice President Shafer. Not that he'd ever counted on getting a promotion as quickly as he had, but just in case, he'd wanted to be prepared. After all, even as assistant press secretary to the vice president, he'd handled highly unexpected questions from reporters. He'd have to study up some more now, and he made a mental note to talk to Calix about who to approach for that.

Across from him, Calix sat on a couch, furiously typing on his phone. Levar had no idea why the president and Calix had requested to meet with him, but he hadn't asked. He would find out soon enough. It wouldn't be about Henley, would it? His stomach clenched. God, they'd been stupid, so stupid. Another mistake like that could cost him his job.

"Thank you, Prime Minister," the president said, then ended the call. He dragged a hand through his hair. "No one ever told me that being president meant being on the phone all day long. That must've been the fiftieth call this morning.

All over the world, heads of state are calling to express their sympathy. Kind of rude not to take those particular calls, especially since we may need their help in the upcoming months."

Calix put away his phone. "I'm sure that will die down after the first few days, sir."

The president let out a sigh. "One can only hope. Anyway, what are we talking about, Calix?"

He grabbed a glass of water, then joined Calix and Levar, whose stomach roiled all over again. He couldn't do this anymore. Seeing Henley was insanity.

"We have a few things we need to discuss, Mr. President. First of all, you need to officially announce your choice for chief of staff."

Choice for chief of staff? Oh, right. Victor Kendall had been President Markinson's chief of staff. That didn't mean that now that Shafer had taken office, he'd automatically keep him. In fact, Levar would put his money on him preferring to work with Kelly and Calix.

"Right. Levar, I'm going to need you to announce that effective immediately, Calix will be my chief of staff. As much as I appreciate Victor, I'm not comfortable with him working as my chief of staff, not after what we found out about how the president was working against me."

Levar was barely able to hide his surprise. Calix was becoming chief of staff? What happened to Kelly?

"Kelly told us yesterday that she doesn't want the job," Calix said, probably noticing the confusion on Levar's face. "She's pregnant with her first child, and when the president was killed, she was in the hospital because of spotting—and yes, she gave me permission to share this with you. The job of chief of staff would bring too much stress for her to combine it with the pregnancy and later a baby. Those were her words, not mine. She's decided to stay in the vice presidential office for now, pending the nomination of a new vice president."

Kelly was pregnant? She was thirty-eight, if Levar remembered correctly, so that had to be a wonderful gift to her and her husband. "That makes sense. I'm happy for her and her husband, and I'm hoping the pregnancy will go well."

"Yeah, we're all keeping our fingers crossed for her," Calix said.

"I asked Calix to step up, and thankfully, he agreed," the president said. "The idea of doing this without him scared the shit out of me, to be honest, so I'm glad he's on board. So sometime today, you can announce this to the press. Maybe don't reveal the pregnancy from the podium, since I'm not entirely sure Kelly has informed her family yet, but I'm convinced the old excuse of personal reasons will work well here. Considering Kelly's record, no one will suspect she was fired. Besides, the press has bigger things to focus on."

"Will do, Mr. President."

"We'll be naming my deputy as soon as possible," Calix said. "I've already reached out to a possible candidate, someone I've worked with in the past who I think would be an excellent choice. But we'll keep you posted on that. Now, let's talk about something that will affect you even more directly. You may have wondered why you were named acting press secretary for the president when the president had a press secretary and even a deputy."

Of course Levar had, but he hadn't asked. Hell, it was only one of the many, many questions he hadn't voiced over the past few days. They'd had more important things to worry about and focus on. "I did, yes."

"Victor found out that Katie was having an affair with

the majority whip, Senator Donaldson. Her deputy knew and covered for her, falsifying White House logs a few times. For obvious reasons, this is unacceptable, and they have both been fired. Unfortunately, the timing of this coincided with the bombing, but President Markinson had already decided to fire her. Sadly, he never got the chance."

"Wow," Levar said. It might not be the most eloquent reaction, but *holy shit*. The press secretary and the majority whip? Damn, that was about the last thing he'd expected. From either of them, for that matter, considering both of them were married. But it also drove home the risk of what he and Henley were doing. They *fired* Katie...and they'd do the same to him.

"The reason we asked you to step up when Ethan was let go was that we wanted you to grow into the role of White House press secretary should President Shafer have won the elections. Clearly, that has all changed now. Unfortunately, your growth trajectory is a hell of a lot steeper than we'd anticipated, but we still want to ask you to formally accept the position of White House press secretary."

Levar's heart skipped a few beats. He had to clear his throat before he could speak. "I'm incredibly honored and flattered, Mr. President. I will gladly accept, but not before I say this. I want to make clear that you are under no obligation to name me. Like you said, no one had expected this to happen, so I may not have what it takes in terms of experience. If you prefer to hire someone with more experience as the press secretary and have me stay on as deputy, I would be more than okay with that."

The president looked at Calix, and then they both laughed. Had he said something funny? "You owe me ten bucks, Mr. President," Calix said.

The president's smile at Levar was wide. "Damn, you just cost me money. Calix said you would try to talk us out of it, and I said no way, but I guess he knows you better than I do."

Levar's cheeks heated. "I'm sorry? I guess? It's just that..."

The president held up his hand. "Don't apologize. It speaks volumes about your character that you wanted to make sure we didn't feel pressured to hire you. I appreciate that. For the future, please know I don't work that way. I haven't met the person yet who can pressure me into anything, so rest assured that the choice to name you as my new press secretary was entirely voluntary and for all the right reasons. Yes, you're facing one hell of a challenge, but I'm confident you'll do a great job. You've already shown how well you can handle the press in the last few days. To be frank, I've been impressed with your briefings."

"Thank you, Mr. President. That means a lot to me."

"So you're officially accepting?" Calix checked.

"Yes, sir. Absolutely, one hundred percent, I'm in."

Calix nodded, a satisfied expression on his face. "Good. That's one problem solved. You can announce that as well today. Or wait, I think I should make that announcement? Should I?"

He looked at the president, who shrugged. "I don't think anyone cares right now, not under these circumstances. Just get it done."

"Finding you a deputy will be a priority, especially since you don't have a backup from the vice presidential office either. Our goal is to appoint you a deputy before the end of the week."

Relief flooded Levar. "That would be good because my call sheet alone is enough to give me a heart attack. Nicole and I have been working around the clock, but it's been crazy."

"Tell me about it," Calix said with a wide smile. "I've stopped looking at my call sheet. I just return the calls I think are most important and let my assistant handle the rest. It's insanity trying to keep up right now."

"Let's bring in the others," the president said, and Calix stepped out for a moment, then returned with the other senior advisors. *Senior advisor.* As the White House press secretary, that now included Levar. Adrenaline pumped through his veins all over again. He was in the Oval Office, working for the president of the United States. *Holy shit.*

"All arrangements for President Markinson's funeral have been made. The date has been set for a week from now. That will give the Secret Service enough time to coordinate the security with the protection details of several foreign dignitaries that will be attending. The British prime minister has confirmed his attendance, and so have the prime ministers of Canada and Germany, the French President, and several other heads of state from key allies. It's going to be one hell of a circus, but we'll have to get through it," Calix announced when the newcomers had found seats.

"I'd appreciate some guidelines on details I can or cannot release to the press about the funeral," Levar said. "I'm sure the Secret Service has security concerns."

Calix nodded. "Yes. I'll make sure someone from the Secret Service contacts you about this. This won't be the same guy you've been liaising with about the investigation into the assassination, by the way. They've appointed a point person to coordinate all security for the funeral."

"Okay. Thank you."

"Mrs. Markinson has asked me to do the eulogy for President Markinson," the president said. "It puts me in a bit of a pickle, considering our disagreements recently. Disagreements that have unfortunately become public knowledge. His staff so far hasn't been super cooperative in making the transition smooth either, so that's a concern."

Calix's eyes darkened, his jaw tightening. "We've heard isolated reports of President Markinson's staff being deliberately uncooperative in transferring responsibilities to our people. The reality is that some of them will need to stay on for now because we need them, but we've decided to let go others because we don't feel they're a good fit for our White House. Please report any instances of insubordination or deliberate attempts at slowing us down to me."

"Mr. President, if you want, I can give the speechwriter some names of staffers who did work for President Markinson who could share some personal stories about him," Levar said. "I have good working relations with his former staff in the communications office."

The president nodded with a grateful smile. "That would be much appreciated. It's hard to ask them to write a heartfelt eulogy when I can't tell them all that much about the man."

"In all fairness, sir, that was mostly his choice," Brian, one of the senior policy advisors, said.

The president let out a sigh. "Trust me, I know, but that doesn't make it easier. It's frustrating to realize how much more we could've achieved had he included me more."

"I still think it was a low blow to do research on possible contenders for the Democratic nomination when you never gave Markinson anything but your full support," Calix said sharply.

The president shrugged. "That's politics for you. At the

end of the day, a lot is decided based on who can get you what you want. In this case, Markinson had counted on me delivering him a bigger win than he ended up getting. I'm not sure why he thought I'd be able to deliver the Senate and the House to him, but I sure as hell tried."

They worked through some more announcements and decisions, and then the president said, "I think that concludes it, right?"

Calix nodded. "Thank you, Mr. President."

The president rose from his chair, and everyone else automatically did the same. "Thank you, Mr. President," Levar said.

"Walk with me," Calix said as they stepped into the hallway.

Levar followed the newly appointed chief of staff into his office—down the hall from the Oval Office—a spacious and light corner room that was easily twice the size of his old office. Calix closed the door behind them. "I'm sorry for the madhouse this will be in the next few weeks and months. Trust me, this was not the transition I'd hoped or planned for, but we'll have to deal with it. How are you holding up so far?"

"I'm good. Don't worry about me. What do you need?"

Calix nodded, relief palpable on his face. "Rhett. The president likes him. Do you think he'd be open to accepting the job of White House photographer? I wanted to check in with you before we approached him, considering the conversation you and I had about his state of mind."

White House photographer? Oh my god, that would be the absolute perfect job for Rhett. "I think he'd be perfect. You know he takes amazing pictures, but he's also good at blending into the background. You rarely notice him, which

I think would be an important asset for a White House photographer."

"I agree. President Shafer liked how unobtrusive he was over the last two days. Plus, he clearly has the qualifications for the job, and the fact that he was at the Pride Parade plays a role as well. He fits into our culture."

"He does. And I think he can handle it. Yes, he's suffered from the effects of that day, as have we all. But he's climbed out of the deep hole he was in and has managed to learn to live with it. He'd do an amazing job, and as his best friend, I'd obviously be over the moon if he got that position."

Calix leaned back in his desk chair. "That, to me, is a crucial reason as well to pick him. You know him. After what just happened, a personal recommendation is worth a hell of a lot more than a standard FBI background check, no matter how thorough those guys are."

"He's trustworthy."

"All right, I'll approach him." Calix's phone rang, and he held up a finger to Levar. "Hold on one second. I told Sheila not to put anyone through, so this has to be important."

He accepted the call, and within seconds, all blood had withdrawn from his face. "What? ... Oh my god. How do we...? Yes, I will inform the president. When can you brief him?... Okay, I'll let his secretary know."

White as a sheet, Calix ended the call. Levar had risen to his feet almost automatically, his stomach clenching with dread. Calix was the most unflappable man he knew, so for him to show this much emotion, the news couldn't be good. Still, he wouldn't ask. It wasn't his place, since it might very well be something that was beyond his need to know or far above his pay grade.

Calix's hand shook as he put his phone on his desk, then

looked at Levar. "We know who's behind the bombing. They just announced their involvement."

Levar knew the answer even before Calix said the words. He couldn't explain it, but maybe it had been brewing in the back of his mind ever since he'd heard the news.

"Al Saalihin has claimed responsibility for the assassination of President Markinson. They're back."

24

Al Saalihin was back.

Henley sat at his desk—more like a glorified cubicle—in his paper's office, his head still reeling after the long press briefing Levar had conducted. It had started great, with Levar announcing he'd officially been named the next official White House press secretary. The applause in the room had been genuine, though Henley had noticed some jealous looks. More than a few reporters had been all too willing to transition to the other side of the podium. Maybe they felt Levar hadn't earned this chance yet, but that was bad luck for them.

Of course Henley had been more than a little curious about the story with Katie Winters and her deputy. From the way Levar had worded it, Henley suspected something hadn't been quite above board. He probably would've looked into it a little deeper if not for the rest of the press briefing, which had made him focus on way more important things.

Al Saalihin was back. How was it possible? They'd said it to each other in New York after the documentary interview.

This unknown terrorist group was responsible for the Pride Bombing and then had disappeared. And now, only weeks after he and Levar had talked about it, Al Saalihin was back.

Levar had been unwilling to divulge much information, for which Henley couldn't blame him. Clearly, the FBI was conducting an ongoing investigation in close cooperation with the Secret Service and the entire intelligence community. But Al Saalihin had officially claimed the attack, and the FBI had deemed the video in which they had done so legitimate. And since this wasn't a group known to claim attacks they had no involvement in, no one had reason to assume they were falsely taking credit for some attack another group had made.

So why were they back? Why now? And why President Markinson? Henley didn't doubt the bombing had been aimed specifically at him. His presence hadn't been a last-minute addition or change in program. The president's attendance at the rally had been announced weeks earlier. Plenty of time to plan this, providing one had already put the necessary orders for materials in place.

So again, why Markinson? Why had they targeted this president? It was the second big terrorist bombing of his term, and unfortunately, one he hadn't survived. What had made this group go after him? That question kept niggling Henley.

The first reports from other news outlets had focused more on the group's general hate for America, which, granted, was fierce. After the Pride Bombing, Al Saalihin had released a lengthy rant against the corrupt American culture, the anti-Muslim sentiments in American politics, and a whole range of other issues that mostly centered around moral things like homosexuality—big surprise there.

For other reporters, it seemed to make sense that for a group like this, taking out the US president was a goal in and of itself, and yet Henley couldn't get past the timing... and that for the second time, they'd targeted this presidency.

Then, of course, there was the how. No information had been released yet about the identity of the bomber or how he had managed to get in. But Henley's gut said it had been an inside job. This hadn't been a lucky attempt. They'd found a way to bring not only a bomber inside but two bombs as well.

He'd searched for his old notes, the research he'd done into Al Saalihin after the Pride Bombing. Messy as he might be in his everyday life, he always meticulously organized his notes, thanks to an internship under a seasoned reporter who had stressed the importance of keeping detailed files that were easily searchable. So he'd read through them again, which had only led to more questions.

They'd been silent for five years, and now they were back. Would it really have taken them five years to plan this? Well, not this specific location but the general approach, the assassination of the US president. Or had they temporarily gone underground after the Pride Bombing to avoid being detected by intelligence agencies all over the world? The US must've called in every favor worldwide and asked about any information about Al Saalihin or Hamza Bashir. So many questions, so few answers.

He stared into the room, only faintly registering other reporters making calls, clacking away on their laptops, and the all-too-familiar sound of a police scanner that was always on. Right before lunch was not the busiest time, which was good because he hated being here when the room was crammed with people.

He took a sip from his coffee, grimacing when the cold, bitter liquid hit his tongue. He got up and stretched, his neck cracking with a satisfying *pop*, then made his way to the break room. Hopefully, someone had made fresh coffee. Thank fuck, yes, he was in luck this time. He poured himself a fresh cup, then rummaged through the basket with snacks and got himself a KIND bar. He'd read they contained way too much sugar to be considered healthy, but he chose to ignore that. It beat the hell out of the donuts he could've also picked, right?

He made it back to his desk, then leaned back in his chair, clicking his pen. Where should he start with finding answers to all his questions? Contact his old sources within the FBI, see if they were willing to share more? He doubted it, though, not after a presidential assassination. No one wanted to be caught blabbing to the press about that. No, he needed another in.

Gus. The retired NYPD detective from New Jersey he'd met when filming the documentary. Gus had mentioned Henley should contact him.

Thankfully, Gus had given him his email address, and using that, he easily traced down his address and phone number. Ten minutes later, he made the call. Gus picked up almost immediately.

"Gus, this is Henley Platt from the Washington Times. We met at the—"

"Henley," Gus said warmly. "I know who you are. After the recent news, I'm not surprised you're calling."

Good. That meant Henley could get straight to business, which was what he preferred. "Talk to me, Gus. What are your thoughts on this?"

"It's crazy, isn't it? First, they managed to pull off the biggest bombing and terrorist in history after 9/11. And now they've accomplished what no one has done since 1963, kill a US president. For a group that is an unknown entity, that's quite an achievement, don't you think?"

"Mm, I agree. No one had heard of them before the Pride Bombing."

"And no one has heard from them since...until now."

"I thought it was a strange coincidence we said as much to each other when we were in New York for the documentary, and now they're back."

"The whole thing doesn't sit well with me, let me tell you."

"I'm sure you still have access to information, considering you were on the JTTF."

"You bet your ass I do. This is all off the record, right?"

"I'll protect your anonymity with all I have."

"Good. Not that I'm willing to share top secret information with you, but I will tell you where to look."

"Anything you've got, Gus. I appreciate it."

"After the bombing, the FBI worked around the clock to investigate Al Saalihin, and literally every government agency you can think of was assisting. What they found was puzzling and has led them to believe that Al Saalihin is not what it seems."

"They're not linked to Al-Qaeda?"

"No one is ready to state it with that much certainty, but it's definitely a possibility. Too many things didn't add up. The bombs were remote detonated, for example. It took Al-Qaeda two days to claim the attack, which shows they didn't know about it. And the cells that publicly expressed their support first were small, relatively unknown groups. How could they have been in the know, but the Al-Qaeda leadership wasn't? Moreover, the NSA picked up an uptick in chatter after the attack, which is uncommon as well. Al-

Qaeda has learned to lie low right after they carried out an attack to avoid being tracked down."

The latter was new to Henley, and he made a quick note to check that with a source he had with the CIA. "What about Hamza Bashir? Is he real?"

"Good question and again, one that's not so easy to answer. He raises questions as well."

"The press speculated that he was wearing a disguise in the video. Was he?"

"Yes. A subtle voice changer too. He's younger than he seems in the video. He also has some inconsistencies in his accent in English that have analysts wonder where he's really from."

Damn, he was striking gold here. "And the three bombers? Is the information that was released about them correct?"

"For the most part, yes, but we haven't been able to track down how they got into contact with Hamza Bashir. The most likely is that they attended some kind of training camp, but no one can find any trace of this. The money trail ends so far as well."

"That's a lot of dead ends after five years."

"Yes, so you can imagine how hard this assassination hit. How did we miss this? Why didn't we pick up any warning signs?"

"I'm still puzzled why they targeted Markinson. Was it simply because he was a US president, or did they have another motive?"

"That's the big question, isn't it? I've been thinking about that ever since I heard the news. Why this president? It's interesting to me because he's not a president who had a strong anti-Muslim platform or even a president with outspoken opinions on the US role in the Middle East. In fact, he's been more reluctant to get involved there than any other president in history. His platform included drastic decreases in defense spending, for example. One would think that would make terrorist groups happy."

"He also hasn't announced any initiatives or changes in foreign policy approach that could be construed as detrimental to Muslim interests, not even that of Al Saalihin. So again, why him?"

"I assume you watched the video a few times, just like me."

Henley rolled his eyes, though Gus couldn't see it. "I have to admit the anti-queer rhetoric was a little hard to stomach, but yes."

"You know what I thought was interesting? Most news outlets and commentators immediately jumped on that as the link between the two attacks. The first attack was on a Pride Parade, which arguably is a fierce expression of the growth in LGBT rights we've seen in the country. And of course, Markinson was the first president who chose an openly bisexual vice president. And yet it seems like such a stupid reason to target him specifically. I don't mean to say that LGBT rights are stupid, don't get me wrong, but why pick that as a reason? Even if you disagree from a religious or moral point of view, it doesn't hurt other countries if the US broadens the right of LGBT people. Why base a terrorist attack on that? It would've made so much more sense if the attack had been because of economic expansion, changes in foreign policy, or anything that directly affects ISIS or Al-Qaeda. I just can't see the logic behind this. I know the investigation will be more focused on the how than on the why, but the why has always fascinated me."

Henley hummed in agreement. "You know what the video reminded me of? Bad movies. It sounded just like the dramatic, over-the-top speech of a villain from a Hollywood B-movie. You know, the ones where the villain takes his time to explain his reasoning for being a villain, basically. Nine out of ten times, you hear a very similar ridiculous rhetoric. Like a James Bond movie, those two-dimensional bad guys who want to destroy the world *just because*. That's what this video sounded like, like a just-because villain. Who would assassinate an American president because he has a bisexual vice president? That just doesn't add up for me."

"I agree. Definitely something worth looking into."

"One more thing. I'm not gonna go into specifics, but see what you can dig up about what the ATF discovered about the components of the bombs used in the Pride Bombing. That's my biggest concern, to be honest."

Henley jotted it down, knowing better than to push. Gus had given him way more than he'd expected already. "Thank you so much, Gus. I hope we'll meet again sometime, preferably under better circumstances. And if you have anything else, let me know."

"You're welcome. And say hi to Levar for me."

Henley frowned. He glanced around, but no one was paying attention to him. "Why would you ask me that? He just got promoted to White House press secretary, and I'm the senior White House correspondent for one of the biggest papers in the country. It's not like I could just walk over to him and tell him this."

Did it sound as weak in reality as it did in his own head?

Gus chuckled. "Keep telling yourself that. I caught the sparks between the two of you. Whether or not you've acted on it, that's your business, but don't try to sell me this bullshit that you're nothing but acquaintances."

Damn. Had they been that transparent? That was a

disheartening thought. "I'll tell him," Henley said with a sigh.

"You do that."

Henley stared at the phone for a long time after Gus had ended the call. Sure, Gus's casual remark about picking up on the tension between him and Levar was worrisome, but he quickly pushed it to the background. Henley's much bigger concern was what Gus had told him.

What if Al Saalihin wasn't what everyone thought they were? What if everything they believed was untrue? If that was the case, then who had been behind the Pride Bombing? And who had really killed Markinson?

25

If Levar had thought his life had been crazy when Shafer had been vice president, he'd clearly been mistaken. The utter and complete chaos of being the White House press secretary the last five days was beyond anything he could've imagined. Granted, part of that was because of the extraordinary circumstances, like the president being assassinated, him having to brief the press on all kinds of unusual materials, and operating without any kind of assistance or deputies.

Nicole was still there, but like Levar, she had to find her way around the White House rather than the vice president's office. Calix hadn't been kidding when he said the learning curve would be steep. Then again, that was true for all of them. Even Calix was struggling to find his footing in his new role. He'd also skipped quite a few steps on the ladder up. President Shafer himself seemed to be conflicted at times, especially about letting go of what had always been his focus as vice president. He simply didn't have the time to keep that on his plate as well, not with everything else going on.

Levar hurried through the West Wing, on his way to Calix for a quick briefing. Apparently, they'd made a new discovery in the investigation into the assassination, and Calix wanted to update him. They'd agreed to do all this in person. The White House network was supposedly the most secure network in the world, but they weren't taking any chances.

Sheila gestured that Levar could walk straight in. Calix was talking to two men he'd never seen before, though he had a suspicion of their identities. And holy shit, they were both *hot*. Like, almost unfair, so attractive. Still, it was more of a clinical assessment than him experiencing any real attraction. That, it seemed, was only focused on the one man he couldn't have.

"Levar, thank you for joining us," Calix said. "This is Assistant Special Agent in Charge Coulson Padman, who is one of the leading agents on the investigation into the assassination."

Levar took his hand, almost wincing at the man's firm handshake. "Pleasure to meet you, Levar. You've done a terrific job briefing the press so far. Much respect because they don't go easy on you," the FBI agent said.

"Thank you, Agent Padman. I appreciate you saying that."

"Coulson, please. I'm not big on formalities...unless I need to."

"I'm Seth Rodecker," the other guy said.

"It's nice to have a face with the voice." Levar smiled. Seth's handshake was slightly less fierce but still somewhat intimidating. He didn't suffer from low self-esteem, but compared to those two, he almost felt ugly. Coulson was like a Norse god, like Chris Hemsworth's brother, and Seth was a tanned, ripped surf dude with a pair of startling blue eyes. Together, they were breathtaking.

"Something has come up in the investigation that Calix thought you should know," Seth said.

Levar had spoken to the Secret Service agent a few times, both on the phone and in person, and he liked the man. At thirty-seven, he seemed to be fairly young to be the Secret Service's point person for the assassination investigation, but so far, he'd proven to be excellent at keeping them up to date. He had a near-eidetic memory, remembering every little detail Levar or Calix told him, and Levar had been impressed by that alone. Almost as impressed as he was by discovering that Seth was the first openly gay Secret Service agent on the first lady's detail—yes, Levar had done his homework on him.

"Okay, I'm listening," he said.

"Obviously, an assassination like this raises a lot of questions about where we as Secret Service went wrong. We've learned a lot from failed assassination attempts over the years, and this has been a devastating blow to us personally as well as to our reputation. The big question we ask ourselves is how. How did the bomber get in? How did he manage to get two bombs in without being detected?"

Seth took a deep breath. "What I'm about to tell you is top secret Secret Service information. We strongly suspect the bomber had inside help from either an employee of the convention center or a cop from the Baltimore Police Department. Or both. We were aware that our biggest deficiency in protecting the president was in large public events. Due to constraints in time and budget, we've been unable to screen every attendee at large events as carefully as we would've liked, and we often have to rely on uniformed officers from local police departments. It left us vulnerable to someone aware of that weakness, someone who also had the means to get inside help. Unfortunately, President Markinson didn't see that as the security threat we felt it to be. We had brought it up several times, but he didn't increase the budget. And even more unfortunately, we turned out to be right. As things stand now, that's exactly what happened. Someone knew our weak spot, and they exploited it. Obviously, that's a statement that can never leave this room. The Secret Service takes full responsibility for this failure in protecting the president, and I don't say that lightly."

Levar couldn't even imagine how the president's agents must feel. Well, those who survived anyway. Four Secret Service agents had been killed right along with the president, giving their lives in a feeble attempt to protect him. The Secret Service had to feel that loss, both personally and as an institution.

Then it hit him. Vulnerabilities in Secret Service protection, especially at large events. He and Henley had discussed this. Henley had detailed this in his articles, based on information from a reliable source. And Henley hadn't shared all he gathered, but he'd still known about this. Someone had told him. What were the odds that the same person had told the bombers? And hadn't Markinson and Shafer argued about the president's Secret Service protection only weeks ago? It almost seemed too much of a coincidence.

"Of course, the argument could be made that since President Markinson had known your limitations and didn't provide you with the necessary support to fix it, the blame for the assassination doesn't lie entirely with the Secret Service," Calix said.

Seth shook his head, his mouth still in a grim line. "It

doesn't work that way. We're always responsible for the president's safety, no matter the constraints. We failed, and that weighs heavily on us."

"I understand," Calix said. "But I wanted to say it anyway."

"I appreciate that."

Levar had to speak up. He had to mention Henley's articles. They were talking about an investigation into an assassination, for fuck's sake. "Henley Platt detailed some of these weak links in three articles last year."

"I was wondering if you'd make the connection yourself, but that's exactly what we wanted to talk to you about," Seth said. "We know you and Henley Platt have worked together on several occasions."

That was one way of putting it, but hell if Levar was giving him anything more. "When I heard about a recent disagreement between the president and the vice president about the Secret Service, I read his articles again. He lists some specific issues, though not the details about the inadequate security at large events."

"Exactly. I checked on our end, and Platt did talk to us about this. We haven't been able to find out who gave him this information. I think it's unlikely his source was a Secret Service agent. I can't rule it out, obviously, but it would be such a massive breach of everything we stand for that I have a hard time imagining one of our agents doing that. Considering how few people knew about this outside of the president's protective detail, that leak was highly worrisome. Platt's articles would've been a good starting point for someone who intended to assassinate Markinson. They clearly laid out some of our biggest shortcomings. Let's just say we were very unhappy when these came out, even though I have to admit Platt didn't report all the information he had access to. His contact with our spokesperson shows that he had many more details he didn't divulge in the articles, and we are grateful for that. However, we did find copies of his articles in the belongings of the bomber, which suggests that they were part of his sources."

Levar leaned back in his chair, dragging a hand through his hair. Oh my god, Henley would be devastated if he found out he'd unknowingly aided in a presidential assassination.

"We can't put the blame on him," Calix said. "As much as we may dislike it, he was doing his job."

"He was." Seth nodded. "And under the circumstances, his articles were more than fair. It *was* news. The disagreement between the Secret Service and Markinson about his protection was real. None of what Platt reported was factually wrong. Obviously, we would've preferred it hadn't been published in the paper, but it wasn't illegal. He didn't lie, he didn't print any classified information, and he did offer us the opportunity to respond, which we declined."

Levar's head was storming with thoughts. Henley had to know this. At some point, someone would make the connection, and it would all come out. In fact, it wouldn't take that long before others would research anything having to do with the president's Secret Service protection, and they would certainly find these articles. If that happened, would the public blame Henley? Could they allow him to be blindsided by this?

Everything inside Levar screamed that he should tell Henley, but he couldn't. Not without permission. He'd already crossed lines he should never have crossed, and he couldn't keep doing that. He'd not only endanger his job but possibly commit a felony by revealing classified information.

"Do we tell him?" he asked Calix. "Henley, I mean. We

have a good working relationship with him, and if this comes out, he'll be under attack. Do we give him a fair warning?"

Calix sighed. "How certain are you that the articles were the inspiration for the assassination?"

Coulson, who had been listening so far, spoke up. "It's an ongoing investigation, but I'm confident in saying that they have certainly played a role."

"Shit," Calix said. "And you both agree with Levar that this will leak?"

"Absolutely," Seth said. "At this point, we're not releasing this information yet, but it won't stay secret. Even our preliminary investigation, before we even had the bomber's name and address, already included these articles. We've known about them since they came out, and they've always been a concern to us. So yes, I'm confident this will come out."

Calix turned to Levar, who had to resist the urge to squirm under his scrutiny. "If you inform Platt about this, can we trust you not to reveal anything more than that?"

Why was Calix asking this? What did he know? Oh God, did he know they'd spent the night together in New York? That they'd hung out at Levar's apartment? This was why it was such a bad idea. He must've guilt written all over him right now. He couldn't lie to his boss, not about something so crucial. Wait, was it crucial? If it was nothing, just attraction, then why did he feel the need to even mention it? Technically, he hadn't done anything illegal. Yet. So why did he feel so guilty?

"Levar?" Calix asked gently.

Levar raised his chin. "You can trust me. I would never put anything above the interests of my job, the president, or even the country."

Calix's face softened. "I know your job comes with perks, but it also has definite downsides. One of those downsides is that it can make friendships hard because you know too much, and you can't reveal it. It's a struggle we all have, and it becomes only bigger when you rise through the ranks like you just did. Like you, my security clearance has gone up considerably, and it's a heady responsibility. If you ever need to talk about how to find a balance in this, my door is always open."

Levar blew out a breath. "Thank you. I'll admit it will take me some time. I'm not afraid I'll say more than allowed to. Dealing with the press for the last two years has taught me to be incredibly careful in how I formulate things, but knowing I'll have to keep my distance from certain people just because of my job...that's not easy."

Seth sent him a kind smile. "I know all about it. Try being a Secret Service agent. The number of things I can't talk about with anyone else is endless."

Coulson hummed in agreement. "It's one of the shittiest parts of the job for sure."

Levar didn't know why that made him feel better, but it did. Calix was right. This job did come at a price, but not just for him. They were all in the same boat. He'd have to decide if that was a price he was willing to pay, but even as he asked himself the question, he knew the answer. He couldn't imagine walking away, not when he had been handed his dream job on a platter, but the president needed him. No way was he deserting him now.

"I'll let Henley know about his articles and tell him to contact you if he has any questions I'm not comfortable answering," he said to Seth.

"I doubt I'll be able to tell him any more than you, but it might make him feel better he can at least try," Seth said. "I haven't met him personally, but from what I understand, he's a good guy."

Calix nodded. "He's always done a fair job in his reporting, especially on Vice President Shafer. I'd hate to see him get criticized over this, especially since technically, this wasn't his fault."

Seth sighed. "No, it wasn't. But my guess is, he'll have a hard time believing that."

26

"You're saying my articles helped the bombers find a strategy to kill the president?" Henley couldn't quite keep the tremor out of his voice. Judging by the look of sympathy on Levar's face, he'd picked up on Henley's distress.

Levar had taken him aside, then back to his office. Henley had known something was wrong when Levar had closed the door firmly behind them.

"Unfortunately, yes. I can't say much more, but the FBI has found evidence that the bombers used your articles to find weaknesses in the president's protection."

Henley closed his eyes, rubbing his eyes with both hands. How could this have happened? He thought he'd been careful to leave out anything too sensitive. Besides, it had been a year. The Secret Service would've had plenty of time to address these issues. How was this his life? How could he be responsible for the assassination of a president?

"It's not your fault." Levar touched his shoulder briefly. "Calix agreed. The articles were fair, even if they were critical. You weren't reporting anything but the facts, and they may not have painted a rosy picture, but that didn't make them any less true."

Henley dropped his arms and opened his eyes again, suddenly feeling twenty years older. "I'm sorry, but that's really not that much of a consolation. The thought that something I wrote contributed to this is... I can't even express it. Devastating, that's what it is. I still don't understand how this could've happened."

Levar hesitated. "You and I both know this isn't your fault. Seth said that ultimately, the fault and responsibility lies with the Secret Service."

Henley frowned. "Seth?"

"Sorry. Seth Rodecker, the Secret Service's point agent on the investigation."

He looked like he wanted to add something, but Henley held up his hand. "I know. That was completely off the record and has to stay between us. No need to say it, Lev. This whole conversation won't leave this room."

Levar sighed. "I hate that we have to keep saying that. I hate that on the one hand, I completely trust you, yet on the other, the voice in the back of my head insists I need to make clear what is for public consumption and what isn't."

Henley waved his hand dismissively. "I understand. You're just doing your job. You'd be a lousy press secretary if you didn't make sure I understood the rules. But I hope you'll believe me when I say that going forward, I won't use anything without your explicit permission. I want you to be able to talk to me, to trust me. This whole thing is crazy complicated to navigate, but I can't lose your friendship."

He scoffed. "If you even still want to be friends with me after this. I may have very well become nuclear just now. Probably not the reporter you want to be seen with."

Levar's eyes showed sadness. "I don't know about

nuclear, but yes, things have arguably gotten even more complicated than they already were. At some point, someone will make this connection, and when they do, you can expect a fallout for you and your newspaper."

Henley nodded. "And for the Secret Service and whomever they suspect to be my source as well. And that's what I'm saying. Once this gets out, you can't associate with me. People will think you're feeding me information."

"I know nothing about the Secret Service, so I'm not too worried about that."

"You should be. Reputation matters, especially for a press secretary. You can't be seen as favoring people, especially when it comes to sharing information with them."

Levar stared at him, a myriad of emotions flashing over his face. "Rationally, I know what you're saying is true, but everything inside me protests against it. I've never played favorites, and you damn well know it. And despite us being...whatever the hell we are, I don't intend on starting now."

Henley's face softened. "I know that, Lev. But others won't, and in this job, in everything we do, perceptions matter. That's why I'm in trouble once this leaks. I can argue I was doing my job and that my coverage of the issue Markinson had with the Secret Service was fair, but others won't see it that way."

Levar's mouth pulled tight. "They will lean on you to reveal your sources. And I can't blame them for wanting to know where you got that information, and I think you'll agree with me after what happened."

"Of course I can understand why the FBI would want to know. But they'll have to get a subpoena because I don't break my sources' anonymity. Once I start doing that, my career as an investigative journalist is over."

Levar frowned. "Investigative journalist? You're a White House reporter."

Funny how almost two years into the job, Henley still considered himself to be an investigative reporter first and foremost. He'd loved working on those articles, even though they'd been only indirectly linked to the White House. That kind of digging totally got his blood pumping faster.

"True, but the code stays the same. We don't reveal our sources. Unless the FBI can make a compelling argument to a judge that revealing my source is crucial to finding out who's behind this assassination, I'm not saying a damn thing. I'm not talking voluntarily. Besides, they already know who's behind the attack, so it's not like they need the information to know who did it."

"No, but they may need it to figure out how the bombers got the specifics. That being said, I understand where you're coming from."

Henley let out a deep sigh as he glanced around the room. The press secretary held one of the bigger offices in the West Wing, probably out of necessity because of the contacts with the press. Often, he and ten other reporters had been crammed in here, trying to get information from Katie Winters. Thank fuck the overwhelming smell of her perfume had disappeared. Chanel No 5 might be a classic, but god, she'd overused it.

A week into the job, Levar had already made the office his. The stacks of papers that had always littered the mahogany desk had disappeared, replaced by neat filing trays, standing next to two pink metal cans holding cheap-ass hotel pens. Henley took one out and grinned when he read the name.

"Comfort Inn, seriously?"

Levar blushed adorably. "I love those pens. They're super handy."

"So you steal them from hotels."

"The Comfort Inn is a motel, and it's not stealing so much as...taking them as a souvenir. I'm promoting them, one could say."

"Sure, tell yourself that." Henley quickly checked a few others. All sported names of motels, restaurants, and conference centers.

He pointed at the fishbowl on the cabinet against the wall. "You inherited Katie's goldfish?"

Levar rolled his eyes. "Apparently, it's a White House tradition that the press secretary has a goldfish, so a few junior staffers got me one. I named it CJ, after CJ Cregg from *The West Wing*."

"Appropriately named."

"I thought so too. I hope I don't kill it because I'm really bad with shit like that."

"No pets?"

"We had a cat for a while, but Rhett always took care of her. She passed of old age, and Rhett didn't want another one just yet."

"How are you holding up otherwise? Are you coping with the pressure?"

Levar smiled at him, one of those sweet, intimate smiles that made Henley feel like they were the only two people in the world. "It's a shit show for sure, but I'm doing the best I can. So far, both Calix and the president seem to feel I'm doing a decent job, so I'm holding on to that. That being said, I can't wait until they've appointed my deputy and a press team for the vice president's office. We don't have a vice president, which, by the way, is a problem all on its own, and a lot of the work I did for Vice President Shafer is still on my plate, even though he's now president. It's like I'm doing the job of four people at the same time, and that's not something I can keep up for long."

"Nor would you want to, I'd hope. You were killing it, but if you don't slow down, you might end up killing yourself."

Levar grinned. "Look who's talking, Mr. My Boyfriend Left Me Because I Was Never Home."

Henley's mouth pulled up in a smile as well. "Touché. I'm the last one to talk, though maybe I have the futile hope that you can learn from my mistakes."

"You mean because of your years of experience on me? Your mature age?"

"Obviously."

They sat smiling at each other for a few more beats, and then Levar said, "I'm afraid I'm going to have to kick you out. My next appointment will be here in a minute."

Henley rose from his chair. "Thank you for giving me a heads-up. You didn't have to, but I appreciate it a lot."

"Take care of yourself, please. You know where to find me if you need me."

You know where to find me if you need me. Levar's parting words played through Henley's head as he walked back to the press room, where he gathered his belongings, then headed back to the paper. He'd need to inform his editor, and this particular conversation was not one he wanted to have over the phone. Toby wouldn't be happy about it, and Henley couldn't blame him.

You know where to find me if you need me. Had it been a casual remark? Something Levar had said out of habit, like a well-meaning but otherwise empty cliché? Or should Henley find a deeper meaning in it? Had it perhaps been an indirect way of letting Henley know Levar wanted him to come to him? No, Levar wouldn't communicate like that.

That was wishful thinking. It had to have been a cliché, a kind gesture on Levar's part, probably because he'd seen Henley's distress. He shouldn't take him up on it. He really shouldn't.

But as the day progressed and his editor expressed his displeasure with recent developments, Henley's mood darkened, and he sank deeper and deeper into despair. He was tired. And if he took a step back and looked at the situation rationally, he had no trouble pinpointing why he felt this way. He'd been working his ass off for way too long, not taking enough rest and time to recover.

Covering the White House was stressful, especially the sensation of always being on the job, never being able to truly take time off. The news never stopped. There might be a lull, a quiet news day, but something was always brewing. And lately, the kettle had almost exploded. No wonder he was getting tired of it.

But even that was just the tip of the iceberg. If he dug deeper, which he usually tried to avoid, something else would become clear. Something he'd refused to vocalize, even in the therapy sessions his editor had forced him to take after the Pride Bombing.

He hadn't been the same since that day. No one who'd been there had been. And in the beginning, that thought had helped him compartmentalize it. Of course he was struggling with the aftereffects of that day. All survivors were. That didn't make him special or make his problems worse than anyone else's.

But over time, it had become harder and harder to deny that maybe, just maybe, his case was a little different than that of most others. He hadn't merely *survived* that day. He had reported on it. And yes, writing all those articles in the weeks and even months after the bombing had helped him process. But that processing had merely taken place on a rational level. He'd very much stayed in his head, if only because the few moments he'd allowed himself to feel all his emotions, their intensity had scared him. He'd carefully kept his heart out of it, but now, for some reason, he couldn't.

Rationalizing his feelings after watching Markinson get killed hadn't been quite as easy. He wasn't sure if he had been the only person in that room who had witnessed both the Pride Bombing and this assassination, but probably not more than a handful of people could say the same. Surviving one big traumatizing experience in your life was a miracle in itself. Surviving two defied all the odds, and that made it hard to reason with himself that whatever he was feeling was normal. In this case, normal didn't exist.

Maybe the only thing he could compare it to was the experience of soldiers who had faced countless battles during their deployment. Not that that was a comforting thought, considering how many veterans struggled with returning to civilian life, with letting go of the horrors they'd witnessed.

Ever since he'd watched that man run up to the podium, Henley's life hadn't been the same. If the Pride Bombing had irrevocably changed his life, the assassination had turned it upside down. Was he brave enough to acknowledge what it had done to him? Did he have enough courage to face these changes head on and deal with them? Right now, the odds weren't in his favor. Hell, the crying fit he'd had in Levar's arms a week ago had been one shaky step away from an actual breakdown.

As he drove home, his thoughts kept playing on an endless loop, jumping from the articles to the Pride Bombing, then to the assassination, then to the conversation he'd had with his source about the gaps in the president's Secret Service protection, then to Gus and his questions about Al Saalihin, then back to the assassination and whether or not he even still had a career. By the time he'd reached his home, his head was pounding.

You know where to find me if you need me.

Was it fair to need Levar? Was it justifiable to reach out to him? The answer to both had to be no, and yet as soon as he'd let himself into his apartment and switched on the lights, Henley found himself staring at his phone. He shouldn't. He really, really shouldn't. Yet his thumbs flew over the keyboard.

I need you.

27

Levar hadn't intended to see Henley again outside of work, but then his text had come in. *I need you.* How much had it taken for strong, proud Henley to admit that? He wasn't the type to ask for help, and the fact that he had meant something. Levar wasn't sure what, but he couldn't ignore that signal, especially after Henley's small breakdown in bed the week before. Henley wasn't okay, that much was becoming clear, and this text was more proof of that.

So he'd replied. *On my way. Text me your address.*

Henley had texted right back. *You don't have to.*

As if he was gonna back out now. *Text me the damn address.*

Henley had, adding a simple red heart.

And now Levar sat on the Metro Red Line, the same one he always took—or the MARC—except he'd have to get off a few stations earlier.

He texted Rhett. *Home late today.*

I thought you were gonna leave earlier tonight. Something happen?

The thought of lying to Rhett wasn't more than a fleeting blip. He didn't lie to him. Ever. Their friendship was too precious for that. Rhett might disagree with what Levar was doing with Henley—he'd expressed his opinions in no uncertain terms after running into Henley on his way out the week before—but he would never betray him. He'd have his back when push came to shove.

I have to make a stop first. No idea how long it will take.

Rhett called instantly, and Levar answered with a sigh. "Don't yell at me. Please."

"Levar..."

"He needs me. He got some bad news today, and he needs me."

"Babe, he can't lean on you. He's got to find someone else."

"I don't think he has anyone else."

"You're kidding me..."

"I'm not. His boyfriend recently broke up with him, his family is in Connecticut, and I don't think he has real friends here."

Rhett sighed. "He should work on that."

"It's not easy when you do what he does."

"I get that, but now he's putting you in an impossible position, and I don't like it. This could cost you everything."

Levar swallowed, closing his eyes for a moment. "I know."

"But he needs you." Rhett sounded resigned now.

"He does. I'm worried about him."

"I love your big, soft heart, babe, but you have got to end this. It can't last, and if it tumbles down, it's gonna crash on top of you. You're gonna get hurt if you're not careful."

Levar bit his lip. "I think it's too late to prevent that."

"Where does he live?"

"Bethesda, close to the Metro station."

"Please text me if you decide to stay the night."

"I will. Thank you."

"I love you, always have, always will. Even when you're being stupid."

Levar smiled. "Love you too."

He could've walked from the station to Henley's apartment complex, probably, but he was way too tired. The five-minute cab ride was much faster and easier.

Before Levar could even press his bell, Henley buzzed him in, so he must've been on the lookout. One flight up and there he stood in the doorway of his apartment, his eyes sunken and dark and his face pale. "You didn't have to come."

Levar rolled his eyes as he gently pushed Henley inside, then followed him and closed the door behind him. He kicked off his shoes and put down his bag. "Then you shouldn't have texted me. I'm not gonna ignore a message like that."

Guilt flashed over Henley's face, and he looked at the floor. "I didn't mean to put pressure on you or guilt-trip you."

"I'm a grown man. I made the decision to come."

Maybe Henley had waited for those words or something along those lines because he stepped close and wrapped his arms around Levar. "Thank you."

Levar held him tight. He didn't like the way Henley shivered in his arms. "What's going through your head?" he asked softly.

Henley took a long time to answer. "So much that I can't stop my thoughts anymore. I keep going in circles. The Pride Bombing. The assassination. My articles and the conversations I had to write those. It's all blending in my head, making me feel like it's all my fault. I know it's not, but my thoughts are spinning and spinning…"

Desperation laced his voice, and Levar's heart went out to him. "Are you gonna invite me in?"

"You're already in."

Levar chuckled. "Into the rest of your apartment? Or do I just make myself at home?"

Henley winced. "It's a bit of a mess. I think?"

The mess wasn't too bad, but what Levar did notice when he stepped into the living room was how cold it was. Not the temperature—though Henley must have the AC turned down low, considering it was ninety degrees outside—but in style and decoration. Light gray walls, dark gray furniture, black cabinets. No colors, no paintings or decorations, no personal touches save a single picture of what had to be his mom and siblings on the cabinet next to the TV. Stylish, yes, but also impersonal, cold. It didn't show anything of Henley himself. The contrast with Levar and Rhett's homey apartment couldn't be bigger. It even smelled sterile here, like disinfectant.

"Where's your bedroom?" Levar asked. Henley opened his mouth, but Levar held up a hand. "Save me the lame joke."

Henley closed his mouth again, then pointed at a door in the hallway. Levar marched in, concluded this room was as boring as the living room, then opened the door to the bathroom. Bingo. "Come on, let's draw you a bath."

"A bath? It's a hundred fucking degrees."

"Not in here, it's not. Besides, we're not arguing about this. For once in your life, Henley, let go. Trust me. Trust me to take care of you."

The fight left Henley's face, and his shoulders slumped.

"I suck at this. I do trust you, but I'm so bad at relinquishing control."

Levar grabbed his hand. "I know, but you're so tired, baby. Just for tonight, surrender..."

"Okay..."

It came out as barely more than a whisper, but Levar understood the magnitude of that single word. "Undress, baby. I'll get the water running."

Henley stared at him for a few beats, his eyes showing the war raging inside him, but then he nodded and turned around. Levar blew out a breath as he hurried into the bathroom. He started the water, then rummaged through the cabinets, hoping for some bath salts or bath bombs. All the way in the back, he found one. Lavender. Perfect. He dumped it in, and within seconds, the flowery smell rose from the water. So soothing.

He stepped back into the bedroom, where Henley stood naked, looking forlorn. As much as Levar had longed to see Henley naked, he'd never imagined it like this. He didn't say a word as he stripped down himself. He'd better not get his nice suit wet. He laid it out neatly on the bed, then took off his tie and shirt as well.

"Those are so pretty," Henley whispered, and Levar followed his gaze to the white lace panties he was wearing. He'd started wearing them to work occasionally, drawing a strange sense of strength and comfort from them. They boosted his self-confidence, even if no one saw them. These were boy shorts style, combining soft silk against his dick with lace trimming around the edges and on his ass. He loved the way they framed his ass cheeks, making them look round and luscious, if he did say so himself.

"Thank you."

"I wish I could..."

Levar sighed. "I know. But I'm here now."

He led Henley to the bathtub, and he allowed it, following Levar's instructions and lowering himself into the water. "Where'd you find the scented thing?"

"In the back of some drawer."

"Logan must've left it. I never use them. Hell, I can't even remember the last time I took a bath."

Levar rolled up a towel and placed it under Henley's head. "Close your eyes. I'll make sure you don't drown."

Much to his surprise, Henley obeyed. The bathroom grew quiet, only the occasional sloshing sound audible when Henley moved. "This feels really good," he finally said, his voice sleepy.

Tears burned behind Levar's eyes at that quiet confession, though he didn't understand why. It *did* something to him, seeing Henley stripped of all his usual defenses, his witty banter. The outside was gone, the masks were off, and what was left was the real Henley. Behind that sharp, brilliant exterior was a vulnerable man, one who struggled mightily with daring to show that side of himself.

He didn't say anything, just sat quietly on a thick towel on the bathroom floor right next to the bath, where Henley was dozing off. After twenty minutes or so, Levar gently stirred him. "Time to get out."

"Do I have to?"

Levar smiled. "First, you didn't want to get in, and now you don't want to leave?"

"I should listen to you more."

"Clearly."

Henley opened his eyes with a sigh, then accepted Levar's hand and scrambled to his feet. He stepped out of the bath and stood in all his naked, dripping, sleepy glory. His eyes were as soft and dreamy as his cock, and Levar's heart tripped in his chest. Henley was pretty damn hot at any given moment, but this vulnerable, pliable Henley? Irresistible.

Levar pushed down his needs and toweled Henley off with a fluffy towel. "I can do it myself," Henley protested.

"Shut up."

"I like you on your knees in front of me." Henley gazed down on him.

Levar grinned. "Dude, I bet you couldn't even get it up right now if I paid you a hundred bucks."

Henley looked from Levar to his cock, then shrugged with a sigh. "Good point."

Levar finished drying him off, then rose. "You don't always have to be witty and flirty. You're hurting. It's okay to stop the banter."

Henley looked away. "I don't know how to do that. It's all I have."

Levar cupped his cheek, and Henley's brown eyes, full of fear and insecurity, met his. "It's scary to drop the tough act and show the real you. I get it. But you can trust me to accept you as you are. I won't walk away."

Henley widened his eyes for a moment, as if Levar's words had shocked him, but then he schooled his features again, his shoulders drooping a little. "I'll try. That's the best I can do."

"It's enough. Come on, off to bed you go."

"Bed? I haven't eaten yet."

"I'll make you something, but you're going to bed."

Henley allowed Levar to lead him to the king-size bed, then help him get in and tuck him in. "Your bossy mode is surprisingly attractive," Henley said.

Levar kissed the top of his head. "This isn't me being bossy. This is me taking care of you, which, I'm coming to understand, is a whole new experience for you. Relax for a bit while I check your kitchen for something edible."

"Eggs," Henley mumbled. "I have eggs in the fridge. And veggies, I think? They may have gone bad, though."

"I'll have a look."

As soon as Levar had stepped out of Henley's bedroom, he had to steady himself by holding on to the wall. He was in so much trouble. What he was feeling for Henley had long passed attraction or even infatuation. His heart was crammed full of all these emotions he couldn't even untangle, but he did know this. He was fucked. Utterly fucked.

28

Washington National Cathedral was packed. Workers had hustled around the clock to prepare the cathedral for the funeral of President Markinson, which would be broadcasted live on national and international TV. Spotlights had been hung on the tall, elegant columns, a control panel had been set up in the back of the church, outside of the view of cameras, and miles of cables had been rolled out and carefully hidden or taped down.

Levar thanked his stars he hadn't been involved other than briefing the media. The White House had an event manager who had been trained to organize a spectacle of this scale, and she'd done an amazing job so far.

The President's flag-draped casket had lain in state at the Capitol Rotunda, where thousands of people had paid their respect under the watchful eyes of hundreds of Secret Service agents, cops, and even FBI. Former statesmen, servicemen and -women, people Markinson had worked with had come from all over the country to say good-bye, as befitting a president who'd served his nation for so long. US

Marines had kept an honor guard from the moment his casket had arrived until the moment it had been carried into the church.

One of President Markinson's grandchildren had walked alongside his casket, dressed in his Marines dress blues, his young, tight face showing no emotion as he helped carry the casket of his grandfather to the front. He'd just joined the Marines a year and a half ago. What a way to start his career in the same armed services branch his grandfather had served in.

Markinson would be buried with full military honors, then laid to rest at Arlington, at his own request. Levar hadn't known, but apparently, when one became president, these kinds of details were discussed and put down in writing, just in case. He wasn't sure when that had become custom. Maybe after the assassination of JFK? Or the attempt on Ronald Reagan's life? After all, that had been a close call. He was daily reminded of it. The White House press room was named after James Brady, Ronald Reagan's press secretary, who had been shot during that attack on the president's life.

Levar looked out over the sea of people seated at both sides of the center aisle, everyone dressed in black or gray. The church was somewhat gloomy due to its design, the only natural light the little bit spilling in from the windows at the top of the tall structure, and the dark clothes and faces only added to this. All the VIPs were seated at the front, including President Shafer with his family, flanked by the former first lady and her family.

Many dignitaries sat behind the former first lady and President Shafer. The prime ministers of the United Kingdom and Canada, the French president, heads of state, and celebrities from all over the world. Even

Markinson's beloved Baltimore Orioles had made an appearance, three star players having a prime spot. Everyone knew Markinson had had a weakness for baseball, watching as many games as he could. He'd been a decent player in college. When he'd pitched the first ball at the opening of the season a few years ago, he'd absolutely nailed it, far better than probably anyone else before him.

"Grieving while in the public eye is not easy," said William Markinson, the president's oldest son, in his eulogy of his father. "But my father wouldn't have wanted it any other way. His whole life was dedicated to serving his country from the moment he enlisted into the Marines until the day he died as president of our great nation. He has made the ultimate sacrifice for democracy, and I, like my family, hope that his sacrifice will not have been in vain."

He gave a last glance at his papers, then raised his head again and addressed the crowd. "I'd like to invite my mother to share her memories. Former first lady of the United States, Mrs. Annabeth Markinson."

Mrs. Markinson made her way to the front, exchanging a brief kiss on the cheek with her son. She looked calm, like she had her emotions under control, though her face was tight.

"Thank you, William, for your beautiful words. You know how much your father loved you kids as well as his grandkids."

Levar frowned. Was it because of nerves that she'd had an edge to her voice? Nothing big, but she'd stressed the you part of the sentence. How much your father loved *you kids*. Almost like she'd wanted to suddenly communicate he didn't love someone else? Levar mentally shook his head. He was reading too much into it. That didn't make sense. By all accounts, the Markinsons had had a good relationship, a solid marriage.

"Being president is all about character," she said. "It's a paraphrased quote from the movie The American President, which Bill and I watched before he became president. He was the senator for Maryland at the time, and I remember us looking at each other and smiling, thinking about how amazing it would be to live out the reality of that movie. Bill had never made a secret about his ambition to become president, and I supported him every step of the way. I thought he had what it took to be an amazing president, and he did. I am proud of what he achieved, and I think we can all agree he made the country a better place."

Unease danced down Levar's spine. It had to be the nerves. The cold, almost emotionless way she delivered her speech had to be because of nerves or grief. Or maybe the White House doctor had prescribed her some kind of anti-anxiety medication.

After all, Mrs. Markinson wasn't known as a terrific public speaker. She'd done it, but she much preferred smaller, more intimate conversations, which was where she was at her best. A crowd like this would have to terrify her, especially knowing that the service was being broadcasted live all over the world, though at a ten-second delay, just in case.

But as Annabeth Markinson kept talking about her husband, about the things he'd done for the country, Levar's unease grew. She was his *wife*. She'd supposedly known him better than anyone else, and yet she talked about him as if she was on a stump speech, promoting him. The man was dead. Of course, highlighting his achievements was natural, but why wouldn't she talk more about who he'd been as a man, a husband, a father?

Mrs. Markinson set her gaze on President Shafer. "Delano, I know Bill was overjoyed when you accepted his proposal to become his vice president. He was in awe of your heroism on that horrific day, that gruesome attack on our freedom, and he was honored to have you at his side. I know he had full confidence in you, and I hope you'll continue to carry out his plans to better our country for everyone."

Yeah, clearly she hadn't been privy to her husband's feelings about then vice president Shafer because otherwise, she would've never said this. Had Markinson flat out lied to her? Or had she simply assumed things, maybe from the way he'd felt way back when he'd first approached Shafer? But why hadn't her staff pointed out the well-publicized rift between her husband and Shafer? It didn't make sense.

After a few more minutes of highlighting what her husband had done for the country, Mrs. Markinson handed the microphone back to Bishop Marshall, who led the service. The National Cathedral was a common venue for funerals of this caliber, but President Markinson had been Episcopalian himself, and he'd actually attended service regularly, so the bishop had a somewhat personal connection with him.

He caught movement from the corner of his eye. Rhett was quietly walking along the outside of the pew Levar was sitting in, holding his camera. Levar marveled all over again at Rhett's ability to become practically invisible. Sure, with his black suit and dark shirt, he didn't stand out anyway, but he could move so unobtrusively you never even noticed him.

Calix had mentioned to Levar how grateful he was he'd recommended Rhett, since his roommate had been doing an excellent job over the week taking pictures of the president and the transition they were still in. He knew from Rhett he loved his assignment as well. Even though it exposed him to people who, under any other circumstance, would've made him incredibly nervous, he'd found a way to blend into the background. Everyone seemed to ignore him, and that worked just fine for him.

President Shafer had spoken first at the funeral, and his eulogy had been good. Somehow, he'd managed to acknowledge their differences in opinion but had painted them as small disagreements, not the blown-up feud the papers had reported. Whether people believed him was the question, but at least it was the polite thing to say at a funeral.

His speechwriter had made Shafer's eulogy a warm, glowing statement about the man's years of service. Even for Levar, who had never particularly warmed up to Markinson, it had brought home that with all his faults and mistakes, Markinson had truly dedicated his life to public service. In that sense, his widow had been completely right, though he still felt it was somewhat odd she'd focused on that.

Then again, who could blame her? No one since Jackie Kennedy had been in her shoes, so she had no role model here, no example, no way of knowing what was best. Maybe talking about him as a statesman helped her keep her emotions at bay, and who was Levar to judge her for that?

As the bishop ended the service, Levar rose with everyone else, and the cathedral was deadly quiet as the Marines took up the casket and, with whispered commands, lifted it, turned around, and in perfect harmony and synchronicity carried it outside. Mrs. Markinson followed the casket with her family, President Shafer falling in step behind her. After that, the guests gradually streamed outside, their conversations hushed.

The group that had been invited to the military service

at Arlington was much, much smaller. For obvious reasons, the famous cemetery was not suitable to host that many people, if only because they might accidentally trample on other graves. Levar had requested to skip that part, and Calix had agreed his presence wasn't necessary there. So Levar waited until it was his turn to file out of his pew and then slowly walked out.

He stopped on his way out and took a long look at the statues of President Lincoln and President Washington on either side of the front door of the cathedral, Lincoln's in bronze and Washington's in limestone, their faces serious and almost regal. Could these men have ever dreamed of the legacy they'd leave behind? Washington had founded the United States, and Lincoln had saved her from herself. What would Markinson's legacy be? Or, for that matter, President Shafer's?

The West Wing was relatively quiet when he walked in, most of the staff still present at the funeral. He quickly headed for his office, where he exchanged his dark suit for a less formal one. He still had a press briefing to do, but he didn't want to do that in the same suit he'd worn to the funeral.

When he poked his head around the corner of the press room to see if they'd gotten back yet—only a handful of reporters had been allowed to attend the military funeral—Henley sat in the back of the room, looking at something on his phone. Levar hesitated. Ignoring him would be the safest option, and yet something about him sitting there, all forlorn and alone, tugged at his heartstrings.

He hadn't spoken to him since he'd been at his house two days ago. He hadn't even texted him, and it had cost him. The man hadn't been out of his mind, but taking care of Henley that night had shown him that he was already far deeper into him than he'd thought, and he had to step back. He had to create distance between them.

He quietly walked over, and Henley looked up from his phone, a smile breaking free on his face. "Hey, you back from the funeral?"

"Yeah. You weren't there? I didn't see you, but thousands of people were there, so..."

"No. My editor didn't think it was a good idea for me to attend. The news about the role my articles played hasn't broken yet, but it could any moment now, so this seemed the safer bet. We didn't want to distract from the funeral in any way."

"I'm sorry," Levar said. "Did you watch the funeral?"

"Of course. I was relieved to see it went off without a hitch. An event of that magnitude is always a little nerve-racking. The number of things that could go wrong is countless, and there's a lot at stake, especially after the assassination."

"For sure. I know people have worked around the clock to pull this off. Literally. I haven't had much sleep myself this week."

Henley's smile was soft. "I hate to say it, but it shows. You're looking a little pale."

Levar rolled his eyes. "Geez, thank you. Just what every guy wants to hear, that he looks tired and pale."

"Part of that is because you took care of me." Henley's voice dropped to a near whisper. "I never got to thank you because I fell asleep, and when I woke up, you were gone."

None of the reactions that popped into Levar's head seemed wise, so he merely shrugged. "You're welcome."

Henley stared at him for a few moments, then let out a sigh and looked away. "I liked the president's speech. He's a good public speaker, so that helps, but the speechwriter managed to hit the right tone, which wasn't easy under these circumstances."

"What did you think of Mrs. Markinson's words?" Levar was relieved Henley had changed the topic.

Henley's eyes narrowed. The casual expression he'd had before morphed into the sharp look Levar knew all too well. As if to underscore the change in their conversation even more, Henley got up from his seat and took a step to Levar. He lowered his voice so nobody would overhear their conversation. "I wonder if you picked up on the same thing I did."

"That depends on what you heard."

"Off the record," Henley said, and Levar loved him for it. "For you and me."

Levar nodded. "Understood."

"I thought her eulogy was cold, emotionless as if she was selling her husband, listing his political accomplishments. A speech like that wouldn't have been out of the ordinary on the campaign trail, but it didn't fit a funeral."

Levar pushed out a slow breath. "Dammit. I felt the same way. It was strange, right?"

"Very strange. Plus, the way she presented the relationship between her husband and Shafer was just...wrong. Either he didn't talk about things with her, which is a valid possibility, but that still makes me wonder why no one told her about the media coverage of the rift between them, or she deliberately chose to lie."

"I don't understand it. Of course, it wasn't the place to make a political statement about any animosity between Markinson and Shafer. But she didn't have to come right out and say those things about how much Markinson's respected Shafer, how proud he was to have him as his vice president. What struck me was that it sounded sincere, which we both know it can't have been, at least not from him. So either she really didn't have a clue of what was going on, or she's a highly accomplished liar."

"Neither option sits well with me. Like you said, she had no reason to be this specific and detailed. She could've made a blanket statement about trusting Shafer to do a good job or something along those lines. This was so explicit it stood out."

"I wonder if others picked up on it as well. The media reported widely on their feud, so they must have questions."

Henley hesitated. "Just in the spirit of being honest and all that... I was working on an article that proved the troubled relationship between them had gone even farther than what we'd reported before, but it got sidetracked when the president was killed."

"You mean more than Markinson considering supporting someone else for the Democratic nomination?"

"Yeah. I doubt I'll even run it now, since it doesn't feel all that relevant anymore, but I have proof Markinson was actively keeping Shafer out of the loop and had instructed his staff to do the same. And Victor Kendall knew about it."

Levar let out a deep sigh. "Damn. I hate to speak ill of the dead, but seriously, what a shitty thing to do."

"It is. But from what I've learned about him, Markinson was petty. He may have genuinely served his country in many ways, but he was also vindictive and petty. And incredibly political."

Levar cocked his head. "How?"

"We both know that to become president you have to know how to play the game. All do it, but some out of necessity. Markinson genuinely loved the wheeling and dealing, though. He excelled at that political game, always willing to compromise, to water down his viewpoints, to swerve a little to the right or the left to appease the right people. For example, in his first campaign six years ago, he positioned himself as the most moderate Democrat ever. He supported the second amendment while proposing cuts to the military budget, he guaranteed Social Security but made clear he didn't embrace Medicare for all, and he talked a lot about values. It's how he managed to get the Democratic nomination because he appealed to the biggest group of voters. He never had much competition from the start. And it's how he managed to win the elections because the contrast with that right-wing nut the Republicans had nominated was too big. He swayed a lot of undecideds to vote for him. I don't think he advocated a clear political philosophy other than catering to the demands and wishes that would get him the furthest."

"In that sense, Shafer is completely his opposite. He knows how to play the game as well, but he's been true to his own values ever since he started in politics."

Henley nodded. "It's something I respect deeply. Anyway, like I said, I don't even know if I'll run this story, since the timing seems ill-advised. And it will make things more complicated for the president."

Levar shrugged. "Yeah, but everything is messed up, complicated, and chaotic already. I doubt an article from you will make that much worse. Besides, he's the president. Whether Markinson liked him or not, whether he'd wanted to support someone else for the nomination or not, it doesn't change that fact. Until the elections, Shafer is it."

"Good point. Speaking of the elections, any movement on looking for a vice president yet?"

Levar laughed. "Pretty sure we just went back on the record, which means I'm not commenting on this."

Henley's look was mischievous. "It was worth a try."

Then his face sobered, but before he could say something else, Levar held up a hand. "Don't. You wouldn't have used anything I said. I *know* you, Henley. I trust you. No matter what happened between us, that didn't change."

Henley's eyes darkened, his gaze intense as he looked at Levar. "Thank you."

He had to walk away now. Levar responded to Henley all over again, the pull almost impossible to resist. The man was like a siren, like Calypso calling out to Odysseus, leading him astray from his chosen path.

Without another word, he turned around and walked away. When he'd taken a few steps, he picked up the last of Henley's whispered words. "I miss you..."

29

Henley was just pulling his front door shut behind him when his phone rang. His stomach sank. Phone calls at seven thirty in the morning rarely meant good news.

"Hey, Toby," he greeted his editor.

He didn't even ask what was up.

"Henley, you need to skip the White House briefing today. The news about your articles broke. We were contacted last night, and our attorney has issued a statement. I'm expecting it to be a big item this morning, so you'd better lie low. I've sent Luther instead."

Henley's stomach clenched. He'd known this was coming, and yet it still came as a shock. Four days. That was how long it had taken the media to discover the link between his articles and the assassination after he'd found out himself. "Yeah, I'd best not show my face there. Otherwise, I'll become the news today."

"Henley, I hate to be rude, but you are the news regardless. The only choice you have is whether or not to respond, and we strongly advise you not to. Keep in mind that when you do respond, you may lose support from the paper, including legal support. I understand this places you in a difficult position, but obviously, management has bigger interests to protect than just your reputation."

"I know. No worries, I won't respond to anything. I know better."

Toby was quiet for a few beats, then said, "Brace yourself. The next few days aren't going to be pretty."

He ended the call, and Henley stood with his phone in his hand. What should he do now? Toby was right that setting foot in the White House today wasn't a good idea. Besides, he'd already sent Luther to cover for Henley, so he'd better work from his office at the paper. It beat the hell out of staying home and feeling sorry for himself. Which he did, but at least the wallowing would be limited when he was in public. Instead, he'd keep working on digging deeper into Al Saalihin, which was proving to be much more difficult than he'd anticipated. None of his sources were willing to talk, not even deep background.

The determination not to take pity on himself lasted until the White House press briefing of that morning started, and Henley watched live as reporters shouted question after question at Levar.

"Can you confirm that Henley Platt's articles about the issues within the Secret Service contributed to the assassination of President Markinson?"

Levar's face was tight, his jaw set in a determined expression. "The FBI investigation into the assassination has revealed that Mr. Platt's articles were one of the many sources the bomber used in preparing for the assassination."

"Will either the White House or the FBI subpoena Henley Platt to reveal his sources?"

"As this is an ongoing investigation, the FBI will explore all options necessary to get information."

"Will the Secret Service take measures to prevent a similar attack from happening on President Shafer?"

"The White House does not comment on Secret Service security details to protect the integrity of the agents who serve and the safety of everyone under their charge."

"Don't you think in this specific circumstance that question deserves an answer? How can the American people be sure that this won't happen again?"

"The White House does not comment on Secret Service policy. Recent events are no reason to deviate from that policy."

The questions went on and on, and Henley's blood boiled as he watched Levar take hit after hit. Had the White House provided Henley Platt with information a year ago? Had President Shafer been aware of the limitations in the Secret Service protection? Had the topic ever come up between President Shafer and President Markinson when Shafer had still been vice president? Did the White House know who Henley's source had been?

Levar had to dodge bullet after bullet, and even though he stayed calm and professional, his cheeks heated up, and he kept touching his scar. Was Henley the only one who noticed that? As the briefing continued, he did it more and more until his hand rested on his chest, his fingertips rubbing the scar. Was it a comforting gesture? An unconscious way he'd taught himself to deal with stress?

Henley could barely keep watching, but he had to. This torturous experience for Levar was on him. Technically it might not be his fault, as obviously, he hadn't killed Markinson, but he sure as hell had contributed to it.

And so his eyes stayed glued to the TV until finally,

Levar called it quits and the cameras went off. God, that had been awful. Guilt flooded Henley. As if Levar didn't have enough to deal with, Henley had made his load even heavier. Funny how that thought bothered him almost as much as the idea that something he'd written years ago had contributed to an assassination.

He'd better call his mom. He didn't want her to have to find out through the news.

"Hey, honey," his mom answered. "I saw the news."

Damn. Too late. "I'm sorry, Mom, I would've—"

"Nonsense. I happened to have CNN on. Otherwise, I wouldn't have caught it. Is it true?"

"The gist of it, yes. Obviously, I never meant for this to happen."

His mom clicked her tongue. "Of course not. And let's not forget that at the end of the day, it's not your job to keep the president safe. That's what the Secret Service is for."

"If the president lets them do their job."

"So that part was on the president. None of this is on you, honey."

Everyone should have a mom like his, unfailingly supportive. "Thank you, Mom. It's so good to hear your voice."

"Not a lot of friendly voices at the moment, I suppose?"

Henley thought of Levar. "No, but I have the support of the people I care about most."

"Good. And if your friends aren't on your side in this, you need better friends."

"Mom, the other day, when I called you after Logan had broken up with me... You said I don't lean on people. What did you mean?"

His mom was quiet for a while. "Are you sure this is the right time to talk about that?"

"I need to know."

His mom sighed, a worried sigh. "Honey, when your father left us, it didn't just break me. It devastated you as well. You were close with your dad, and him walking out on you and never looking back crushed your sense of safety."

Henley's throat tightened. Why had he wanted to know again?

"You were fifteen, but you grew up in a matter of days. You were the oldest, and you stepped up, taking care of Joel and Sabina while I rebuilt our life. I leaned hard on you, Henley. Maybe too hard. We all did. And you were so strong, so mature, that I never questioned myself if you could handle it."

"Mom, you had no choice. None of us did. He left, and you did what you had to do to survive...and so did I."

"I know you did, but in hindsight, I have to wonder how it affected you... I think what you learned was that you couldn't trust people, that you couldn't afford to emotionally invest in them again because they could leave you. You figured that if people relied on you, it was much safer than the other way around. You've kept yourself at an emotional distance, honey. Not from me or Joel and Sabina but from others. From your partners, your friends."

Henley closed his eyes, his mom's words sinking into him, penetrating his heart. "That doesn't make me sound like a nice person."

"You have such a big, caring heart, honey. You're the strongest man I know. You're just scared of getting hurt again, and who could blame you after what your father did?"

Henley wiped away a tear that had spilled. "I don't understand it, Mom. How could he do that? How could he turn his back on us? I never saw it coming."

"Neither did I. Looking back, I recognized signals, but I never expected this. He was a good dad right up until the day he left."

"You know what hurt the most? That he left us. I know that sounds harsh, but people get divorced. I understand that. But if he was tired of being married, if he'd fallen out of love with you, why did he also abandon us? He never even contacted us."

"That's the part that still upsets me the most as well. What kind of man walks out on his kids? I wish I could help you understand, but I can't, since it still doesn't make sense to me, all these years later."

Henley rubbed his eyes. "But you think that's what fucked me up? Him leaving?"

"I hate to be blunt, but how could it not? How could something as traumatic as that leave you unaffected?"

"So that's why I haven't been able to keep a relationship?"

Another long pause. "That and you tend to go for a certain type."

Henley frowned. "I have a type?"

"All your partners have been super nice and smart. Accomplished in their own fields. But they've also been… soft. They all leaned on you, never the other way around. And with every relationship, you pulled back further."

Was she right? Her words were like daggers, each one hitting him deeper. They hurt, yet somehow, the pain felt good. Light. Freeing. It seemed to indicate that even if he couldn't fully admit it yet, she was on the right track. "I don't like how that makes me sound."

"You did the best you could, honey, but I think it's time for you to have an honest look at yourself and decide if this is how you want to live your life. You deserve better. You deserve more."

"Mom...thank you. Thank you for loving me and for being there."

"Oh honey, loving you is so damn easy. You're such a wonderful man...and one day, you'll meet someone who loves you the way you are, even with your faults and weaknesses. Someone you can be yourself with. Someone you trust enough to lean on."

For minutes after he'd ended the call, Henley sat with his phone in his hand, his mom's words playing through his head. Was she right? Had he unknowingly sabotaged his relationships by closing himself off? With Logan, he could see it. The trust hadn't been there from the start. He'd liked him and had certainly liked the sex and the convenience of having a boyfriend, but he'd never trusted him enough to truly share himself.

But when he looked farther back, his heart grew cold. The pattern was there, and rather than improving, it had become stronger over the years. With every relationship that had ended, he'd closed himself off more and more. How had he never realized this? It was so fucking obvious that shame filled him. No, he hadn't done it on purpose, but how the fuck had he missed this?

Levar was different, though. Henley had leaned on him, hadn't he? He'd allowed Levar to take care of him, more than he'd ever permitted Logan. Hell, he'd bawled his eyes out in front of Levar. And Levar wasn't even his boyfriend. Or maybe that was why it had been easier—because he wasn't. Had he unconsciously decided the risk was less because they couldn't be in a relationship anyway? This was all so fucking complicated.

He lasted an hour before he gave in and called him. Levar picked up almost immediately. "Hey."

"That was brutal this morning."

"You watched? I saw your paper sent a replacement."

Henley chuckled wryly. "Yeah, my editor didn't think it was a good idea for me to show up. Imagine that."

"Smart choice."

"I'm sorry," Henley said softly. "I know those are empty words, meaningless ones, but I need to say them. I'm sorry."

Levar let out a deep sigh. "None of this is your fault. I've told you before, but I will say it again. You were doing your job. I get that you feel guilty. I'd feel the same in your shoes, but just because you *feel* responsible doesn't mean you are."

Wasn't that the truth? "Rationally, I know the blame always lies with the perpetrator, in this case the bomber or the terrorist organization behind him. But emotionally, it's going to take me a while to shake off the guilt that I somehow contributed to this."

"They didn't decide to kill Markinson based on your article. That wouldn't make sense at all. They must have made him a target, then done research on how to get to him, and that's where your analysis came in. Would Markinson still be alive if you hadn't written that article? I don't know. Fact is that he knew about it and didn't feel it warranted a higher budget, so in a way, he was responsible as well."

Henley rubbed his temples. "How long do you think this will take to die down?"

"That depends on how much the Secret Service finds out in the next few days and weeks and how much of that they'll release to the public. If they find more evidence that suggests an important role for your article, it could take a while. If it turns out it was just one in a long list of sources, it may die down quickly."

"Yeah, figures. You did good, though. You remained very calm and professional."

Levar stayed silent for such a long time that Henley checked to make sure the connection hadn't been broken somehow.

"It bothers me that you're being blamed," Levar finally said. "Especially because we both know how big Markinson's role in all this was. He knew security for big events he attended wasn't as it should've been, and he didn't care. He forced the Secret Service to let people in without a thorough screening. And yet I can't say that. I talked to Calix about it, but he made it crystal clear."

"The White House doesn't comment on Secret Service policy," Henley said softly, his heart somehow lighter with the knowledge Levar had wanted to defend him.

"Yeah. Especially not after an event like this. The less information outsiders have about the president's protection or any changes in security policy after the assassination, the better. We wouldn't want Al Saalihin or any other terrorist organization to get ideas about trying this again."

"I get it, and it's the right call."

"So was publishing your articles. Your source revealed much more than you put on paper, so you have nothing to blame yourself for."

"Too bad that in the end, it didn't matter."

"You don't know that. You don't know what mattered and what didn't. But even if it did, that wasn't your responsibility. What you reported were facts. It was the truth. An uncomfortable truth and one that the White House, let alone the Secret Service, would've very much preferred to keep under wraps, but the truth nonetheless."

Levar's words lightened Henley's heart even more. Why would fate be so cruel to give him this special connection with the one guy he couldn't pursue? Or was he so attracted to him because it was safe somehow? "Thank you. And thank you for taking the time to talk to me."

"Henley..." Levar was quiet for a few beats. "Please keep in mind that your calls to my phone are part of the official White House phone logs."

He didn't need to say more. Henley understood the implied warning all too well. He couldn't call him like this too often. Even though they'd be careful with what they said and wouldn't cross any lines, outsiders wouldn't know that, and the appearance would be bad for both of them. "I know. I won't bother you anymore."

"You're not bothering me."

Henley let out another deep sigh. "Bad choice of words. I understand what you're saying, Levar. I get it, and you're absolutely right. It's just that..."

"Yeah," Levar said softly. "I wish things were different too."

30

He shouldn't be here. Levar made no illusions about the stupidity of him showing up again at Henley's apartment, and yet here he was. He pushed down the million reasons why this was a bad, bad idea. Henley needed him. Again. And Levar was unable to resist, especially knowing how rare it was for Henley to be this vulnerable.

He'd sounded so sad when he called, so defeated and down. What did it say about Levar that that had gotten to him? If Henley had outright asked him to stop by, he would've said no. If Henley had asked for anything from Levar, chances were he would've been able to hold him off. But he hadn't. He hadn't asked, hadn't demanded, hadn't expected anything. He'd called, and somehow, he'd given Levar the impression that even listening to him had been enough for Henley. How could he not ache for him, knowing how much he hurt?

Levar probably should've warned Henley he was coming. Showing up unannounced was even stupider than calling and asking if Henley wanted him to come over. So why hadn't he? Maybe because if he had asked, Henley would've pointed out that he shouldn't, and Levar hadn't wanted to give him that opportunity. He hadn't wanted to hear it because he'd heard it all before. He *knew*.

Before he could talk himself out of it, he knocked on the door, his heart racing as he waited. When the door opened, Henley looked baffled to see him. "Levar? What are you...?"

"Can I come in?"

For one horrible moment, Levar feared he had misjudged the situation. What if Henley had sought comfort with someone else? What if he had someone he could be with?

But Henley opened the door wide and gestured. "Of course."

They stood awkwardly in the hallway, gazing at each other. The AC was turned down as low as before, and Levar shivered. Or was that because of nerves?

"I had to come," Levar finally said, his voice barely more than a whisper. "I couldn't stay away."

"Levar..."

"I know. You don't need to tell me. I know."

They stared some more, and then Henley hugged him, and Levar went willingly. The first kiss was gentle, almost sweet, Henley tenderly exploring Levar's lips as their bodies melted against each other.

"I can't believe you're here," Henley whispered against his mouth. "Again."

"I can't believe I came. Again."

Henley cupped his cheek, the gesture infinitesimally tender. "We don't have to do anything. You being here is enough."

Levar leaned into his touch. "I know."

Hand in hand, they walked into the living room, which

was even more of a mess than last time. "If I'd known you'd come by..." Henley bit his lip, a bit embarrassed.

Levar smiled at him. "You would've impressed me with your cleaning skills? Because nothing is sexier than a man who knows his way around a vacuum cleaner and Lysol?"

Henley laughed. "Something like that. The truth is that I'm a slob, at least when it comes to my personal life."

Levar waved his hand dismissively. "So am I, mostly due to lack of time. If I weren't rooming with Rhett, I'd need to hire a cleaner, but he keeps our place immaculate."

"Maybe I need to find me a roommate like that."

"Or a new partner." Levar wasn't even sure why he'd said that.

Henley's smile held sadness. "I'm not interested in anyone else."

Anyone else. That implied he was interested in Levar, right? God, the games they played. The clever words and the teasing, the flirting and the banter. What did all of it mean? At the end of the day, friendship was the best they could do, and even that was debatable. "Yeah, same," he said.

Henley sank onto the couch, then tugged at Levar's hand until he followed his example. As soon as he sat down, Henley pulled him against him, then rolled both of them onto their sides so they faced each other. "I meant what I said. You being here is enough. More than anything, I didn't want to be alone. Not today."

"More than anything, I didn't want you to be alone today. I'm sorry. I know this is —"

Henley placed a finger on his lips. "No more talk about politics or work or any of it. Let's leave the world outside for a bit. Do you think we can do that?"

"Yeah, we can do that."

Henley traced Levar's nose with his index finger. "You

have such a cute nose." He tapped the tip. "It makes me want to play boop-boop games with you, just like I do with my nephew and nieces."

Levar smiled. "How many do you have?"

"Four. One nephew, three nieces. The one boy is from my brother, Joel, the three girls from my sister, Sabina. They're all under ten years old. I'm their uncle who spoils them rotten. Very stereotypical, I know, but what can I say? It works for all of us. I'm the world's worst babysitter, since I genuinely don't give a crap about them eating healthy or all of that. So I get to spoil them and have fun with them, then deliver them back to their parents to do the serious stuff."

Levar laughed. "I bet they love you to pieces. I would've loved an uncle like that."

"No siblings?"

"One. An older brother, but he doesn't have kids. He's... he was diagnosed with autism years ago, and while he's successful in his career and has a girlfriend, they've decided they don't want kids. He is very set in his routines and needs that structure, so he's scared that having a child would be too disruptive for him and he wouldn't be able to adjust to it."

"I can respect that choice," Henley said. "I wish there wasn't such a taboo in our society on people deciding not to have kids for whatever reason. I hate it when people get the guilt trip or are being shamed for making a choice like that. It's not like buying a car or a house that you regret later. Having a child is irreversible, so I always appreciate it when people make that decision consciously."

"Would you ever want kids?"

Henley looked pensive. "You know, up until a few months ago, I would've vehemently said no. But lately, I've been wondering. Maybe it's because I'm getting older, I don't know."

His eyes narrowed slightly as he looked at Levar, who merely grinned. "No old man jokes, I promise. But what has changed? Is it because of your last relationship?"

"I wouldn't have wanted to have kids with Logan, that's for sure. Our relationship would've never survived that. But today, I realized it might be time to reprioritize."

Levar frowned. "Reprioritize? I'm not sure what you mean."

Henley's eyes were a little sad as he met Levar's gaze. "Today was a reminder that my career is finite. Maybe even fragile. Oh, I'm not going to get fired over this. I have the full support of my paper, as I should in this case. But as a reporter, I'm only one scandal away from getting sacked, and it's not easy to come back from that. Without my career, what would I have? What would be left of me?"

Talking like this, their faces only inches apart and their bodies practically plastered against each other, was strangely intimate. Maybe even more than kissing or having sex. Levar felt vulnerable, stripped of his defenses, and Henley appeared open as well.

"You're much more than your career," he said. "Otherwise, I wouldn't be here."

"If not for my career, we might be more," Henley said, and Levar couldn't argue with that. Henley sighed. "But I get what you're saying. I used to feel the same way, but...I don't know. I'm not feeling myself today. I had a conversation with my mom, and it's... It's shaken me up, that's for certain."

Levar stroked his jawline with his finger, Henley's stubble a pleasant rasp. "Do you think you need to talk to someone?"

"Maybe. Probably. I tried therapy after New York, but I

didn't get much from it. In all fairness, that was most likely due to me not being invested in it. I went because my editor told me to, not because I wanted to talk."

Levar smiled a little. "That sounds like you, all right. Maybe you should give it another try?"

"Talking about it makes me so sad and frustrated. Angry. Like grieving all over again for what we lost that day. Then again, my mom suggested I might have some other issues as well, so I probably should force myself to go."

Levar stayed silent. There was little he could say to Henley that the man didn't know himself. And he was right. Therapy was useless unless someone wanted it, unless he was willing to invest his energy in it.

The silence between them lasted, but Levar didn't feel uncomfortable as he kept looking at Henley. Somehow, being together was enough right now, though why, he couldn't even explain. Something about being in Henley's presence made him feel better, made the heavy weight on his chest lighter.

He must've dozed off at some point, jolting awake when Henley said, "You need sleep."

Levar blinked a few times. "I think I *was* sleeping."

Henley's smile was sweet. "It was fun watching your eyes flutter shut. You were clearly fighting it."

Yeah, no shit. Even now, Levar could barely resist the temptation to close his eyes again. "I'm exhausted."

"Stay."

That had Levar's eyes wide open.

"Stay. Just tonight. No sex, nothing weird. Just sleep. Together."

He shouldn't. "Yes."

Henley rolled off the couch first, then pulled Levar up

and into his arms. His hug was gentle, comforting. "Thank you. Thank you for everything."

Levar wrapped his arms tightly around Henley's neck, smiling when Henley bent over and lifted him into his arms. Such a sweet, romantic gesture. If only...

If only they weren't who they were. If only they didn't have the jobs they had. If only...

For now, this would have to be enough. Being together, if only for a night.

31

Henley woke up early, and it took him a few moments to figure out who was plastered against him. Levar. In his bed. His arm was flung around Henley's waist as if preventing him from escaping, and his head was on Henley's shoulder. Henley's morning wood presented itself with fervor, but he ignored it, instead giving preference to the mushy feelings in his belly.

Levar was a snuggler. He was softly snoring, little puffs of air and smacking noises, and Henley found it the most adorable thing ever. How was it possible that he liked from Levar what had irritated him from previous bed partners? Not something he wanted to think about too long.

Last night had been perfect. No pressure, no demands, just Levar being there and holding him, even though he'd been exhausted himself. Luckily, they'd both slept through the night, so at least Henley hadn't robbed him of his sleep. Fuck knew the man would need it in his job.

But it was six in the morning, which meant he'd have to wake him up. Levar couldn't afford to be late at work, and he'd want to take a shower for sure. He caressed his hair. "Time to wake up, baby," he whispered.

Levar stirred, his body going tense for a moment. "What time is it?" he mumbled sleepily.

"Six."

"Oh god. I could sleep for hours more."

"I know."

Levar snuggled closer, and Henley's heart warmed. Levar wasn't ashamed of what had happened. Somehow, it would've hurt Henley had he jumped out of bed and left him. Moreover, he was as hard as Henley, and he wasn't hiding that either.

"Did you sleep well?" Levar asked.

"Mmm, perfect. You're a little snuggler, aren't you?"

"Does it bother you?"

"Not at all." To prove his words, Henley tightened his arm around Levar. "I'd be happy to lie like this all day."

Except he couldn't. Not just now, but ever. Being together wasn't an option for them, and that thought sobered him.

"Is it okay if I take a shower?"

"Of course. If you don't want to go home, I'm sure I have a shirt you can borrow. It might be a little loose around your neck, but if you wear a tie, no one will notice."

"Please tell me you have one without pink flamingos on the collar."

Henley smiled. "I do."

"Good, because that would be hard to explain if people saw it. I'm very much not a pink flamingos guy."

"You have no idea what you're missing."

Levar chuckled. "I'll take your word for it."

"We could shower together?" Henley said after a pause.

"Henley..."

He heard the quiet protest in that one word. "You're already here anyway. What does it matter now? At least let us get the most out of this moment."

Levar groaned. "You're such a bad influence...and way too persuasive for your own good."

"I heard 'yes, please' in that, correct?"

Levar laughed. "Yes, asshole. We can take a shower together."

He rolled off Henley, and Henley stretched out and switched on the light on the bedside table. He got his first look of a barely awake Levar, who was propped up on his elbow, gazing at Henley. His hair was too short to look messy, but his face still had crinkles, and his eyes were sleepy.

"You're adorable when you just wake up," Henley said.

"I'm adorable, period."

"True. Let me rephrase that. You're even more adorable when you just wake up."

Levar's eyes sparkled. "Better. You're a morning person, aren't you?"

"Yup. The second my alarm goes off, my eyes are open, and my brain fires up instantly."

"I need about two minutes or so, but then I'm up and at 'em. Good thing you caught me before I was fully awake, or I might not have taken you up on your offer for a shower."

"You severely underestimate my powers of persuasion."

"You severely underestimate both my willpower and my stubbornness." Then his face softened. "Though both seem to be in short supply when I'm with you."

They stared at each other, the all-too-familiar electricity zinging. They moved at the same time, reaching for each other, and then their mouths slammed together. Their kiss had no finesse. It was all tongues and lips, hot wetness that made Henley's cock even harder.

Henley hauled Levar atop his body, his hands possessively splaying across his ass cheeks. He wasn't wearing panties. Why the hell wasn't he wearing panties? These white Calvin Kleins were so fucking boring on him.

He broke off the kiss, panting. "I disapprove of your choice of underwear."

Levar's eyes, so hot and heated before, mellowed. "I only occasionally wear panties to work."

"You should. It should be a rule that you never wear anything else because they look so damn hot and sexy on you."

"Thank you."

Levar had barely gotten that out when Henley took his bottom lip between his teeth and sucked. Oh, the sound Levar made. Sexy. Sinful. His gorgeous blue eyes darkened again, showing the same lust that thundered through Henley's veins. He surged back into his mouth, the kiss so frantic their teeth clacked.

His hands slipped under Levar's underwear, the skin of his ass cheeks so soft. He kneaded as he kept kissing him, moaning when Levar brought his weight down on his cock and ground into him. This time, he wanted more. "Fuck me," he panted against his lips. "Please, baby, fuck me."

For a terrifying moment, he thought Levar would turn him down, but instead, he said, "I'm fine the other way around as well."

"No. Need to feel you."

"I don't have much time."

Henley snorted. "With how hard I am, I'm gonna blow my load in no time."

That made Levar chuckle. "Lube and condom?"

Henley gestured at the bedside table. Levar rolled off him, and he missed the contact instantly, a shiver racking his body. He dragged down his underwear, and his cock slapped against his stomach.

"I love that sound," Levar said huskily. He rolled back, throwing the lube and the condom onto the bed. "I also love that look. You're gorgeous."

His eyes hungrily took in Henley's body, and almost automatically, Henley arched his back and slowly fisted his cock.

"Mmm," Levar hummed in approval. He made quick work of his own underwear, and this time when he pulled Henley against him, no more barriers existed between them. Their kiss was softer now, deeper, as heated skin met heated skin and hard cock met his equally aroused counterpart. Levar slid half off him, then broke off the kiss and grabbed the lube. With quick moves, he squirted out some onto his fingers, and without hesitation, he found Henley's ass.

Henley pulled up his legs, spreading wide for him. With strangers, he preferred to top, but with Levar, he had no issues bottoming. He trusted him. He had from the beginning. Strangely enough, it didn't bother him that they didn't have time to explore each other's bodies at an unhurried pace. He needed him, and this way, he didn't have to wait.

He let him in with ease, his body eagerly anticipating what was coming. Levar brought his slick finger inside him, first one, then two. Their eyes met, and Henley shuddered.

"You good?" Levar checked, and Henley loved him for it. This amazing man was always so considerate. So tender and caring. So giving. This time, Henley would make sure Levar found pleasure as well.

"Impatient."

Levar smiled. "That makes two of us."

Three fingers burned, but he took it. It had been a while, and his ass was reminding him, but it was fine. He'd feel it the rest of the day for sure, but that thought wasn't a deterrent either. He didn't have to say he was ready. Levar seemed to feel it, pulling back his fingers and wiping them on the sheets, then picking up the condom. He put it on with practiced moves, then slicked himself up.

"How?" Levar asked.

"Like this."

Levar nodded as he took position between Henley's legs. When he pressed against Henley's hole, Henley breathed out and let him in. Those first few seconds always stung, but Levar waited and gave him time to adjust. Then he sank in with shallow thrusts, deeper and deeper until Henley's ass was on fire, burning and glowing with the sensation of being fucked for the first time in months.

It felt right, like Levar belonged there. The tightness in Henley's chest loosened with every thrust, with every inch Levar sank farther inside him, as if the discomfort grounded him and distracted him from everything he'd been struggling with.

"God, you're tight. I'm not hurting you? Your body is squeezing me like it never wants to let go."

"You're saying it as if it's a bad thing."

Levar's eyes heated up. "The way you're feeling, it's good I have to leave in a few minutes, or we'd be doing this all day."

The words that bubbled up inside Henley would ruin everything. They'd remind them that this could never work, and he didn't want to think of that right now. So instead, he dragged down Levar's head and kissed him, pouring every ounce of his frustration into his mouth, his lips, his tongue. Levar kissed him back, surging into Henley's mouth until

Henley wasn't sure anymore where he ended and Levar began.

His moves started gentle and slow, then picked up speed until Levar ran out of breath. Their heads an inch apart, stealing each other's breath, they moved as one. Levar gave, and Henley took. He met him thrust for thrust, inch for inch, his needy ass begging for more. All pain and discomfort were gone, his body lighting up like fireworks now, every move driving him higher and higher.

Other words pushed forward now. Begging words. Pleading ones. He feared he'd say too much still, and all he allowed were sounds. His body vibrated as whimpers pushed past his lips, breathy groans and shaky, choked sounds in the back of his throat. "Fuck... Lev... So good."

His pulse beat in his ears, in his cock, in his heavy balls, so full and tight. His hips lifted off the bed, meeting Levar's thrusts. "Close," Levar warned him between clenched teeth.

"Same."

Henley wrapped his hand around his dick and forgot about teasing himself. He needed to come. Right fucking now, the pleasure almost unbearable. His eyes snapped close, the sensations too overwhelming. Levar's pants danced over his heated skin, interspersed with low moans that had Henley's belly quiver.

Levar sped up, his strokes becoming faster and jerkier. Henley tightened his grip on himself. One, two tugs and then he flew. Levar slammed into him, but Henley was already gone, his cock jerking in his hand, his body taut as a bow as he emptied his balls into his hand, spilling between them with rope after rope of cum.

Inside him, Levar's release spurted hot into the condom, and Henley mourned the thin barrier between them. He'd never been the type to appreciate the sensation of fresh cum in his ass, mostly because it was such a fucking mess to clean up, but with Levar, he wanted to feel it. He wanted to feel everything.

Levar slumped on top of him, and he held him. Silence descended as their heaving chests grew quieter, and the sweat on their bodies evaporated. Henley had so much he wanted to say, but he couldn't voice any of it. So instead, he held Levar close and pressed his mouth against the scar on his neck. "Thank you."

32

Would it ever get old, working in the White House? Technically, the West Wing wasn't the actual White House, but still. That building was only a short walk through the Colonnade—the forty-two-second commute, staffers called it—and its grandeur spilled into all the surrounding buildings. Would he ever get to the point where he was so used to this that walking into the Oval Office didn't fill him with a sense of awe? Maybe, but if so, Levar was nowhere near that point yet.

After a rocky start—completely understandable, considering the chaos of how they'd made the transition from the vice presidency to the presidency—staff briefings were now, three weeks in, running efficiently. Calix sent them the notes at seven AM every workday, and the meeting started at nine sharp. Levar appreciated that Calix had brought so much structure and organization into the workplace. It made navigating the insanity of their jobs a little easier.

Staff briefings usually included Calix, Levar, and a handful of senior advisors. Some of those positions still had to be filled, so the group would maybe grow with a few people more, but at least the small size made for short, effective meetings right now. The president attended whenever necessary. They usually held them in the Cabinet Room, but when the president was sitting in, like today, they gathered in the Oval Office.

"Let's get started," Calix said. "First point on the agenda. The president and his family will move into the residence tomorrow."

President Shafer nodded. "We offered Mrs. Markinson more time to make the transition to civilian life, but she indicated she wanted to leave the White House as soon as possible. Her belongings were moved out yesterday, and our things are being moved in today."

"I'll announce it in this morning's briefing." Levar made a note on his legal pad. "Can I get some details about personal touches that have been made to the residence?"

Calix nodded. "I've already spoken to the head usher. He will bring you up to speed on some of the furnishings and paintings the first lady has picked out."

The president looked a little uncomfortable. "It feels silly to talk about paintings and curtains when the reason we're moving in is so sad."

"I understand, sir, and I even agree, but the press will ask. I'd rather have answers for them."

"Fair enough," the president said. "Just downplay it as much as you can. I'd like the focus to be on the content, not the outward stuff. It will only distract from our message."

"And that brings us to one of the key decisions we'll have to make over the next few weeks," Calix said. "We'll have to name a vice president. And with all due respect, but we'll have to be fast about it too."

The president let out a wry chuckle. "What Calix doesn't want to say but is implying is that we are one red steak too much for me away from a Republican president, considering the Speaker of the House is a Republican. Good thing my wife is always on my case about eating healthy and working out."

That earned him a round of chuckles, including Levar's. He appreciated the president's dry sense of humor.

"We've come up with a shortlist, but for obvious reasons, this cannot leak. Levar, I'm counting on you to immediately let us know if the press catches wind of any of the names," Calix said.

"I will, but keep in mind that if the shortlist contains names of people everyone would expect to be on that list, the press will speculate about them anyway, even if technically no one has leaked their names."

"Of course, and we have a few of the usual suspects on the list for sure. But we also have some people who may not seem a logical choice, and those are the ones we'd like to keep out of the press for now."

"The choice won't be as straightforward as we'd like," the president said. "Here, as in all things, politics will play a crucial role. As much as I have my ideas and preferences about my vice president, the reality is that it will have to be someone who can get confirmed in the House and the Senate, and that won't be easy. He or she will almost automatically be my next running mate, and thus the most logical candidate for the elections after I've fulfilled my term limits. The Republicans know this, so if we propose too strong a candidate, they will block it for sure. This means we may not be able to get our first or even our second or third choice but will, unfortunately, have to settle for someone who is, at the moment, not as well known."

"Brian is running point on this," Calix said.

Brian nodded. "We're in the process of vetting the people

who are on our shortlist. We've eliminated a few candidates already because we discovered some skeletons in their closets, ranging from votes on important policies, which makes their record debatable, to personal issues that could be a liability. Our main objective is to find a candidate who complements the president in terms of experience and background, and we'd very much like to give preference to a candidate who represents a minority, whether in gender, race, social-economic background, or other aspects."

"Diversity is one of my key pillars," the president said. "I'd like to assemble a staff that is as diverse as possible in every way."

Levar looked around the room and marveled all over again of the group of advisors the president had assembled. For way too long, politics had been the playground for old, straight, white men, but they were changing that. This room represented multiple ethnicities, had men, women, and a transgender man, and when it came to the rainbow, the president's staff covered every possible color combination. More than anything, that made Levar proud.

The White House was by far the most inclusive workplace he'd ever been a part of. The gayest White House ever, the press had already labeled it when Shafer had still been vice president. They'd have a field day with all the new people that were being hired for critical positions. Of course not all of them were on the rainbow, but they were highly diverse, and Levar loved it.

"That's it for today." Calix thanked all those present. "Levar, can you walk with me to my office?"

"Thank you, Mr. President," they all said, then walked out of the Oval Office, past the president's secretary. Levar's stomach cramped as he followed Calix through the hallway to his corner office, where the chief of staff closed the door behind them.

"Am I in trouble?" Levar tried to joke, but Calix wasn't laughing. He pointed toward a chair, and Levar sat. Calix sat down behind his desk.

"I don't know. Are you?"

Levar shifted in his seat. What was this about? It had to be about Henley. God, he'd been so stupid. What was it about him that he couldn't stay away from him? He hadn't seen him again since he'd left Henley's apartment very early in the morning over a week ago. He'd taken a shower after that spectacular round of sex, and then they'd said good-bye with a last kiss. They hadn't spoken, but they had texted. Nothing overly sexy or flirty, but the undertone was there. It was always there.

"Levar, I'm going to be completely honest and upfront with you. I have concerns about your relationship with Henley Platt. Big concerns. I haven't mentioned these to anyone else yet, because I wanted to talk to you first and give you a chance to explain. Please, tell me this is not what I think it is."

Levar had never felt smaller in his life, his shoulders hunching as he took a deep breath. "To be honest, I don't know what it is. We started as friends, but now...I don't know what we are. But yes, I've been seeing him."

Calix's face softened. "I appreciate your honesty, Levar. I hope I don't have to explain to you that a relationship between the two of you can't happen. Not under any circumstance, not with both your jobs."

Levar nodded. "I know. It's a complete conflict of interest." He raised his head and met Calix's eyes. "But I want you to know I've never stepped out of line when it comes to my job. He and I have an understanding about what has to stay between us."

"I'm relieved to hear that. Not that I expected anything else from you. Look, if you had still been on the vice president's staff, it still would've been an issue, but not to the extent it is now. You're the White House press secretary, Levar. You can't have a relationship with a White House correspondent."

"I know."

"I won't offend you by asking for more details. Though as much as I'd like to claim it's none of my business, it really is, considering you work for me. I don't want to lose you, Levar. Please, don't be stupid. Whatever is going on between the two of you, you have to break it off. Even friendship is a gray area. Do you understand me?"

"I do." He swallowed. "I don't want to defend myself, but I just want to say it's more than just chemistry or attraction. He's..."

How could he put into words what was happening between him and Henley when he didn't even know himself? Yes, chemistry and attraction did play a huge role, though that was more how it had gotten started than what was fueling it now. He *liked* him. He really, really liked him. When he was with Henley, he felt...beautiful. Appreciated. Funny and smart and cute and sexy. And good. He felt good when he was with him, and he'd never felt that with anyone else before.

"The fact that feelings are in play makes it even worse," Calix said softly. "And I'm sorry for you. I really am. But it can't happen."

"I promise I'll break things off. Out of curiosity, how did you find out?"

Calix chuckled. "I'm the White House chief of staff. I've

discovered that comes with a shitload of information I didn't have before, so there's not a whole lot I don't know. But in this case, I already had my suspicions earlier, and then a staffer mentioned seeing you two on the train to New York. Combined with how you reacted when we talked about him..."

Levar's stomach roiled. "Thank you for speaking to me directly."

"Levar, I've said it before, and I want to make it crystal clear. We don't want to lose you. You're a crucial member of the team, and we want you to succeed. But this relationship needs to end. Now."

Levar nodded, even as his heart broke into a million pieces. "I'll take care of it."

33

When Henley came home and saw Levar waiting for him by his apartment door, his heart jumped up with joy. But as soon as he caught the expression on Levar's face, that instantly dissipated.

"I'm not going to like this conversation, am I?" Henley said quietly.

"No. Can I come in anyway?"

Henley opened the door and let him in. An hour earlier, Levar had texted if he could stop by, but of course, he hadn't said for what. Henley hadn't been stupid enough to think it would be anything resembling a booty call, but the grave expression on Levar's face promised the exact opposite. As if life didn't suck badly enough, what with the news about his articles and now the FBI leaning on him to reveal his sources. He was expecting a subpoena at any moment now.

"You want something to drink?"

Levar shook his head. "I can't stay."

Yeah, this wasn't good. Henley shoved his hands into his pockets. "Why don't you say what you came here to tell me?"

"I think you know what I'm going to say."

Sadness filled Henley. "Yeah. I think so."

"Calix asked to talk to me today about my relationship with you, and I told him the truth."

Henley swallowed, his throat suddenly tight. "I'm assuming Calix wasn't happy?"

"He told me to end things."

"Kinda hard to end something that never was."

Levar sighed. "Things don't need a label or definition to exist. You and I may not have ever gotten to the phase where we figured out where this was headed or even what it was, but we both know it was more than acquaintances or having a professional relationship, and that's all that matters."

Levar was right. Of course he was. He'd been right from the start, but that didn't make it any easier. "No more friendship, then?"

"Nothing. A professional relationship, that's all we can have." Levar had been almost emotionless so far, but now that façade broke. His eyes filled with sadness, his face mirroring the anguish Henley felt inside. "You know this is not my choice. And I can't even begin to tell you how hard this is."

Henley didn't think but grasped his hand and, when Levar allowed him, laced their fingers together. He brought Levar's hand to his lips and pressed a soft kiss on it. "I do know. I may not be in the same position as you are, but we've been navigating a minefield from the start. And despite telling myself that, despite knowing it had to end, I couldn't do it. So I do understand."

"I didn't want this to happen. I wish..." Levar's voice broke.

"I know."

"I debated with myself all day about what I should do. I

told Calix I'd break things off, but throughout the day, I kept wondering if it was the right call."

Henley frowned. "What do you mean? What other choice would there be?"

"Quitting my job."

The words burst into him like a grenade, and Henley was speechless. Quitting his job? Levar had seriously even considered quitting his job? How was that even possible? How could he have even entertained the possibility? He was the White House press secretary. That was not a job you gave up, not because of a relationship. Especially not because that relationship wasn't even defined.

"You can't quit," he said. "I'd never expect you to."

Levar's smile was sad. "I know you wouldn't, but that's a double-edged sword. On one hand, I appreciate you not expecting me to quit for you, not putting pressure on me in any way. But on the other hand, what does it say about us, about what we have, that it's not worth sacrificing a career for?"

"I don't think it says something about what we have at all. This is not about how much our relationship is worth to you. This is about having a career option you couldn't even have dreamed of years ago, and yet here you are. You've been promoted to the job you've always wanted. The fact that you value that more than exploring whatever is happening between us isn't a judgment on our relationship. It's proof of how much your job means to you, and if it didn't, you wouldn't be the person I..."

The person I had fallen for, he wanted to say. Because he had. Despite their stubborn refusal to use labels, despite their insistence this wasn't a relationship and they weren't boyfriends—and technically, they weren't, since they'd never had so much as a date—he'd still fallen for him. Hard. When had that happened?

It didn't matter. Levar was right. This had to end. His feelings would go away over time. Look at what happened with Logan. Henley had loved him. Maybe not as much as he should, maybe not as much as Logan had wanted him to, or as much as Logan had loved him, but his feelings for him had been valid and real. And yet only a few months later, he didn't even spare him a thought. That was the plus and the downside of feelings. As quickly as they could grow, they could disappear as well, which was exactly why they weren't worth sacrificing a career for.

"The president needs me. I know that sounds like a horrible cliché, but with everything that's going on right now, I can't quit my job. I still don't have a deputy. They've only just hired someone for the vice president's communications office, and we're already struggling to stay afloat as it is. Despite the circumstances, I'm beyond excited that Shafer is now president. The first openly bisexual president in history. I can't walk away from that. This man is going to make history, and I want to be there when he does."

Henley looked at their hands, still laced together. "I agree. The president needs you, and I know you'll do an amazing job. You're making the right call, even though we both hate admitting it."

They stared at each other, their eyes saying everything words couldn't express. Henley tugged on Levar's hand, and he stepped into Henley's embrace. He held him close, breathing in his smell, reveling in the sensation of his body pressed against his own. "I'll miss you," he whispered. "I'll miss you so freaking much."

"I'll miss you too. You have no idea how much I wish things were different."

"We could have been good together."

"We could have been special. We were."

They let go at the same time, and Levar's eyes were as moist as Henley's. Henley gave him a sweet smile as he caressed his cheek. "Promise me one thing. Promise me that if you find someone else, you won't settle for someone who makes you hide who you are. You're beautiful, and the memories I have of you and your sexy lace lingerie are some of the best I have. I'll always treasure that image. Don't settle for anything less."

Levar leaned in and kissed him, a tender, light kiss that nevertheless sent Henley's heart aflutter. "I promise. Thank you for appreciating me the way I am. Take good care of yourself, okay? I worry about you."

"I know you do, and I appreciate it. I promise I'll try."

One last touch, one last look, and then they let go. Without another word, Levar walked out, and Henley closed the door behind him. His apartment suddenly felt cold and empty, and with a sense of complete dejection, he dropped onto his couch, pulled a blanket over himself, and closed his eyes. It would take time, but he would get over this. He always had. Why would this be any different? A few weeks from now, he'd look back on his time with Levar and appreciate the beautiful memories they had made together. All he had to do was be patient and wait it out.

But God, he hoped it wouldn't last long because the cold fist around his heart, clenching his insides until he wanted to scream, was not something he wanted to endure for long.

34

"Let's start," Calix said, and the Cabinet Room grew quiet as the president's chief of staff sat down and looked around the table. "We have a ton to discuss, so let's keep it short and on topic. Levar, why don't you kick things off?"

Levar nodded. "My new deputy is starting today, Ginger Bryant. She comes from the Department of Education's Office of Communications and Outreach. Please give her a week or so to settle in."

"I'm glad we found someone to lighten your load," Calix said.

"Me too." Levar chuckled. "My to-do list was reaching cataclysmic proportions."

"My deputy is starting today as well." Calix gestured to his right side, where a serious-looking black guy was sitting, his notepad ready in front of him. "I'd like you all to meet Terrell Lewis. He and I worked together when I was Senator Shafer's chief of staff, and he worked for Senator Marshall. I'll be catching him up this week, and after that, he and I will decide on a division of duties so we both have a clear caseload of responsibilities."

A chorus of greetings and acknowledgments went around the table, and Terrell smiled at them. "Thank you. I can't tell you how excited I am to work here."

"Wait till you see your office. That excitement will instantly be cut in half," Brian joked.

Terrell grinned, which completely changed his look into something mischievous. This guy had a sense of humor, Levar could tell. He'd need it here. "I saw it. It's about half the size of my previous office, but I think I'll manage. The surrounding real estate is pretty sweet and more than makes up for it."

"Okay, onto the real issues. The Republicans are beyond pissed off that Senator Donaldson and Senator Farrah, the majority leader, have resigned," Calix said with a sigh.

"The Democrats didn't force the majority whip to resign," Sakura, President Shafer's senior political advisor, said. "That came from within the Republican Party itself. They were furious he'd had an affair with Katie Winters not only because they were both married but also because she's a Democrat. And the majority leader dug his own grave, since he knew about the affair and silently condoned it. None of that is on us."

"That may be so, but they're unhappy about the whole thing. Sakura said it looks like Senator Thune will succeed Donaldson and Senator Mackay will become majority leader."

Levar winced. Mackay. Oy. He was a hardliner, an old-school Republican who'd risen to fame in the nineties and still bore a grudge that Bill Clinton hadn't resigned after his impeachment.

Sakura nodded. "My sources on the Hill tell me that the new majority leader and the Speaker of the House are distinctly unhappy about the changes in both their leadership...and in the White House. With President Markinson, they knew what they had, and in some ways, they could work with him. With President Shafer, things have become much more uncertain for them, and his distinctly pro-LGBTQIA+ agenda makes them uncomfortable."

"Well, their homophobia makes me uncomfortable, so there's that," Brian quipped.

Levar chuckled along with everyone else.

"The problem is that right now, they hold one powerful card," Sakura said. "The VP nomination."

"Will they really put that on the table?" Levar asked. "I may sound naïve, but aren't we constitutionally required to have a VP?"

"Yes and no. With the next presidential elections still two years out, but the midterm elections coming up in a few months, they're gonna drag this out as long as they can. Right now, if something were to happen to the president—god forbid—the Speaker of the House would be next in line. That's one of their guys, and so is the one after that. As soon as they confirm a vice president, they're a step farther away from power."

"But if they wait too long, they might lose the majority in the House and the Senate in the midterms," Brian said. "The polls are in our favor. If that happens, the new Congress will confirm the VP, and we might be able to get a much more progressive candidate."

"Which is why they're not gonna wait that long. They'll ask us for candidates, then take their time vetting them, then tell us they reject them and ask us to come up with new ones, and right before the elections, they'll saddle us with the weakest candidate they can find." Sakura's tone had grown sharp.

Damn, that was next-level politics. Levar should be used to it by now, but these kinds of games could still shock him. "What is my response when the press asks me about it?"

Sakura glanced at Calix. "Tell them that the White House is still vetting VP candidates but that we have confidence the Republican leadership will recognize the constitutional importance of affirming a vice presidential candidate when the time comes. Any deliberate delay tactics would be an affront to the memory of President Markinson."

Levar whistled between his teeth at Calix's statement. "That last part is hardball. The press is gonna jump on that. They'll want to know if that's what the Republicans have been doing and if so, if I have proof."

Calix smiled. "It's our warning shot across the bow. They need to know they can't fuck around with us on this."

"And when they press you about it, add that a failure in Republican moral leadership doesn't mean the White House should have to pay the price for that," Terrell said. Levar loved that he was unafraid to speak up.

"I like that," Calix said. "Puts the blame right where it belongs. This whole Donaldson thing is their problem, not ours."

"Katie Winters was on our payroll, though," Brian said. "Not that I want to put the blame with her, but..."

"She wasn't an elected official. Technically, her mistake was lying about the affair and falsifying the official logs. If she'd come clean about it, it wouldn't have been an issue. Clearly, we wouldn't have been happy about it, but she didn't run on a strong pro-family platform," Calix said sharply.

"Clear." Levar scribbled down some notes. He'd also have to ask Nicole to do a recap on the rules about the lines of succession in case he got questions about that.

"One last thing. President Shafer is actively recruiting an advisor on domestic affairs with a Muslim background. He feels this will send a signal to the country that the jihadists don't represent all of Islam. If any of you have any people you know that fit the bill, let me know. Levar, we expect you may get questions about this. We'll work up some language for you."

Damn right, he'd get questions about that, and Levar was grateful for the heads-up.

They quickly checked off the rest of the items and managed to be done in under half an hour. "Levar, can you hang back for a moment?" Calix said after he'd dismissed them.

Levar's stomach clenched. Had he done something wrong again? He'd stayed away from Henley. It had damn near killed him to see Henley sit in the back of the briefing room and not be able to so much as acknowledge him, but he had managed. He hadn't texted him, hadn't called him, had kept his distance in every way. It had cost him, especially after noticing Henley didn't look good, but he'd kept his promise to Calix.

"I'll meet you in my office in a few, Terrell," Calix said, and after his new deputy had left the room, it was just Calix and Levar.

"What's up?" Levar asked, his hands clammy.

Calix's mouth pulled up at the corners. "Relax. I'm not here to scold you."

"No?"

"Do I have reason to?"

Levar immediately shook his head. "I've broken things off and kept my distance."

"God, I sound like your dad." Calix laughed at himself.

"Then what did you want to talk about?"

Calix's eyes softened, and he put a hand on Levar's shoulder. "I wanted to make sure you're okay. You look tired, and I'm worried we're working you too hard."

Levar cast his eyes down. How could he tell Calix what was keeping him up at night without sounding like an idiot? It was so childish, so high school-like.

"Or are you hurting over the breakup?" Calix's voice had dropped to a volume so low no one else walking by would be able to hear it.

"We weren't together, so it's not really a breakup."

"Yeah, somehow, I'm starting to doubt that. Either way, that wasn't what I asked."

Levar shuffled his feet. "It's... I'll be okay. It'll take a little time, but I'll be fine."

The lies he told to himself and others.

Calix squeezed his shoulder. "I'll keep an eye on you, Levar. You're doing a great job, but you know I care as much about you being okay as you doing good work."

Levar met his eyes as he nodded. "Thank you. I appreciate that."

After Calix had walked out, it took him a few minutes to compose himself enough to get back to his office and do his job. Experiencing heartbreak for the first time in his life might be an essential part of growing up and all that crap, but it fucking sucked. He should've gotten this particular experience done and over with years ago. Maybe then he would've known how to handle this.

A week after breaking things off, he was still hurting. No

matter what he did, his heart still beat heavily in his chest, his eyes were one sad thought away from tearing up, and his mood brewed like he had a permanent black cloud hanging over his head. God better have mercy on the reporter who would piss him off today. Things were not looking good.

35

Henley installed himself on the couch for another rerun of NCIS. The show was far from realistic, but who the hell cared? It was mindless entertainment, and fuck knew he could use some of that. Life sucked donkey balls, and a night of TV with a bottle of red and a cheese platter would hopefully distract him from the gloomy reality of being depressed and on his own. Again.

Twelve days had passed since Levar had broken things off, for good this time, and Henley felt fucking awful. Still. How the fuck had he ended up alone? He was turning forty in a few weeks, and here he sat on his boring couch in his boring apartment on a Friday night, about to get sloshed, as the British would say, all by himself. Dark was an understatement for how he was feeling. Permanently pissed off seemed more accurate.

Plus, down. Heartbroken. He'd never been the type to mope, but he sure was moping now. God, he was one glass of wine away from doing a full Bridget Jones rendition of *All By Myself*. He was a sad, sad motherfucker, but he couldn't even muster the energy to care.

The icing on the cake was the subpoena he was about to get slapped with, which would force him to reveal his source for the Secret Service articles. He still hoped the judge would deny it, considering the case his paper had made in their appeal that the articles weren't essential in finding out who had assassinated the president. He wasn't holding his breath, but one never knew.

He'd just poured himself a liberal amount of red wine when his phone rang. The temptation to let it go was almost impossible to resist, but he couldn't. Not with his job. He muttered a curse and answered his phone without even looking at the number. Nine out of ten times, that was useless anyway. He got so many calls from people who weren't in his contacts.

God, he hoped it wasn't a marketing call. He was *so* not in the mood for that. "Hello?"

"Good evening, is this Henley Platt?"

"Yes, it is. What can I do for you?"

"Mr. Platt, this is Professor Rudy James from Georgetown University. I'm the dean of the School for Journalism. We've met on a previous occasion."

Henley sat up straight, putting down his wine. "Yes, I remember. The Edward R. Murrow Awards Dinner last year."

"Yes. I was wondering if you had a few minutes for me."

"Absolutely, Professor James. What can I do for you?"

"We have an upcoming vacancy at our department, and I wanted to gauge your interest. The position would be for assistant professor, and you'd be primarily teaching classes in investigative journalism, as well as mentoring students during their internships."

Henley blinked a few times. Assistant professor at Georgetown University? That was a career move he'd never even considered. "I'm flattered that you would ask me, but if I may be so bold, why me?"

Professor James chuckled. "You cut right to the chase, huh? We have multiple reasons, really. The first is obviously your experience in investigative journalism and the awards you've won. My sources say you're up for a Pulitzer Prize again this year, and I wouldn't be surprised if you walked away with it. That series of articles on the most powerful lobbies in DC was excellent and a classic example of thorough, almost old-fashioned journalism. It embodied the spirit of Woodward and Bernstein, and I'm not exaggerating."

Henley's cheeks grew warm, the feeling spreading to the rest of his body. "Thank you, Professor James. Coming from you, that is high praise."

"Another reason is that I've heard nothing but wonderful feedback from students who have interned with you. You've shown to be a great mentor for young people, and all of them have come back enthusiastic about their career and with an enormous load of experience and wisdom. I've also heard you speak on several occasions, and you're a talented teacher. The online class you did on interview techniques is one I still use in my curriculum."

Henley blew out a long breath. Wow. He hadn't seen this coming. "I'm almost getting embarrassed with all the praise."

"You shouldn't be, but I know it's hard to listen to somebody else sing your praises. Look at it from the bright side. At least you won't have to convince me of your qualifications. I already know you have them."

"So why approach me directly? Why not put the job up on whatever website you guys use and have an open application process?"

"We will if our initial search doesn't result in securing the right candidates. But to be honest, the number of people who are qualified to teach at the level of our school is limited. And most of them are outside of DC and probably won't consider moving here. You're already in town, you know your stuff, and it would be a perfect combination for you with whatever you would choose to do at your paper, since this is not a full-time position."

"How many hours are we talking?"

"On average, two to three days a week. Officially, twenty hours, but it can be a bit more or less depending on the season."

"So what you're saying is that I could combine this with something else, like working at my paper."

"Absolutely. Most of our faculty members have two jobs like that, and to be honest, we prefer it. Once we work in academics full time, it's easy to lose contact with reality and become so isolated we resemble that infamous ivory tower. We want to prepare our students well to work in the real world, and to do that, we need people who have ongoing real-world experience."

"With all due respect, but that's not something I can combine with my position as White House correspondent."

For the first time, Professor James hesitated. "No," he said finally. "And that's a decision you'll have to make. But I'm sure that someone with your résumé would have no trouble whatsoever finding something more suitable."

Henley frowned. "Something more suitable?"

"I didn't mean to suggest that your current position isn't suitable for you," Professor James said quickly. "Though I do wonder if, in the long term, it holds the attraction you're experiencing right now."

"I'm not entirely sure what you mean."

"You made fame as an investigative reporter, and some of your best work has been in politics. But I can't help wondering how much of that is simply because you're working in DC, which, by its very nature, has a political focus. Or is it the politics itself that interests you the most? The White House beat certainly is appealing and glamorous, but it can also be tedious and somewhat of a routine."

Henley chuckled wryly. "With the previous president being assassinated, I'd hardly think routine and tedious is the right description."

"Oh, I agree. But let me ask you this. Wouldn't you love to cover the assassination, dig deep into the Secret Service investigation? Talk to your contacts in all the law enforcement agencies to find out what they know? Maybe give a shot at figuring out who was behind it? Or would you rather sit in the White House briefing room day after day as things in there slowly return to normal? Yes, President Shafer is still fresh and new right now, but how long will he stay that way? How long until his presidency becomes routine for you, a matter of daily reporting on whatever policy proposal the president has and how Congress is either fighting him or supporting him?"

The White House beat as a routine. Henley had never looked at it like that, but now that Professor James had presented it in those terms, he couldn't help but wonder. Did the man have a point? Was that why he'd been off his game the last few weeks?

He'd blamed the Pride Bombing commemoration, the assassination, the whole thing with his Secret Service articles that had blown up and made him the center of attention. The conversation with his mom hadn't helped, as the thought of him being emotionally distant had stuck with him. And obviously, he'd blamed his complicated relationship with Levar and their ultimate breakup. He'd thought all of those were the reasons why he hadn't felt as good about his job as before. But what if Professor James was right?

Questioning his job seemed almost sacrilegious. Being a White House correspondent had been his dream. He could still recall the first time he'd set foot into the James S. Brady Press Briefing Room, filled with a sense of awe he couldn't even put into words. How could one walk those hallowed grounds and not feel impressed?

Yet in a way, he did. The glamour and the novelty had worn off. Sure, every now and then, when he checked into the White House and entered through the lobby, it dawned on him all over again how privileged he was, what an incredible opportunity he had to become part of history. It was hard not to when everything around him reminded him of where he worked, of the importance of that building both in history and for the future. And yet...

"You've given me food for thought. I'll give you that," he finally said.

"I'll take that as a positive development," Professor James said. He had patiently given Henley the time to gather his thoughts. "We're not in an awful hurry. You'd be replacing Professor Milton, who is retiring, and since we know well in advance when his last day will be, we've started the recruiting process early so we can make sure we can find a candidate who fits our high level of standards."

"That's good to hear. So, what would you expect of me? What does this process look like?"

"For now, just think about it. Consider your options and determine if this is something you'd be interested in. We don't expect a firm commitment from you even in the next step. If this is something you're willing to entertain, we'd love to invite you to meet the rest of the faculty, to have a look at the program as it is being taught right now, and decide if you'd be a good fit. We think so, but that doesn't exclude you from making that judgment yourself, obviously."

"Okay, that sounds good. Pretty noncommittal, if I may say so."

"Absolutely."

"Just out of curiosity, am I the only one you're speaking with about this?"

"At this point, yes. We have a shortlist, but you were at the top, and we'll give you at least a week to decide before we move on to our number two."

"Thank you. I'll let you know for sure. I appreciate you approaching me. Not sure if I already said that. It's definitely a privilege to be even asked, considering the stature of your program. It would be a great honor to be a part of that."

He was rambling a little, suddenly filled with a need to express that he damn well realized this job offer was anything but ordinary.

"I appreciate you saying that. Thank you, Mr. Platt, and I look forward to hearing from you."

Henley slowly put his phone down. Teaching journalism at Georgetown? Wasn't that the craziest thing he'd ever considered? Wait, *was* he actually considering it? How could he, after finally realizing his dream? People would kill and die for the job he had, so how could he just walk away?

No, he couldn't. Even thinking about it made his stomach clench. Letting go of his dream would be insanity. He let out a deep sigh and pressed Play on NCIS. Hopefully, Gibbs could distract him enough to forget about how much everything sucked.

36

"Henley, can you tell me why you're here?"

Henley looked around the therapist's office. The room was about as nondescript as he could've imagined. Pale yellow walls, blue carpet, sparse furniture that looked like it came straight from whatever office furniture mail order system every other office ordered from, a couple of framed diplomas on the wall, and of course, the inevitable comfortable chair.

He turned his attention back to the therapist, a surprisingly attractive guy with thick-rimmed glasses. Much younger than Henley would've expected as well. "Is 'because my editor told me to' a valid answer?"

A faint smile tugged at the corners of the man's lips. "I wouldn't say valid, but it's truthful, which is always a good place to start. Why did your editor tell you to go to therapy?"

Yeah, that had been a pleasant conversation. *Not.* If he hadn't respected the hell out of Toby and the man's decades of experience, Henley would've rejected his remarks out of hand. "Henley, I'm worried about you," Toby had said.

The first time, he'd waved dismissively. The second time,

he'd frowned and told him he was fine. Apparently, neither had convinced him, and the third time, Toby had flat out told him he wanted him to sit down and talk to someone. He'd considered that a mere suggestion until he'd been told when and where to report for an appointment. Not a suggestion, then. A directive.

He'd never admit it, but he'd been somewhat relieved Toby had given him no choice. His conversation with Levar about therapy and talking to someone had kept playing in his head, but the step to actually do something about it had been too daunting.

"He says he's worried about me. By the way, what do I call you? Dr. Whitman?"

The therapist shrugged. "Frankly, I really don't care. You can say Doctor, you can say Mr. Whitman, or you can call me Oren."

Henley raised an eyebrow. "Really? The wide collection of diplomas and various awards on the wall suggests otherwise."

Oren's smile widened. "That's not for me. That's for my clients, who, for reasons I probably don't need to explain to you, seem comforted in the knowledge I do hold several degrees and have the qualifications to do this."

Henley chuckled. He could appreciate his dry sense of humor.

"Now that that's settled, maybe you could tell me why your editor was worried about you."

Henley's smile faded. He took a deep breath. "Lately, I've had some setbacks. Apparently, I've been off my game, as he called it, and he thought I needed to talk to someone."

"Did he specify what you needed to talk about? I mean, we could start with your childhood, talk about your misspent youth, your relationship with your parents, and any sexual frustrations you might have, but it may help if you at least have an idea of what the issue is."

Henley liked the man. "My childhood was happy right until the moment my dad walked out on us, but my mom is amazing, and I love her to pieces. I'm out and proud as pansexual, and I have no sexual frustrations other than that I'd like to get laid, but that's probably not going to happen anytime soon, so we might as well talk about something else."

He had thrown in the offhand pansexual comment on purpose. No matter how much Toby could pressure him into talking to someone, he flat out refused to spend his money—or the paper's money, in this case—on someone who wasn't queer-friendly. If he couldn't be himself, he was out—pun intended.

Oren smiled. "That saves me a lot of time. No Freudian analysis for you, then."

"Nope. So I guess I'd better explain what I think is the issue, at least according to my editor."

Oren leaned forward, his blue eyes intense. "Before you do that, Henley, let me make something clear. I'm well aware you didn't book this appointment. I've worked with your paper before, and I'm their standard referral when they feel any of their people need a session. However, that's where your paper's involvement ends. I do not report back to them, not about the content of our conversations nor any possible diagnosis. HIPAA fully applies here, no matter who pays the bill. So I hope you'll talk about whatever is bothering you, but if it's something else than what your editor thinks, that is fine. And if you don't want to talk at all, that's your prerogative as well."

"I had therapy before. I didn't get much from it."

Oren nodded. "That's not uncommon. I can think of many reasons why therapy won't work."

"I was required to go then as well."

"That's definitely one of the main reasons. You can't force someone to talk or even to open themselves up for introspection. People have to be ready and willing. Otherwise, it's a colossal waste of time on both ends."

That, they at least agreed on. "I haven't decided yet if I'm willing to do it this time."

"Fair enough. I figured you would at least give me the courtesy of a first appointment to see if I can change your mind."

Oh, this guy was good. Calm, rational, basically using Henley's arguments before he could employ them himself. He could not only respect that but admire it as well. "The first time I was forced into therapy was after the New York Pride Bombing."

Oren leaned back in his chair, folding his hands and placing them in his lap. "You were present that day."

"I was, and as you can imagine, it was far from a pleasant experience."

"Actually, I can't imagine what that must've been like, but I'll take your word for it."

He wasn't asking questions. Oh, Oren was paying attention all right, definitely listening to every signal Henley was emitting, but he wasn't bombarding him with questions like his previous therapist. Hypocritical as it might be considering his profession, Henley hated it when every answer he gave, every statement he made, every question he asked, was answered with another question. Of course he understood the whole core idea of therapy was to make someone reflect on their lives, on their choices, but that didn't mean he didn't want an outright answer every now and then.

"I was also present when President Markinson was assassinated."

"Wow," Oren said, and somehow, the genuine emotion in his voice comforted Henley.

"Yeah, talk about bad luck."

"Yes and no. For anyone else, yes, I would've said it was bad luck. But considering your job, wouldn't it be reasonable to assume that these kinds of situations, no matter how horrible, are part of what you do?"

"I'm a political reporter, the White House correspondent for my paper, in fact. Politics are not usually this violent."

"True. I guess it would be more applicable to foreign correspondents who are deployed to cover wars. Still, I'd think that being witness to a lot of unpleasant situations is par for the course with a job like yours."

Was it strange that Henley had never looked at it that way? He should have. It was a reasonable viewpoint that his job would expose him to awful affairs. He'd just never been interested in covering wars or any kind of violent events. From the get-go, he'd been more of an investigative reporter, and while he'd read a lot about horrible incidents, he hadn't experienced them. With those two big exceptions, obviously.

"That may be so, but you can't tell me that I should've expected to watch a man get killed right before my very eyes."

"No," Oren said with a sigh. "No one could've expected that, if only because we haven't seen anything like it in almost sixty years. It was a big shock to the whole nation, but to watch it live? Like I said, I can't even imagine."

"It felt like I was observing," Henley said quietly. "When the bomber ran forward, it felt like my brain was detached from my body, like I was watching from afar. I couldn't move, and if my survival had depended on me acting, I would've been dead."

Oren's eyes were kind now. "How far away were you?"

"I don't know. I was sitting to the side in the press section. Some of the reporters who were closer to the front got hit with shrapnel..." He swallowed. "...and body parts. But I was too far away for that. I just sat there, frozen to my seat."

"It must've been pandemonium."

"Everybody was in full-blown panic, people trampling on each other to get out. The explosion was so loud it almost pierced my eardrums. We were inside, so it echoed and filled the hall. I guess people were scared there could be another bomb. Not without reason, not after the Pride Bombing."

"That is still one of the most chilling aspects of that day. The sequence of the bombs was deliberately aimed at making the survivors fleeing from the first blast walk straight into the trap of the second and the third bombs."

Henley nodded. "The goal was to maximize the body count, and they succeeded."

"Why was your editor worried about you? Did he mention that?"

Henley couldn't help but roll his eyes. "He said I was off my game. Distracted, unfocused, delivering sloppy work—his words. Denise, his assistant, had told him I looked like crap. In fact, I think her exact words were that I looked like I hadn't slept in two weeks and hadn't showered in a month. Something along those lines."

Oren cocked his head, his blue eyes never leaving Henley's face. "Had you slept? Showered?"

"Of course I shower. Every day. What kind of question is that?"

"No judgment. Just trying to ascertain the facts here. If your hygiene routine hadn't changed, why would she have said that?"

"I don't know. Because Denise is prone to worrying? She's overreacting? Not because she's a woman," Henley quickly added. "I'm not that stereotypical, but I've known her for a few years, and she does tend to worry about people."

"But she must've had reasons to point it out to her boss. If nothing had changed, why would she have talked to him about you?"

Henley gave a one-shoulder shrug. "I may have worn the same clothes a few times, which I usually don't do, but I didn't feel like doing laundry. Whatever. And I guess I need a haircut, but I just haven't had the time to book an appointment yet."

"Sounds reasonable. How often do you usually get a haircut?"

Geez, the man was asking questions now, wasn't he? Yet they didn't feel like probing questions, the kind of stuff that made him think. But if it made the man happy to know his self-care routines, Henley saw no harm in telling him. "Usually once every three weeks. I'm not a TV reporter, but I do have high visibility in the White House, so I like to look as presentable as possible. And with my hair, keeping it short and neat is a better look."

He dragged a hand through his hair and frowned. It was much longer than usual. How long had it been since his last haircut? His last one had been...before the assassination, for sure. When had he seen his barber? Geez, it was coming up on eight weeks. Had it really been that long? He'd better call him right after this.

"I've met Toby, and he doesn't strike me as the type to make things up," Oren said.

Henley held up his hands in defense. "Hold up. I never said anything about him making things up. All I said was that he drew the wrong conclusions from whatever he saw as evidence, based on his own and his assistant's observations. Just because it's been a while since I've had a haircut doesn't mean they should be worried about me."

"So all she noticed was that your hair was longer."

"Well, I mentioned the sleep thing. She thought I looked like I hadn't slept in forever."

"Have you? Are you sleeping well?"

Henley hesitated. "Define sleeping well."

"In my experience, if you have to define what it means to sleep well, that means you're not."

"I've had a lot on my plate. It's been... The last few months have been intense. I had personal stuff happening, and then the Pride Bombing memorial, the assassination, everything."

"The Pride Bombing memorial? You attended?"

"Yeah. But a few weeks before, I went to New York City to..."

What an amazing weekend that had been. Filming the documentary had been a mixed experience, moments of relief and connection combined with stress and sadness at the memories of that day. But what had made the weekend so extraordinary was the time he'd spent with Levar. And of course, the same could be said for the memorial. The commemorative ceremony itself had been intense, and he'd had to close off his emotions a few times to prevent himself from showing too much. But the time with Levar afterward had been...

God, he missed him. He'd never expected to miss him as

much as he did, not after Logan walking out on him and him barely noticing the difference. How was it possible that a few weeks with Levar had made him miss him so much more than two years with Logan? It didn't make sense. They'd never been boyfriends officially, hadn't lived together. Hell, they'd never even been on an official date. And yet he missed him. Horribly.

"Tough memories?" Oren asked.

Henley shook his head to push down the thoughts of Levar. "That commemoration wasn't easy for those of us who attended."

"I believe you. You also mentioned personal stuff?"

"Yeah, my boyfriend broke up with me and moved out."

Oren's eyes widened slightly. "How long were you guys together?"

"Two years."

"Did you see it coming?"

"In hindsight, yes. At the time, no. But I don't blame him. He wanted a boyfriend who was home, who could spend time with him, who would make him a priority, and that wasn't me. My career is too important to let it be pushed to second place."

Funny, the spiel that had once sounded legitimate now came across as fake, even to himself. His mom's words kept playing through his head.

"Fair enough," Oren said. "Though I am curious why you would mention it as something that had contributed to you not sleeping well if it wasn't the heartbreak it could be."

Why had he mentioned it? Henley frowned. He wasn't even sure. Maybe it had been because he'd been thinking of...

He'd been thinking of Levar. How much he missed Levar. It hit him like a lightning bolt. He was suffering from a broken heart. How incredibly cliché and stupid was that?

He'd already struggled with the aftermath of the Pride Bombing and then with the assassination and the role his articles had played. Discovering he'd self-sabotaged his previous relationships had floored him, as had the realization that his father walking out on him might have fucked him up more than he'd ever dared to admit.

All that had been crappy, but it hadn't been what had kept him up at night. It had been Levar. Losing Levar had been the proverbial straw. He missed him so much it physically ached and consumed his thoughts. He was suffering from a broken heart. How the hell had that happened?

37

He was pathetic. Absolutely, one hundred percent certified pathetic. At least he was honest enough to admit it. Levar popped a Lindor white chocolate truffle into his mouth while his I'm-so-sad playlist started all over. Seconds later, Toni Braxton's amazing voice filled the room as she begged her man to un-break her heart.

Un-break a heart. Now, there was a concept Levar could get behind. He'd pay a damn fortune not to have his heart broken into a million pieces and then stomped on. God, why had he never felt this way before? He'd had boyfriends in high school and one in college, but breakups with them had never resulted in feelings this intense.

Mildly annoyed, maybe. Pissed off the one time his boyfriend had cheated on him because who the fuck risked his relationship with his very cute boyfriend—if Levar did say so himself—to blow the very straight captain of the college football team. Ugh, so pedestrian and cliché. That, more than anything, had angered him, the high school-movie feel of it all. Sans the happy ending, sadly.

And a happy ending seemed out of the realm of possibilities for him entirely. He'd never looked for a relationship, not seriously anyway, but now that he'd lost whatever the fuck this complicated thing with Henley had been, he *ached* for it. How was that possible? How could he miss what hadn't been, what he'd never had?

"It's time for an intervention," Rhett said as he marched into the room. "Alexa, stop."

"Hey, I was listening to this," Levar protested.

"You were wallowing while listening to depressing-as-fuck music. Big difference."

"I worked hard on compiling this playlist, I'll have you know."

Rhett raised an eyebrow. "Babe, you're listening to Toni Braxton. You made a fucking broken-heart playlist."

"I call it my I'm-so-sad playlist."

Rhett rolled his eyes. "Yeah, and none of these songs is gonna make you feel better."

"Nothing is gonna make me feel better," Levar mumbled, and to his credit, Rhett didn't roll his eyes again or even sighed. Instead, he dropped onto the couch next to Levar and curled up to him, then pulled him against him. Usually, it was the other way around, but this felt nice.

"You're really hurting, aren't you?" he asked softly.

"I don't know what's wrong with me that I feel this way, that I still feel this way after three weeks. Maybe I'm overly tired or stressed, and that's making it worse." Jeez, pathetic was way too kind a word for this.

"Or maybe your feelings for Henley are much deeper and stronger than you realized."

He refused to even consider that option because if he did, that meant he had no solution, no way out of this. "I just need a few good nights' sleep."

Rhett shot him a look that made crystal clear how he felt about that statement, but at least he was kind enough not to say it. He stroked Levar's hair. "Why didn't you ever have a serious boyfriend before?"

Levar frowned. "I had Kirk."

"Dude, that was in college. You're thirty-two now. That's ten years of no boyfriends. You're smart, cute, successful, so what's up with that?"

"I never met a guy who was worth investing more time in. Like, the sex was fine, but none of them captivated me enough to try for more."

"Are you that critical? I'm just wondering."

You haven't had a boyfriend either. The words were on the tip of Levar's tongue, but he held them back. They were unfair and way too harsh. Rhett had issues, and none of them were his fault. Confronting him with those simply because he asked questions that put Levar on the defense was low and mean, and he wouldn't become that person.

"Maybe? I don't know. It's just that between scoring regular hookups for the sexual release and having you at home, I guess my needs were met?"

"What do I have to do with anything?"

Levar hesitated. "I guess having you as my roommate meant I had someone to come home to? Someone to take care of?"

He winced as his last words registered. God, he hoped Rhett didn't take it the wrong way.

"You do take good care of me," Rhett said, his voice soft. "You're a nurturer, always have been. I don't know what I would've done without you."

Levar had always been the strongest one in their relationship, but after the bombing, he'd really had to become Rhett's rock. He'd done it with love, helping Rhett find a way to cope with the trauma of that day. They'd done research together, had found him a good therapist, and they'd implemented the man's coping strategies, like picking a scent that grounded him. It was why their apartment always smelled of vanilla, why Rhett always had a vanilla stick on him. Small things, but they'd helped Rhett find his way back.

"You'll never have to find out because I'm not going anywhere. Even if I will have a boyfriend someday, that still doesn't mean I won't be there for you."

Rhett's smile was sweet and sad at the same time. "I know, but it shouldn't have to be that way. I shouldn't need you as much as I do."

"You know I don't mind."

Was that the right thing to say? He could deny Rhett needed him, but that would be a lie.

"I know you don't, and you never made me feel otherwise. It's just... I'm an adult. I have been for a long time. I shouldn't need you to the extent where I'm hindering your love life."

"You're not, babe. You haven't been."

"What if you do get a boyfriend? What would that mean for me?"

"He'll have to accept that you're my roommate, so either he can be down with that, or he can take a hike and become my ex-boyfriend."

"You're so damn loyal." Rhett let out a shaky sigh. "But if you keep putting me first, you'll never find someone."

"Honestly, I've never missed it. Not until..."

"Henley was different."

"He was. He is. He's... I'd say he's perfect for me, if not for the pesky little detail of him being a reporter."

"It's so unfair. It's totally reasonable, don't get me wrong, but it's so unfair that you finally have that connection with someone, and it's with the one person you can't be with."

Levar held on to him tighter. See? This was why he hadn't needed a boyfriend. He had Rhett, who was the best friend in the world and all kinds of empathic and supportive. Because of that, he dared to ask him the one question he wouldn't ever bring up with anyone else. "Do you think... If it's love what I feel for him, if he's like my big love, would he be worth quitting my job for?"

Rhett met his eyes straight on. "I don't know. It sounds like way too big a sacrifice to make, but I don't know the first thing about love. All I know is that you're weeks into the job you always dreamed of. This is the most important thing you'll ever do in your life. You have a seat at the table, a voice with the president. How can you walk away from that?"

The thought made Levar's heart ache, but then he thought of Henley, and his heart hurt even more. "The president needs me. That's the thought that keeps swirling around in my head, and that's what I told Henley as well. After everything that has happened, the president needs people around him he can trust...and I'm one of them. They've entrusted me with a massive responsibility, and to walk away from that would feel like a betrayal to them."

"I agree," Rhett said. "And if that's what you told Henley as well, then why are you still questioning it?"

"Because it fucking hurts. It wasn't supposed to last this long, to hit me this hard, to ache to the point where I do play Toni Braxton on repeat."

"Oh, babe..." Rhett hugged him tight. "I'm so sorry you got your heart broken. Wanna get some vanilla ice cream? I think we have half a tub left in the freezer."

"Yes, please."
Un-break my heart. If only.

38

"Henley!" His mom's face and voice communicated her surprise when she opened the door and found Henley standing there. "What are you doing here?"

That was the big question, wasn't it? For someone who wasn't impulsive in the least, Henley's decision the day before to take a day off and hop onto a plane to Hartford was rather unusual. Both the last-minute decision and the fact that he'd actually gotten on a plane.

"I needed to talk to you," he said.

His mother's hand flew to her heart. Boy, that had sounded rather dramatic, hadn't it? "Nothing serious, no worries," he quickly added.

"Next time, you may wanna lead with that, son. You damn near gave me a heart attack."

"Sorry, Mom," he said meekly. "Can I come in?"

She slapped his shoulder. "Don't ask stupid questions. This is still your home."

He followed her into the cozy kitchen, where she made him a strong cup of coffee, exactly the way he liked it, and a much sweeter one for herself. They settled at the kitchen table, which had always been the place for serious conversations. He'd come out there, age seventeen. It was where he'd told his mom he'd gotten into UConn and would be staying close to home. And they'd been sitting around the kitchen table when his mom had told Henley and his brother and sister that their father was not coming back.

"What's wrong, honey?" his mom asked once she'd sat down as well, looking worried.

"Mom, is it possible to think you want something more than anything, and then when you have it, it turns out it's not like you imagined?"

She studied him, seemingly searching for something. "Why don't you stop asking hypothetical questions and tell me what's bothering you?"

"I don't know what to do." His throat tightened unexpectedly. "I've gotten a job offer, and it's amazing, but it's not what I'd expected or imagined for myself, and I have the job I always dreamed of, except..."

She took his hand in hers, the firmness of her touch steadying him. "Except it's not what you imagined it to be?"

"How is that possible, Mom? I don't understand it. How can I not love covering the White House?"

He was ashamed of the whine in his tone, but his mom showed nothing but understanding. "Because sometimes, how we imagine things is not how they turn out in reality. Trust me, I know all about that. But tell me. How did this come about? What happened?"

What happened... The question of the century. So much had happened, but what had caused what? What had been the catalyst? The Pride Bombing commemorative ceremony? The assassination? Discovering that the bomber used his articles? Or...Levar?

It all came back to Levar. No matter how Henley reasoned, which way he went in his thoughts, he always ended up with Levar. He couldn't stop thinking about him, couldn't stop missing him and aching for him.

"I met someone," he said.

His mom's eyes lit up, and god, he loved her for that. Six exes later, and she was still rooting for him to find true love. "What's their name?"

"It's super complicated. He's... Our jobs aren't compatible."

"He's a competitor?"

"Levar Cousins, Mom. I'm in love with Levar Cousins."

His mom's mouth dropped open for a moment, but then she caught herself. "Oh, honey..."

"Yeah, tell me about it."

"Why don't you tell me about it? About him?"

"He's..." Henley couldn't help smiling as he thought of Levar. "You'd love him, Mom. He's smart and passionate, funny and caring. He's strong and doesn't take crap from anyone. But above all, he's kind and so sweet and nurturing. When that whole shit storm went down about my articles, he came over to my place and took care of me."

"He took care of you?"

Henley nodded. "He drew me a bath, and then he made me a veggie omelet because I had nothing else in the fridge."

His mom squeezed his hand. "You leaned on him."

"He makes it easy. What does that mean? That I can do with him what I've never done before? Is it because I'm aware of it now? Or is it because of him?"

His mom huffed. "Just because you're aware of a problem doesn't mean it's solved."

"So it's him."

"Is he different than your previous partners?"

Was he? He'd never even known he had a type until his mom had pointed it out. They'd all been weaker than him in some area. Needier. In itself, being needy wasn't wrong, but it had always put him in the position of the provider...and he'd always let them down because he hadn't been able to give them what they truly needed.

"I think so. He's strong and doesn't need me for anything, and I mean that in the good sense."

"Does he like you back?"

"He does, but we can't be together. Our jobs clash, and I understand. He's got the chance of a lifetime, and he can't walk away from that. And I..."

"Ah. Now I understand. He made you take a step back and look at your job differently."

"It's not as glamorous and rewarding as I thought it would be. A lot of it is routine, as someone recently pointed out to me. I'd never thought of it like that before, but he wasn't wrong. And since Levar can't quit—I wouldn't even let him—I've been thinking if maybe I should... Tell me I'm not crazy."

His mother's smile was sweet. "Of course you're not crazy. You're in love. This is what people in love do."

"But am I right? Is it the right thing to do? Is it worth it?"

Her face sobered. "You're asking the wrong person, honey. I loved your father with all I had, and in the end, that wasn't enough. I know that doesn't sound encouraging, but I want to be honest with you. Love is not a guarantee. But if you don't take the chance, you'll miss out on what could've been amazing. And, honey, if I had to make the choice again, I'd marry your father all over again. How could I not when he gave me the three of you? Just because he broke my heart doesn't mean it wasn't worth it."

Henley's eyes grew moist. "A broken heart is the most horrible feeling in the world. I miss him so much, Mom, and we weren't even together. It's like a part of me is missing, and I don't understand how it happened."

His mom teared up as well. "You've never done anything halfway in your life, so when you fall in love, you do it with all your heart."

"But that's why I'm so conflicted about quitting my job. It feels like failing."

"You said you had a job offer?"

Henley told her about the position at Georgetown, and her eyes grew wide. "Assistant professor? Honey, that's amazing! How is that failing?"

"Because I have the job everyone covets, and I'd be walking away from it."

"Does it make you happy?"

The question hit him straight in his heart. Could it really be that simple? He hadn't been happy in a while, not since… He wasn't even sure. Since he'd accepted the job in the first place? Except for when… "Levar makes me happy. I'm happy when I'm with him."

"There's your answer, then."

"That simple?'

"Yes, that simple. Listen to your heart rather than your head. Your heart knows what it wants, even if your head is arguing against it."

"What if I'm too fucked up? What if Logan was right and I am emotionally unavailable?"

His mom shook his head, smiling. "Then you fix it. You seek help, and you work hard to learn how to open up. Didn't you tell me Levar already liked you?"

Henley's heart went all warm and fluttery. "He does. I think he loves me."

"Then what the hell are you still doing here?"

Excellent point. Then again, his mom had always had a way with words.

He made a call from his mom's house, then took a flight back home that same day.

He showed up when almost everyone had left already, and Toby was as surprised to see Henley as his mom had been. "I thought you'd taken the day off?"

"I was." Henley plopped down into a chair across from Toby's desk in a small, stuffy room without windows. Being an editor didn't come with the perks of a corner office. "I needed some time to think, but I've come to a conclusion, so I figured I'd share it with you."

Toby raised an eyebrow. "Something tells me this isn't good news."

"Maybe not, but I think you won't be surprised."

"You're quitting."

Henley nodded.

"That's a big decision. I assume you have something else lined up?"

"I've been offered a job as assistant professor at Georgetown, teaching investigative journalism. It's a part-time position, but Time magazine already approached me a few months ago for a position as an investigative journalist, so I think I'm gonna take them up on that offer."

Toby's face cracked open in a smile, in itself a rarity. "Assistant professor at Georgetown. That's amazing, Henley. I'm so excited for you. Proud too because I feel like I've watched you grow. It's a great step."

"Was I right? You're not surprised?"

"No, I've seen this coming. You know, when you were hired for the White House beat, at first, I thought that was the most brilliant decision ever. I've always been a fan of your work, and you've shown over the years you're a fantastic reporter with the tenacity needed to do a good job, as well as the ethics and the writing skills. But you weren't happy. You haven't been for a while."

"I didn't know. I never realized it until recently, but you're right. I don't know why because I've always wanted that job, but it wasn't what I thought it would be."

"As glamorous and exciting as it sounds, the White House beat is a routine. It's a song and dance with the press secretary, with spokespersons for the government on all levels. They try to sell something, you try to see through their sales techniques and spin, you give it a twist, throw in some opinion, and that's it. It doesn't have the depth you're so fond of."

Hearing Toby say this was bittersweet. Also, somewhat humbling to realize that he'd seen what Henley had been blind to for so long.

"I tried to figure out what I loved about this job, spent hours thinking about it, analyzing it. In the end, it came down to the investigative part of it. That's what I love about what I do. Not the day-to-day stuff, not reframing whatever the government has decided on in a way that fits the bigger narrative. It's digging deeper. Like, despite the controversy it has triggered, the articles I did on the Secret Service last year. That's the kind of stuff I live for. Those are also the kind of articles I'm truly proud of. Or more recently, the rift between then president Markinson and Shafer. It might not have been the scoop of the century, but I was the first to report on it, and I loved trying to figure out what was going on. I absolutely love that part. The rest? Not so much."

Toby nodded. "I figured as much. I debated talking to you about it, but I wasn't sure if that was the right course of action. First of all, it would be kind of shooting myself in the foot, since chances were that me speaking up would lead to you leaving, as you've proved just now. But more importantly, I questioned if you were ready to hear it. People don't need to hear this from someone else. I could've told you, and maybe you would've taken it seriously and thought about it, but it wouldn't have had the same impact as discovering it yourself."

"I'll admit it caused an identity crisis. This was my dream job, and then to learn it wasn't what I thought it would be, it's... It's a bit of a disillusion, really. It's disappointing to have to conclude that what I've worked for and thought I wanted all these years isn't the best fit for me."

"I can imagine. And obviously, I'm sad to see you go. Your contribution to this paper has been phenomenal, and I'm proud to have had you on our team. But the choices you've made sound like they'd be perfect for you. Though I'm surprised you didn't go for a full-time position with Time magazine."

Here was his perfect segue to share about his other bit of news. How would Toby take this? His editor had never breathed a negative word about Henley being pan, but Henley had no idea if he was queer-friendly or not. Well, he was about to find out. He took a deep breath. "About that... It probably wouldn't have been my first choice, if not for another factor that has played into this. I'm in love with someone, and his job caused a direct conflict of interest with mine. When it came down to the choice between losing him and keeping a job that involved political Washington or quitting, I chose him."

Toby blinked a few times. "Damn, son, you surprised me after all."

He didn't look angry, more stunned, so Henley plowed

on. "I might as well tell you who it is because it'll come out soon anyway. It's Levar Cousins."

Toby's eyes widened, and he whistled between his teeth. "Holy shit, Henley. That's a massive conflict of interest. For both of you, but especially for him."

"We tried to stay away from each other because we both knew our relationship had disaster written all over it, but we couldn't. He's just...he's worth it. I don't know how else to put it. I never thought myself to be the kind of guy who'd make the grand gesture, and yet here I am."

"It's damn hard to be irate with you when you tell me that."

That was as good as he would get from Toby, and he'd take it. "I wanted to be honest with you, also because I need to be taken off the White House beat immediately."

"Consider it done. I'm sure you can find something to work on in those last two weeks, so we'll talk more about that another time."

"I'll sit down with Luther and Adriana and share everything I know with them to make sure they're set up for success."

"We'll make it work."

"Thank you," Henley said, the last bit of stress leaving his body. "And I am sorry about the legal trouble I've caused with those articles."

Toby waved dismissively. "That's par for the course as a newspaper. Our lawyers aren't done fighting it yet."

"Thank you. You know I appreciate you all having my back on this."

"Don't mention it."

It was done. He'd quit his job. Now all he had to do was tell Levar and convince him to give them a shot.

"I'm out of here again. I have something to prepare for tonight."

Toby grinned. "Romantic date?"

Henley rose from his chair. "Something like that. It's more of an 'I just quit my job for you without telling you first, so I really hope you feel the same way about me as I do about you' kind of thing."

39

You have a visitor.

Levar frowned as he read the text. He was still on his way home, the train about ten minutes out from his station. *You have a visitor.* Why wasn't Rhett simply telling him who was there? Had his parents shown up? No, he'd said visitor. Singular. But who could it be? If it had been any of his friends, Rhett would've simply used his name. They'd been sharing an apartment long enough that they didn't have any friends the other didn't know about. Hell, most of the friends they had were friends to both of them, considering how long they had known each other.

Who is it?

He stared at the three dots. What was taking Rhett so long?

I'm not sure I should tell you. He didn't ask me not to, but now I'm doubting whether I made the right call warning you.

Warning him? What the hell was going on, and why was Rhett being so secretive? Why wouldn't he simply say who... Oh. Suddenly, Levar knew who it was.

Is it Henley?

This time, the answer came much faster. *Yes.*

Okay. Thanks for letting me know.

Do you want me to ask him to leave?

Levar smiled. Sweet Rhett. He hated confrontation, so for him to offer this was a sign of their friendship.

No, it's fine. I've got this. You may want to stay in your room, though.

Should I be worried about fighting or fucking?

Levar rolled his eyes, though the question wasn't unreasonable, considering the history between him and Henley. Why had he even come to his place? Hadn't they agreed to stay away from each other, to not reach out to each other anymore? Lord, if the man kept showing up, it would make things so much harder. And Levar already missed him enough as it was. Hell, the first thing he'd done when he stepped into the briefing room was checking to make sure Henley was there. He hadn't been today. Levar had wondered about it. Henley had sent his replacement before, and yet somehow, Levar had worried. Was he sick? Had something happened? The urge to text him had been almost too strong to deny, but he only had to remind himself of Calix's strong warning to stop himself from making that mistake.

So why had Henley shown up again? And more importantly, why was Levar already excited to go home now, when he hadn't been five minutes ago?

Fighting. Definitely fighting. There will be no more fucking.

Can I quote you on that?

Rhett knew him too well. *You can never quote me on anything. You should know that by now.*

Rhett's answer was a crying-with-laughter emoji. Fucker.

As he got off the train and made the short car ride home, he went through all kinds of scenarios in his head. Maybe

Henley had come to apologize, though for what, Levar had no idea. Or maybe he wanted to talk to him off the record about something. No, he wouldn't do that. He wouldn't come to his apartment unannounced if it was business, so to speak. It had to be something personal. But what could be important enough for him to break their mutual agreement?

By the time he walked up the stairs to his apartment, he still didn't have any answers. He found Henley in the living room, chatting with Rhett, who had apparently given him something to drink. "Hi," Levar said stupidly. Why did his tongue feel so heavy all of a sudden, his brain so foggy?

"Hi," Henley said back.

Maybe it wasn't just Levar who was affected.

Rhett rose from his chair, laughing. "I'll consider that my exit cue." He looked at Levar. "I'll be in my room with my noise-canceling headphones on. Do whatever you have to do and come get me if you need me."

When he walked past Henley, Levar grabbed him by his wrist and made him stop. "Thank you."

How had he ever gotten so lucky with a best friend like Rhett, who knew him like no one else and accepted him just the way he was?

Rhett smiled at him. "You're welcome."

Levar waited until the door closed behind Rhett, then turned to Henley. "At the risk of sounding incredibly formal, but what can I do for you? I'm hoping, really, really hoping that you have a good reason for showing up."

Henley got up from the couch, and they stood across from each other, maybe three feet between them. It was ten kinds of awkward, and yet Levar couldn't move.

"I do have a reason," Henley said. "Though now that I'm here, I'm wondering if I just made the biggest mistake of my life."

Biggest mistake of his life? What had he done? "Why? What happened?"

Henley took a deep breath. "I quit my job."

Levar's mouth dropped open, and it took him a few seconds to get his brain functioning again. "You did *what*?"

He couldn't have heard that correctly, right? Henley hadn't just said that he…

"I quit my job. I gave my two-week notice this morning, but as of today, I'm off the White House beat."

Oh. My. God. Henley had legit quit his job. A thousand thoughts at once assailed Levar, all of them accumulating into one single word. "Why?"

Henley took another deep breath, then stepped forward and grasped Levar's hand. "For you. I quit my job for you so I could date you. See you. Be with you without having to hide or worry about the consequences. If that's what you want."

"I have to sit down for a moment." Levar felt lightheaded. Henley held on to his hand as he guided him toward the couch, where they sat down next to each other. "I don't understand," Levar said slowly. "You quit your *job* for me?"

Henley nodded. "Yes. I missed you. I missed you so fucking much, and it didn't make sense because we weren't that serious. Hell, we weren't even officially dating. So I told myself it would go away, but it didn't. I told myself that I was overreacting, that I was being dramatic about it, but that didn't help either. I tried everything I could think of to forget about you, and nothing worked. You're the one I want."

Levar swallowed. "You quit your job for me?"

A smile tugged at the corners of Henley's mouth. "You gonna keep asking me that?"

"Until my brain can process, probably."

Henley squeezed his hand. "I know this sounds crazy.

Maybe I *am* crazy. I don't know. But I felt that if I didn't at least try to make it work with you, I'd always regret it."

"You quit your job for me. I can't get over that fact. This was your dream job, everything you'd always dreamed of. You told me yourself that when you started doing journalism in college, the White House was your goal. How can you walk away from that?"

"Because my dream was wrong. My dream was naïve and fueled by an expectation of what it would be like that didn't match reality."

Levar frowned. An expectation that didn't meet reality? "I thought you loved that job."

"Up until a few weeks ago, so did I. But something changed. Something made me look at it differently. The Pride Bombing commemoration, the assassination I witnessed, talks with my mom and a session with my therapist, but above all, spending time with you. They say that you don't know what something is worth until you've lost it. I guess that cliché was true for me as well. I hadn't realized how much you had come to mean to me until I lost you. But the reverse was true as well. I hadn't realized how complex my feelings were about my job until I started considering leaving it."

"I thought you were happy covering the White House. What changed? What did you realize? Help me understand."

"I love investigative journalism. That's the part of the job I'm crazy about. Everything else? Not so much. Only I didn't see that. I don't know if I didn't want to see it because I felt I had to like it or because I was too busy with the day-to-day aspects of the job to ever step back and analyze it, but the truth is that I haven't been happy for a while."

"So, are you quitting because you don't like the job

anymore, or are you quitting because you want us to try if we can work together?"

Henley nodded slowly. "Fair question, and it's probably half and half. Missing you as much as I did was the catalyst to step back and question myself and my motivation for my job. But if I hadn't cared about you as much as I did, I might've quit this specific job, but I would've stayed with the paper, probably covering politics in general. But in order to see you, I had to walk away from all of it. Otherwise, the conflict of interest would've still been there, and that was unacceptable to me."

Warmth spread through Levar's chest. "You really quit your job for me."

Henley laughed. "I did."

Levar gave himself a mental shake. "I need to stop saying that because I'm starting to sound like a parrot."

"I can live with the parrot part, but I'd love for you to give me some indication of whether or not my decision makes you happy."

Was he kidding? Didn't he know the magnitude of that gesture? "I missed you so much it physically hurt. I never understood all those sad songs about heartbreak until now."

"I'd expected it to feel the same as when Logan broke up with me, and that was after a two-year relationship. But whereas I missed him more in a practical sense, I couldn't stop hurting for you. I couldn't stop thinking about you, couldn't stop wondering what we would've been like had we had a chance, couldn't stop dreaming about a future with you. It's all kinds of crazy, and I know I sound borderline obsessive, maybe, but—"

"I feel the exact same way. I can't explain it, but I've never been attracted to someone the way I am to you."

"So if I asked you officially out on a date, you would say yes?"

Levar's face cracked in a big smile. "I would." Then he grew serious. "But not yet. I have to talk to Calix first. I have to be honest with him and ask for his permission. I can't do this behind his back. He'll find out anyway, and it'll look ten times worse than it is, but aside from that, he trusts me. I can't break that trust."

"I understand. It speaks to your integrity. But what if he's still not okay with it?"

Levar's heart sank. Would Calix still have an issue with it, even if Henley wasn't working for the White House anymore? "You haven't told me what you're going to do instead."

Henley slapped his forehead. "Sorry. I completely forgot about that detail. I've been offered a position as assistant professor in investigative journalism at Georgetown, and I may also be working for Time magazine, but that's still in the works. I'm off the White House beat, so there shouldn't be a conflict of interest. Yes, we may have to agree not to talk about certain aspects of our work, but I think we can both manage that."

"Assistant professor? Henley, that's amazing. I'm so proud of you."

"I'm super excited. They approached me. Can you believe it? Out of the blue. In fact, they had the best timing ever because if they'd asked me a year ago, I would've flat out turned them down. But their timing was impeccable, since I was in the middle of this whole crisis about you and me, about my job, about what I wanted in life, so it was the perfect opportunity."

"Thank you. I don't even know if I could ever thank you or even try to express what it means to me that you did this, but I want to at least try. Knowing that you cared enough about me to make such a life-changing decision is... It's everything."

"I don't need your gratitude. I needed to take this jump, this risk. If I hadn't, I would've always regretted it."

"I'll talk to Calix first thing tomorrow, and as soon as I know, I'd be proud and happy to go on a date with you."

"I'd better make it something good, huh? Lots of pressure here, considering I just poured my heart out to you."

Levar leaned in, cupped Henley's cheeks in both his hands, and looked him deep in the eyes. "No pressure whatsoever. No expectations. Just you and me. That's all I need."

He pressed a soft kiss on Henley's lips, then pulled back immediately. God knew that if he held on too long, he'd get sucked right back into that attraction, and he couldn't. Not until he'd talked to Calix.

Henley cleared his throat. "I'll be counting the hours."

"Me too," Levar said. Fuck, he'd never meant words more than those.

The next day, Levar hung back after their morning staff meeting. "Did you need something?" Calix asked.

"A few minutes of your time, if you have them."

Calix narrowed his eyes as he looked at Levar, but then he nodded. "Sure. My office."

"What's up?" Calix asked as soon as they had reached his office and closed the door behind them.

"Henley Platt has quit his job as a White House reporter," Levar said.

Calix, who had been shuffling some papers on his desk, stopped, then gazed at Levar in shock. "He has *what*? Are you serious?"

"Yes. He quit yesterday. He's off the White House beat as of immediately, and he'll be leaving the paper in two weeks."

Calix folded his hands behind his head. "I'll be damned. I have to admit I didn't see that coming. Why did he leave?"

Levar merely lifted one eyebrow.

Then a smile spread across Calix's face. "He did it for you? He did it so the two of you could be together?

Levar nodded, smiling broadly himself. How could he not when he thought of what Henley had done for him, for them? "He accepted a position at Georgetown University, and he's hoping for a part-time position with Time magazine, but not in national politics."

"No more conflict of interest," Calix said.

"Not according to Henley, and I agree with him."

"And you're telling me this, why?"

God, he was going to make him say it? Calix's eyes sparkled, though, so Levar was pretty sure of his chances. "I'm telling you because I'd love to have your permission to officially date him. Out in the open."

Calix shook his head, laughing. "God, I feel like a father who's talking to his child's suitor, who's asking him to pursue them." Then he grew serious. "But I appreciate you coming to me. And of course you have my permission under these circumstances. Let me talk to White House Counsel, though. I just want to make sure we don't need any kind of NDA or something in place. And I may make a quick call to the ethics committee, just to give them a heads-up."

"That's fine. Do whatever you need to clear the way for us."

"You really like him, hmmm?"

Levar took a deep breath. "I think we may be past the *like* stage. Somehow, somewhere along the line, I've fallen in love with him."

40

All systems go.

Henley read the text from Levar again. All systems go? What did he...? Oh. *Oh.* Finally!

He hadn't seen Levar since he'd told him he quit his job a week ago. He hadn't talked to him either. All they'd exchanged were short texts, mostly updates from Levar, who had refused to see Henley again until he had permission. Henley respected the hell out of him for that.

Calix is talking to the Office of White House Counsel.

Calix is checking with the ethics committee.

And now finally, the text he'd been waiting for. *All systems go.*

A rush of happiness filled him. Exhilaration. How long had he waited for this? Weeks at most, and yet it felt like months, years. His whole life. Gah, this whole being-in-love thing was making him cheesy and sappy, and yet it felt so good, so normal.

Can you come over after work? he texted him.

Yes. Not sure what time.

Anytime. I'll wait. I'll wait forever, he wanted to add. More sappiness. Where had cynical Henley gone?

Can I stay the night?

Yes, please.

I'll stop by home real quick and grab a change of clothes... including some underwear fitting for this momentous occasion.

Henley swallowed. *Yes, please.*

Shortly after eight, the doorbell rang, and Henley opened it to find a beaming Levar at his door. He pulled him inside, then hugged him tightly. Levar dropped the small bag he'd been carrying onto the floor and clamped his arms around Henley. "Hi."

"Hi."

"God, I missed you," Henley said.

"I missed you too."

"Let me hold you just a little longer."

"As long as you want."

When he'd finally had his fill of him, Henley loosened his grip and brushed his lips against Levar's, a featherlight kiss that sent his stomach aflutter. "I can't believe I get to do this now."

"It's not like we never kissed before."

"Yeah, but we don't have to sneak around anymore. I don't have to feel guilty for kissing you."

"True. And you're not scared that the forbidden element was part of the attraction?"

Henley froze for a moment. "No! No, of course not. What... Why would you think that? Is that how you feel?"

Levar put his forehead against Henley's. "No. I'm sorry. It's just that you've given up so much for us to get here, and I don't want you to be disappointed."

Henley cupped his cheeks and looked him deep into his

eyes. "I don't think I could ever be disappointed in you. You're..."

God, he was going way too fast, wasn't he? They hadn't even had an official date yet, they were still in the hallway, for fuck's sake, and here he was, about to blurt out the serious stuff. The things that ultimately led to wedding vows and death do us part. He'd never felt this way, and if nothing else, that told him it was real. He'd already taken the jump by quitting his job. He might as well go all in now.

"I love you," he said quietly, still holding Levar's cheeks. Levar's eyes widened. "I'm in love with you more than I ever thought possible and definitely more and deeper than I've ever been before with anyone. You're it, baby. You're the one for me."

Levar's face broke open in a beautiful smile. "I love you too. It's crazy and way too fast, but it's real."

Henley's heart settled down, the fear of rejection gone now. "It's very real."

"Kiss me," Levar begged, and Henley didn't need to be told twice.

He drew Levar's body against his own and covered his mouth with a searing kiss. Everything he felt, he poured into his kiss, his caresses, his touch. He probed him deeply, exploring his mouth, his lips, teasing his tongue. He tasted his toothpaste, the faint flavor of coffee. But above all, he tasted Levar. His essence filled his mouth, his body, his soul.

Levar clung to him, his arms wrapped around Henley's neck, their bodies pressed together. He kissed Henley back as if he was starving for him, his touches as eager as Henley's. He thrust his tongue into Henley's mouth vigorously, meeting him stroke for stroke, gasp for gasp.

The core of his body tensed with need, his cock throbbing and pulsing, and he gyrated his hips and ground into Levar.

"I prepped," Levar whispered against his lips.

"Yeah?" Henley was stupidly happy with that. Such a small act in itself and yet so meaningful to him. It meant that Levar wanted this, wanted him, that they were on the same page.

"I'd love for you to top me..."

"God, yes. A thousand times yes."

"I'm also wearing something especially for you..."

Okay, Henley was done standing in the hallway. "Bedroom," he said, and Levar grinned when Henley grabbed his wrist and tugged him along.

Henley drew his shirt over his head as he walked, then kicked off his pants and underwear. He'd already been barefoot, so by the time he walked into his bedroom, he was naked and ready. He turned around, and his breath caught in his throat. Levar had undressed as well, leaving him in a pair of red silk panties. He stretched his arms above his head, making the silky fabric pull tight around his hard cock. Sweet Jesus and all the saints.

"God, you're sexy," Henley growled. "Seeing you in those panties makes me want to tear them off...with my teeth. Very caveman-like, I know, but there you go."

"Wait till you see the back..."

Levar slowly turned around, revealing a lacy triangle at the top of his crack and then nothing but a very thin strip of material down. The flared end of a butt plug was sticking out of his hole. Levar looked over his shoulder, his expression pure sex. "You like?"

This man was *his*. The knowledge sent a rush through Henley. "I've never seen a man sexier than you. Let me touch you, baby," he begged. "Let me fill you."

Levar closed the distance between them, and they kissed again, hungry mouths seeking and finding. They stumbled into bed, their hands clawing at each other, caressing naked skin, exploring and stroking. Heated skin found heated skin, their bodies growing slick.

Henley nibbled on Levar's bottom lip as his hands brushed over the silk of his panties. The sensation of cupping his hard cock through that soft fabric was so amazing. It felt sinful, dirty, and judging by the way Levar's cock pulsed in his hand, Henley wasn't the only one turned on by it.

"I want to fuck you wearing your panties. If they tear, I'll buy you new ones. Hell, I'll buy you ten new pairs. From now on, you can't wear anything else but these. I'm making that a rule."

Levar laughed, but the heated look in his eyes told Henley how much he loved it. "Yes."

"Yes, what? To panties every day?"

"That's still under advisement. But yes to fucking me wearing these. You have no idea how hot this material feels against my cock."

Henley stroked his cock through the silk. "I wanna see how they look on you when you spill all over them."

"Then get going."

Henley didn't dawdle anymore but grabbed lube and a condom from his nightstand. He ripped open the condom wrapper.

"Can I do it?" Levar sat up.

Henley nodded, and Levar scrambled to his knees. He kissed the tip of Henley's cock, smiling deviously as he licked a drop of precum of the slit. An act he'd performed so often himself now became incredibly erotic to Henley as Levar slowly rolled the condom down over his cock, holding him tightly, his hands so warm and soft. His touch was almost reverently, his eyes blazing with want.

When he fisted him a few times to spread the extra lube, Henley clenched his teeth. "Keep doing that, and it'll be a long time before I'm inside you as you'll have to wait for round two."

Levar laughed, but he let go of him and rolled onto his back, spreading his legs wide. Unashamed, he presented himself, his cheeks sporting a slight blush, and that red silk so gloriously hugging his erection. Henley palmed his dick again, loving Levar's moans as he rubbed himself against Henley's hand.

"I bet you could come just from that," Henley whispered. "Just from rubbing that sexy cock of yours against my hand."

"Easily." The word came out hoarse.

"Someday, I'll do that. I'll take the time to discover what pleasure I can bring you with just a pair of silky panties... I can wrap them around your cock and jack you off with it."

"Mmm, yes."

"Or I could use them to wipe off my cum, then have you put them on."

"God, you're dirty."

"Pot, meet kettle. You're a dirty man underneath those prim suits, Levar Cousins."

"*Your* dirty man."

Cheesy? Hell yes. But damn if that simple statement didn't make Henley's heart go wild. *His* dirty man. He liked that far more than he probably should.

He stroked Levar's thighs, reveling in the way he gasped when Henley came closer to his cock, to his ass. So responsive.

"Can I...?" He pointed at the plug.

"Yeah."

He gently pulled it out, then dropped it onto the sheets. He pressed a thumb against Levar's hole, smiling when it reacted by pulsing.

"I know that technically we have all night, but I don't have all night." Levar sounded just a tad whiny.

"You in a hurry?"

"Do you mind? I haven't had a good dicking in, like, forever."

Henley snorted. "I see how it is. I've been reduced to one part of my body."

"Oh, I appreciate your brilliant conversation, just not right now."

Henley smiled. God, he loved him. "I think I can accommodate you...with a good dicking."

The way Levar looked at his cock made it twitch. "I have faith in you."

Henley took position between Levar's legs. He reached down, took his rock-hard cock in his right hand, and directed it to Levar's ass, pushing aside the thin strip of his thong. Oh, he was so slick and hot, so welcoming. He plunged deep with one penetrating thrust, Levar letting him in with ease. He filled him completely, their bodies flush together. The soft silk rubbed against his stomach, and the combination with the hardness captivated in that thin material was wonderfully arousing.

Face-to-face fucking. While it had been too intimate at times with his previous partners, he wanted nothing else with Levar. He wanted to see every expression fly over his face, every emotion in his eyes, catch every sound he made as Henley brought him pleasure. And the way Levar was watching him now, his eyes sultry and blazing with want, he didn't even consider looking away.

"I'm gonna make you feel so good," he promised.

"You already do. "

Levar curled his legs around Henley's waist, and Henley sank in deeper, so deep until he didn't know where he ended and Levar began. Their faces were inches apart, their eyes locking, their breaths mingling. Desire rippled down his spine, filling every cell of his body. He wanted him so much.

He pulled out and slid back in, slow and deep and precise. Levar's eyes crossed, and he squeezed around Henley's cock in reaction. A low grunt burst from the back of Henley's throat, raw and primitive. "Do that again."

He drove home again, and Levar clenched around him. "This?"

"If you keep that up, we won't even get to the dicking part."

"You better get started, then."

Henley hung over him, panting against his neck as he thrust his cock in hard. Levar clawed the sheets, his back arching off the bed. "Ungh," he moaned, moving against Henley.

Henley planted his knees and leaned in with his weight to force himself in deeper. He wanted every inch of him, every part of his body. He wanted to claim him, which was ridiculous and more alpha male than he cared to admit, but it was the god-honest truth. Levar was his, and he was Levar's, and fuck everyone who had an issue with that.

He rotated his hips, screwing in deeper and grinding against Levar. It also brought friction for Levar's cock, which lay swollen between them, imprisoned by the panties Levar was still wearing. Tightness gripped his balls, clenching, making them so heavy and full.

He pushed himself up on his arms and watched as he sank into Levar, his cock disappearing into his body. The red panties were almost obscene, the way they stretched around Levar's cock. Henley palmed him and squeezed. After a few tries, he found a rhythm where his hand rubbed Levar in the same cadence as he fucked him. The position wasn't the most comfortable, and he wouldn't be able to keep it up for long, but holy shit, did it feel good. He wanted to see Levar flood those panties with his cum. Drench them.

His breath hitched in his throat, and his strokes became hard and fast. He couldn't wait any longer. His head tilted back in ecstasy as he chased his release, going by pure instinct now. He moved faster, hammering him, pounding, his hand squeezing and rubbing him until he exploded. Intense spasms gripped the base of his cock, electrifying his balls as he unloaded into the condom.

His hand clenched around Levar's cock. Levar let out a strangled cry, and then he, too, was coming, soaking his panties. As soon as he'd caught his breath, Henley rolled them over, pulling Levar on top of him. He let out a satisfied sigh. God, that had been...spectacular. He splayed his hands across Levar's ass cheeks, the silk of his underwear now wet between them and yet so arousing.

Henley held him, Levar's body limp on top of his own. He inhaled his unique scent. He loved that he knew what Levar smelled like, what he tasted like and sounded like. He knew him, and yet they'd only just begun their journey together.

Minutes later, Levar slid off him with a groan, and Henley turned onto his side. The panties were soaked in the front, and he touched them with a finger. "My dirty man."

Levar grinned. "Going alpha on me?"

"It's damn hard not to when you look like that. It makes me want to do things to you. Bad things. Dirty things."

Levar slowly licked his lips. "Okay, I guess I can tolerate the alpha posturing in that case."

He really was perfect. "I want you to meet my mom."

Levar let out a tired laugh. "Bad segue, Platt. If the thought of doing dirty things to me makes you think of your mom, we need to have a serious conversation."

Henley just kissed him until he ran out of breath. Much easier. Also way more fun.

41

Levar felt like a high school boy again as he waited for Henley to pick him up for their official first date. He'd been out since middle school, and while he hadn't dated a lot, he had been on a few fun dates. And whenever he had waited for his date to arrive, he'd felt the exact same combination of nerves and excitement that were coursing through him right now. Funny how that had stayed the same twenty years or so later.

He didn't have to wait long, as Henley pulled up exactly on time in a sleek black BMW. "Good morning," Levar said as he got in and immediately wanted to slap himself. Why was he always so awkward initially whenever he and Henley met up? It was like his brain needed a few minutes to reboot.

Henley leaned over the middle console, and Levar gladly obliged his wordless request for a kiss. "I like waking up much better when you're in my bed," Henley said, his voice still a bit gravelly.

Levar smiled at him. "Ditto."

"Glad we have that established. Maybe we can do something about it."

Levar laughed. "I'm sure we can work something out."

Henley was smiling as he drove off.

"So where are we going?" Levar asked.

"I thought it would be fun to explore a bit of scenic history and get out of the city. With that hint, can you take a guess?"

"Scenic history outside of the city... That could literally be ten different things, probably more."

"True. I'll give you another hint. We're heading toward Virginia."

Virginia. That still left open a lot of possibilities. "A Civil War site?"

"Nope. You have to go back a little further in history."

"How much further?"

Henley rolled his eyes at him. "Like I'm going to tell you that. You gotta do some of the work yourself."

Further back than the Civil War. In Virginia. Levar frowned. What was there from before that time? Something from the early settlements? Or... "Mount Vernon."

"Bingo. Have you ever been?"

"Once, on a school trip. As you can imagine, I didn't pay a whole lot of attention."

"Good. That means you'll be able to appreciate it even more. It's one of my favorite spots. I can't explain why, but I find it very soothing. It's rural, it's got a great view over the Potomac, and I love how they've made history feel alive there."

Levar liked that Henley was taking him to a place he loved himself rather than something he'd never been to. It made it personal, like he was sharing a little bit of himself.

They chatted during the ride to Virginia, Henley taking

the back roads instead of the Beltway. Smart choice. It might be longer in terms of miles and maybe even time, but at least they'd have a scenic view.

The parking lot at Mount Vernon was filling up, though they still had no trouble finding a spot. "On the weekend, you have to get here early," Henley said. "It can get crazy busy, and you really don't want to be here around Christmas or for the Fourth of July. It's overcrowded then, though I do have to admit it's fun as well. On the Fourth especially, they have all kinds of demonstrations and a big firework show. Plus, they're shooting real cannons and old guns."

He parked the car but left the engine running. "We're not getting out of the car?" Levar was confused.

"In a minute. I wanted to give you something first."

"You brought me a gift?"

"I did. I hope I got it right, but I wanted to make today special to celebrate the occasion of our first official date."

Henley reached behind his chair and pulled up a paper bag, one of those colorful gift bags with tissue paper on top. "You even wrapped it all beautifully," Levar teased.

"Are you kidding me? I love those gift bags. You just throw stuff in, put some of that paper on top, and call it a day. I don't have the patience to actually wrap presents unless it's a book or DVD. Those I can do."

Levar laughed. "I'll make sure to ask for books and DVDs for Christmas, then."

He took out the yellow tissue paper and peered into the bag. What had Henley gotten him? Something made of fabric. He reached inside and pulled it out. "Oh my god." His cheeks flushed as he stared at the gorgeous black lace panties. They were see-through lace at the front and had the softest silk material at the back. And they were manties, designed to be worn by people with a dick.

"They're amazing," he said softly. "Henley, this is so beautiful."

When he looked up from the panties, Henley was beaming at him. "I'm so glad you love them. Do you think I got the size right? I had to guess a little."

Levar held them up again. "Yeah, these should fit fine. Where did you get them?"

"Online. I would've loved to buy them in person, but I was running short on time, and this store promised two-day delivery. They came through. The reviews were amazing, so I was hoping they'd turn out to be as spectacular as they looked in the picture...and they did."

"I can't tell you how much this means to me. Not just that you brought me a gift but specifically this gift."

"You know I love your affinity for lingerie. You look so sexy in panties, baby. So absolutely stunning and beautiful. If you never were to wear anything else again in your life, I'd be a happy, happy man."

Levar had to clear his throat before he could speak, a sudden tightness affecting his voice. "I'll make sure to model these for you and thank you in the proper way." He leaned in, and their kiss was warm and full of promises.

He put the panties back in the bag, his heart almost filled with longing to put them on, then placed them under his seat where they'd be safe.

"Let's explore," Henley said as he turned off the engine. They got out, and he locked the car.

Levar couldn't remember much from his previous visit, and he took it all in with excitement. Henley paid for the two of them, and they walked onto the grounds. The sky was bright blue, a few fluffy clouds contributing to the almost idyllic picture. If not for the people around them, it almost felt like they'd stepped back in time.

"I'd forgotten how stunning that first look is," Levar said as they strolled toward the mansion.

"Like many people did back then, the house was designed to impress visitors," Henley said. "Kind of like how DC was built to impress foreign visitors and show the grandeur of the new American states, Washington designed Mount Vernon in a way that would make it look expensive and stately. What I like is that it's not over the top. It still feels like a farm despite the expensive interior. It fits the surroundings."

They joined the tour group Henley had already signed them up for, and Levar enjoyed the fascinating walk through the main mansion. The tour guide was dressed in clothes from Washington's time, which added atmosphere, and he wasn't just knowledgeable but spoke with passion and excitement. Levar couldn't imagine having to do the same spiel every day and still sound like it was all fresh to you, but the guy pulled it off.

"I'm amazed every time at how colorful it is," Henley said as they peered into a room called the Blue Room. The combination of the blue wallpaper with intricate flowers on its walls and four-poster bed with white-and-blue curtains was almost headache inducing, but it certainly qualified as colorful.

"Was that uncommon in that time?"

"Depending on how much money people had to spend and what kind of room it was. From what I understand, they invested more money in guest rooms and rooms they knew visitors would see than in behind-the-scenes rooms, which were decorated sparsely and painted in boring, cheaper colors. Makes total sense from their point of view."

After the tour, they headed to the back porch, where they stood watching over the Potomac. "Say what you want, but the man certainly knew how to pick a prime spot for a house," Levar said.

"I think his father chose the location. I don't remember all the details, but I'm pretty sure his father started a very modest and small house here before George Washington took over. And it took him a couple of decades to enlarge it to what it is today. What's interesting is that he played a major role in the renovations, designing stuff and overseeing every step. Whereas a lot of homeowners would've let someone handle that, he was involved himself."

"He certainly had taste, then. I can't say I'm an expert, but I really like what he built here. The farm was almost self-sufficient, but he also tried to impress visitors but managed to make it not feel over the top or pretentious. And like you said, the colors are gorgeous."

Henley took his hand, lacing their fingers together, and tingles spread through Levar's body. Such an innocent gesture, and yet it meant so much. They kept holding hands as they explored the grounds, ambling through the gardens, the farm, and a distillery Levar had forgotten about from his previous visit.

By the time they'd seen pretty much everything, the visitors had swollen to less comfortable numbers, crowding the grounds, so Levar wasn't sad when Henley hinted it was time to go. "What's next on the schedule?" he asked Henley.

"I made a reservation in the Mount Vernon Inn restaurant next door for lunch. I figured we would spend a few hours here and get hungry, and there's not a whole lot around other than the restaurant."

"I think I saw a sign for a food court?"

Henley looked horrified. "If you think I'm taking you to a food court on a date, we need to talk about your standards."

Levar laughed. "I appreciate your standards, trust me."

The restaurant was a short walk, and the hostess brought them to a private table in the back. They were early enough for lunch that the restaurant was only half-filled, the soft murmur of quiet conversations providing a pleasant backdrop. Levar might not have the money to afford it often, but he loved restaurants that didn't have a bar and blaring TVs.

The menu made it hard to choose, but Levar settled for crab cakes as an appetizer and pan-fried snapper with crispy maple bacon Brussels sprouts as a main. Henley opted for crab soup and grilled duck.

"Thank you, this has been amazing," Levar said as the waiter had taken their orders.

"I'm glad you like it. It was a bit of a gamble, but I figured that if you truly hated this, I might have to reconsider our relationship."

"Good thing I passed that test, then, huh?"

"I had no doubt you would, just for the record."

"I apologize for the clunky and inelegant segue, but would it be okay if we talked a little about what you expect going forward?" Levar asked.

"I'd love to talk about that. And it's not an easy subject to bring up, so you're forgiven for the lack of sophistication here."

"You know how busy and crazy my job is. I don't have to explain that to you. It does worry me, though, what that might mean for our relationship."

"Fair enough. My hours will be much more regular now, so at least one of us has a more or less stable schedule."

Levar cocked his head. "You don't think it will become a problem, me working so much? After all, it's what broke you and Logan up."

A look of sadness flashed over Henley's face. "You know,

on the surface, that might've been the issue, but I think the real problem was much deeper. We wanted different things in life, and the bottom line was that I didn't care for him as much as he did for me. I'm almost ashamed to admit it, but in my defense, I really thought I did love him. But now that I've met you...it puts things in a different perspective. The truth was that Logan was right. I didn't make him a priority, and I should have. All I can say is that if I had felt the same way about him as I do about you, I would have."

"But does that mean you want the same for me? Are you expecting to be my number one priority?"

Henley shook his head. "No, because I know you can't promise me that. You work for the president. That trumps everything, and I understand that. I know you'll be working a lot and irregular hours too. I can live with that, but I hope you can promise me one thing."

"What?"

"Technically, you could be working for President Shafer for ten years. This won't count as his first term, so he could be reelected twice. Ten years is a long time to be waiting for you to slow down. So all I'm asking is that you'll consider setting a deadline. A date for both of us so we know what we can look forward to. I can take a lot, but it would help me if I knew for how long."

It wasn't an unreasonable request. Besides, no way in hell would he be able to keep this up for ten years, let alone combine it with a relationship. Nor did he want to. He might've only been doing this for a few weeks, but it was long enough to be acutely aware of the toll this job would take on his personal life as well as on his health.

Yes, having someone to come home to would make a difference because as much as he loved Rhett, coming home to him wasn't the same motivator as it would be with

Henley. But he'd still be working a lot more than before, a lot more than what most people would consider normal. So yes, Henley's request was more than reasonable.

"I think I can make that promise. One full term. Six years max, and I'm out. But to be honest, I can see myself leaving even before that. I don't think anyone could keep this pace up for long."

"Six years is good for me. Especially when you say it might be less."

Levar nodded. "Less, definitely not more. I want this, Henley. I want this with you, and while I'm not ready to give up my job right now, I know I'll have to compromise as well, and I'm willing to do that."

"I wouldn't want you to quit your job. You were born to do this, and I love seeing you find your footing. You'll shine, and I'll be watching you every step of the way, cheering you on."

42

Henley had been told to leave Levar's apartment for half an hour, and so he did, walking over to a coffee shop nearby and taking some time there reading the papers. So far, his fortieth birthday had been amazing with Levar making him breakfast in bed, then spending a few lovely hours together just chatting and reading, watching some TV, and more chatting.

They'd picked up lunch from his favorite deli and had spent the rest of the day lounging. Rhett had been there until lunch, but then he'd gone into work, explaining the president had asked him to shoot a family portrait. Afterward, he was heading to a friend's house for dinner. He'd wiggled his eyebrows at Levar in a way that told Henley something was up.

His timing to turn forty on a Sunday had been excellent if he did say so himself. All thoughts of work were pushed to the back of his head, and the simple act of being with Levar and enjoy it was all the birthday present Henley would ever need.

Not that Levar hadn't gotten him a present. He had. An

amazing, expensive fountain pen that made Henley want to sit at his desk and write, just for the joy of using it. Levar knew him well to buy him a gift like that, and Henley loved that thought.

But right before dinner time, Levar had Henley told to get lost for half an hour—though he'd worded it more politely than that. Henley had no idea why, but he didn't ask. Duh. Obviously, Levar was planning something, so he'd discover soon enough. That had to be why Rhett had made himself scarce as well. Sure, they could've gone over to Henley's apartment, but he much preferred to be at Levar's place. He'd never realized how much he disliked his apartment until now.

His phone dinged. *You can come back.*

He was almost giddy with anticipation as he hurried back. What had Levar planned? A birthday dinner? If he managed that in half an hour, he'd have to have it catered. Besides, he wasn't that good a cook, as he'd admitted himself. Neither of them were.

A surprise party, then? Nah, that was equally impossible to pull off in such a short time, and Henley didn't even have that many friends. Not enough for a party anyway. So what was left? He hadn't come up with a plausible option when he opened the front door, using the key Levar had given him a few days earlier. "Levar?" he called out.

"I'm in the living room!"

Henley closed the door, kicked off his shoes, and walked into the living room. As soon as he did, music started playing. He came to a full stop. Henley swallowed as he let his eyes roam over Levar's body. He was wearing stockings. Shimmery, black stockings that were attached to a...was that a black lace garter? Was that was it was called? Henley wasn't sure, but oh my god, it was the sexiest thing he'd ever seen.

Levar's cock was straining against a thin bit of see-through black lace that did nothing to hide his erection. And his chest was covered in…it wasn't a bra, so much, but maybe a male version of it? A black lace bralette that offered tantalizing glimpses of his nipples, the fabric clinging to Levar's skin, framing his smooth chest.

And then he danced. Henley had never thought of Levar as ungraceful, but the fluidity of his moves took his breath away. Levar held Henley's eyes as he dipped and swayed his body, showing off his skin and the gorgeous lingerie covering it. His hips swirled, his stomach taut and teasing, and Henley licked his lips, his cock growing to steel in seconds.

Levar floated around, showing off the thin strip of lace between his ass cheeks as he shimmied his hips again, rolling and dipping, swaying and undulating. He peeked over his shoulder with a cheeky grin as he showed off his backside, sinking low on his haunches, baring almost everything.

"You're breathtaking," Henley said, proud that he'd finally found words. "God, seeing you like this is…the sexiest thing ever. I have trouble breathing, and my heart rate is through the roof."

"You like your present?" Levar beamed, never losing his rhythm.

"Best. Present. Ever. In fact, it should be my birthday every day."

"Such a greedy boy," Levar teased him, gripping him by his shirt as he moved against him, rubbing and sliding against his body. Henley's hands ran up and down Levar's arms, then caressed his belly, his back, as he kept twirling and twisting.

Levar turned around again, pressing his almost bare ass cheeks against Henley's crotch. Henley palmed Levar's ass and squeezed the soft flesh. Levar pushed against Henley's hands, and Henley's whole body was on fire. He loved him. God, he loved him. The all-encompassing feeling washed over him, leaving him panting as much as the sexy dance.

Levar stretched his hands up behind him and gripped the back of Henley's head, rubbing himself against Henley's weeping cock. "If you keep doing that, this will be over way too soon," he warned him, and Levar chuckled as he let go and stepped away.

He shook his ass at Henley. "I wasn't done dancing for you yet."

"God have mercy," Henley said breathlessly.

Levar spun around. Eyes sparkling, he slid his hand down his chest and grabbed his own dick, letting out a moan that shot straight to Henley's balls. He held his inner thighs, then sunk low on his heels, opening wide to show Henley all of him.

Henley wiped the sweat off his forehead, his hand shaking. "Shit, baby, I'm losing it here."

The music ended, and Levar stopped moving, his chest heaving. "I wanted to show you how much I appreciate your love for my penchant for lace and silk."

"Where the hell did you learn to move like that? Not that I want to see you change careers, but you could make a fortune as a stripper."

Levar laughed. "YouTube, believe it or not. Watched a few videos, practiced in front of my mirror, then figured it was good enough."

"It was more than good enough. It was amazing. Breathtaking. Absolutely perfect...and arousing."

Levar stepped close to him again, his gaze dropping to Henley's crotch. "Yeah, I noticed you were...interested."

"That's one way of putting it. But, baby...that dance in itself was a gift. I don't need anything else."

Levar slid his hand into Henley's crotch and massaged firmly, and Henley bucked against his hand. "Levar..."

"Hush, baby... This is my show, my gift to you."

Henley let Levar peel off his shirt, then unbutton his shorts, which slithered to the floor. His underwear came next, and he stood naked, pulse racing and heart beating fast as he awaited Levar's next step. Levar walked him backward until Henley toppled down onto the couch, spread out for Levar to pleasure...and torture.

Levar sank to his knees next to the couch. His wet lips kissed Henley's neck, then sucked gently on his throat before moving lower. A startled cry burst from Henley's lips when Levar took his nipple into his mouth, swirling his tongue around the hard bud. Steel and velvet, heat and wetness, the sensations too much to even process. Had he ever been made love to this thoroughly?

"I love you," he said, almost desperate with the need to say those words out loud.

"Mmm, baby, I love you too."

Levar's first touch was gentle. He ran his index finger up and down Henley's cock, sending flare-ups of electricity all through his body. "You have such a beautiful cock."

"Yeah?" Henley was ridiculously pleased. "I'm not exactly...*built* down there."

He was average, which might be fine in itself, but he'd never felt his cock was one of his best features. Of course, he'd never been a man who was satisfied with average, so why should this be any different?

"It's the perfect size. Not so big it's prohibitive but nice and thick and with that perfect upward curve."

Henley's belly heated up. "Thank you."

Levar's mouth ghosted over his cock, so close he could feel his breath without actually touching him.

"Can I blow you?" Levar asked, his eyes so dark they were navy blue now.

"God, yes."

Levar ran a path from his belly button down to his cock, where he licked off the drop of precum at the tip. Tingles danced down Henley's spine. Levar's warm lips blazed a trail to the sensitive skin of his thighs and sucked on his skin until Henley shivered. He continued his exploration, nipping his skin, scraping the flesh of his balls with his teeth, and all Henley could do was gasp.

Levar folded his hand around Henley's base and brought his mouth down. His lips wrapped around his cockhead as he used his tongue to tease his crown and slit. He suckled, the sensation sending spikes of desire through Henley. He'd never make it long, not after that dance and the way Levar was touching him now.

Levar took him in deeper, his hot mouth engulfing Henley's cock. He'd died and gone to heaven. Logan hadn't been a fan of blow jobs, so it had been a while since he had one, and this was... "Fuuuuuck..." he grunted, the sound rising from deep inside him.

Levar moaned around his cock, clearly deriving pleasure from blowing Henley, and that made it all the sweeter.

"Ah...fuck!" Henley's pulse spiked as Levar's hot mouth slid up and down his cock, sucking hard. He held on to

Levar's head, his fingers digging into his skull. "God, you're good at this."

Levar's right hand circled Henley's nuts, cradling them, then rolling them in his palm. His left hand was still firmly wrapped around the base of Henley's cock, and oh my god, how he wished for a third hand so Levar could finger him. He'd always loved having his ass played with during a blow job.

As if he'd read Henley's mind, Levar let go of his nuts and slid backward, his dry finger pressing against his hole. Henley arched his back, moving into his touch. Levar's hand disappeared, and a whine slipped off Henley's lips as Levar's mouth plopped off his cock, and he let go of Henley completely.

Levar chuckled. "Just getting the lube, baby. Be patient."

"Impossible with how good you make me feel."

Levar slicked up his fingers. Then he was back, his mouth on Henley's cock and pressing his finger against his hole. He bore down, and Levar's finger sunk in deep, going straight for his sweet spot. "Holy shit!" Henley grunted. "Oh god...fuck!"

Levar fingered his ass thoroughly as he sucked Henley's cock hard, his cheeks hollowing, pumping the base with urgency. Henley wasn't gonna last long, not with this multi-front assault on his senses. He worked his hips, sliding into Levar's mouth with deep strokes. And fuck, the *look* on Levar's face, the way his eyes held Henley's... Maybe even more arousing than his mouth, his hands, his touch.

He didn't even have time to warn Levar, his orgasm barreling into him. He spurted into his mouth, and Levar coughed, then bravely tried to swallow it all. By the time Henley was done, Levar had cum all over his face, and fuck if that wasn't the sexiest sight ever, especially with him still wearing that lacy thong.

"Happy birthday, baby." Levar beamed.

Henley kissed him reverently, tasting his own cum as much as Levar's sweat. "Best birthday ever."

43

"Boardwalk with three houses." Henley's voice was stuffed to the brim with glee as he held out his hand to Rhett. "Pay up."

Levar laughed at the sheer annoyance on his best friend's face. "It's totally unfair I land there again for the third time in a row. This game is cursed."

"Cry me a river, but you'll still have to pay." Henley curled his fingers in a "give-it" gesture.

Levar had thought no one could take board games more seriously than Rhett, but it seemed he'd found his match in Henley. Rhett grumbled as he counted his money, then threw it onto the board with a sigh. "That's it. I'm out. You bankrupted me, Platt. Capitalism won once again. Hope that makes you happy."

For a moment, Levar worried Henley wouldn't see past the fake-gruff attitude, but his boyfriend—and how amazing did that sound—just sent Rhett a blinding smile. "Pleasure doing business with you, Foles. Anytime, any day."

Rhett burst out laughing. "It's so much fun playing with you. You play to the death, unlike Levar here. I approve."

Henley shot Levar a big grin. "He has other talents, though."

Rhett rolled his eyes. "I'm sure he does. The walls here aren't that thick, you know."

"Which is why you have the noise-canceling headphones," Levar pointed out.

"At two in the morning? You guys need to sleep like normal people."

Henley and Levar looked at each other, then chuckled. "Pretty sure we'll never be normal people."

"Well, can't you guys go over to your apartment to fuck?" Rhett asked Henley.

Something flashed over Henley's face. "We could…"

It had come out way more serious than Levar had expected, and Rhett picked up on it as well, sending Levar a sideways glance. "I wasn't serious," Rhett said. "I was just teasing you. I don't mind you being here at all."

"Are you sure?" God, had Henley ever looked this vulnerable and insecure? Levar's heart ached for him. "Because I don't want to make it look like I'm trying to come between you or break up your friendship."

"I know. No one could anyway. Levar and I are… We're connected in a way that can't be broken."

Levar loved the strength in Rhett's statement. How blessed he was to have him as a friend.

"Good. I just…" Henley bit his lip, another highly uncharacteristic gesture for him. "I like being here much better than my own place."

No wonder, Levar thought, but he didn't say it. Henley's apartment might technically be more luxurious, but it was also cold in every sense of the word.

"You're welcome here, and I'm sorry if my teasing made you feel otherwise." Rhett looked all kinds of guilty.

Henley held up his hand. "You're good. It's just that... I talked about this with Oren, my therapist, this week. About the concept of home and what it means to me."

Rhett glanced at Levar. "I can go to my room if you want?"

Levar shook his head, but before he could say anything, Henley said, "No. Please stay. Unless you want to leave. I don't ever want you to feel like you can't be in your own home. And maybe this is important for you to know about me, I don't know. It certainly made me think."

Levar scooted over on the couch so he could snuggle up to Henley. "What did Oren say?"

Henley had agreed to go to therapy once a week, and so far, he'd been quiet about it but positive when Levar asked.

"We talked about home as the definition of a safe place, somewhere where you feel like you belong and where you feel safe and connected. My mom was my safe place, especially after my dad walked out. And even in college, she functioned as my home. But when I moved to New York, the city became my home. I loved it. Loved the fast pace, the opportunities, the gay subculture, everything. And then..."

Silence descended.

"And then that day happened," Rhett whispered. He'd understand like no one else. "And it took away your safety."

"Yes." Henley's voice was hoarse. "I'd never thought of it in those terms until recently, but the bombing robbed me of the sense of feeling at home and safe. I was adrift, and even moving to DC didn't help me to find that back."

"I know what you mean," Rhett said. Levar was so proud of him for talking about this when it was so hard for him. "After...after Pride, I had to leave New York. I had panic attacks and was afraid even to set foot outside. When Levar suggested moving to DC, I jumped on it. But even after moving here, it took me a long time to feel safe again."

"How did you get it back, that sense of home and safety?" Henley asked.

Rhett nodded at Levar. "Levar. He became my safe place until I was rooted again. He's... Look, I don't need to tell you how amazing he is, but he saved me. Literally, without him, I wouldn't be here, and I will never, ever forget that. He's the best friend someone could have."

Levar's eyes grew moist. Gah, that had hit him straight in the feels. "Right back atcha. I love you to pieces."

"I wish I'd had someone like that." Henley sighed, then seemed to shake himself. "No, I should say I wish I'd allowed someone to be that for me. I haven't been good at letting people in, which is why I kept losing partners."

"Is that because of the bombing?" Rhett asked.

"No, that's because I have safety issues on another level as well, as Oren pointed out to me this week. Trust me, I hate and admire him for it in equal measures. My father walked out on us when I was fifteen. Out of nowhere. One moment we were happy, and then he was gone, and he never looked back. It crushed me, and as Oren made clear, it caused me to distrust people and to lose my sense of safety, even with those I loved. My mom and my brother and sister, that was it. I didn't let anyone else in, and with every breakup over the years, I closed myself off more. That's why the bombing affected me so profoundly on that level. It reinforced a pattern I'd already established. I was scared, and that was my way of protecting myself."

They'd said it before, and this proved it once again. The casualties of that day lay far beyond those who had been killed or physically injured. It had forever changed them in ways that might take them years to figure out and recover from. Heal. It would never be gone, but they'd learn how to live with the scars.

"But you're aware now," Rhett said. "So that's a big step already."

Henley nodded. "And for some reason, it's different with Levar." He gazed at him, the love radiating from those brown puppy eyes. "I've felt safe with him from the start, and opening up to him was easy."

Rhett smiled at them both. "He's become your home."

Levar teared up all over again, even more when Henley said, "Yeah, he has. He's become my everything."

He couldn't have imagined a declaration of love more beautiful than that. "I love you." He couldn't manage more. Words failed him to express what he felt inside. It was too big, too beautiful, too magical to describe.

"God, I love you." Henley's answer was equally simple, but it was all that mattered. And there it was again, that crackle between them, that zing in the air. Chemistry, sparks, attraction, whatever they called it, Levar hoped it would never go away.

"Rhett..."

Rhett grinned. "I'll be in my room, wearing noise-canceling headphones. Have fun."

Levar had the best friend in the world...and also the best boyfriend. Knowing that you were loved the way you were, maybe that was being home meant. And he'd never felt more at home than now, lying in Henley's arms, bringing his mouth up for a kiss that would lead to much, much more. He couldn't wait.

∽

Keep reading in Friends, book two in the White House Men series!

FREEBIES

If you love FREE novellas and bonus chapters, head on over to my website where I offer bonus scenes for several of my books, as well as as two free novellas. Grab them here: http://www.noraphoenix.com/free-bonus-scenes-novellas/

BOOKS BY NORA PHOENIX

🎧 indicates book is also available as audio book

White House Men

A romantic suspense series set in the White House that combines romance with suspense, a dash of kink, and all the feels.

- **Press** (rivals fall in love in an impossible love)
- **Friends** (friends to lovers between an FBI and a Secret Service agent)

Perfect Hands Series

Raw, emotional, both sweet and sexy, with a solid dash of kink, that's the Perfect Hands series. All books can be read as standalones.

- **Firm Hand** (daddy care with a younger daddy and an older boy) 🎧
- **Gentle Hand** (sweet daddy care with age play) 🎧

- **Naughty Hand** (a holiday novella to read after Firm Hand and Gentle Hand)
- **Slow Hand** (a Dom who never wanted to be a Daddy takes in two abused boys)
- **Healing Hand** (a broken boy finds the perfect Daddy)

No Shame Series

If you love steamy MM romance with a little twist, you'll love the No Shame series. Sexy, emotional, with a bit of suspense and all the feels. Make sure to read in order, as this is a series with a continuing storyline.

- **No Filter** 🎧
- **No Limits** 🎧
- **No Fear** 🎧
- **No Shame** 🎧
- **No Angel** 🎧

And for all the fun, grab the **No Shame box set** 🎧 which includes all five books plus exclusive bonus chapters and deleted scenes.

Irresistible Omegas Series

An mpreg series with all the heat, epic world building, poly romances (the first two books are MMMM and the rest of the series is MMM), a bit of suspense, and characters that will stay with you for a long time. This is a continuing series, so read in order.

- **Alpha's Sacrifice**
- **Alpha's Submission**
- **Beta's Surrender**

- **Alpha's Pride**
- **Beta's Strength**
- **Omega's Protector**
- **Alpha's Obedience**
- **Omega's Power**
- **Beta's Love**
- **Omega's Truth**

Or grab *the first box set*, which contains books 1-3 plus exclusive bonus material and *the second box set*, which has books 4-6 and exclusive extras.

Ballsy Boys Series

Sexy porn stars looking for real love! Expect plenty of steam, but all the feels as well. They can be read as stand-alones, but are more fun when read in order.

- **Ballsy** (free prequel)
- **Rebel** 🎧
- **Tank** 🎧
- **Heart** 🎧
- **Campy** 🎧
- **Pixie** 🎧

Or grab *the box set*, which contains all five books plus an exclusive bonus novella!

Kinky Boys Series

Super sexy, slightly kinky, with all the feels.

- **Daddy** 🎧
- **Ziggy** 🎧

Ignite Series

An epic dystopian sci-fi trilogy (one book out, two more to follow) where three men have to not only escape a government that wants to jail them for being gay but aliens as well. Slow burn MMM romance.

- Ignite 🎧
- Smolder 🎧
- Burn 🎧

Now also available in a *box set* 🎧, which includes all three books, bonus chapters, and a bonus novella.

Stand Alones

I also have a few stand alones, so check these out!

- **Professor Daddy** (sexy daddy kink between a college prof and his student. Age gap, no ABDL) 🎧
- **Out to Win** (two men meet at a TV singing contest)
- **Captain Silver Fox** (falling for the boss on a cruise ship) 🎧
- **Coming Out on Top** (snowed in, age gap, size difference, and a bossy twink) 🎧

MORE ABOUT NORA PHOENIX

Would you like the long or the short version of my bio?

The short? You got it.

I write steamy gay romance books and I love it. I also love reading books. Books are everything.

How was that?

A little more detail? Gotcha.

I started writing my first stories when I was a teen...on a freaking typewriter. I still have these, and they're adorably romantic. And bad, haha. Fear of failing kept me from following my dream to become a romance author, so you can imagine how proud and ecstatic I am that I finally overcame my fears and self doubt and did it. I adore my genre because I love writing and reading about flawed, strong men who are just a tad broken..but find their happy ever after anyway.

My favorite books to read are pretty much all MM/gay romances as long as it has a happy end. Kink is a plus... Aside from that, I also read a lot of nonfiction and not just books on writing. Popular psychology is a favorite topic of mine and so are self help and sociology.

Hobbies? Ain't nobody got time for that. Just kidding. I love traveling, spending time near the ocean, and hiking. But I love books more.

Come hang out with me in my Facebook Group Nora's Nook where I share previews, sneak peeks, freebies, fun stuff, and much more: https://www.facebook.com/groups/norasnook/

My weekly newsletter not only gives you updates, exclusive content, and all the inside news on what I'm working on, but also lists the best new releases, 99c deals, and freebies in gay romance for that weekend. Load up your Kindle for less money! Sign up here: http://www.noraphoenix.com/newsletter/

You can also stalk me on Twitter: @NoraFromBHR

On Instagram:

https://www.instagram.com/nora.phoenix/

On Bookbub:

https://www.bookbub.com/profile/nora-phoenix

Or become my patron on Patreon: https://www.patreon.com/noraphoenix

ACKNOWLEDGMENTS

This book was long in the making, and I owe a ton of gratitude to everyone who helped me make it better. First of all, my PA and cover designer Vicki Brostenianc. We had at least fifty revisions before we settled on this cover, and she patiently (usually anyway) endures my perfectionism, haha.

Tanja Ongkiehong made the book shine. It's always a pleasure to work with her, and this time was no different.

My usual beta readers Abbie, Amanda, Kyleen, Tania, and Vicki did a great job with the beta reading, pointing out some plots issues. You have, as always, my gratitude.

Layla did a great job sensitivity reading and made a good suggestion that really improved the book. Thank you so much for doing this. You know how much that meant to me.

Sabrina offered a local's perspective and corrected some errors that would've made it less accurate in details, so much gratitude for that.

And last but not least, I owe a freaking mountain of gratitude to Nonny, who gave me the perspective of a federal agent and made the book a hundred times better and more accurate. Thank you so much.

Printed in Great Britain
by Amazon